Secrets of the Night

Una-Mary Parker

MILTON KEYNES
COUNCIL
THIS ITEM HAS BEEN
WITHDRAWN FROM
LIBRARY STOCK
PRICE
50P

MILTON KEYNES LIBRARIES		
		727 698

HEADLINE

Copyright © 1998 Cheval Associates Ltd

The right of Una-Mary Parker to be identified as the Author of
the Work has been asserted by her in accordance with the
Copyright, Designs and Patents Act 1988.

First published in 1998
by HEADLINE BOOK PUBLISHING

First published in paperback in 1999
by HEADLINE BOOK PUBLISHING

10 9 8 7 6 5 4 3 2

All rights reserved. No part of this publication may be
reproduced, stored in a retrieval system, or transmitted,
in any form or by any means without the prior written
permission of the publisher, nor be otherwise circulated
in any form of binding or cover other than that in which
it is published and without a similar condition being
imposed on the subsequent purchaser.

All characters in this publication are fictitious
and any resemblance to real persons, living or dead,
is purely coincidental.

ISBN 0 7472 5688 8

Typeset by
Letterpart Limited, Reigate, Surrey

Printed and bound in Great Britain by
Mackays of Chatham PLC, Chatham, Kent

HEADLINE BOOK PUBLISHING
A division of Hodder Headline PLC
338 Euston Road
London NW1 3BH

This book is dedicated to all the friends whose talent and expertise made the parties we organised together over the years such tremendous fun. They include Duncan MacArthur, the best Banqueting Manager ever; John Plested for his brilliant originality with flowers and decorations; Nigel Tulley, who with The Dark Blues produces music no party should be without; Bryn Williams, the Top People's Toast Master who makes sure everything runs smoothly; and many others too numerous to mention.

Thank you for your help then and for giving me the inspiration which helped me to write this book.

Tuesday

18 June 1996

One

Nancy Graham moved house every three years because by then her neighbours had stopped talking to her. This time she was more than glad to go. As soon as she saw the marquee going up on the lawn of Highfield Manor, not three hundred yards away from her cottage, she knew that this was yet another village event to which she had not been invited. When she'd first moved into Cherry Tree Cottage, the Rutherford family had seemed a friendly lot, and she'd quite looked forward to getting acquainted. In the beginning they had invited her to a drinks party, but Douglas Rutherford had been dismissive of the advice she'd given him on growing roses, and Julia Rutherford hadn't been at all gracious when Nancy had suggested their drawing room would seem lighter if she changed the colour of their curtains.

People are so unappreciative, Nancy reflected, as she stood on a stool in her bedroom window, watching as men hauled at the ropes of the white canvas, like the sails of a boat on a silent sea, until it was upright. And BIG. She blinked rapidly. One hand, glittering with diamond and emerald rings, clutched claw-like at her glazed chintz curtains to steady herself. With the other she shaded her delicately made-up eyes from the sun which slanted into

3

her room through the beeches that divided her garden from theirs.

Her knowledge of the family, gathered and absorbed as if by osmosis, enabled her to work out now what was happening. Douglas and Julia had been married twenty-five years, their eldest daughter, Anna, was about to be twenty-one . . . and their eldest son, William, was nearly eighteen. It didn't take Nancy more than a brief raising of her pencilled eyebrows to cotton on to the fact that they were going to give a party, an enormous bash, very likely a ball. And once again she had been Left Out.

It was the story of her life and Nancy simply couldn't understand why. If anyone had a grievance it was her. No one knew how much stress she'd suffered by living next door to the Rutherfords. And in spite of her constantly complaining how inconsiderate they were being, they still continued to cause her annoyance so that sometimes she thought they were actually doing it on purpose! Their constant comings and goings, not to mention that of their endless stream of guests, drove her demented. They swished up and down the gravel drive in their racy cars at all hours of the day and night, without a thought for her, living in a cottage not fifty yards away! And what had they done to cut down the noise made by their dogs and horses and music, after endless requests from her? Nothing.

Then they let William and his friends play tennis at the most unsociable hours, so that the *plock-plock* of the ball hitting the racket gave her a headache, while their nine-year-old son, Michael, was allowed to charge around on his bike, constantly going *dring-dring* on the bell. As for Anna . . .! Surely a girl on the eve of her twenty-first birthday should have ceased to frolic in the swimming

4

pool with her flock of friends, giggling and shrieking in the annoyingly silly way all young girls have?

Nancy Graham compressed her thin lips and the wrinkles around her mouth deepened as she reflected bitterly on the bad manners of her hellish neighbours. Thank God, by this time next week she'd be installed in her new house. It was just five miles away because she liked this part of Hampshire and had no intention of moving into another county. The trouble was, though, by now she was beginning to run out of villages.

Autocratic in bearing, superbly well dressed and bejewelled, coiffeured and manicured twice a week, Mrs Philip Graham, as she liked to be called although she'd been widowed fifteen years before, acted as though she was royalty. Her long-suffering husband had been an extraordinarily delightful and easy-going man and people had often wondered how he'd managed to live with Nancy for thirty-nine years, without even the distraction of children to lighten the atmosphere.

When, at last, his great heart had stilled, leaving her forever on her own, she'd been instantly aware that his charm, which had protected her like a cloak throughout her adult life, had gone. There was no one to defend her now with the firm but quiet loyalty that Philip had always shown. She would have to fight her own battles. Fortunately, this presented no problem. Having been the instigator of most of the contretemps that arose with anyone who displeased her, standing up for herself came naturally to Nancy, although Philip had been too nice, or too weak, to realise it. She'd held the all-powerful trump card, too. Their money was hers, inherited from her father. Not many people wanted a head-on collision with five million pounds.

Then Lloyd's of London had suffered the unthinkable, or 'The Crash' as she referred to it, and a big chunk of her fortune disappeared into the sea along with the oil spill from the *Exxon-Valdez*, and Mrs Philip Graham wasn't so rich anymore. Refusing to 'down grade', referring to it instead as 'wanting a simpler life', she had lived in a series of small cottages since Philip's death. If the exteriors were plain, the interiors were like the inside of a jewel box: filled with exquisite objects that glowed and glittered against a background of cream silk wall coverings and burgundy velvet furnishings, giving a whole new slant to the estate agent's use of the description 'bijou'.

Nancy Graham stepped down carefully from the stool, and gave an aggrieved sigh. Moving again was the most fearful bore, but she wasn't altogether sorry to be going. There was something very shady about the Rutherford family, for all their apparent devotion to each other. Something told her they were heading for trouble, and judging by the gossip in the village, she thought she knew what it was.

When Julia Leonard married Douglas Rutherford in June, 1971, she had no idea that by the eighties they would be wealthy, thanks to the string of restaurants he'd opened, or that by 1987 he would be listed in *The Sunday Times* colour supplement as 'one of the hundred richest men in the country'.

With a flair for business, though no culinary experience, he'd bought a run-down café on the corner of Lots Road and King's Road, in the Fulham area of London. He'd called it Lots and turned it into a bistro with red-checked tablecloths and candles jammed into empty wine bottles. Then he created an amusing menu that recommended customers to: 'Have Lots! Lots of pasta. Lots of salad. Lots of creamy puddings'.

Spurred on by its instant success, he opened a second bistro, ten minutes' walk away in Hollywood Road. Here he was competing with several other established restaurants, but he reckoned on picking up customers when they couldn't get in anywhere else, and he was right. He called it Hollywood, covered the walls with pictures of famous film celebrities, and devised a 'Dine with the Stars' menu, which included a starter called the Jane Fonda Appetiser, (light, lean and worked-over), the Robert Redford Main Attraction (a tender steak with something on the side), and the Joan Collins Final Indulgence (a dark rich smooth chocolate *pot*, with a dash of fiery Cognac).

By 1978 he'd opened a third theme restaurant, this time designed for people with children. Not only was there a special menu aimed at two- to ten-year-olds, but there was also a crèche on the floor above where babies could be left in the care of trained nannies. Waiters were dressed as clowns and trapeze artists, sometimes performing simple conjuring tricks or juggling with apples and oranges, and the atmosphere was relaxed and jolly. For the first time in London, there was a place for parents to eat which actually encouraged them to bring their children and The Kitchen became a huge success, propelling Douglas into the limelight. His career as an innovative restaurateur had taken off and there was no stopping him. The *Evening Standard* gave him his own cookery column, he was offered a regular spot on breakfast television, where he became the Family Cook, slotted in on alternate days with the Family Doctor, and suddenly, from not knowing how to boil an egg, he found himself an adept chef whose name had become synonymous with family values and How To Keep the Family Happy by Feeding Them Well. After years of hiring the best chefs from all over Europe, he had to learn fast and he did. Douglas became a kitchen hero and restaurant writers gave his bistros rave reviews.

At the beginning of 1979, he and Julia bought Highfield Manor, on the outskirts of a village called Stickley, near Stockbridge in Hampshire, a place Julia hoped would provide the peace and quiet she'd begun to long for, but which instead turned out to be the perfect photogenic setting for the 'successful Rutherfords and their children, Anna, three, and William, one'.

Sunday colour supplements featured the four of them in either the enormous pine-fitted kitchen, amid glittering copper pans, in the garden where Douglas grew herbs for his restaurants as well as his home – according to the public relations blurb – or relaxing in their elegant drawing room, playing a family game of Monopoly.

It was a heady time and Douglas enjoyed every minute of it. By the mid-eighties he owned restaurants all over the country. In 1986 he floated his company, Bistroesque Ltd, on the Stock Market, and before the bubble burst, sold all his shares for a cool £60 million.

Sensing that people would soon want something altogether different, he bought a disused cinema in Lower Regent Street, and converted it into his first megarestaurant, which seated three hundred people. With state-of-the-art kitchens, visible through the slatted walls down one side, ultra-modern decor, live music in the evenings, a delectable *nouvelle cuisine* menu and reasonably priced wine list, Futures was an instant hit. As far removed from a homely kitchen as it was possible to be, the mode was all glass and glitter, with waiters gliding about like skaters on speed. From noon, when the atmosphere was as heady as the champagne cocktails, and the *beau monde* filled every table, greeting each other with shrieks of delight, until the evening when the *jeunesse dorée* took over and live music belted out as the money came rolling in, Douglas congratulated himself on having once again correctly judged the mood of the moment and made the right decision. This was where the future lay and so far his only rival was Sir Terence Conran, who'd had a similar idea.

By 1996 Sir Terence had opened Quaglino's, Bibendum, Mezzo, and was planning to open Bluebird the following year, but Douglas Rutherford, not yet knighted but working on it, had opened Futures, Trendy's, Smart's and Butterfly. The majority of his clientele were half his age but that didn't worry him. With a team of young chefs and designers, he reckoned he had the scene sussed. Nothing fazed him now and that included this party he and his wife were giving to celebrate their Silver Wedding Anniversary, and the twenty-first and eighteenth birthdays respectively of Anna and William. They also had nine-year-old Michael, an unexpected but welcome later addition to the family.

Julia, of course, looked upon the ball as a private family affair, but for Douglas it was much more. Photographers from *Hello!* and *OK!* magazines were coming, and so were Richard Young from the *Daily Express* and Alan Davidson from the *Daily Mail*. He'd also invited the social editors of *Tatler* and *Harpers & Queen*.

There was no way he could let a public relations opportunity like this pass without ensuring it would be covered by the press.

★ ★ ★

From her desk in the study of Highfield Manor, Julia watched through the window as the tent was erected by the marquee contractors. The guy ropes were taut now, and the iron pegs had been hammered savagely into the once virgin lawn. Soon the garden would be unrecognisable, filled with an alien area of white canvas shelters which would house kitchens, storerooms for drinks, portaloos, and changing rooms for staff, apart from the main marquee where on Saturday night three hundred people would dine and dance.

Julia and Douglas were used to entertaining but she felt this party was going to be special. Smiling to herself, she found it hard to believe how quickly the last twenty-five years had passed. She'd been only nineteen and a student at St Martin's School of Art when she'd met The Dashing Douglas Rutherford, as her half-brother Christopher teasingly referred to him, at a dinner party. It had been love at first sight. A bolt that came from nowhere and was to pin her forever to his side and his bed, like a butterfly to a velvet pad. Even now, when he came into a room, her heart still contracted with an exquisite pain. His closeness made her grow weak and filled with desire, the smell of his skin and his hair almost made her faint. She loved him with every cell of her body, and she knew she could never look at anyone else. Douglas was her love, her life, her very reason for being, and when she had the morbid thought that he might die before her, she already felt sick with grief.

'How's the seating plan coming along?' Anna shouted from the garden, as she passed the open window.

Julia blinked, remembering the job in hand.

'It's nearly finished,' she called back, pulling the large

white sheet of paper towards her again. There were going to be thirty round tables, each seating ten guests, and each had to be hosted by either one of the family or a close friend, so that no one would feel they were at an 'inferior' table. Julia was always thinking of other people. If it wasn't her husband and family, it was the animals, or someone in the village who might need a helping hand, or a charity that needed support. In spite of their wealth, she had kept her feet on the ground, never forgetting how broke they'd been when they'd first married. On occasions, Douglas had even waited on tables at Lots, while she'd been out at the back washing up.

It was all such ages ago and they'd come such a long way, but they'd done it together, she reflected. They'd done everything together, standing by each other every inch of the way. That was what was so wonderful. That was why this party was so thrilling. A celebration of love and friendship and a loyalty nothing could break. Surrounded by Anna and William and Michael, it was going to be a truly marvellous night.

Suddenly Julia seized her pencil and added 'Michael' to her list as one of the table hosts. Why not? Even if he was only nine he could be trusted to behave and it would encourage him to develop a sense of responsibility.

Then she strolled into the garden to see how it was all going. Petite and very slender, with black shoulder-length hair, and large, very dark eyes, set in a pale face that still looked young because of her fine bone structure and high cheekbones, she made an elegant figure in a navy blue trouser suit with a long jacket, a silk scarf in vivid blues and greens slung casually around her neck.

'How are you getting on? Can I get you some coffee? Tea? A cool drink, perhaps?' she asked, sweetly.

'We're OK, thanks,' the foreman replied with a grin. 'We're nearly finished for today. Tomorrow we'll be laying the flooring. It'll look a lot better then.'

'I can't wait!' She clasped her hands together, as enthusiastic as a young girl. 'I'm not allowed to see the decorations, you know, until Saturday night. My husband wants to give us all a surprise.'

Douglas had commissioned John Plested and his versatile team at Town & County Flowers to design the themed decor, lighting effects and floral arrangements for the marquee, and for the past four months there had been endless meetings between them, with drawings being considered and rejected, designs discussed and colour schemes talked over. At last Douglas had given the go-ahead but everyone involved was sworn to secrecy and all he would tell Julia was: 'Think fantasy, think magic and something out of this world. Nothing like it has ever been done at a private party before,' he'd added tantalisingly.

She looked around the cool empty space, like a blank canvas waiting for an artist to paint a fabulous picture on its vast surface, and longed to know what had been planned.

'What a pity we can't keep this up permanently. It would make a marvellous extra room,' she joked.

'Your husband could start another restaurant in it, perhaps,' the foreman jested.

Julia raised finely arched dark eyebrows.

'Oh, he wouldn't think it was nearly big enough. You couldn't get a thousand people in here!' she retorted with mock reproof.

'Bloody old bat!' Anna exclaimed, crashing the phone back on to its cradle.

Julia, coming in from the garden, paused in the french windows of the study and looked enquiringly at her daughter.

'Who was that, darling?'

Anna cast her eyes to heaven. 'Who do you think it was, Mummy? Who else complains all the time about everything we do?' She flopped on to the sofa, and wriggled her bare toes. The soles of her feet were black from running in and out of the garden.

'Mrs Graham, I suppose. Oh, dear! What did she say?'

'She said she's phoning the police in Stockbridge, and planning to get an injunction from the noise abatement people to stop us giving the party. She says it's not as if it's going to be held during the day. She said we'll disturb the whole village *all* night and no one will get a wink of sleep.' Anna scowled at her mother defiantly. 'I'd like to throttle the old bat!'

Julia frowned. 'I knew we should have invited her, but your father wouldn't hear of it. I wonder if it's too late?'

Anna pulled off the white scrunchie that held her hair back and, bending forward, shook her head so that her long fair tresses fell into a silky cascade which she scooped up expertly and secured once more. Looking at mother and daughter an onlooker would never have thought they were related. Anna was totally her father's child: big-boned and grey-eyed, with bronzed skin and blonde hair. Beside her, Julia looked as fragile and dainty as a humming bird.

Anna said dryly, 'If you ask her now she'll know you're only doing it to stop her making trouble. Anyway, why can't we get an injunction to shut *her* up?'

'We've got to do something.' Julia's brow puckered and her eyes looked troubled. 'This is serious. I'd better get on to Daddy right away. You were polite to her, I hope, darling?'

Anna's scowl dissolved into a smile. 'Of course I was, Mum. I'm not entirely stupid.'

'It's a pity she's not leaving Cherry Tree Cottage before the party.' Julia returned to her desk and, sitting down again, picked up her mobile phone. Douglas was at Butterfly today, lunching with a free-lance journalist called Stephen Parsons who was doing a piece for the August edition of *Tatler*. But this was something she urgently needed to talk to him about, so she'd have to interrupt.

He answered immediately. 'Hello?'

'Darling? Sorry to disturb you, but we have a problem.'

His tone was brisk. 'Yup. What is it?'

While he listened to her, his eyes were noting everything that was going on around him. Butterfly was his latest venture and he liked to keep an eye on every detail. He glanced first at the two pretty young women who greeted the clients as they arrived and were trained to remember the regulars by name as they discreetly checked the reservations. Douglas knew that people could be intimidated by large noisy restaurants so he continued to watch, to make sure the customers were taken to their table immediately, unless they chose to drink at the mirrored bar first, and that they were swiftly offered the menu. Waiters must be knowledgeable about that, and the wine list, too, but at the same time had to remain unobtrusive. Douglas continued to listen to Julia, saying 'Yup' occasionally but watching all the time. The presentation of the food was something else he was fanatical about, so that it looked as wonderful as it tasted. 'Like painting a picture on a plate,' as he described it.

14

There was a buzz about Butterfly that spelled success. He noted that the clients still looked happy even when they were presented with their bill, a sure sign they would come again.

'I'll deal with it when I get home later,' he said at last.

There was a pause before Julia answered, 'Mightn't that be too late? Mrs Graham gave Anna a hard time on the phone and it sounded as if she meant business. Suppose the police prohibit us from playing music?'

Aware that Stephen Parsons was listening to what he said, although he was trying to look absorbed in breaking his bread roll into small pieces, Douglas spoke non-committally. 'I'll deal with it. It's no problem. Everything else OK?' He sounded up-beat, energy radiating from him like heat.

'Everything's fine.' Julia's voice was small, very feminine.

His was warm and husky, promising more than the cool brevity of his words. 'See you later then. 'Bye.' Then he smiled at the journalist as he returned his mobile to his pocket. 'Sorry about that. There's always something happening with four major restaurants to run.'

Stephen Parsons stopped reducing his bread to fine crumbs and looked alert again. 'I know you own three places apart from this new one, but how extensive is your actual involvement in the others?'

Douglas shrugged expansively. 'They're each as important as the other. I visit all four every day, and usually have lunch in one of them. Sometimes dinner, too. Standards have to be maintained and the staff kept constantly on their toes, and I make all the major decisions – from approving a new dish to the choice of napery and cutlery. I also audition musicians to play in the evenings . . . I utterly detest muzak and think whoever dreamed it up, ought to be shot!' He laughed easily. 'And I work closely with the architects on the design of a new restaurant. The Look. I want people coming for the first time to recognise it instantly as one of mine.'

Stephen Parsons, gazing around him at the awesome space that made him think of busy railway stations in the rush hour, smiled politely.

'And I control all the finances, of course,' Douglas added.

'Of course.'

Douglas shot him a wary look. Did he detect a touch of sarcasm in the journalist's voice? He had a love-hate relationship with the press. He did his own PR these days, not trusting anyone else to speak on his behalf, not even when he'd told them what to say. Journalists had a way of taking things out of context, in his opinion, and working to their own agenda, burrowing like rats into forbidden territory. He didn't trust any of them.

For the next hour, as they ate grilled goat's cheese salad with pickled damsons, followed by salmon smoked in a wok with orange zest, fresh fronds of dill and rice, and then plum and kirsch fool, Douglas told Stephen Parsons only what he wished him to know and no more. At two-fifteen exactly, he brought the interview to an end.

'Forgive me, but I'm due at a meeting in ten minutes and it's on the other side of London!' he said, giving Stephen the impression that he'd already spared him more of his valuable time than he should have done.

In fact, Douglas was anxious to get down to Stockbridge to sort out Mrs Graham. He would not let the old bitch screw up their party. As he headed out of London in his new thirty-thousand pound TVR sports, he decided there were several options open to him. He could offer

Mrs Graham a night in any hotel of her choice, perhaps the Ritz or the Savoy, all expenses paid. Or he could go straight to the police and tell them to pay no attention to her grumbling; the whole village knew what a pain she was. Or he could offer her financial compensation for having her night disturbed. One thing was certain: under no circumstances whatsoever was he going to invite her to the party.

Douglas Rutherford considered Highfield Manor to be his greatest trophy. He wanted to be able to give his children all the material advantages his parents hadn't been able to offer him and his brother, and that included a beautiful home, but he also wanted something that would be a visible symbol of what he'd achieved. The memory of the ugly red brick, semi-detached 1930s house he'd been brought up in still made him shudder. The moment he'd seen Highfield he'd known it was exactly what he wanted. Entering it for the first time was like the breathless excitement of falling in love, a sense of tumbling ecstasy that left him dazed. He snapped it up immediately, gazumping another couple who were also after it though he never told Julia that bit. The day they moved in was one of the happiest of his life, and there had not been a single day since when he hadn't felt delight at owning such a place.

It was a long, low, mellow brick house of elegant symmetrical proportions, with an imposing porticoed entrance. Through the double front door one stepped straight into a large square hall, in the centre of which Julia always arranged a huge display of flowers on an oak table. To the left, the L-shaped drawing room, decorated and furnished in pastel shades, had windows overlooking the garden on three sides. Douglas had cleverly divided the room into four seating areas, each effectively screened from the others by tall orchids placed on side tables.

To the right of the hall was Julia's sitting room, pretty and feminine with its crisp colour scheme of blue and white, and next to it was the study which commanded a view of the lawn where the marquee was today being erected. Behind the hall lay the panelled dining room which could seat twenty-four guests. When they gave a dinner party the glossy expanse of the mahogany table, surrounded by matching Georgian chairs, reflected crystal and silver, candlelight and flowers, and a centrepiece overflowing with fruit. Beyond this another large room had evolved over the years from playroom to 'music room', as Douglas referred to it. In spite of there being a grand piano at one end, however, it was the beat of Oasis that belted out from the hi-fi nowadays when Anna and William asked their friends to stay. Secretly, Douglas longed to call it 'the ballroom', because at least eighty people could have danced on its polished parquet floor, but he knew Julia would think that pretentious.

Upstairs, the fourteen bedrooms and twelve bathrooms were rarely unoccupied, although none of the staff lived in the main part of the house. Morgan, the butler, and his wife, the cook, had a large flat above the kitchen, breakfast room, larder and utility room, at the far side of the building.

Douglas had never stopped to count the cost of doing up and maintaining Highfield Manor. It was the house of his dreams and what he'd always wanted. A setting for a rich man who had worked hard to give his family the best. And if the house was the symbol of his success, the garden in which it was set was the crowning glory. It had a tennis court, swimming pool, large stables and acres of romantically designed lawns and flower beds, with winding stone-edged camomile paths bordered with lavender, that led to secret corners where love seats, framed by archways, were hidden from view by tumbling showers of roses. To either side of the drive, towering rhododendrons formed an opulent spring display of white, pink and red blossoms, though for the rest of the year Julia hated them, begging Douglas to cut the gloomy things down and plant something else. In her more fanciful moments she had the strangest feeling they were barring her way to paradise.

On the afternoon of 18 June, Douglas had no such notions as he headed for Stockbridge. He listened to the first day's racing from Royal Ascot on the radio, wishing he and Julia had gone this year as usual, and in his mind went over the final details for Saturday night. Everything had to be perfect. He felt his reputation was on the line. After all, if a top restaurateur couldn't organise the best party of the year, who could?

For Douglas's parents, Pat and Reggie Rutherford, this was a week they'd been looking forward to for a long time. Reggie, a retired accountant from Derbyshire, was extremely proud of both his sons, but while Peter had done well academically and was now headmaster of St John's Court preparatory school near Salisbury, it was Douglas who had made the money, become a high-profile media figure and led a glamorous lifestyle. Reggie rather enjoyed being referred to as 'Douglas Rutherford's father'.

Pat, on the other hand, was looking forward primarily to seeing all her grandchildren again. She'd always been particularly close to Anna because when she'd been three, Pat had looked after her for two weeks after William was born; she loved to help out because it made her feel needed. During those weeks she'd really felt herself bond with the little girl and couldn't help regarding her as the daughter she'd never had. Then along came Sweet William, as she always called him, a dear boy with a truly loving temperament. The third child, an afterthought born nine years later, turned out to be as appealing as he was unexpected, and 'Little Michael', as she called him, quickly became his granny's Little Darling – and knew it. But Anna was special, the brightest and the best so far as Pat was concerned, with a rainbow spirit and a warmth that filled you with gladness just to see her.

In Pat's suitcase a flat leather case nestled under her sensible cardigans. It contained a pearl necklace with a diamond clasp. She'd saved up for a long time to buy it for Anna and hoped she would like it and wear it often. Of course Pat had other granddaughters, too. She mustn't forget them. Peter had married soon after Douglas. His wife was a rather demanding woman called Leonora, who regarded herself as superior to the rest of them. Their daughters, Cressida and Sasha, were nineteen and twenty respectively. Nice girls, Pat thought, but nothing out of the ordinary. Not special, like Anna.

'It's lovely the whole family is going to be together this weekend, isn't it?' she remarked to Reggie as she finished her packing. She'd bought herself a new dress for the party, navy blue silk with long sleeves and a V-neck. She liked it because it wasn't showy.

Her husband rubbed his white moustache, which he'd been trimming with Pat's nail scissors because he couldn't find any others.

'When did Douglas say everyone was arriving?' he asked. They'd been invited tomorrow, Wednesday, but he knew Peter couldn't get away mid-week during termtime.

'I think Leonora is bringing Cressida and Sasha on Friday afternoon and Peter's joining us all on Saturday.'

'Then there's Julia's family,' Reggie reminded her as he gave his moustache a final satisfied stroke. 'They'll all be staying, too.'

Pat shook her head though her newly permed white hair remained rigid. 'I don't know how she manages. So many people in the house. And all the arrangements for the party to be made.'

'Douglas will be looking after all that,' Reggie said proudly. 'You can rely on him. He'll put on a wonderful show, Mother.'

Leonora Rutherford held up the evening dress she'd bought and hoped its sheer glamour would outshine whatever Julia was going to wear to the party. Julia always looked extremely expensively but deceptively simply dressed. During the day she wore understated trouser suits by Armani, and for the evening favoured Amanda Wakeley. For some reason that Leonora couldn't fathom, Julia didn't go in for glitter or bright colours or plunging necklines or sexy splits up the skirt. Leonora's smile was smug with self-satisfaction. She'd got *all* that in the Gianni Versace model she'd bought at Pandora's, the famous dress agency in Knightsbridge. And who was to know it was second-hand and had cost her only a fraction of its original price?

The strapless peacock blue satin top fitted her to perfection, accentuating her bust, and the straight skirt slit to the thigh was really sexy. A *ton* of crystal and sequin embroidery encrusted the bodice, formed a panel down the front and edged the hem. Every time Leonora looked at it she smiled, remembering someone had once said: 'In his collections, Versace knows every sequin personally.'

Peter hadn't seen it yet, and would probably think it too flashy – that is, if he noticed what she was wearing in the first place. Leonora's once lovely face, marred now by a network of fine lines tracing her discontent, gazed at herself in the long bedroom mirror and felt the sting of bitter regret. She never had the opportunity to go out and wear dresses like this. She was wasted in her present life. When did she ever get to meet anyone interesting, or famous, or amusing? She never went anywhere. Instead, she was stuck with Peter in this boring school full of boring little boys, and she hated every minute of it. For a long time now she'd nagged him about wanting a little flat in London, but Peter always said they couldn't afford it. What did they need a place in London for? he'd asked. They lived in a spacious flat that was a part of St John's Court School. Wasn't that enough?

The day the iron really entered Leonora's soul was when Peter happily bought a flat in Fulham for Cressida and Sasha, and they started living the life she'd wanted for herself. When she heard about it, she'd locked herself in the bathroom in a paroxysm of tears. Torn between gladness for her girls, and jealousy that they would enjoy the opportunities she herself longed for, Leonora stormed at a God she didn't believe in, and wished she'd never had children in the first place. Then she could have left Peter a long time ago.

It simply wasn't fair, she thought, desperately. Life was passing her by before she'd ever really lived. She was still only forty-six. There was a whole world out there, to be enjoyed and experienced, while she was stuck in rural Wiltshire, having to be polite to tedious parents. It didn't help to know that Julia, her sister-in-law, was having a terrific time as a major player on the London and Hampshire social scenes.

'The trouble,' Leonora said to herself, as she hung up the Versace dress, 'is that I married the wrong brother.'

Two

It was nearly five o'clock and the contractors had finished laying the marquee floor. They were hot and exhausted, having started work at dawn, and were casting longing glances in the direction of the pool. Julia, coming out of the house and realising they were now faced with the long drive back to London, immediately suggested they have a swim.

'There are plenty of spare bathing trunks in the pool house,' she told the foreman, 'and I'll have some beer ready for you all afterwards.'

They needed no persuasion. While they luxuriated in the cool water, Morgan brought out cans of chilled Carlsberg, glass tankards and bags of crisps, which he set up on a table on the terrace.

'I'd no idea it would be such a big job,' Anna remarked, as she and her mother went to thank the men after their swim for all their efforts. 'Thank God the weather's been fine. What would have happened if it had rained?'

The men grinned, and the foreman replied: 'We would have had to stay inside to keep dry. It doesn't matter if it rains now.'

'Don't even mention rain!' Julia protested, laughing. 'I'm relying on its being a balmy night with a full moon.'

25

'The forecast says it's going to be hot and dry, doesn't it?' Anna asked. She had secret hopes for Saturday night; hopes that her boyfriend, Petroc Tregain, would choose her birthday celebrations to ask her to marry him. In the past few weeks she'd even allowed herself to indulge in fantasies of how it would be, with Petroc leading her by the hand along the grassy avenue to the rose garden, then kissing her before he murmured those longed for words. It would, she reasoned, be such a perfect occasion to announce their engagement. After all, they had been going out for nearly three years now and were looked upon as a steady item amongst their friends.

When Anna had left Benenden, she'd decided she'd rather 'get on' with her life than take a gap year. She didn't want to go to university either. She wanted to get a job and start earning money so she could be independent. Douglas admired this attitude because it reminded him of how he'd been at her age; eager to carve out a career for himself, anxious to make his mark in the world and feather his financial nest. He immediately bought her a three-bedroomed flat in Chelsea, his only proviso being that she must share it with two girlfriends, and they must all contribute to a mortgage in lieu of rent. Thrilled, Anna enlisted two of her school chums, Henrietta Walters and Camilla Holland, and within a year they'd all taken a course at Queen's Secretarial College, found themselves jobs and created their own social life. They gave frequent dinner parties, enlarging their group of mutual friends as they did so. They could squeeze eight round the table in their bright little kitchen, and each cooked one of the courses.

One evening, Henrietta's boyfriend Richard asked if he could bring a chum. That was the first time Anna had met Petroc. At first she hadn't particularly liked him; thought him rather arrogant and supercilious. But then she realised his languid and slightly condescending manner was a cover for acute shyness. Once she got to know him better and had met his family who came from Cornwall, she found him warm and funny and very kind. Broad-shouldered, with dark curling hair and penetrating hazel eyes, he was also very sexy. During the next few weeks they kept bumping into each other in the Trafalgar in the King's Road, which was a favourite haunt, until one evening it struck Anna with breathtaking force that she'd fallen in love with him. She also realised, almost at the same moment, that Petroc felt the same way about her.

Now, after nearly three years of being an item, she was frustrated that he seemed no nearer committing himself than he'd been at the beginning. He continued to live in his flat in Battersea, sharing with two friends, while she remained in Chelsea with Henrietta and Camilla, and the future was never discussed. He never even brought up the subject of marriage and as he was now twenty-seven and had a very good job in a computer company, she wondered what he was waiting for? After all, he loved her, of that she was sure. Camilla had suggested Anna give him an ultimatum: marriage or they end their affair. Henrietta went so far as to suggest Anna should do the proposing, but she shrank from that idea and was now pinning all her hopes on Saturday night. Surely, with a few gentle hints, Petroc would realise it was what they both really wanted?

'So you've got a house full of people staying for the party, have you, Mrs Rutherford?' The foreman's remark to her mother cut across Anna's day-dreaming.

'Yes,' Julia replied. 'There'll be twenty-one of us for the weekend.'

The foreman whistled through pursed lips.

'How do you make it twenty-one, Mummy?'

'With all the grandparents and aunts and uncles and cousins, plus Petroc, and William's girlfriend Stephanie, and my old friend Caroline . . .'

'Wow!' said Anna, stunned. She hadn't realised. She tried to multiply twenty-one breakfasts, lunches, teas and dinners over the coming few days and realised that was why a tented extension had been added on to the house, leading off the back door from the kitchen, with mobile cookers, an industrial dishwasher, and several large worktops.

'Mrs Morgan isn't going to be doing it all, is she?'

'Lord, no!' Julia threw back her head, laughing. 'Daddy is sending down two chefs, from Trendy's and Smart's, and a dozen kitchen helpers and waiters. We're putting them up at The Red Lion, and they'll arrive each morning in time to do breakfast for us all.'

Julia continued to look serene because catering had been her life ever since she'd married Douglas and to her it was just a job, but Anna blushed, feeling guilty at what must look like an ostentatious show of wealth.

'Well, everyone's welcome to share my scrambled eggs,' she said with rather more force than she'd intended. 'I'll be too sick with nerves by Saturday to want to eat anything!'

At that moment Douglas came briskly across the lawn from the direction of Nancy Graham's cottage. He was scarlet in the face.

'Of all the pig-headed, obstinate, trouble-making old bitches, that one takes the *biscuit*!' he spluttered in fury.

'I've spent nearly two hours trying to pacify her, reason with her, bribe her and practically threaten her, but it's made no difference. She's determined to make trouble on Saturday night.'

Julia looked up at him and asked calmly: 'Did you try inviting her to the party?'

Douglas spun round. 'How could I possibly do that? At this late stage? It would look so rude.'

She suppressed a smile, knowing he would get even more annoyed if she appeared amused by his attitude. 'So what can we do?'

He looked determined. 'I'm going to get the police on my side by going to them before she does. I'm sure a big donation to one of their funds would make them turn a deaf ear for the night. If she gets to them first she'll embellish the situation with wild accusations of my trying to rape her while the band played on, or something!' He strode around, waving one of his strong, square hands airily, and the workmen laughed. Douglas always loves playing to the gallery, Julia reflected, and her dark eyes were tender as she gazed at him.

Anna stood up and faced her father, a younger, feminine version of him, even to the shape of her tanned hands which were adorned with silver rings on each finger. 'Will it be all right, Daddy?'

He stopped and looked at her, grey eyes to grey eyes, in recognition of a kindred spirit.

'Of course it will, my pet. Saturday will be a night we'll remember for the rest of our lives!'

A week later Anna remembered those words, but if someone had told her then what was going to happen she wouldn't have believed them.

At eight o'clock the family sat down to dinner, cooked by Mrs Morgan and served by her husband. This was the last evening they'd be on their own until after the party because Douglas's parents were arriving tomorrow, and on Friday everyone else, including Julia's parents, would be arriving during the day.

William, fresh-faced and excited about the celebrations which were partly to mark his coming-of-age, talked volubly about his approaching gap year, during which he planned to back-pack around the world with an old school friend.

'I reckon we can do the whole trip for about five thousand pounds, but we'll need to take plastic with us for emergencies,' he said importantly as he spooned chilled Vichyssoise into his mouth. William was a large and gangling youth who had also inherited his father's genes and was currently going through a phase of knocking things over and tripping up on his size twelve feet.

'Sounds like you're planning to stay at five-star hotels instead of youth hostels,' Anna protested, laughing. 'Five thousand pounds is an awful lot of money.'

William turned scarlet, so that his blond hair looked white at the roots. He turned on her in fury.

'No, it's not,' he retorted. 'I bet the dress you're wearing on Saturday night cost at least half that.'

'No, it didn't!' She glared at him indignantly. 'It cost one thousand.'

'One thousand!' squealed Michael, his soup spoon wobbling perilously in mid-air. 'What a waste of money! I could buy a really good bike for that.'

The others smiled indulgently. Michael was always trying to sound grown-up, and it was no secret that he would do anything to defend his elder brother.

'Why can't you wear one of the dresses you've already got, Anna?' he continued belligerently. His dark eyes, so like Julia's, flashed critically at his sister. 'No one will be looking at you anyway.'

'That's enough, Michael,' Douglas said quietly.

'But William *is* going to need a lot of money to go travelling,' he insisted, determined to have the last word.

Julia smiled peaceably. Michael was the only one of her children who was like her and she felt a strong affinity with him, although she tried not to let the others see it. Michael was bone of her bone, blood of her blood, and she knew exactly how to handle him. 'We want William to travel safely, too, darling, and sometimes that will mean staying in hotels, though not necessarily five-star ones. We'll make sure he has enough money for the trip.'

'I didn't go travelling at all,' Anna remarked.

'That was because you wanted to get a job here,' Douglas pointed out.

'And because you couldn't bear to tear yourself away from Petroc, once you'd met him,' Michael added. 'I'm never going to fall in love.' He cast his eyes upwards. 'It really messes up your life.'

William ignored his little brother and looked thoughtful. 'Stephanie says she'll wait for me. I hope she does. Six months isn't all that long.'

'It's a long time when you're young,' Julia said. 'When I first knew your father, I thought a weekend away from him was an eternity.'

Douglas smiled down the length of the polished table at her. 'You still do,' he chided gently. Their eyes locked, and he said with a twinkle in his eye, 'I think we should all have an early night. The next five days are going to be pretty hectic, and the florists are arriving at nine o'clock in the morning.'

Michael looked horrified. 'But won't the flowers be dead by Saturday?'

'It will take them three days to set everything up and then they'll add the flowers to the decorations at the last moment. Remember, the theme is going to be very elaborate and a surprise for everyone. You ain't seen nuttin' yet!' Douglas crowed with boyish enthusiasm.

'And how much is *that* going to cost?' Michael demanded like a querulous old man, as he stomped upstairs to bed.

Anna lay awake for a long time that night, so excited about the ball that sleep was impossible. They'd never given a really big 'do' before, drinks parties or garden parties for a hundred or so guests hardly counting by comparison. And her mother had bought her a wonderful blue chiffon dress, with shoes to match. Would Petroc think she looked beautiful? What a pity they wouldn't be able to sleep together this weekend, she reflected with a flash of resentment. Although her parents knew that they often spent the night together in London, and Julia had even taken her to see her own gynaecologist before she went on the pill, when Anna came home to Highfield Manor it was made very clear that she and Petroc must have separate rooms and there was to be no creeping around the corridors in the middle of the night. Their old-fashioned attitude infuriated Anna, and she'd once accused them of being hypocritical, of not minding what she did so long as she did it discreetly, but they'd stuck to their guns. Even if she and Petroc got engaged at the party, she'd still end up alone in her room, while he'd be in one of the guest rooms.

Nancy Graham peered out of her bedroom window for one last peep before getting into bed. Through the beeches the marquee now looked like a great white whale sleeping in the moonlight. It loomed curiously immobile; even the wind that ruffled the grass and swished through the leaves didn't cause it to move an inch. For once the house was quiet, too. All the lights were out. Nothing more was going to happen tonight.

Getting into her double bed with its ivory brocade headboard and matching bedcover, a jaded relic of a time when she had endured the feeble fumblings of the late Philip Graham, Nancy pondered on her confrontation earlier in the evening with Douglas Rutherford. He'd made her so angry with his swaggering arrogance, and the confident way he'd assumed she'd jump at the offer of a night at the Savoy, that she'd decided it was time he was taught a lesson. To complain to the police about the noise on Saturday night would be to let him off far too lightly. She knew for a fact that five thousand pounds was the maximum fine for a breach of the peace and to Douglas Rutherford that would be mere petty cash. Her mind worked with swift cunning. Maybe she would do a little research into all the village gossip she'd heard when she'd first moved to Cherry Tree Cottage. A little gentle coaxing, some encouragement here and there ... The owner of the local village store could usually be persuaded to talk, and as the Rutherfords were giving this big party on Saturday she could bring up the topic of Douglas quite naturally. Without arousing suspicion.

Nancy Graham smiled to herself. With a firm click she switched off her bedside light and settled down to sleep, but it evaded her. She was too busy planning her neighbour's downfall.

Wednesday

19 June 1996

Three

On Wednesday morning Julia was awakened at six o'clock, by the heavy pattering of rain. Turning over in the enormous double bed, she opened her eyes and groaned inwardly. Beside her, Douglas slept on. Sleeping the deep sleep of an untroubled mind, she thought with envy, looking at his bulky outline. Her husband was one of those fortunate people who were able to shut out all the worries of the day the minute his head touched the pillow. He never read in bed, or talked, and on the nights he made love to her he remained totally alert until, with a final embrace, he kissed her goodnight, rolled over, and was lost to her. Julia hadn't slept well since . . . She sat up in the bed and decided it was better to get up and get on with the day than lie there tormenting herself with the what ifs of the world. The way to a nervous breakdown was paved with what ifs . . .

Sliding out of the bed so as not to disturb Douglas, who didn't like being awakened before seven o'clock, she pulled on her white cotton dressing-gown and crept out of their room. Downstairs, she made herself some coffee, instant because it was quicker, and turned on the television. Over the years Julia had discovered two ways of dealing with the feeling of angst that sometimes brought her to heart-pounding consciousness at dawn. The first was to get into a vertical position; once her feet were on the ground she felt more in control of her life. The second was to distract herself with breakfast television.

The more banal the programme the better. But today she had a real reason to concentrate on the screen; she wanted to see the weather forecast for the next few days. She was desperate for the party to be a success, not only for Anna and William's sake, but for her own and Douglas's too. At one time she'd been convinced that they'd never make it. It had been touch and go . . . but reaching this anniversary was like setting the seal on the success of their marriage, something no one could take away from them. And a wonderful success it had been. Wrapping her hands around the mug of coffee, she kept her eyes fixed on the screen, forcing her fears aside and facing the day with her usual sweet complacency.

In a few minutes Mrs Morgan would be darting around the kitchen getting breakfast for everyone, a tiny slim figure with short grey hair who could only find clothes to fit her in the children's department of any store, and whom Douglas referred to as a 'geriatric anorexic'. 'She's no advertisement for her own cooking,' he'd observe dryly. A few minutes later her husband, who acted as butler and driver and was in charge of the maintenance of Highfield Manor, would appear, dapper and with his remaining hair smoothed neatly over his bald patch, to lay the table for breakfast, each knife, fork and spoon arranged with military precision.

It was still raining, hissing on the leaves and splattering against the windows. Across the lawn, the marquee stood damply against the jewelled grass. It did not look promising.

'Good morning, ma'am,' Mrs Morgan said gaily as she charged over to the Aga. 'Chilly this morning, isn't it?'

'Yes. I'm worried about Saturday.'

Mrs Morgan stared at her, small grey eyes round with astonishment. 'It'll clear by Saturday,' she replied dismissively.

'I hope so.'

''Course it will. And the garden could do with a drop of rain. Make it nice and fresh.' She banged the kettle down on top of the Aga. 'Another cup of coffee, ma'am?'

Julia shook her head. 'I'm fine, thank you,' she replied, already feeling better. By the time she'd finished her coffee, and heard that 'A showery start to the day would give way to warm sunshine', no one would have guessed how anxious and depressed she'd been when she'd awakened. It was part of Julia's nature to keep her problems and worries to herself. Even Douglas didn't know how almost every morning she had to struggle to emerge from her private prison of depression. The only boon was that it wore off as soon as she got going, and as the day passed she felt increasingly better.

Douglas was up and about to have his bath when she returned to their room.

'Look at that bloody rain,' he boomed.

'It's going to clear and be sunny later on,' she informed him, seating herself at her dressing-table and brushing her long hair.

'What? God gave you an assurance?'

Julia nodded, smiling up at him. 'In person!'

He kissed her hard and swiftly on the mouth. 'In that case I'll cancel the insurance policy against a storm on Saturday night.'

'Don't tempt providence, darling.'

His eyes dwelt lovingly on her fine, neat features. 'Maybe you're right. Listen, I've got to rush. I've got a meeting at Butterfly at nine-thirty.'

Julia caught his hand. 'Will you be away all day?'

'I've got lunch with another bloody journalist. Be home again by five, I should think. Anyway, I'll be on the mobile if there are any panics here.' As he entered their bathroom he shouted over his shoulder, 'Don't forget John Plested and his team will be here to start the decorations.'

'I know. And your parents are arriving during the afternoon, too.'

Douglas spun round, looking shocked. 'Christ! For the moment I'd forgotten. I'll get back as soon as I can, darling. And explain to them I'm flat out with the restaurants. They'll understand.'

Julia nodded, knowing that was true. Pat and Reggie Rutherford would forgive their darling son if he cheated at games, robbed the Bank of England or committed mass murder.

'Can you talk? Or is your boss breathing down your neck?' Anna asked in a low voice. It was early afternoon and, aching to talk to Petroc, she'd phoned him at his office.

'He's still at lunch,' her boyfriend replied easily. 'Stupid old fart! He never gets back to the office until after three-thirty. So how's everything going?'

'I'm missing you, sweetie,' she said mournfully. 'I haven't seen you since Sunday and now it's Wednesday. That's three whole days.'

'Well, I'll be down on Friday evening.'

'I don't think I can bear to wait that long, and even

then . . . oh, God! There'll be masses of people around all the time, so we won't be able to . . . you know. Are you missing me?'

'Yes. Of course.'

'Really, really missing me? Like I'm missing you?'

'Yes, Anna. Of course I am.' Then his voice dropped to a whisper. 'I can't talk now, the office is full of people.'

She couldn't keep the disappointment out of her voice. 'Is it? Can't you go to another phone?'

'Not really. It would look odd.'

'Oh, Petroc! This is real agony. I wish I'd stayed in London this week instead of coming down here. I love you so much. What are you going to do this evening?'

'Don't know yet. I'll probably go to the pub for a drink. Watch some TV or something. What are you doing?'

'The usual things. Grandma and Grandpa are arriving today. Everything's going very well for Saturday. It's going to be the most fantastic party.'

'That's good.'

'I can't wait for you to get here.'

'Yup.'

'Is there anything wrong, Petroc? You sound sort of . . . I don't know, strange.'

'Everything's fine, but I ought to go now. I've got masses of work to do.'

'You sound tired,' she said sympathetically.

'I'm knackered,' he agreed.

'So I'll see you on Friday? In time for dinner?'

'Yes. I should get to you about seven-thirty, if the traffic's not too bad.'

'I can't wait! 'Bye, sweetie. Love you lots.'

''Bye. See you Friday.' There was a click and he was

gone, his warm, richly timbred voice no longer thrilling her, the chance to talk to him over. With a sigh Anna wandered back into the garden, wondering how she was going to get through two more days without feeling his arms around her; his kisses, hot and demanding; his strong hands, gentle but searching. Deep inside her there was a real physical ache of longing for him. Then she felt another flash of irritation that her parents insisted they have separate rooms. Didn't they realise these were the nineties? If she couldn't be with Petroc on Friday night she would *die*. Well, she *would* be with him. As soon as everyone had gone to bed she'd creep along to his room and stay there all night. And if she got caught, it was too damn' bad!

'Hello, Grandma! Hello, Grandpa!' Anna came hurtling down the front steps of Highfield Manor and flung her arms around Pat and Reggie Rutherford, just as she'd done when she was a little girl.

Pat searched the grey eyes, so like Douglas's, to see if there was any vestige left of the little child she'd known so well when she'd been small; the child she'd often bathed and put to bed and read stories to when Douglas and Julia were both working in their first restaurant. Her one regret about the passing of time was that her children and grandchildren had grown up so quickly, and in doing so had seemed to grow away; like the climbing branches of a vine, still attached to the roots but stretching out along their own chosen paths. It appalled her to realise that Anna even drove her own car now; instinctively she felt her granddaughter should still be holding her hand to cross the road.

'Hello, my sweetheart,' Pat exclaimed, kissing the

peach-soft cheeks. 'Don't you look well!'

'It's chaos here,' Anna replied cheerfully, 'but at least it's stopped raining.'

'Look at that!' Reggie paused to look at the marquee, from which banging could be heard and billowing red silk glimpsed through the opening. 'It's big enough, I must say.'

Anna tucked her arm through his. 'None of us is allowed inside because Daddy wants the decorations to be a surprise on the night,' she explained. 'Mummy's on the phone but we're going to have tea in a few minutes.' She led them into the house, and across the hall to the drawing room.

'It's a bit like being back-stage before a performance,' Reggie observed, glancing around at stacks of gilt chairs, bales of fabric, boxes of candles, dozens of lanterns, crates of bananas, and even a few Grecian-style stucco pillars and statues. In his younger days, before he'd set up his own accountancy business, he'd worked in the accounts department of the Royal Opera House in Covent Garden and loved to reminisce about those days, and tell thrilling stories about what went on behind the scenes. Like the occasion in 1965 when all Maria Callas's costumes for a performance of *Tosca* went missing just two hours before curtain-up.

'Most of the stuff will be going outside,' Anna told them, 'but John had it put in the hall this morning because the lawn was soaking wet, and there was no room in the marquee, at the moment.'

'John . . .?' Pat enquired.

'John Plested. The floral designer. Ah! Here's Mummy.'

Julia, in cream linen trousers and a long matching jacket, came hurrying out of the study. 'Pat darling, I'm sorry I wasn't there to greet you. I was stuck on the phone and couldn't get off.' She kissed her mother-in-law fondly on each cheek before turning to Reggie whom she also adored. 'Reggie, you're looking well! It's lovely to see you both. Come into the drawing room where it's fairly peaceful. I can't tell you what it's been like this morning! Everything, including the crockery and glasses for three hundred people, was delivered two days early, and nobody knew where to put it because the units in the mobile kitchen haven't been set up yet.'

'Isn't Douglas here to help?' demanded Reggie.

Julia's smile was indulgent. 'He's far too busy with Butterfly to stay down here all week. He's been having journalists to lunch every day. You know what it's like when he opens a new restaurant. But he'll be home in an hour or so.'

Pat settled herself in one of the pastel-covered arm-chairs by the fireplace, which in the summer overflowed with arrangements of flowers and leaves from the garden. Thin and neat in her plain brown skirt and blouse, she looked as eager as a sparrow.

'So tell us all that's happening, dear,' she said to Julia, adjusting her glasses. 'When is everyone arriving?'

'Well, you're the first of the family to arrive, because we haven't seen you for ages and this is a good opportunity to catch up, but the rest are turning up on Friday. After which all hell breaks loose!' Julia replied cheerfully. 'We'll have twenty-one people staying, and three hundred coming to the party.'

Pat shook her head, but she looked excited. 'What a lot of organising that's going to take! When I arrange a trip up to London for the local Women's Institute, *that* drives me crazy, and I'm probably only making arrangements for thirty or forty people. It's the logistics that are a nightmare,' she added knowingly, as if her experience was vast.

'Tell me about it!' Julia laughed. 'My main worry is the parking. If it rains any more the meadow is going to be a quagmire and I reckon there'll be at least a hundred and twenty cars.'

'You've got parking attendants?' Reggie asked, ever efficient.

'Yes, six. Then, apart from all of us and the guests at the party, we've got to cater for dozens of waiters and barmen . . . arrange for tons of ice to be delivered late on Saturday afternoon . . . finalise the seating plan . . . oh, my God!' Julia's hands flew up to cover her already pale cheeks. She turned to Anna, her expression stricken. 'The Lindsays phoned this morning to say they could come after all, and I've forgotten to include them on the seating plan . . .'

Anna rose. 'I'll do it now. Are they to go on any special table?'

'Don't, for God's sake, put them with Martin and Carina Buckman. Rosemary Lindsay's brother broke up Carina's sister's marriage last year. They don't speak.'

'Right.' Anna nodded her understanding as she hurried out of the room.

'Was it wise to ask them in that case?' Pat enquired anxiously.

Julia shrugged her shoulders. 'Nearly everyone I know seems to have been involved in an affair or a divorce. We'd have no guests at all if we tried to keep them all apart.'

'Well, I'm glad to say there's been none of that in our family,' Reggie remarked grimly. He didn't believe in

45

divorce. Took an even dimmer view of 'living in sin', unmarried mothers and abortion.

Julia gave a tight, fleeting smile. She believed in the sanctity of marriage, too, but she was more liberal-minded; to her it wasn't so much what people actually did as the spirit in which they did it, and if real love was the motivating force behind anyone's actions, then that should be taken into account.

'The moment of truth will come,' she remarked smoothly, 'when the toast master announces dinner, and everyone takes their seats. I think I'll lock myself in the loo and only come out when I'm sure I haven't left anyone out by mistake.'

'I could help you check the list,' Pat offered brightly.

There was only a fractional pause, not discernible to her in-laws, before Julia replied. 'Thank you, Pat. That would be most helpful.'

Vivien Leonard had been greatly looking forward to her daughter's twenty-fifth wedding anniversary party, until a heart-stopping moment when she discovered the lump in her breast. It *couldn't* be . . . Oh God, surely not! But it was there, no bigger than a large baked bean firmly fixed under the skin; it didn't hurt and it wasn't red. Both bad signs. An icy feeling swept through her like a tidal wave and, weak with fear, she sank to her knees in front of the tall cheval-glass in her bedroom.

Vivien, now sixty-eight, had been a great beauty in her youth. In the forties, she and Barbara Goalen had been the two top models who had made the profession accept-able, even for aristocratic girls. As Vivien Strong, she became *Vogue*'s favourite model, gracing the glossy pages of the magazine each month, photographed in the latest

Paris fashions. With her eighteen-inch waist, long slim legs and dainty feet that easily slipped into size four shoes, she inspired thousands of women to try and emulate her. But few could match the porcelain skin, the exquisite bone structure, the rich chestnut hair.

When Dior's New Look was launched, Barbara Goalen and Vivien Strong were the models who most perfectly displayed the wasp-waisted suits with their ankle-length skirts, jaunty hats decorated with flowers, feathers and veils, very high-heeled shoes and kid gloves dyed to match. By the end of her second modelling season, Vivien became engaged to the wealthy Prince Guido Aldrovandi Falsini. After a lavish London wedding she went to live with him in his *palazzo* just outside Rome where Julia was born the following year. She had inherited her mother's exquisite looks but her father's fine-boned frame and dark hair and eyes, and the combination was enchanting. They both doted on her and took her everywhere with them as they divided their time between London and Rome.

Not surprisingly they soon dominated the social scene. Vivien, now able to afford the sort of clothes she'd modelled in the past from Dior, Balmain and Givenchy, overshadowed all the other women, and in spite of his diminutive stature, the sheer charisma of Guido's personality made other men fade into the background. They were the international set's most starry couple, the darlings of the society pages, the epitome of fairytale happiness; a romantic prince and princess who lived in a sixteenth-century palace and were blessed with beauty and wealth, and an enchanting baby daughter.

Then in 1953 tragedy struck. On a business trip to Lucerne, the private light aircraft in which Guido was travelling crashed into a mountainside. There were no survivors. Vivien was devastated. For several days she was under sedation while Julia was looked after by her nanny. Then it was discovered that Guido had been on the verge of bankruptcy at the time of the crash and had been on his way to see a Swiss banker, a friend of his late father's, to see about a loan.

With her whole world collapsing around her, Vivien returned to England. The *palazzo*, with its priceless furniture and paintings, had been seized, together with her jewellery and furs. She had nothing but what she stood up in, and a four-year-old daughter to support. Living with her parents in London, she tried to get back into modelling while they looked after Julia. But a new breed of model was storming the catwalks and filling the fashion magazines; more relaxed, natural-looking girls, with fuller figures. The hothouse orchid had been replaced by the wild rose and Vivien realised she no longer fitted in. She took what work she could get, mostly in fashion houses where the pay was low and the hours long. Then, one day, when she was modelling for the Rhavis sisters in their Mayfair salon, a rich client came in accompanied by her brother. Her husband was abroad and she wanted a man's opinion before buying clothes for Royal Ascot.

And that was how Vivien came to meet Simon Leonard. Later he told her that he'd fallen in love with her the moment she'd glided into the salon, wearing a cream silk suit with a large cream hat. After an old-fashioned courtship which involved him sending her endless bouquets of flowers and notes, Vivien agreed to marry him.

'I'm not in love with him,' she told her parents, 'but I

like him and he's very kind. He also loves Julia, so I'd be a fool to turn down a chance like this.'

Simon Leonard was rich, but not flamboyantly, vulgarly rich as Guido had once been. He bought a house with a garden in a quiet Kensington street, gave Vivien a car and a generous allowance, and in return she ran his house and entertained his friends to perfection. She did something else as well. She fell in love with him, deeply, utterly and passionately. And when she bore him a son, Christopher, two years later, their happiness was complete. At times she wondered what she'd ever seen in Guido, so all-consuming had her devotion to Simon become. Her only fear, over the years, was that fate would take him away from her, too.

And now this. Vivien looked into the mirror and saw the fear in her own eyes. Surely she was too old to have breast cancer? Didn't it strike women in their forties and fifties? Sick with anguish and shock, she staggered over to the bed and lay down, despair washing over her, dragging her down with its undercurrent of terror. What was she going to do? Her first thought was to protect Simon. She wouldn't say a thing, pretend everything was all right, and then go to the doctor secretly next week; get through the weekend first; act normally at Julia and Douglas's party.

I must not spoil everyone's weekend, she told herself firmly.

A few minutes later she rose again, tentatively feeling her breast once more in case she'd made a mistake. But the lump was still there, and all the reassuring tales she'd heard of lumps turning out to be non-malignant cysts evaporated from her mind like the dawn mist; she was certain this was cancer.

Only one tiny thought brought her comfort. It probably meant she would die before Simon.

'So long as my wife never finds out,' Christopher Leonard murmured as he stroked Barbara's long gold-streaked hair, which felt silky and sensuous between his blunt-tipped fingers. It was lunchtime and they were lying on the kingsize bed in her Park Lane apartment.

'You could say you've got to stay in London on Friday night because you have a client flying in from the States,' Barbara replied, quick as a flash.

'I suppose that's the only thing I *can* say,' Christopher agreed, 'but I had promised my mother and father I'd give them a lift down to Julia's party.'

'They won't mind, will they? Can't they hire a car?' she asked in a wheedling voice.

'I suppose so. I could arrange for a chauffeur-driven car to take them.'

Christopher was a successful lawyer, a partner in Blumfield, Morgan and Coleridge, solicitors in Gray's Inn, and enjoyed a standard of living that was the envy of many of his friends. He and his wife Oonagh were on the A-list for the best parties in town and practically every month their photographs appeared in the social diaries of *Tatler* and *Harpers & Queen*, champagne glasses in hand, inane smiles pinned to their faces. He could easily afford to send his parents down to Hampshire in a limousine, and arrange for a car to bring them back to London on Monday, too. It wasn't as caring as taking them down himself, but they'd understand. They'd always backed him in whatever he did, and everything he did they thought was marvellous. Unlike Oonagh. If she ever found out about Barbara she'd make sure he was ruined professionally, socially and financially. In fact, she'd go for gold with the determination of an Olympic contender.

Barbara slid her hand between his thighs, instantly arousing him again.

'If you stayed in London on Friday night, darling,' she whispered, 'surely you wouldn't have to get down to your sister's dance until late on Saturday afternoon, would you?' Her hand slipped higher. She reflected that she'd have liked to have gone to Julia and Douglas Rutherford's dance, too, but she'd never met Chris's sister. Only Oonagh, and of course his wife hadn't known who she was.

It had been at the opening of the O'Hagan Gallery in Cork Street, an occasion for rubber-necking and trying to get photographed talking to someone important, when she'd glanced over to the entrance to see who was being greeted by an explosion of flash bulbs. With a sense of shock she realised it was Christopher with his wife. Barbara knew it was Oonagh Leonard; she'd seen that cold gamine face with the neat dark hair staring at her from dozens of photographs. 'Chic' was how Nigel Dempster described her in his column, and chic was what she was, from her Paloma Picasso gold earrings, teamed with a little black Chanel dress, to her Manolo Blahnik high-heeled, fuck-me shoes.

Christopher spotted Barbara at the same moment but not by the merest flicker did he acknowledge her. She skirted carefully around the couple until she saw them talking to someone she knew. Then she glided up to join the group, forcing an introduction. Oonagh nodded at her politely but her eyes said, You're someone who is of no use to me so I needn't bother talking to you. Christopher's eyes took on a blank look and he merely muttered, 'How d'you do?' before turning away. When Barbara saw him a few days later in her flat, neither of them referred to the incident.

'I have to go now,' he groaned, looking down at himself. 'Look what you're doing to me.'

'Then I'll stop,' she replied lightly, withdrawing her hands. She turned to face him, all tanned and golden with nipples like ripe raspberries and tousled blonde hair falling about her small childlike face. 'Save it for Friday night.'

'I want you now.' His eyes were filled with longing, his voice yearning.

'You've just had me, darling. And I'm always here for you,' she said softly.

Christopher gave her a sad smile and slid off the bed to go and have a shower. It would be fatal to carry the smell of another woman back to Oonagh. The trouble was, the whole situation had become much more complicated than he'd intended. When he'd first met Barbara at a drinks party, to which he'd gone alone because Oonagh had been unwell, he'd been very attracted to her. She was sweet, sexy, and a trust fund babe with time on her hands and money with which to enjoy it. Her father had given her the swish flat for her twenty-first birthday and she had no need to work. One thing led to another and before he knew it, he'd taken her to bed within weeks of their first meeting. She confessed to liking older men, and added that she hadn't had a steady boyfriend for the past year. Before Christopher knew it, he found he'd fallen in love with her, utterly and hopelessly. So much so, he was even dreading having to go away for this weekend. How was he going to survive without her tender kisses, the gentle expression in her blue eyes, and the wondrous things she did with her hands and her body?

★ ★ ★

Nancy Graham's day had been most satisfactory. As far as she could make out, from her little chat with Mr Harris, who owned the village store, a lot of things had happened in the village some sixteen or seventeen years ago.

'Around the time the Rutherfords moved into Highfield Manor,' he murmured, as he took down Nancy's order, larger than usual he noticed, to be delivered the next morning.

'Really? Better make that three pounds of sugar,' she added encouragingly. 'What sort of things?'

They were interrupted at that moment by another customer coming into the small shop, but as soon as she'd gone, Nancy, ordering more goods than she really wanted, persisted with her questions, and Mr Harris was quite willing to indulge in talk. He ended by saying sourly: 'Disgraceful, it was! We're not used to people like them around here.'

It was obvious he hated the Rutherfords, but it hadn't escaped even Nancy Graham's notice that the reason he didn't like them was because they brought down all their supplies from London, and never purchased so much as a box of matches from him.

'I think I'd better have a large washing-up liquid, six bars of Lux and two cans of furniture polish,' Nancy continued, asking as an afterthought: 'And then what happened?'

She was startled by the strange look he gave her.

'She went and died, didn't she?' he said abruptly, and at that moment someone else came into the shop.

'You're home very late?' Oonagh's voice rang out sharply

from the drawing room as Christopher let himself into their Kensington house that evening.

'It's only just gone seven,' he retorted mildly.

'We're expected at the opening of Theo Fennell's new jewellery store in a few minutes,' she said, coming and standing in the drawing-room doorway, as straight and upright as a telegraph pole in her black dress, and about as seductive, he thought, looking at her perfect geometrically cut hairstyle and the hard black outline of the kohl around her eyes. His mind was filled with the memory of wildly tangled blonde hair and softly smudged blue eyes, dazed with passion. His heart ached with despair.

'I'll go and change my shirt. I'll only be a moment,' he said, turning to climb the curved staircase.

'Don't you want a shower?' Oonagh asked, surprised.

'I'll leave it for now. It'll make us late,' he lied, taking the steps two at a time. To get away from her. To have a few moments on his own in which to think about Barbara.

They took a taxi to the party, so that he wouldn't have to find a parking space and so he could drink.

'By the way, I'm arranging for a hired car and driver to take you and my mother and father down to Julia's on Friday afternoon,' he said conversationally, as the taxi trundled down Gloucester Road. 'I've got to stay in town. Some important clients are flying in from the States and I've got to give them dinner, but I'll join you all on Saturday.'

There was a long, icy silence in the cab. Christopher looked at Oonagh. Her face was white with anger.

'You've forgotten, haven't you? You've bloody well forgotten,' she said coldly.

'Forgotten what?' He racked his brains but couldn't think of anything.

'What week do you think this is, for God's sake?'

'Week?' He stared at her blankly. He had no idea what she was talking about.

'Ascot week, you fool!' she shouted, her voice harsh. 'And you promised me . . . *promised* . . . that we could go on the Friday, because you said you were too busy to get away the other days.'

Christopher had never seen her so furious. 'Well . . . there's always next year,' he said feebly.

'Next year?' Enraged eyes met his. 'Not only have I bought a new outfit and hat, but I've arranged that we meet Delia and Tony Hammond, Richard Seeley and Monica Pembroke, and Mark and Lucy Miller. We're all having a picnic lunch. I *told* you, Chris. We discussed it. We decided we'd need our car and the Pembrokes would take theirs, but the Hammonds decided to hire an estate car, because none of us has room for all the picnic tables and chairs and everything.'

Christopher felt stunned. He'd completely forgotten about it, so engrossed was he in other ways of spending his time away from the office.

'Oh, God!' he exclaimed.

'You're taking me to Ascot and that's that,' Oonagh snapped. 'Cancel whatever else you've fixed. I will not be let down on a day like this.'

Christopher gritted his teeth, knowing he'd now have to spend Friday night in London with Oonagh. 'What about my parents? Julia's invited them for Friday. She wants to give them time to settle in before the party.'

Oonagh shrugged. 'Send them down with a driver, as you'd planned. Only don't expect *me* to go with them.

You and I can drive down on Saturday. That'll be time enough, anyway.'

Oonagh wasn't particularly looking forward to the weekend, although she liked parties. The problem was she'd never got on with her sister-in-law, finding her smugness at her perfect life deeply irritating. Julia never stopped saying how lucky she was to have Douglas, and how much she loved him, and how wonderful Anna and William and Michael were, and how blessed she was as a mother. It made Oonagh want to throw up. Life wasn't that perfect for anyone. Certainly not for her.

So far as she was concerned, Christopher was OK as a husband in that he was quite good-looking, dressed well and had charming manners. But as a lover . . .! Or a companion . . .! He was permanently distracted by work, the charm was switched off as soon as they were on their own, and he never talked to her about anything. Theirs was a brittle relationship, as shallow as their lives and as false as their smiles for the paparazzi, but what else was there? Their only child, Timothy, was nineteen and at Edinburgh University, so he didn't need her. And if Oonagh ever felt a pang at having an empty nest, there was always the compensation of having a very active social life. It was wonderful how lots of champagne and making small talk with strangers could soften the edges.

It was six o'clock at Highfield Manor and everyone was looking exhausted. Julia had spent the afternoon finalising the seating plan; at least she hoped this was the final arrangement, but last-minute acceptances kept coming in, and Anna and William kept wanting to alter where their friends were sitting, and long telephone conversations revealed couples who had fallen out in the past twenty-four hours and couldn't possibly sit together, or others who seemed, most inconveniently to Julia, to have suddenly fallen in love, and were desperate to sit together.

The numbers had also gone up: to three hundred and eleven.

'What an odd number,' Julia said, puzzled.

'That's because Squiffy Melrose is coming on his own now,' Anna said, au fait with what Julia referred to as 'the Young List'.

'Shouldn't we find a girl for him?'

Anna threw back her head, laughing. 'He'll probably bring someone at the last moment, knowing Squiffy.'

Julia frowned in irritation. 'That's exactly what I *don't* want to happen. Where will she sit? There won't be a place for her!'

'OK, Mum. Chill out. Does everyone have to have a place card? Why don't you just do it for your lot? Then William's and my friends can sit where they like?'

'That'll cause chaos,' Julia exclaimed. 'You'll end up with all the plain girls on one table, and those who are already friends huddled together on another, not talking to anyone else, while you'll have your favourite chums with you . . . it's out of the question.'

'I don't see why.'

'Our most important job is to make sure all our guests are looked after and have a good time. It's not enough for us to enjoy ourselves, you know. The guests come first,' Julia added firmly.

'I'm not going to enjoy it at all at this rate,' Anna wailed. 'The next thing you'll say is I can't sit next to Petroc.'

'Of course you can sit next to him, but what I'm saying is we must make sure everyone is looked after before we go dashing off to enjoy ourselves.'

At that moment John Plested put his head through the open study window, leaning heavily on the sill with his arms. 'We've done all we can do for today,' he said. 'So I think we'll be off.'

Julia sprang to her feet. 'Not until you've had a drink,' she exclaimed. 'Come in. Bring the others. You must be absolutely exhausted.'

Ever the hostess, she asked Morgan to bring glasses, white wine and mineral water into the study so that when John appeared with the rest of his team, she was on her feet, ready to greet them, looking as fresh as she had that morning.

'Elaine, how are you? Hello, Georgie, come and sit down. Andrew, Ruth, Graham ... come in! What will you have to drink? Ah, Gail! Lovely to see you. Have some wine; you're not driving, are you? Graham, you're driving? Oh, you don't drink anyway? That's lucky! I'm dying of curiosity to know what you've all dreamed up in the marquee!'

'Don't raise your hopes too high, you may think it's a nightmare when you see it,' John chuckled.

'It'll certainly get people talking,' Elaine observed, cheerfully.

'I don't think we've ever done anything quite like it,' Andrew agreed.

'We must get lots of photographs taken, before the guests arrive,' Julia commented excitedly. Watching her, they marvelled at her energy and genuine enthusiasm, as she topped up their glasses, and handed around a bowl of cashew nuts.

When Douglas returned from London a few minutes later, it sounded as if a full-scale party was under way.

'Starting already?' he quipped, putting his head round the door.

'Darling!' Julia hurried over to greet him. 'I didn't hear you arrive. What sort of a day did you have?'

'OK.' He kissed her lightly on the lips. 'Is that a drink I see before me?' he misquoted, looking at the bottles of wine.

Julia swooped forward, picked up a glass and filled it. 'There you are. I was just saying, I'm longing to see what they've been doing in the marquee.'

Douglas grinned. 'Only three days to go! And then – WOW!' He looked at John and the others, his eyebrows raised. 'Everything going to plan? Are we on schedule?'

'I like the royal *we*!' Anna said laughingly. 'You haven't so much as picked a flower, Daddy.'

'Wait until I get going,' he retorted robustly. 'Oh, by the way,' he turned to Julia, 'I'm staying down here for the rest of the week . . .'

Her face lit up, and her eyes blazed with delight. 'Darling! That's wonderful. Oh, it will be so lovely to have you at home. What a relief . . . I thought I was going to have to see to all the last-minute arrangements by myself.'

He slid his arm around her waist. 'As if I'd leave you to do everything,' he said, eyes lingering on her.

'Watch it, Ma,' Anna warned jokingly. 'He'll have you running around after *him* all week if you're not careful.'

Douglas threw back his head and laughed, catching Julia's hand and swinging it, and John and the others saw the public persona of the man in action; larger than life, expansive, generous, manipulative and a born host, whether in one of his restaurants or in his own home.

Julia laughed too. She suddenly felt gloriously carefree.

The party really was going to be fun. It would be an exciting night of revelry; an occasion they would remember forever; a celebration of enduring love, of family life, warm friendship and loyalties. She squeezed Douglas's hand tighter.

'I expect we'll *all* be running around after your father,' she remarked happily.

Vivien replaced the received later that evening and turned to Simon. 'That was Christopher. He's very kindly fixing for a chauffeur-driven car to take us down to Julia's on Friday,' she told him. 'Isn't that nice?' Almost as if he knew, she thought.

'Very nice,' Simon agreed from the depths of an armchair, where he was comfortably ensconced, watching television. 'I thought we were going down with Oonagh?'

Vivien smiled. 'He thought so too, but he'd forgotten it's the last day of Royal Ascot. Oonagh has arranged for them to meet up with friends for a picnic. They're coming down on Saturday instead. More coffee, darling?'

She'd taken special care with her appearance for dinner so that Simon, who'd been playing golf, would not guess the inner turmoil and shock she'd been suffering all day. It also made her feel better to know she looked good. Luckily she'd kept her figure; velvet trousers and a cream silk shirt made her look years younger than sixty-eight, and she had few wrinkles. Too soon to become an old woman. Too soon to die.

I'll beat this thing, she swore to herself, filled with determination as she looked at herself in the mirror. God, she thought, casting her eyes to heaven, don't rush me. I'm not ready yet.

Thursday

20 June 1996

Four

Three days to go. Everyone was revving up for Saturday night, in various stages of hysteria. Douglas, bounding about, supercharged on adrenalin, was bellowing, albeit charmingly, at anyone who got in his way. Julia, looking thinner than ever, had an almost ethereal quality as she flitted around, complaining that she wouldn't be able to put the place cards on the tables unless she was allowed into the marquee at least three hours before kick-off.

In the house, Anna had been detailed to make sure all the spare rooms had extra blankets, flowers, mineral water and magazines, while the bathrooms had to be kitted out with everything from piles of fluffy towels to hangover cures. William and Michael, considered too oafish by their mother to do anything dainty, were delegated to help Peters, the gardener, weed the flower beds, rake the gravel drive and manicure the edges of the lawn.

'What can I do to help?' Pat Rutherford bleated from time to time, but her cries went unheard as the others dashed around, high on purpose and self-importance. 'Be back in a moment,' they said breathlessly, and then were not seen again for hours.

'We'd do better to let them get on with it,' Reggie said

sagely. 'When everyone else arrives tomorrow, we can talk to them.'

'Talk?' Pat rather wished they'd delayed their own arrival until tomorrow. She hated feeling useless.

'Entertain all their other guests, dear.'

'But they're not expecting guests, it's just family,' Pat replied rather tartly.

'So we'll talk to them,' Reggie said patiently. 'Anyway, I think there are going to be some guests. Isn't Anna's boyfriend coming to stay? And an old friend of Julia's? Caroline something?'

Pat shrugged her shoulders and pulled her bright green cardigan closer. 'What time is it?'

He consulted his heavy wrist watch. 'A quarter-past eleven.'

'It's going to be a very long day,' she said hollowly, wishing she was a part of the whirlwind blowing through Highfield Manor; realising, though, that old age was beginning to prevent her from being a part of anything.

'Are you all right, John?' Julia asked anxiously. He was balancing what looked like a Corinthian column on his shoulder as he made his way across the lawn in the direction of the marquee.

'I'm fine.' He chuckled. 'It's only fibreglass, weighs just a few pounds.'

'I wish I could see what's happening inside,' she said longingly, falling into step beside him.

John raised his eyebrows and his brown eyes twinkled.

'Perhaps it's better that you don't,' he said darkly.

'Am I really going to have a terrific surprise on Saturday?'

Again the chuckle, huskier than ever. 'More like a huge shock, I'd say.'

Julia grinned. 'Thank God I trust you!'

'You might not after this,' he quipped back. 'Your husband's really gone to town this time.'

His business partner Elaine rushed past at that moment, her arms full of laurel leaves, painted gold.

'My goodness!' Julia exclaimed. 'What's Douglas staging? *Julius Caesar?*'

'No, my darling,' his voice boomed, coming up behind her. 'Looking at you, more like *Romeo and Juliet* . . . or Julia, should I say?'

'Oh, Gawd! I'm off,' said John, charging into the marquee, dragging the Corinthian column after him.

Julia took her husband's arm, trying to detain him for even a few moments. 'How's everything going?'

'The caterers have arrived to equip the mobile kitchens,' he announced with satisfaction, 'and the shippers we use have just delivered something like a thousand bottles of Moët & Chandon, all the wines for the dinner, and whatever else we need . . .'

'A *thousand* bottles?'

'It'll keep for another occasion if we don't drink it all on Saturday,' he remarked breezily. He glanced at his wrist watch, his obsession with wanting to know the time at all times becoming marked today. 'The tables should be here soon. Now where the hell are the gas cylinders?' he asked with sudden irritation. 'Nobody can do anything in the kitchens until the gas arrives.' He gave Julia an absent-minded pat on the hand. 'I must go and find out what's happening, darling.' And with that he shot off.

She watched his broad-shouldered backview as he strode away. Douglas was never more in his element than when he was organising things, she reflected, whereas she was happier being directed, being told what to do, not having the responsibility of having to make decisions. Her domain was the home, it was her nest, but even here Douglas's touch could be seen in the way the rooms were decorated, and the style in which they entertained; and of course their flat in London, small, minimal and functional and only used for odd nights when they stayed in town, was almost entirely his creation. There was only one area which he surprisingly left to her, or in reality to Mrs Morgan, and that was the cooking, saying that his life revolved around trying out new recipes and designing menus, not to mention having to eat a restaurant-style lunch almost every day. All he wanted when he got home was something simple: 'Glorified nursery food, that's what I want,' he told Julia. 'Something warming and comforting and countrified.'

Later that morning, Nancy Graham hired the local taxi to take her to the village of Longford four miles away. She knew nothing about it and had never been there before; she wasn't even sure if she had the right address. Mr Harris hadn't been certain whether it was Cranberry Cottage, Meadow Lane, or Wishford Cottage, Cranberry Lane. 'I know there's a Cranberry somewhere in the address,' he'd said, smoothing his hands down the front of his crisp white cotton coat. He wore a fresh one every day.

'I don't approve of sloppy dressing,' he'd explained when she first remarked how nice it was to see a shopkeeper properly dressed. 'Especially when handling food. People may call me old-fashioned, but it's the way my father and my grandfather dressed when they had this shop, and I sees nothing wrong with it.'

Nancy Graham, who had old-fashioned ideas herself which she referred to as 'having standards', fervently agreed with him. That had been the start of their customer-and-shopkeeper relationship, and she particularly liked Mr Harris because he 'knew his place and showed respect'.

It was the same with Mr Miller, the local taxi driver, whom she'd used in the past to take her to the station.

'He's one of nature's gentlemen,' she once remarked to the vicar, making him wonder if she considered *him* one of God's gentlemen. 'He always calls me Ma'am, and carries my cases. I really cannot tolerate this terrible new habit of calling complete strangers "love",' she added despairingly.

Now as Mr Miller's old Ford Capri rattled along the winding country lanes, Nancy enlarged on her problem of not being entirely sure of the correct address.

'Do you know Longford well?' she asked.

Mr Miller shook his bald head. 'I can't say as I do, Ma'am. It's a bit off the beaten track. Don't lead nowhere, if you know what I mean. I've had the odd person pick me up at the station and ask me to take them to Longford, but it hasn't happened very often.'

'It's Cranberry something – either cottage or lane. Is Longford a big village?'

'About the same as Stickley, I'd say. But more scattered, like. What's the name of the people, Ma'am?'

Nancy Graham bit her narrow bottom lip with vexation. 'I don't know.'

Mr Miller slowed down the car with ill-concealed astonishment, but remained silent.

'I'm calling on a friend of a friend,' she explained hurriedly. 'I – I don't actually know them.'

'Then it's no good looking them up in the phone book, is it? To get the address?'

'I'm afraid not.'

Mr Miller sighed gustily. 'Oh, well, we'll drive around until we find the right place.'

'I'll be wanting you to wait for me while I . . . er . . . while I see these people, and then you can take me back to Stickley,' she added firmly.

And I bet the old bag doesn't even give me a decent tip, Mr Miller sighed to himself as he pressed his foot down hard on the accelerator.

'I'm seeking refuge,' said Julia, hurrying into the drawing room and closing the door behind her. Her in-laws looked up expectantly, their expressions like dogs that had been shut up too long and were hopeful of being taken for a walk.

'What's happening?' Pat asked eagerly.

Julia flopped down into a chair and kicked off her shoes.

'The place is crawling with people, there's cases of drink everywhere, loud music is pounding out of a radio in the electrical company's van . . . and this isn't even the party! What the hell's it going to be like on Saturday?'

Reggie rose from the sofa, laughing. 'Sounds like the celebrations have already started. Anything I can do to help?'

She looked at him gratefully. 'Could you get Douglas to stop running around for a moment and come in and have some lunch? It's only a snack in the breakfast room, but I do think he ought to stop and eat something.'

'Leave it to me,' he said immediately, hurrying from the room.

'What can I do, dear?' Pat asked plaintively.

'Oh, Pat, darling.' Julia sounded contrite. 'What a terrible hostess I'm being. You've been sitting here all morning . . .'

Pat blinked rapidly and her mouth trembled. 'It's so horrid, being old. One feels so useless . . . as if one's day was done.' A tear slid down her cheek and vanished into the folds of her green cardigan.

A moment later Julia was sitting beside her on the sofa, putting her arms around her. 'You mustn't think like that,' she admonished gently. 'Douglas and I want you both to relax and enjoy yourselves and not be worn out, as we undoubtedly shall be, before the party even begins,' she said, thinking rapidly.

'I'm relying on you,' she continued, smiling brightly into her mother-in-law's sad face, 'to help me look after everyone tomorrow. We've got people arriving from lunchtime onwards, and they're not all just family either. You and Reggie are so good at making things go with a swing and making people feel welcome. I know Douglas and I are going to get caught up in a million tiresome queries for most of the day, and it would be such a relief if I knew everyone was being looked after.'

Pat beamed with obvious delight. 'In that case, you'd better give me a list of who's expected,' she said, 'and which rooms they're sleeping in.' She looked around the drawing room, and it was obvious she was feeling revitalised by having something to do. 'Perhaps there should be a drinks tray in here, dear, so Reggie can offer people a drink when they arrive?'

'An excellent idea,' Julia agreed. 'Let's go and have some lunch, and then afterwards I'll give you a list of who's coming and which rooms they're in.'

'Will Morgan have a list as well? So he knows where to

put their luggage?' Pat was already on her feet, cardigan discarded, raring to go.

Julia looked at her, wide-eyed. 'I can see where Douglas gets his organisational talents from,' she observed. 'Come on, Pat. Let's have a chicken sandwich and a glass of wine and get down to work.'

'It's my fault as much as yours, but we must make sure your parents aren't neglected. They were feeling really left out of things,' Julia explained to Douglas as she took him a plate of sandwiches in the garden because he insisted on staying with 'the workers', who had already been given a picnic lunch, set up on a trestle table on the lawn.

'Oh, God, I hadn't realised. Are they all right now?' With his shirt open and his sleeves rolled up to the elbow, looking hot and dishevelled, he couldn't imagine a worse fate than being 'left out of things'.

'Yes. We're having something to eat in the breakfast room and they're fine. And I'm arranging for them to help us tomorrow with everyone arriving to stay.'

'Tomorrow,' Douglas told her gravely, 'is going to be hell on horseback. All the preparations have got to come together then. If they don't, we're fucked. By tomorrow night, everything's got to be *in situ*, so that on Saturday all that has to be done is to assemble the dinner and add the fresh flowers to the decorations. Oh, and set out the fireworks for the display at midnight.'

Julia nodded, knowing he was secretly enjoying every minute, and the more chaotic the better. 'Have you seen Anna, by the way? I can't find her anywhere.'

'I haven't seen her for hours. Wasn't she supposed to be checking all the bedrooms?'

'I gather she's done that. Oh well, if you see her, tell her to come and have something to eat.'

'OK, I will.' He grabbed her hand. 'Stay and talk to me.'

Julia leaned forward and kissed him sweetly on the lips then pulled away gently. 'I must get on, Douglas. I've got to drive Michael into Stockbridge this afternoon to have his hair cut.'

'I bet you're popular.'

'Oh, yeah, he's thrilled to bits,' she laughed. 'I'm flavour of the month.'

It had been her special place when she'd been a child, but Anna reckoned it must have been eight years since she'd last climbed up into the broad supportive arms of the old oak at the far end of the orchard. She remembered the last time vividly; she'd been due to go to boarding school the next day, and overwhelmed by the thought of leaving home, having to go into an unknown environment amongst people she'd never met, her nerves had given way and she'd hidden amongst the golden leaves of autumn, to sob her heart out.

The oak tree had been her bolt-hole in times of trouble, ever since she could remember. When she'd been scolded by her parents for some childish misdemeanour, when her pet guinea pig had died, when her beloved nanny had left . . . during all these moments of sorrow, she'd slipped away and clambered up the familiar tree to curl up in its strong embrace until she felt ready to face the world again.

As on that last day, when the autumn leaves had cloaked her from sight, so now did the fresh green mantle of June. Anna's first instinct had been to fly to this private sanctuary when she'd received Petroc's phone call.

Numbed still, and in shock from what he'd said, it was too soon for tears; they would come later. It was also too soon to face her family and so she remained there, her face buried against her bent knees, hands clasped around her ankles, knowing they'd be wondering where she was, but unable to bring herself to go back into the house. It was the cruel timing of Petroc's statement that wounded her most at this moment. How could he? On the eve of her twenty-first birthday, when her parents were giving the party of a lifetime, so they could all celebrate together . . . how *could* he choose that moment to ring her up and say he wasn't coming because he was unsure where their relationship was going, and he thought they should cool it for a while and see less of each other?

Bewildered, Anna tried to grapple with her tortured thoughts which were scuttling around her mind like rats in a maze. What had happened? Why had Petroc changed his mind since she'd seen him four days ago? Could he have met someone else? Would he come back to her? What could she do to *make* him want to come back to her? As for her hopes of his proposing marriage on Saturday night . . .! What a stupid romantic idiot she was even to have had such fantasies. Then came the worst thought of all. Perhaps she'd been kidding herself all along? Maybe he'd never been as much in love with her as she was with him?

At that thought her breath caught on a sob and her eyes brimmed with tears. She'd loved him so much, and now she was going to have to get through Saturday night without him. Everyone would guess what had happened, of course. There would be pitying glances, and over-cheerful remarks about how nice she looked, and William would make sure that lots of his friends danced with her, and everybody would be so bloody busy trying to cheer her up, that she'd want to scream.

For a moment it crossed her mind that she could go back to London and not stay for the party at all; but then she realised her parents would be upset, and so would her grandparents, and her friends. Oh, shit! she thought, as the tears suddenly poured down her cheeks and her body was wracked with sobs. Why did this have to happen now? Why, in God's name, couldn't Petroc have waited until after the party? Selfish bastard! Fucking selfish toe-rag!

Anger energised her, gave her purpose. She couldn't stay here, hiding up a tree forever. And why should she? He was the one who ought to go into hiding. Clambering down, she hunted through the pockets of her jeans for a tissue, her anger bubbling. What right had Petroc to behave like this, after their closeness during the past three years?

Striding towards the house, she heard her name being called. It was her father, sitting on an upturned tea chest, eating a sandwich and looking exactly like Pooh Bear. He was waving frantically at her.

'Anna, darling! Where have you been? Your mother's been looking for you. Lunch is ready.'

She walked slowly towards him, dabbing her nose on a damp ball of tissues. As soon as he saw her expression he got to his feet, and spoke anxiously.

'What's wrong, my precious? What's happened?'

Anna's face crumpled as she stumbled into his arms. 'It's . . . it's Petroc, Daddy. He's d-dumped me.'

'He's *what*?' Horrified, Douglas hugged her close. 'What do you mean . . . dumped you?'

'He phoned a while ago. He's not coming to the party.'

Tears streamed down Anna's cheeks. 'He says he doesn't think we have a future together.'

Douglas gripped her by the shoulders, forcing her to look into his face which was scarlet with rage. 'I'll kill the little bastard!' he said through clenched teeth. 'Wait until I get hold of him. I'll make sure he doesn't *have* a future.'

'No, Daddy, please. You'll only make it worse. He might come back to me. He said we should cool it for a time, but eventually he might . . .' Her voice trailed off, and she buried her face in his shoulder. Right now she couldn't bear to face the thought of never being close to Petroc again. She loved him so desperately, had for such a long time, and all her future dreams and plans included him. Without him, she felt she was facing a black, bottomless void.

'Let's go and find your mother, my pet,' said Douglas, leading her towards the house. 'This is a terrible thing to happen. I could do with a stiff drink.'

In silence they crossed the lawn, and seeing them through the kitchen window, Julia hurried out of the house, realising something was wrong.

'What's happened?'

'Bloody Petroc's said he's not coming to the party,' Douglas barked, gruffly. 'Seems he's having second thoughts about going out with Anna.'

'Oh, no!'

Feeling like a fragile parcel, she felt her father gently release his grip on her as her mother took her in her arms.

'My poor baby. Look, we'll go upstairs where it's quiet,' Julia said. 'Come along. Tell me what's happened.'

Douglas watched sorrowfully as they went indoors, Julia so slim and tiny beside her daughter, who had started to sob again. Then he went into the study and poured himself a large glass of brandy. 'Shit! Oh, shit!' he muttered, pacing around. 'Why did the little fucker have to do this now, for Christ's sake?'

At that moment his father put his head round the door. 'What's up?' he asked worriedly.

'Would you believe that Anna's boyfriend has only gone and chosen this week, of all weeks, to bloody go and chuck her?' Douglas exploded in fury. 'She's in a dreadful state. I'd like to wring his neck.'

Reggie sat down on the arm of the brown leather sofa. 'Oh, God, that's rough on the poor little thing. Have they had a fight or something? If so, it'll probably blow over by . . .'

'He's dumped her, Dad,' Douglas said succinctly. 'I wanted to ring him up and give him a piece of my mind, but Anna won't let me.'

Reggie nodded, sagely. 'Better not to interfere. They'll probably work things out for themselves. You know what the young are like.'

Douglas sighed heavily. 'I suppose so. Oh, dear, what a shame. I did so want everything to be perfect on Saturday. Now this has cast a blight over the whole proceedings. Anna's going to be miserable, and Julia's going to be miserable because she'll be worried about Anna. The whole night's going to be spoiled,' he added disconsolately.

'Well, we must keep cheerful,' Reggie said firmly. 'You might give me a brandy, too, old boy. We've got to keep the show on the road.'

'Dad, this isn't Covent Garden.' Douglas poured a second brandy and topped up his own glass at the same time. 'If we weren't past the point of no return, I'd cancel the whole thing.' He stared out of the window at the marquee, looking momentarily deflated.

'Rubbish, Douglas,' Reggie said sternly. 'If I know Anna, she'll put on a brave face on the night, and so will Julia. We all will. We must. Three hundred people are expecting to be entertained and given a night they'll never forget. You wait and see. It will still be a marvellous evening, in spite of this.'

'I hope you're right, but it's an awful disappointment, isn't it? I mean, it's bound to ruin the evening for Anna, not having Petroc here.'

The study door opened and Pat appeared, looking from her husband to her son and then back to her husband again.

'What's going on? Reggie, why are you drinking brandy at this hour?'

As briefly as possible, Douglas explained what had happened.

'Then Anna's better off without him, if that's the way he behaves,' she retorted, angrily. 'How dare he do this to her, on the eve of her birthday party? It's the most disgraceful thing I've ever heard.'

'Yes, dear, we know that,' Reggie said soothingly. 'But we're just going to have to make the best of it because there's nothing we can do.'

'He should be horse-whipped!' Pat exclaimed. She couldn't remember when she'd last felt so angry. That her own sweet Anna had been hurt in this way upset her deeply. Anna was such a good, kind girl and she deserved the best. Pat had only met Petroc a few times and hardly knew him, but at this moment she hated him. And then she wondered if it was because she'd only had sons that she felt so particularly close to Anna? Douglas and Peter had always been able to look after themselves; besides which, neither of them had ever been chucked by a girl.

'It's all right, Ma,' Douglas said consolingly. 'Plenty more fish in the sea for someone like Anna, and we're going to have to brace up for her sake, you know. As Dad said, the show must go on.'

Pat pulled away from him impatiently, dabbing her eyes fiercely. 'Men!' she scoffed. 'What do they know about it?' Then she turned and stalked out of the room, her back held straight.

Reggie and Douglas looked at each other. Reggie spoke first.

'Pat's always had a soft spot for Anna, you know,' he whispered, in case they could be overheard. 'She's bought her a string of pearls for her birthday present, with a nice diamond clasp. Saved up for ages to get it.'

Douglas's eyes softened. His parents didn't have that much money, having always steadfastly refused financial help from him, so his mother must have made sacrifices to have bought Anna such a valuable gift.

'That's very sweet, Dad. I know Anna will be thrilled.'

Reggie smiled proudly. 'I'm giving William some cuff links, myself. There's a lot of good in that boy.'

'He's very like you, actually.'

'Is he, d'you think?' Reggie beamed broadly. Then he slapped Douglas on the back. 'Everything's going to be all right on Saturday night, old chap. Just you wait and see.'

'I hope so,' Douglas replied, wishing now that he felt more sure. A sudden blight had descended on him and he supposed it was because of Anna's bad news. Or maybe he was just tired. Downing the last of his brandy, he glanced at his watch for the umpteenth time, then hurried back into the garden. There was still a lot to do and not a moment to lose.

Nancy, back in her house again after her excursion to Longford, watched as Douglas crossed his lawn towards the marquee. Through eyes narrowed with cunning satisfaction, she observed the preparations in progress. What a lot of people seemed to be involved, she reflected. And what strange things they were carrying into the tent! Statues, pillars, trees, large mirrors . . . how odd. And then . . . surely not? A little winding staircase attached to what looked like a balcony? What *were* they doing? There seemed to be a lot of equipment, too. If she hadn't known there was going to be a dance, she'd have thought it was a film set. There even seemed to be some arc lights, and a lot of electric cables spread out on the grass.

How amusing, she reflected, that whilst Douglas Rutherford was getting everything ready for what he thought was going to be the best party he'd ever given, he was actually preparing for his own downfall . . . with a little help from her, of course.

Oh, yes. Her trip to Longford had been even more successful than she'd hoped. She'd found who she was looking for and *that* had been most interesting. Now everything was set to do Douglas irreparable damage. It might even ruin him, she thought hopefully, relishing every moment of her planned revenge.

It filled her with profound satisfaction to realise she was the author of his ruin; she'd suffered three years of hell having the Rutherfords as neighbours, and blamed Douglas as the head of the family. Sometimes she wondered how she'd stood the disturbances for so long. Days of being driven crazy by annoying and persistent noise

was as nothing compared to endless nights of sleepless-
ness. There had been moments when lack of sleep, and
the knowledge that other people were enjoying themselves while she lay alone and unwanted, nearly caused
her to do something violent, like throwing a heavy object
through one of their windows. How ineffectual the local
police had been, too. While she boiled with rage, her
blood pressure soaring to what she was sure were dangerous heights, they were tip-toeing around, advising the
Rutherfords to 'keep the noise level down'.

Well, what she'd done today might well keep their noise
level down for a very long time. And, oh! how she was
going to enjoy Saturday night.

Nobody felt much like talking as they sat down to dinner
that evening. Anna, pale and puffy-eyed, did her best to
be cheerful, but it was obviously an effort and after a
while she lapsed into silence, and scarcely touched her
food. Meanwhile Douglas and Julia did their best to chat
to his parents, and William talked about the day's win-
ners at Royal Ascot, which he'd watched on television
that afternoon. But with the exception of Michael, a
definite blight had descended on everyone, and Julia
wondered how soon she could suggest they all went to
bed.

'At least we're on schedule with all the arrangements,'
Douglas informed them, as Morgan filled their glasses
with an excellent claret to go with the roast lamb Mrs
Morgan had prepared.

'What has to be done tomorrow?' Julia enquired.
'Apart from welcoming our house guests.'

'Tables and chairs set up in the marquee, the final
touches put to the decorations, the lighting checked, John

is going to make a start on the actual flowers, the mobile kitchens will be made operational . . . there's still a hundred and one things to be done.' He sounded tired and harassed.

'Where are the ladies going to leave their evening wraps?' Pat enquired.

'In the house. Wraps will go in here, we've got rails coming, and we'll move the dining-room table to one side,' Julia explained.

As soon as dinner was over Anna escaped, unable to bear it anymore. She shut herself in the study whilst the others had coffee in the drawing room. She had to talk to Petroc. Ever since this morning she'd been torturing herself, desperate to know why he had done this dreadful thing to her. How was she supposed to react? Sit and wait patiently until he decided he wanted to see her again? Anger stirred in her blood. She would not be treated in this cowardly way by a man she'd loved, and who had professed to love her. Her hands shook as she dialled his number. For a moment she almost hoped he'd be out so she wouldn't have to talk to him, but with a suddenness that startled her, she heard him speak.

'Hello?'

'Petroc . . . it's me.' Anna's voice wobbled although she tried to control it.

'Hi!' He sounded surprisingly relaxed and normal.

'We . . . we have to talk, Petroc. You can't just ring up and say you're not coming to the party – just like that. There has to be a reason? And a jolly good one.' She decided not to mention his telling her earlier that he thought they ought to cool it a bit. 'It's rude, to say the least,' she added spiritedly.

There was a long pause before he replied. 'I just think

it's better if I don't come,' he said guardedly.

'But *why*? What's the matter?'

'Like I said, Anna, I think we should have a breather. From each other, that is. Give ourselves a bit of space. And time.' He spoke haltingly. She knew him well enough to understand that he was embarrassed and feeling awkward. Well, so what? she thought. I'm feeling a lot worse.

'Why don't you speak plain English instead of all that psycho-babble?' she snapped furiously.

'I am speaking plainly. I don't know how to speak any plainer,' he enunciated slowly, as if his patience was sorely strained.

'Well, I don't know what you're talking about,' she lashed back. 'You're behaving in the most extraordinary way. We've had this party planned for *ages*. It's my twenty-first, for God's sake! What do you think you're playing at by announcing you don't think you'll come? You're supposed to be my boyfriend. How dare you think you can treat me like this?' She was beside herself with rage now, no longer caring what she said or how he might react. Apart from the hurt he was inflicting on her, she was going to be humiliated at her own birthday party because her boyfriend, whom everybody knew about, had decided not to turn up.

'You can go screw yourself for all I care!' she screamed down the phone. 'I don't give a damn if you fucking come or not.'

'Do you think Anna's going to be all right?' Julia whispered, as she and Douglas lay in bed later that night. 'When I saw her coming out of the study she was in a terrible state.'

'What, worse than this morning?'

'Yes. This was anger as well as grief. All she would say was that she'd finished with Petroc and never even wanted to hear his name again.' Julia snuggled closer for comfort, moulding her body against his. Douglas put his arm around her, planting a kiss on her cheek.

'You know what the young are like,' he said reasonably. 'It will all have blown over by Saturday.'

'I'm not so sure. Poor Anna. She's so in love with him. I just hope to God he hasn't met someone else.' The wretchedness in Julia's voice made Douglas, who'd begun to feel sleepy, alert again.

'I don't suppose he has,' he said calmly.

'Why not, though? He's a very attractive young man and he's always been very popular with girls. I've often thought there must be times when that makes Anna feel insecure.'

Douglas felt genuinely amazed. 'Why on earth should it make her feel insecure? She's pretty and jolly and good company . . . not like those anorexic models who never smile and never look as if they're enjoying themselves. Any young man in his right mind would prefer her.'

Julia's voice was strained. 'I agree, but Anna is wife material. That's not the same as being a sexy little number to have fun with.'

There was a moment's silence before her husband spoke. 'I like her just the way she is.'

'Of course. So do I. But we all know men can stray, and I don't want her to get hurt.'

Douglas groped for her hand, found it, and squeezed it hard. 'None of us wants her to get hurt, darling. I think Anna is probably stronger than you realise.'

'Maybe.'

'Falling in and out of love and getting hurt is all a part

of life, sweetheart. A part of growing up. She'll learn more from getting hurt than from always being happy,' he added softly.

Julia didn't answer. She would have done anything to have spared her beloved daughter the pain of rejection, jealousy, and the agony of self-doubt and loss of confidence that was bound to follow. Maybe breaking up with a loved one did teach you about life, a 'learning curve' Anna and William would have called it, but it was something Julia had always fervently hoped her daughter would never have to endure. She and Petroc had seemed so settled; it had appeared it was only a matter of time before they got married. What could have happened to make him change his mind? Julia closed her eyes, feeling Anna's misery, empathising with her so that it became her hurt, too.

'Are you OK, darling?' Douglas asked, stretching his hand out to feel for her face, to stroke her cheek. He could sense her anguish as she lay silent and still in the darkness beside him.

'I'm fine,' she said quietly, kissing his fingers as they trailed gently across her mouth. 'We'd better get some sleep, don't you think? Tomorrow's going to be hectic with everyone arriving.'

'You're right. Good night, my darling.'

Entwined in each other's arms, they settled for the night in their nest of downy pillows and Irish linen and lace. Douglas was asleep within minutes but Julia lay awake for a long time.

Petroc Tregain was also having difficulties in getting to sleep, in his flat in busy Battersea. His room overlooked the Albert Bridge Road, and the traffic crossing the bridge between Battersea and Chelsea never seemed to stop. Great trundling lorries thundered through the night and made the old Victorian house shudder down to its foundations. Sometimes he wished he'd picked one of the two back bedrooms, occupied now by Philip Stockton and Max Welby, old friends from his days at Harrow, but the front room had been bigger with a nice view over Battersea Park and he hadn't realised, at the time, that the traffic went past all night.

Tonight, though, something else made him fidgety and wakeful. Anna's irate phone call earlier in the evening had shocked him. She was usually so . . . so amenable and loving. Always ready to fall in with his plans; clinging even. A sweet, meek girl who was always jolly and laughing and whom life seemed to have endowed with a path as smooth as silk. And then, suddenly, there she was on the phone, screaming abuse at him, and he felt thoroughly confused. The reason he'd backed out of going to the party was because he was feeling pressured to get engaged to her on Saturday night and simply wasn't ready to commit himself to her, or to anyone else for that matter. He probably should have explained but he didn't want to make a heavy deal of it. Surely, he had reasoned before he'd called her that morning, it was better to suggest he skip the party and they have a . . . well, a sort of sabbatical from each other for a while? It sounded reasonable enough to him, and at the time she'd just said very quietly and calmly that she understood and it was OK. For a moment he'd felt a bit miffed that she wasn't more upset, but then you could never tell with girls. They played all these games, pretending not to care when they did, doing stupid things to make you jealous, but he hadn't thought Anna was like that. That was why he loved her; she was so straightforward and in your face. No messing around. Until now.

Why was she behaving so oddly? he reflected, pumping his pillow which seemed to have turned into a sackful of bricks during the past three hours. It was so unlike her to make a fuss and get all emotional. After all, it was only a party . . . although he had to admit this was a fairly special party. Oh, God! He didn't know what to do now. He wasn't absolutely sure, either, if he loved her enough to get involved in something as serious as marriage. She was too . . . well, too sweet; his grandmother had once dismissed her as 'a doormat' and said he should get himself a girl with spirit. Well . . . Anna had certainly shown spirit on the phone tonight; there was even a touch of the fishwife in her irate delivery. It had made him see her from a new perspective. Perhaps she wasn't all amiability after all?

If only Philip, who knew Anna's flatmate Henrietta, hadn't told him that Anna apparently had 'high hopes Petroc would propose on Saturday night'. That had really unnerved him. Now he didn't know what to do. Another lorry rumbled past. It was three o'clock in the morning. Shit, was he ever going to get to sleep?

For Julia's mother, Vivien, there was no sleep at all. All she could think of, as she lay beside Simon in their canopied bed, was how she was going to get through the weekend. The car Christopher had arranged to take them to Highfield Manor was picking them up at two o'clock. They'd arrive in time for tea. Whatever happened, she mustn't let anyone see how stressed she felt. She comforted herself with the knowledge that at least she wasn't in pain. Nevertheless, it wasn't going to be easy to disguise her distress from Julia. Then she remembered something. Something that might help.

Sliding out of bed so as not to wake Simon, she crept into the bathroom and opened the mirror-fronted medicine cabinet. Yes! They were still there. A bit out of date, maybe, but they'd probably be all right. When her beloved dog, Jemima, had died, two years ago, she'd been so distressed her doctor had prescribed a short course of tranquillisers. In fact, she'd only taken them for two days and then Simon had whisked her away for a surprise holiday in the Caribbean and so the moment of grief had been assuaged and the pills forgotten. Now they were exactly what she needed. She reached for the bottle gratefully. ONE TO BE TAKEN THREE TIMES A DAY, she read. Upending the bottle, she saw there were enough to see her through the coming week. Thank God! At least she'd be able to control her tears of panic, preserve her dignity and not be a nuisance to everyone else.

Friday

21 June 1996

Five

The first thought that struck Julia as she awoke was that there was only one more day before the party and still so much to do. From the moment she got out of bed, she'd be swept along on a torrent of arrangements to be made, decisions to be taken, details to be finalised. And throughout the day there'd be a steady stream of people arriving for the weekend and culminating in a dinner party for twenty tonight. She peered at the small travelling clock on her bedside table. It was half-past six. For a moment she lay on her back in contemplation, realising she felt surprisingly excited. In fact she couldn't remember when she'd last felt so elated and had looked forward to a day with such delight. Had it been Christmas morning when she'd been a child? Or her wedding day, knowing that Douglas would be waiting for her at the top of the aisle? Or Anna's christening, when she'd held her first baby with such enormous pride?

There was no way Julia could go back to sleep now. She sprang out of bed with alacrity and rushed over to the window, trying not to make a noise and disturb Douglas, but so filled with enthusiasm it was hard not to exclaim with pleasure when she carefully parted the curtains and saw the rosiest pink dawn she'd ever seen, the air clear and pure, the lawn a-glitter with dew.

There was no time to lose. Slipping into jeans and a navy tee-shirt and a pair of trainers, she hurried from the bedroom and ran down the stairs to the kitchen. It might never happen again, but today she felt about twenty-two and full of joy and anticipation. This was really going to be the most marvellous weekend of their lives.

'Darling! You're up early?' she exclaimed, as she entered the kitchen and found Anna sitting at the table, sipping a large mug of coffee.

'I didn't sleep at all,' she replied dolefully. She looked pale and miserable.

'Oh, sweetheart!' Julia put her arms around her and kissed the crown of her head. 'I'm so sorry about Petroc.'

'He's a sleazebag,' Anna remarked. 'Once I get used to the idea of being without him, I'll probably think I had a lucky escape, but right now . . .' Her eyes brimmed and she wiped them impatiently with the back of her hand. 'I could *kill* him for doing this, just before the party. He must have known it would cause an upset.'

'I know,' Julia replied sadly. The loveliness of the day seemed to have fragmented into tiny icy particles in the last few moments; a reminder of the fragility of happiness. She shivered. She'd never forgive Petroc for choosing this exact time either. For a moment she contemplated phoning him and telling him to come to the party no matter what; he could always discuss the future with Anna afterwards. But she'd never interfered in either Anna's or William's romantic relationships, and she was loath to get involved now.

'Why don't you have a hot bath, darling?' she suggested instead. 'By the time you come down I'll have some eggs and bacon ready for you.'

Anna rose wearily, drained her mug and then went over and put it in the sink. 'I couldn't eat a thing, Mum. Thanks all the same. Bloody men!' she added fiercely. 'Who needs them? I'm going to enjoy myself tomorrow night if it kills me.' Then she stomped out of the kitchen, a look of determination on her face.

Mrs Morgan came bustling through the door at that moment, and while Julia drank her coffee, she watched the place take on the familiar, behind-the-scenes atmosphere of one of Douglas's restaurants. Two of the kitchen staff from Butterfly, and two from Futures, who had spent the previous night at The Red Lion in the village, had arrived and were soon hard at work preparing dinner while Mrs Morgan got on with the breakfast. Morgan, meanwhile, was setting a tray for Pat and Reggie Rutherford, so they could have breakfast in bed.

The fragrant aroma of coffee brewing, bacon sizzling, and croissants warming in the oven soon filled the air, making Julia feel hungry. On impulse, she helped herself to a croissant, spread it with apricot jam, and filling her mug with fresh coffee, strolled into the garden. No one had arrived yet to complete the decorations, and the stillness of the morning was only broken by the piercing song of a thrush, high up in an oak tree.

'What are you doing up so early, my pet?'

Julia looked up and there was Douglas, leaning out of their bedroom window, grinning down at her.

'Hello, darling,' she called back. 'It's going to be a fabulous day.'

'Hang on a minute.' He disappeared inside, and a few minutes later came padding out of the house, through the study french windows. He was tying the belt of his navy blue silk dressing-gown and his feet were bare.

'Hello,' she said again, softly and welcomingly.

For answer, he kissed her on the mouth then sat down beside her on the stone steps that led down to the lawn.

She held out her mug to him. 'D'you want a sip?'

Douglas shook his head, smiling mischievously. 'I've just hijacked my parents' breakfast tray. Morgan's bringing it out now.'

Julia looked up in time to see him placing the large tray on the garden table on the terrace.

'Oh, Douglas . . . how could you?' she asked, laughing.

'Morgan will fix them another one,' he replied easily. He reached for her hand and pulled her to her feet. 'Come on. There's grapefruit, boiled eggs, toast so we can have soldiers, and lots of fresh coffee. We can't start the day without a proper breakfast, and what could be nicer than to have it out here, just the two of us on our own, with the sun coming up?'

Julia almost felt guilty at being so happy when Anna was so miserable, but nevertheless she allowed Douglas to lead her to a seat by the table. Smiling, she looked into his eyes.

'I do love you,' she said impulsively.

'I know,' he replied complacently. 'Lucky, isn't it, that I love you too?'

'Very lucky.'

'Twenty-five years, eh? Who'd have thought it?'

'I did,' Julia replied, in a quiet but firm voice. 'I was determined we'd stay together. Quite determined.'

Douglas handed her an exquisitely prepared grapefruit, each segment cleanly divided and a tiny sprig of mint on the top.

'Eat up, or you'll fade away before tomorrow night,' he commanded.

They had just finished their breakfast when 'the gang', as Douglas referred to John Plested and his team, arrived in force.

'Miss Keaveney, what have you there?' Douglas hailed her with theatrical aplomb, as he stood in his dressing-gown on the terrace, waving his arms at her.

Elaine Keaveney doubled up with laughter. 'Cherubs,' she replied, indicating the bundles under each arm. 'Big fat golden cherubs.'

Julia's eyes widened. 'Is there no end to what you're putting in that marquee?' she joked. 'I don't think we're giving a dance at all, I think we're putting on a production of *Le Nozze Di Figaro*.'

'It wouldn't surprise me,' John quipped, 'the way things are going.'

Michael emerged from the house, tousle-haired and in his school pyjamas. 'Mummy, what's all the noise for? It woke me up.' Barefoot like his father, he trotted across the terrace and plonked himself on Julia's lap, where he curled up, yawning.

Douglas pulled the cord of his dressing-gown tighter and followed John and Elaine over to the marquee. 'See you later, darling,' he said. 'I want to see how it's going.'

'All right.' Julia knew she wouldn't see him again for ages. She turned her attention back to Michael. 'Shall I butter you some toast, darling?'

'No, I want Coco Pops,' he whined.

'Please, Mummy.'

'Please, Mummy,' he echoed unenthusiastically.

'Let's go to the kitchen then,' she said, lowering him gently to his feet, realising the excitement was already getting to him. 'I think a rest this afternoon would be nice, don't you?'

'I don't want a rest!'

'We're all going to try and get a rest,' she lied. 'It's going to be a long weekend and we don't want to be tired, do we?'

He looked up at her, enraged. 'I'm not a baby!' His eyes were scornful. 'If I'm old enough to . . . to host a table, I don't need to rest.'

'Oh, dear, I hoped we might watch a video together after lunch.'

'What video?' he asked grudgingly.

'Whatever you choose,' Julia replied diplomatically.

Michael didn't reply, but she knew she'd won the battle. Lying on the sofa in her bedroom after lunch, with some space-age epic on the box, he'd be asleep within ten minutes.

In London, Julia's half-brother, Christopher Leonard, waited until Oonagh was in the bath before he crept quietly into the drawing room, which was at the far end of their flat, and tapped out Barbara's number on his mobile phone. She answered on the second ring, her voice soft and breathy.

'Hello?'

'Darling, it's me.' Christopher spoke in a low voice in case Oonagh overheard him. 'How are you?'

She sounded sleepy. 'Missing you, my love. Missing you dreadfully.'

He groaned, feeling himself becoming aroused even by her voice. 'We can at least spend the whole evening together.'

'Oh, bliss. What time will you be back from Ascot?'

'If we leave before the last race then we should be back by six-thirty, seven at the latest. I've said I've got to dine with American clients.'

'But will you be able to stay the whole night?' Barbara asked longingly. 'Please say you can, darling.'

Christopher looked up and a cold rush of dread swept through his body as he saw Oonagh coming into the room.

'. . . I'll do what I can,' he said, trying to keep his voice steady and business-like, casual even, 'but this is not a straightforward case and a lot will depend on counsel.'

Barbara took her cue from him and, thanking him, hung up a moment later.

'Who were you talking to?' Oonagh enquired. She was draped in a pale blue towel, worn like a sarong, and her short black hair clung wetly to her head.

'A client,' he replied briefly. 'I'm going to have my bath. What time are we leaving here?'

'We must go at ten-fifteen, we're meeting them in the car park at noon,' she replied coolly. 'You'd better hurry.'

'Which car park?'

Oonagh raised exquisitely defined dark eyebrows. 'Number one, of course.' She spoke as if there were no other car parks at the race course.

'Thank God for that! I don't fancy walking for miles before the racing even starts.' Christopher wandered off to have his shower, his thoughts still with Barbara. Thank God Oonagh hadn't heard him saying anything intimate to her. Meanwhile he'd have to get through the usual picnic lunch, consisting of coronation chicken with salad, with a bunch of shallow socialites, during which he'd drink too much champagne from boredom, watch the Queen and her family travel up the course in open carriages, no doubt half-hidden by umbrellas in pouring rain and a force-seven gale, and then lose his money on five races, in spite of several tips given him by the Queen's trainer. Oonagh was going to love every second of it, of course, from the first mwa-mwa of air kisses and colliding hat brims, as she tottered on her high heels around the Enclosure, to the moment when he finally had to drag her away from her avid social-climbing because he didn't want to get stuck in a three-hour traffic jam back to London.

An hour later, as Christopher and Oonagh glided along the M4 in their Rolls Coupé, their son Tim was catching the Piccadilly Line at Heathrow, having taken the shuttle from Edinburgh, on his way into London and Waterloo station, where he'd get a train to Stockbridge. He'd told his Aunt Julia that he'd get a taxi from the station to Stickley because he wasn't sure what time he'd be arriving. He liked to feel independent, to come and go as he pleased, and on this occasion was particularly anxious to avoid being caught up in his mother's plans. She was always wanting him to meet the 'right people', or go to the 'right party', and never stopped dropping names.

Reading politics at Edinburgh University, where he'd be for four years, was, Tim felt, the best thing that had ever happened to him. At nineteen he no longer had to come home for the holidays, thus avoiding Oonagh to whom he'd never been close, and he planned to travel, with financial help from his father. Christopher was generous and could afford to be, especially as Tim was their only child, and although he never said anything, Tim was certain his father understood his need to escape the nest. Secretly he wondered if his father might not like to escape with him.

The taxi driver, who seemed to know exactly where

Stickley was, set off at a brisk pace.

'I was only there the day before yesterday,' he informed Tim chattily. 'I picked up an elderly lady from a house bang next door to Highfield Manor. I saw a great white tent on their lawn. Like a Big Top it looked. Are they giving a party?'

'Tomorrow night,' Tim said. 'It's my aunt and uncle's wedding anniversary, and the birthday of two of my cousins.'

'Very nice, too. My lady passenger, Mrs Graham was her name, said she was worried about the noise. Thought she'd probably have a sleepless night. But I expect they've sent her an invite like, haven't they?'

Tim, sitting in the back, rather wished the driver would keep his eyes on the road instead of cocking his head to look at his passenger through the windscreen mirror.

'I don't know,' he replied. 'I don't know who's been invited, but I think they're having about three hundred people.'

'Blimey! Quite a shindig. No doubt you'll be dancing the night away, eh? I was a great dancer in my youth. Mrs Graham said there was going to be a big dinner, too. She seemed to know all about it, so I expect she's been asked. Well . . .' He gave an asthmatic laugh. 'That's *one* guest I won't have to drive home, seeing as she only lives next door.'

'Quite.'

Tim gave the driver a generous tip when they arrived at Highfield Manor because he was so glad to be rid of him. If there was one thing he disliked it was being cornered by someone chatty. He supposed it was because it reminded him of his mother.

'Tim! My dear Tim! How lovely to see you.'

He turned to see his aunt standing in the doorway, her arms outstretched.

'Hello, Julia.' He kissed her on both cheeks and got a whiff of tuberose and jasmine, which suited her perfectly.

'Come in, Tim. I'm longing to hear all about Edinburgh and how you're enjoying it. Your parents aren't arriving until tomorrow, you know.' As she talked, she led him into the drawing room where Pat and Reggie were sitting, bright-eyed and eager to entertain arrivals.

'Now, you're in the blue room, on the second floor,' Pat told him, as soon as greetings were over. 'Would you like me to show you?'

'Perhaps you'd like a drink first?' Reggie suggested, hurrying over to the drinks tray which Morgan had placed on a round table in the bay window.

'Er . . .' Tim looked from one to the other, and then to Julia.

'Or maybe a cup of coffee, Tim?' she said diplomatically. 'You know where the kitchen is, why don't you pop along and help yourself? Mrs Morgan will be delighted to see you again.'

With a quick smile of relief, he escaped and shot down the corridor. He was quickly enveloped in wide smiles and warm smells, and platefuls of homemade cakes and biscuits which were shoved across the freshly scrubbed kitchen table in his direction by a thrilled Mrs Morgan, who had known him since he'd come to stay as a small boy.

The happiest school holidays Tim had ever spent had been at Highfield Manor, and although he was nearly two years younger than Anna and a year older than William it had never seemed to matter.

'Mrs Morgan, you're determined to make me fat,' he

laughed, as she popped a meringue on to a plate and put it down in front of him. He found it was as crisp as snow on the outside but gorgeously soft and gooey in the centre.

'Bliss,' Tim said, munching. At that moment William came into the kitchen, very obviously having just got up.

'Wotcha, me old mate!' he greeted Tim with an affectionate slap on the shoulder. 'I see you've already got round Mrs Morgan with tales of starvation. Does nothing change in this world?'

'And I can see you've just got out of bed, you lazy scumbag,' Tim retorted good-humouredly. 'I'll have you know I was up at six o'clock this morning, to catch my flight.'

'Poor diddums!' William gave him another friendly punch. 'Any chance of some breakfast, Mrs Morgan?'

'Breakfast was over three hours ago,' she replied with mock severity. 'We've got to cook lunch for ten people, so don't go thinking I can start doing breakfast again.'

William pretended to look deeply hurt. 'Oh, Mrs Morgan, how can you be so cruel to me? This is *me*, William. Your lost lamb. And I'm starving.' His bottom lip quivered.

'I'll give you starving,' she said, seizing a frying pan and putting it on the stove. 'What's it to be? Four rashers and two eggs?'

'Mrs Morgan,' he said solemnly, 'I'll remember you in my will.' Then his voice reverted to normal. 'How come we're ten for lunch? Who's coming?'

She started ticking off on her fingers. 'There's your ma and pa, and your grandparents, and you, Anna and Michael . . .'

William nodded. 'That's seven, and with Tim eight. Who else?'

'Mr Sullivan and his lady friend, Miss Schemmel.'

'Ah!'

'Who are they?' Tim asked.

'Roger Sullivan. You know, Dad's best friend. He's going out with an American interior designer called Pammy Schemmel. She's positively skeletal and the last time she came here told Mum the drawing room had cold vibrations and wasn't user-friendly. Lectured Mum for two hours on feng-shui and karma and all that crap.'

'Where's Anna?'

William gave him a secret warning look. 'Around,' he said carefully. 'Tread warily,' he added in a whisper.

'What's up?'

'Boyfriend trouble.'

'Not Petroc?'

William nodded.

'God, I thought they were fixed for life.'

'Unfortunately so did Anna.'

'Bad timing, eh?'

'Couldn't be worse. Hush, I can hear her coming.'

Tim listened to the clumping of platform shoes along the corridor. A moment later Anna burst into the kitchen. She was wearing black stretch pants that resembled leather and a white polo-necked jersey.

'Hi ya!' she greeted Tim, throwing her arms around his neck. 'When did you arrive? Shit, it's so good to see you.'

'Hi ya! You're looking terrific,' he added, thinking that she really did. She was wearing make-up, which she didn't usually do, and was certainly acting sparkily.

'I'm fine,' she replied lightly. 'Let's go into the garden, it's so hot in here.'

As they wandered off, cousins and old friends who were delighted to see each other again, William raised his eyebrows and looked at Mrs Morgan.

'She seems happy enough,' he commented.

'She's being brave,' the cook replied, breaking a second egg into the sizzling pan, 'but all that muck on her face doesn't deceive me. That's put on to hide her tears. It's a damn' shame, if you'll excuse my French.'

Roger Sullivan brought his car to a standstill outside the front door of Highfield Manor, and looked across to the activity surrounding the marquee.

'Jesus, tomorrow night's going to cost a bomb,' he remarked as he switched off the engine. 'Douglas is really pushing out the boat this time. Look at the size of that marquee.'

Pammy Schemmel, unbuttoning her cashmere jacket with claw-like hands, glanced through the windscreen. 'I guess he can afford it,' she drawled. Her narrow face was heavily freckled; her hair, which was scraped back into a chignon, was an ugly plum-coloured shade of red. But she was wearing two thousand dollars worth of cashmere and silk, and a few more thousand dollars worth of gold around her neck and in her ears and this accounted for her supreme self-confidence. As an interior designer, working in a world of illusion, she was her own cleverest invention. Even her freckles resembled designer markings.

Roger nodded, grimacing. 'Unlike me, Douglas hasn't had to fork out two lots of alimony.'

Pammy's laugh was harsh. 'I expect he's managed to have his cake and eat it. You know, cheated here and there but never got caught. Never been divorced. A smart guy.'

Roger didn't reply. It was none of Pammy's business anyway. He certainly had no intention of enlightening her on the private life of his oldest friend.

'Let's go and find them,' he said instead, getting out of the car.

Douglas had already seen them arrive, and was hurrying towards them, hands outstretched.

'Roger, great to see you!' he exclaimed warmly, as both men swung their right arms in a circle before connecting in a handshake. Then with the grace of a born host he turned to Pammy, whom he privately didn't like, and kissed her on both cheeks.

'Pammy, my dear, welcome. Now, why don't we have a drink on the terrace before lunch . . . unless you'd rather go to your room first?'

They chose the terrace, where tubs overflowed with great clusters of pink geraniums and cushions of white impatiens sprouted from stone urns at the top of the steps down to the lawn. Douglas's parents were seated under a large cream sunshade talking to Julia, who jumped to her feet in welcome as soon as she saw them.

'Roger! Pammy! How lovely to see you.' Like Douglas she did not like Pammy either, but as she seemed to be a fixture in Roger's life these days, there was nothing for it but to appear pleased to see her.

'How about a large jug of Pimm's before we have lunch, darling?' Douglas suggested, putting his arm around her waist.

Pammy watched, through narrowed eyes, his manner and body language with his wife. It had been the same the last time Roger had brought her to stay. He was obviously devoted to her, but was there something more? Guilt, perhaps? And a devotion that was too good to be true?

Especially after twenty-five years.

'I'll get Morgan to make up a couple of jugs,' Julia replied, and in her Pammy noticed an almost ardent desire to please. Now she really does love him, she thought. And, boy, is she co-dependent!

'What number in the car park are Delia and Tony?' Christopher asked, as they approached the race course.

'Number one, I told you,' Oonagh snapped, taking a quick look at herself in the sun-visor mirror. She was wearing a pale lime green silk suit and her hat, chosen with care, was a single large silk rose, worn at an angle over one eye, and held in place by cunning little lime green leaves and a froth of veiling.

Christopher snorted with impatience. 'I know it's number one car park, but what number is their space?'

'Oh!' She looked blank for a moment, smoothing the short hair at the nape of her neck with gloved fingers. 'I don't think Delia said.'

'For God's sake, Oonagh! There'll be hundreds of cars, we don't want to have to walk around the whole place to find the right spot.'

'I remember now. She said we should meet by Richard's car. He's near where we'll be parked. In row H.'

'Well, I suppose that's something. God, look at all these crowds. It's going to be hell today.'

'It wouldn't be fun if there weren't any crowds,' she pointed out, determined to enjoy herself.

The traffic crawled, bumper to bumper, surging like bees to a honeypot of pleasure, the most exalted turning into the number one car park, the others finding their place in two, three, four, five or even further beyond. Oonagh gazed with competitive interest at the outfits of hundreds of other women, and was reassured to find none looking so good as herself. There was no doubt her picture would appear in the shiny sheets of *Harpers & Queen* and *Tatler* and hopefully *Vogue* as well. Like royalty, she sat upright in their Rolls, smiling at no one in particular but keeping her face at an angle that was becoming to her jawline.

They found Richard Seeley and his girlfriend, Monica Pembroke, almost immediately. They had given a lift to Mark and Lucy Miller, and were already into the second bottle of champagne. They were all friends of Oonagh's rather than of Christopher, and there was a little awkwardness at first because both couples were much younger than them. Oonagh was acting girlishly which annoyed Christopher, who suddenly felt old beside Richard and Mark, especially when he realised with a shock that Barbara was younger than any of them. Barbara . . . Oh, God, sweet Barbara. He looked around at the rows of neatly parked cars, and the glamorous groups clustered around tables set with silver and cut crystal glasses, and wondered what the hell he was doing here, with a wife he no longer loved and a bunch of her friends he didn't even like? Despair swept over him and he felt physically sick with longing. Life meant nothing unless he was with Barbara. That was a fact there was no denying. He took a gulp of champagne to suppress the ache in his heart, and immediately Richard Seeley seemed to pop up in front of him, an eager smile on his young face and a bottle in his hand.

'I say, old chap, your glass is empty. Can't have that, can we?' He laughed as if he'd said something funny. 'Let me fill you up, eh?'

Christopher looked at him with eyes that felt a thousand years old and his smile was wintry. 'Thanks.'

Oonagh gave a shrill little cry. 'Here they are! Here's Delia and Tony. And with a *van load* of food!'

A Shogun estate car had stopped just yards away and the Hammonds were jumping out, hugging and kissing the others, and then with the driver's help unloading collapsible tables and chairs, picnic baskets and cold boxes, and two cases of Bollinger.

Christopher went politely forward to help, not understanding the urgency with which this simple exercise was being carried out. 'Where's your parking space?' he asked Tony Hammond.

'Er . . . well . . .' Tony gave a forced laugh. 'There's been a bit of a mix-up, actually. We thought we'd have lunch here, by Richard's car – it's more central. While the driver goes and parks ours for us.'

Christopher frowned, puzzled, and then it all became clear as he glanced at the estate car's windscreen. Number four car park, it said, making him realise the Hammonds had probably never been granted a space in number one in the first place but were too embarrassed to admit it. Amusement at the situation really cheered him up. How typical of Oonagh's friends, he reflected, and how unbelievable that anyone should care where they parked their car.

'I think I'll have that top-up, after all, Richard,' he said, holding out his empty glass with a grin.

'Oh, absolutely,' Richard brayed inanely.

Mrs Morgan had prepared one of her special luncheons, knowing that the chefs would be taking over the catering for the rest of the weekend and that the dishes would be what she called 'very restaurant' and 'towny'. In spite of its being June, she knew Mr Rutherford would like to start with a light vegetable soup, made with chicken stock, and then go on to fish pie topped with creamy mashed potatoes and fresh mangetout from the garden.

'Exactly right,' Douglas beamed as Morgan served them. He'd laid the table earlier and had arranged three low bowls down the centre, filled with paeonies, delphiniums and love-in-a-mist. When John Plested had glanced in through the dining-room windows as Morgan was putting the finishing touches, the butler had stared defiantly back at him as if to say: The flowers indoors are *my* territory.

'What's happening this afternoon?' William enquired.

'Yes, is there anything we can do to help?' Tim asked eagerly.

'Can I trust you to put out the place cards, seeing that I'm not allowed into the marquee?' Julia asked.

'They're not allowed either,' Douglas said. 'No one is allowed to see what's going on until tomorrow night.'

'But *when* tomorrow night, Douglas?' she said, an edge of desperation in her voice. 'You're making me very nervous, you know. I feel I'm completely out of control . . .'

He laughed uproariously. 'Oh, my sweetheart. What a lovely thought. You, completely out of control . . .'

Pammy, watching, actually saw a flush creep up Julia's cheeks and thought: Can she really be embarrassed?

'You know what I mean,' Julia said, laughing too, but her eyes were pleading.

'Don't tease, Douglas,' his mother said firmly. 'Your teasing will get you into trouble one of these days.'

He turned grey, glowing eyes on her. 'Me – tease? How

can you say that?' he said playfully, hands held up in surrender.

'Daddy, you're a terrible tease!' Anna exclaimed.

'You're the worst tease in the world,' Michael said in a loud voice.

'He only does it to annoy,' Reggie Rutherford remarked.

'That's right,' agreed William. 'Do you remember the time you said my birthday party had been cancelled, half an hour before all my friends were due?'

'And you wept,' Anna reminded him.

He looked at her indignantly. 'I was only seven.'

'And didn't you enjoy it all the more when you found it hadn't been?' Douglas reminded him. 'And you found Mummy and I had given you the bike you wanted? And your birthday cake was a big chocolate castle?'

'But it was awful for him for a few minutes,' Julia said sadly. 'I couldn't bear to see his disappointment.'

'There! See how Mummy always sticks up for me,' William said triumphantly. 'Anyway, when *are* we going to be allowed to see inside the marquee?'

'I bet it's going to be as big a disappointment when we do . . . like an . . . an anticlimax . . . as when . . . as when William was told his birthday had been cancelled,' Michael said, red in the face from the effort of making such a long sentence.

'If you'll all stop attacking me I'll tell you exactly when you're allowed to go in,' Douglas announced dramatically.

To Pammy's amazement, she being the only one at the table unfamiliar with the way he orchestrated the people around him, everyone was instantly silent, all eyes fixed on Douglas's face.

'As you know,' he boomed, as if he were addressing a large audience, 'the guests have been invited for eight o'clock, and so everyone who is staying in the house will be given drinks in the marquee at seven-thirty, *precisely*. But I will be taking my bride over at seven-fifteen, so we can have a few minutes on our own to drink a private toast to each other in the setting I – with a little help from John Plested – have created.'

'Oh, Douglas . . .' Julia's eyes were suddenly bright with unshed tears. 'That's so romantic.'

Shit! Pammy said to herself. This dame is off the sodding wall!

'Let's go for a walk,' Anna suggested to Tim as soon as lunch was over. She needed to get out, get away, have a breath of fresh air, and knew Tim would understand if she didn't want to talk. They'd always been in tune with each other's feelings which was why he was such a good companion.

'Fine,' he replied.

While the 'oldies', as she referred to them, went back to the terrace for coffee, Douglas complaining that there was still a hell of a lot to do, Anna and Tim slipped out of the Manor via the back door.

'Let's go this way,' she suggested and led him along the camomile path, where, to one side, tall beeches formed a screen which afforded them privacy in the garden.

'So, tell me about Edinburgh . . .' she began, and then jumped, startled, and gave a little scream.

'What is it?'

Anna ignored him. She was staring angrily through the trees, where an old brick wall divided their property from Cherry Tree Cottage.

'Will you stop spying on us!' she said loudly. 'What the hell do you want?'

Intrigued, Tim saw the face of an elderly woman peering at them over the wall. She was looking defiantly at Anna, her immaculately made-up face set in lines of disapproval.

'I'll thank you not to talk to me like that! You're a very rude gel. I'm merely doing a little gardening, in my own garden, and so far as I know there's no law against that,' she snapped.

'You were snooping! You're always snooping and complaining . . .'

'Any more from you, young lady, and I shall call the police. You're harassing me on my own property . . .'

Anna turned away in disgust. 'Come on, Tim.' She strode on ahead of him.

'Who was that?' he asked, catching up with her.

'The local busy-body, Mrs Graham. She's an absolute menace. Everybody hates her. We're afraid she's going to make a scene about the noise tomorrow night. Daddy's tried to pacify her but she's determined to make trouble.'

'You haven't invited her, then?'

'Invited her? That woman has been making our lives hell for the past three years with her complaints. Nothing we do is right. Anyway, she's moving out next week, thank God.'

'That's good,' Tim said peaceably. He could see Anna was very upset and rattled, which was unlike her, and guessed Mrs Graham wasn't the only reason. They walked on until they were deep in the woods where the trees grew high above their heads, arched like the roof of a cathedral and equally quiet and peaceful.

Anna hadn't spoken for a while and he noticed that she

kept her face averted. When they came to a clearing she suddenly sat down on a fallen tree trunk and put her head in her hands.

'Oh, Anna . . .'

'I'm sorry,' she sobbed apologetically.

'Don't be. Let it out.'

'It's Petroc . . .'

'I thought as much.' He squeezed her shoulder and sat in sympathetic silence, letting her weep.

'Have you got a hanky?' she asked, after a few minutes. 'I never seem to have one when I need it.' She was groping fruitlessly through the pockets of her jeans.

'Here you are.'

'Thanks, Tim.' She took the dark green paisley-patterned handkerchief from him, grateful for its size and the fact it smelled pleasantly of after-shave. 'Oh, shit! I thought I was making such a good job of being brave and now I go and do this,' she added after she'd blown her nose. 'Bloody Petroc! I hate him at this moment.'

'You've had a fight?'

Anna shook her head. 'Not really. He dumped me, so I rang him back and told him what I thought of him, and now of course I'll never get him back.' She turned to face Tim, her eyes red-rimmed and her nose pink. 'And would you believe, I was naive enough to hope we might get engaged tomorrow night? How could I have been so stupid?'

'You don't sound as if you've been stupid at all. After all, you've been together for several years, haven't you?'

'Yes, and I've done everything I can think of to make him happy, and make him like me.' She started to cry again, great tears streaming down her face and plopping on to her denim-clad knees.

Tim hesitated for a moment then decided to speak.

'Could that be part of the problem, do you think?' he asked.

Anna looked up sharply, clearly shocked. 'How could it be?'

'Maybe he's someone who needs a bit of a challenge,' he said carefully.

'But I wasn't all that easy,' she said defensively. 'I refused to go to bed with him for quite a time, because I wanted to be sure we really loved each other.'

'I wasn't just thinking of the bed thing. You're such a sweet person, Anna, so easy-going and, well . . . easy to get on with. Maybe . . . I don't know, but maybe you always let him have his own way. That sort of thing,' he added lamely, hoping he hadn't already said too much.

She was silent for a moment, deep in thought. 'That was because I wanted him to love me,' she said at last.

'Men are perverse creatures, you know. Sometimes they want what they think they can't have. Sometimes playing hard to get, in the platonic sense, turns a man on.'

'What would you know about that, Tim?' she asked rudely. 'You're only nineteen. How many girlfriends have you had?'

'A few.'

'I bet! What? A couple of dates at the cinema, and the odd dinner in a restaurant, and suddenly you're an expert on how to conduct a relationship?' She spoke scornfully and with bitterness, and Tim realised he'd rattled her cage. He'd never seen her like this before, and it struck him that it made her a much more interesting person than the placid, cheerful girl he'd always known.

'So what are you going to do now?' he asked calmly.

Her shoulders slumped again, anger spent. 'What the

hell can I do? I've blown it. He'll probably never speak to me again.'

'Lots of other fish in the sea.'

'Maybe.' They sat in silence once more then she rose and stretched, as if she'd been sitting for a long time. 'I suppose we'd better get back. We've got people arriving and I should be helping Mummy.'

'OK.' There was nothing more to say. They walked slowly back and Anna seemed more composed. He'd obviously given her something to think about, though, because just before they got to the house she looked at him, her expression perplexed.

'Can one really be too nice to men?' she asked tentatively.

'I think one can try too hard to please,' he said slowly. 'And that applies to men, too. They can end up getting trampled on, the same as girls.'

Julia's mother and step-father had arrived by the time they got back.

'My darling girl,' Vivien Leonard said warmly, as soon as Anna appeared. She'd been warned by Julia not to mention Petroc and so, what with that, and the tranquillisers which she'd swallowed with vodka before leaving London, she was unusually effusive and gushing. 'Isn't this all exciting, darling? And you've got such a large houseparty as well. We *are* going to have a fun weekend, aren't we?'

Anna smiled weakly, and then kissed Simon Leonard whom she always called 'Papa'. Tall and white-haired with a white beard, she'd thought of him as a Father Christmas lookalike ever since she'd been a small child.

Everyone was still gathered on the terrace, entertainment being provided by the comings and goings of John

Plested and his team, and the caterers as they unloaded their vans in the drive.

'It reminds me of the old Covent Garden market,' Reggie remarked nostalgically, as he regarded the stacked crates and boxes containing dozens of different types of flowers, and large selections of fruit, vegetables and salads.

'It all smells wonderful,' Pat agreed, 'but where on earth is everything going to go?'

'No problem,' Douglas said cheerfully, as he grabbed a crate of peaches. He was thoroughly enjoying himself, priding himself on being a 'hands on' organiser, one of the workers, while assuring Julia that of course he wouldn't be worn out by tomorrow night.

'I've never watched preparations for a party on this scale,' Vivien observed, sitting down beside Pat in a deck chair.

'Interesting, isn't it?' she replied, 'I've often been behind the scenes in one of Douglas's restaurants, and it's amazing how everything falls into place. All that food is going to go in the mobile kitchens which are attached to the marquee,' she added in a knowledgeable tone, having just watched her son head in that direction with the peaches. 'And of course the flowers are to decorate the marquee. Douglas won't let any of us see what he's planned until just before the party starts tomorrow night. It's to be a surprise.'

Vivien looked at Pat. 'You must be so proud of him.' It was a statement not a question.

Pat flushed with gratification. 'Of course I am. And I'm proud of Peter, too. Unfortunately, he can't be here until tomorrow afternoon, but Leonora and the girls should arrive at any moment. Reggie and I are really very lucky with our family,' she added, face filled with pride.

'More than lucky, I'd say,' Vivien said generously. 'It's obvious you've brought them up very well. I'm so happy that Julia has Douglas. And to think they've been married twenty-five years! He's been a fantastic husband, and a marvellous father to Anna and William and Michael, too. I feel very blessed to have him as a son-in-law.'

Pat looked bright-eyed. 'He's a good boy,' she said, as if she were referring to a ten-year-old.

'Is Granny all right?' Anna asked her mother in a low voice. It was four o'clock and the activity in the house and on the lawn had reached the frenzied stage when time was running out and it looked as if they'd never get anything finished in time.

Douglas was red-faced and sweating, barking orders and in his opening-a-new-restaurant mode, while Mrs Morgan and her husband were trying to keep their temper in the face of an invasion of their territory by a dozen restaurant staff.

'I think so, darling,' Julia replied, wrestling once again with a seating plan, this time for tonight's dinner in the dining room. 'Shall I put Tim next to you? And then if I put Roger on my right . . . no, Simon should go on my right . . . Oh, dear, then I'll have to put Reggie on my left and that'll offend Roger . . .'

'For goodness' sake, Mummy, does it matter? We don't have to be formal, do we?'

'It's not a case of formality, but making sure all our guests are looked after,' Julia remonstrated gently.

'But it's such a performance! You're not going to put their names on little cards, are you?'

'With so many people, it's the only way to avoid chaos,'

Julia said. Then she looked serious again. 'Why do you think there's anything wrong with Granny? She seemed in very good form to me.'

'I wondered if she'd been drinking.' Anna wandered down the length of the dining-room table, which Morgan had already set with a white damask cloth, gold and dark blue Venetian wine glasses which Douglas and Julia had brought back from a trip to Italy, and an antique gilt épergne overflowing with fruit. 'She seems so . . . so animated,' she added, leaning forward to straighten a spoon.

'Drinking?' Julia's voice rose in astonishment. 'Who are you talking about? My mother or Daddy's?'

'Mummy, you know I always call your mother Granny and Dad's mother Grandma. I'm talking about Granny. She seems to be all over the place.'

'Oh, don't be ridiculous, darling. Granny never drinks . . . well, not what I'd call drinking. Just the occasional glass of wine, perhaps. You're imagining it. I expect she's just excited about being here with all of us for the weekend.' As she spoke, she put small cards on which she'd written names in front of each place setting.

Michael came roaring into the room at that moment, on his rollerblades. In knee and elbow pads, loose-fitting knickerbockers with a reinforced seat and a baseball cap, he did a circuit of the table before coming to a wobbly halt beside his mother.

'Michael, how often have I told you not to come indoors in those things?' Julia admonished him. 'You'll ruin the floors.'

'But Dad told me to come and get you.' His face and hands were grubby and he was full of self-importance, intent on carrying out his father's instructions.

'They're here,' he said flatly.

'Who are?'

'Leonora and Cressida and Sasha. They're talking to Dad in the garden.'

Julia quelled the pang of dread she always experienced when Leonora's name was mentioned. Much as she liked Douglas's brother, Peter, she found his wife both threatening and rude. Following Michael into the garden, she braced her shoulders and assumed a welcoming smile. Leonora was talking to Douglas, smiling up into his face with a coquettish expression on hers.

'Leonora! How lovely to see you,' Julia exclaimed, doing her best to sound pleased, but their eyes locked for a moment of frozen dislike and with a sinking heart Julia realised they were once more in combat.

She turned to kiss Cressida and Sasha. They were sweet if rather lumpen, and completely overshadowed by their mother. Greeting Julia shyly and awkwardly, they soon reverted to gazing around the activity on the lawn in awed silence.

'Let's all have some tea,' Julia suggested, suddenly realising this was going to be a very long weekend. 'Would you like a swim first?' she asked her nieces.

Although they were nineteen and twenty respectively, they looked at their mother as if for permission.

Leonora nodded. 'Why don't you? You don't often get the chance to stay in a house with a swimming pool, do you?'

Julia felt her jaw harden at this attempt to rouse sympathy.

'Surely they can use the school swimming pool?'

'Peter doesn't really like them using it. It's meant for the boys,' Leonora retorted, and turned abruptly back to

Douglas, ignoring Julia's presence. 'You must have worked so hard to organise all this?'

'We've all been working hard,' he replied easily. 'If you'll excuse me now, I've got to check on the mobile kitchens – make sure the cookers are working.'

She made to follow him. 'Can I see what's going on?'

He laughed, shaking his head. 'Nobody's allowed backstage. Not even Julia,' he added firmly.

Julia smiled, and then felt instantly appalled by her own feeling of triumph. Why did Leonora bring out the worst in her? It wasn't because she flirted with Douglas; it was a joke between them that he did not find his sister-in-law attractive. It wasn't even Leonora's snide remarks; they were obviously based on jealousy and rather pathetic. It was her sheer competitiveness that seemed to be catching.

It was now five o'clock and the full heat of the day seemed to have settled on the afternoon, reducing the older ones, still sitting on the terrace, to a state of torpor. Shrieks of laughter were coming from the pool as Anna, Tim, William and Michael joined their cousins in a swim. To Julia it seemed like a long time since the morning. Remembering her early elation she felt a sense of melancholy now at the passing of the hours and the speed with which life slipped away, never to be recaptured. Watching the members of her own and Douglas's family, gathered together with all their children for this special weekend, it saddened her to think that the best moments pass the swiftest, and in that instant become the past. I'm getting morbid, she scolded herself, as she heard a car coming up the drive. It was William's girlfriend, Stephanie Harris, a sparky blonde with a mind of her own and a huge personality.

'Hi!' she shouted through the open window as she brought her car to a swerving halt and jumped out to greet Julia as if they were the same age.

'Hi, Stephanie!' They hugged each other warmly and Julia led her towards the pool. 'How are you?'

'Glad as hell to be here.' Stephanie flashed her a wide grin. 'I wanted to get out of London before the Friday-night traffic built up, but it was still pretty bad.'

'That reminds me . . .' Julia glanced at her wrist watch. 'My brother Christopher and his wife are supposed to be arriving sometime soon. You go on to the pool, darling, you'll find William there. I'm just going to make a call to see what time they're arriving.'

'Where the hell *is* Oonagh?' Christopher fumed, looking at his wrist watch again. 'I told her to meet us by the car at five o'clock.'

Richard, who had opened another bottle of champagne, shrugged vaguely. 'She and Monica said they'd only be five minutes.'

'But whose box did they go to?'

'I don't know. Oonagh met this couple, and they invited us for a drink, and I said I couldn't because I was meeting Delia and Tony by the Tote . . .' Richard sipped his drink thoughtfully, and Christopher groaned.

'I told her we had to leave well before the last race,' he said furiously.

'The traffic's going to be bad no matter what time we leave,' Richard reasoned.

'I have to get to dinner . . .' Barbara will be waiting . . . ready to make love . . . oh, God, I want to be with her so badly. He gritted his teeth and scanned the rows of parked cars that stretched away into the distance. He was looking for a silly hat with a big pink rose but there was no sign of it.

'I'll tell you what,' Richard said suddenly, 'why don't you go ahead if you're in a hurry? I can bring Oonagh back in my car.'

'But you've got Mark and Lucy Miller . . .'

'It's no problem, old chap! The girls can have a good gossip in the back and Mark can come in the front with me.'

Christopher's face filled with gratitude. 'You're sure?'

'No probs, old boy. You get off.' Richard waved an arm expansively and for a second it struck Christopher that he was probably over the drink limit . . . but the traffic would be crawling so there was really no risk . . . and he'd probably sober up a bit by the time they set off.

'Well, thanks, Richard. Will you explain to Oonagh that I simply had to get back? It's a business dinner, you know. Tell her I waited and waited . . .'

Richard clapped him on the shoulder. 'Leave it to me. We'll probably all go out to dinner when we get back, so we'll take her with us. You hurry along now.'

Christopher needed no further encouragement. After a firm handclasp of thanks, he hurried off with a glorious feeling of escape. When his car phone purred loudly five minutes later he swore. Nothing was going to make him go back, though. He'd tell Oonagh he was stuck in traffic on the motorway and couldn't turn round. Cautiously he lifted the phone to his ear, cursing himself for ever having installed it in the first place.

'Chris? Is that you?'

Relief made him dizzy for a moment. 'Julia!'

'Hello, Chris. I was just wondering what time you were arriving? Dinner isn't until eight-thirty, but . . .'

'Oh, fuck!' He sounded genuinely regretful. 'I'm most awfully sorry, Sis, I should have let you know. Oonagh insisted we went to bloody Royal Ascot today, and now I've got to go to a business dinner . . . she's getting a lift back with some friends, so we'll be going down to you tomorrow. Does that muck up your plans completely?'

'Oh, Chris! How could you?' He could tell she was disappointed. 'I've got the whole family here. Tim arrived earlier, and Mummy and Simon. We're having a family dinner party tonight and it won't be the same without you.'

'I'm really sorry, Sis. I really am. I've been . . . well, I have problems at the moment and I'm totally disorganised. Sometimes I don't even know which day of the week it is.'

'What is it, Chris? What's wrong?' Her voice was sharp with anxiety. 'You're not ill, are you?'

He smiled to himself, as he manoeuvred the car into a gap in the traffic. 'I've never been better. I'll tell you all about it tomorrow . . . but, Julia?'

'Yes?'

'Don't mention anything to Mum and Simon, will you? And certainly not to Tim. How is he? Did he say if he likes Edinburgh?'

'Your son is a credit to you, Chris. He's as nice as ever, and he's doing a wonderful job cheering up Anna . . .'

'What's wrong with her?'

'Boyfriend trouble.'

'Oh, lor'!'

'I know. So you'll be down tomorrow? Come in the morning otherwise I'll hardly see anything of you. And you don't have to rush back early on Sunday, do you?'

'I'm not sure. It depends,' he replied carefully.

It was only after they'd said goodbye that he realised, with amusement, that she'd never asked after Oonagh, or mentioned her once.

'What do you mean . . . he's left?' Oonagh's face looked suddenly drawn and pale with anger.

Richard laughed nervously. 'He waited for you, but he was worried about the traffic. He's got a business dinner to get to, hasn't he?'

The others grouped around awkwardly, realising this was a social crisis. Husbands did not zip back to London, abandoning their wives in the middle of Berkshire, even if they had been assured she would be given a lift. It simply wasn't done.

Pride kept Oonagh composed, but her mouth was tight in the face of this public humiliation though she tried to make light of it.

'He works far too hard,' she said, unable however to keep the bitterness out of her voice. 'But if you can give me a lift, Richard, that would be most helpful.'

'But why don't you come with us?' Delia Hammond interjected. 'There'd be much more room in the estate car, and as we have a driver we can all relax on the way home.'

Oonagh hesitated. It would be preferable to go with the Hammonds than to be squashed in the back of Richard's car.

'And we can all meet up in London for dinner,' Tony Hammond added. 'We can go to The Collection, it's always fun there.'

So far as Oonagh was concerned, that settled it. 'Thank you,' she said gratefully.

'Are you sure?' Richard didn't want to be blamed by

Christopher for failing to keep his promise to give her a lift.

'Absolutely!'

'Well,' he turned to his girlfriend, Monica, and Mark and Lucy Miller, 'shall we get going then? The last race has just started, and we'll be ahead of the traffic if we leave now.'

Agreeing that was a good idea, goodbyes were said all round, Oonagh kissing those who were leaving with precise care so as not to smudge her lipstick or mess up her pale green veiling. Then Richard got into his car and they waved as it bumped slowly across the grass, lost to them among the hundreds of other cars still parked in neat rows.

At this point, Oonagh realised she, Delia and Tony were on their own, with the remains of the picnic. The tables had already been folded up and so had the chairs, and they'd been placed beside the stack of baskets and containers which now held nothing but a few left-overs from lunch, and the dirty dishes.

'Is there any champagne left, Tony?' Delia asked.

'I'll have a look and see,' he replied as he started rummaging.

'Your car is picking us up here?' Oonagh remarked, feeling it was a foolish question, but anxious to subdue her sudden feeling of foreboding.

Tony nodded cheerfully. 'Yes. I told the driver to come and collect us after the last race. Ah! An unopened bottle!' With triumph he withdrew a bottle of Moët & Chandon from one of the boxes. 'I'm afraid all the glasses are dirty, though.'

'Never mind.' Delia sounded breezy. 'I don't suppose any of us have foot and mouth.'

'Perhaps we could sit down while we're waiting?' Oonagh suggested, eyeing the stack of chairs. Her shoes were causing her acute pain and she wished she could slip them off.

'I don't know that it's worth it,' Tony demurred. He glanced at his wrist watch. 'The car should be along in a few minutes.'

From the distant roar of thousands of people cheering the winning horse past the post, Oonagh realised with relief the last race was over. It was getting a bit chilly, and the sun had been obliterated by heavy clouds. People were already beginning to leave, parting with effusive good-byes, piling into their Daimlers and Rolls-Royces and Bentleys, the women unpinning their big hats and fluffing their hair with relief, the men removing their grey toppers and tail coats, and exchanging them for comfortable blazers. Her eyes, already tired from searching the crowds for the past five hours in the hope of seeing a familiar face, now scanned the vast car park in search of a dark blue estate car. The champagne, which earlier had pleasantly stimulated her senses, now formed a layer of sour acidity in her stomach. She'd kill Christopher for this. For her humiliation. For her discomfort. For not looking after her as a husband was supposed to. This was his revenge, of course, for having to spend the day at the races. He'd probably planned to dump her here all along, knowing her friends would be forced to take pity on her.

For a moment Oonagh felt like crying with vexation. Tony, she noticed, was looking at his watch again, and frowning. Only Delia, always sweetly stupid, seemed unconcerned. She was prattling on about the fashions she'd seen in the Enclosure, and how some of the hats were too big to get through a doorway.

Twenty minutes later the estate car still hadn't turned up.

'Perhaps he's stuck in traffic?' Delia suggested when Tony expressed his annoyance. 'There are so many cars getting out of the car park, he probably can't get in.'

Oonagh, watching with such concentration her head now ached, wished it was that simple. Now that so many had left she had a clear view of the two distant exits, and whilst it was true cars were queuing up to leave, there was certainly room for a vehicle to enter.

'If he's not here in another ten minutes I'll have to walk to number four car park and fetch him,' Tony said irritably, helping himself to more champagne.

'Oh, sweetie, it's *miles* away,' Delia exclaimed, her eyes stricken. If he'd suggested he'd have to climb the Himalayas she couldn't have looked more distressed. 'You can't go all that way. He's sure to come soon. Perhaps he doesn't realise it's over.'

'Surely he'd be curious at a mass exodus if the racing wasn't over?' Oonagh observed tartly.

'Well . . . he's foreign,' Delia replied as if that explained everything.

They waited another twenty minutes. Whereas there had been around a thousand cars earlier in the day, there were now only a few dozen. A chill breeze was whipping across the exposed field and there was a definite air of melancholy in the atmosphere. With reluctance Tony put down his glass and decided to go in search of their hired car.

'Take care,' Delia called after him.

It was half an hour before Tony returned. He was on his own, looking pale and tired, and his shoes were dusty.

Delia rushed forward, all commiseration and sympathy. 'Sweetie, what's happened? Where's the car?'

'It's not there. He's gone,' he replied succinctly.

'*Gone*?' Delia and Oonagh shrilled in unison. Then they stared at him in stunned silence. 'Gone?' Oonagh echoed faintly.

'Gone.'

'Did you look in the right car park?' Delia bleated.

Tony gave her a filthy look. 'I ended up looking in car park number one, number two, number three, number four *and* bloody number five. I also looked in the driveway of various private houses, and our car and our bloody driver are nowhere to be seen. He's *gone.*'

'What shall we do now, sweetie?' Delia asked.

Oonagh, realising that they were lumbered with two six-foot collapsible tables, eight chairs and an assortment of picnic baskets and cold boxes, was probably for the first time in her life unable to say a thing.

By seven o'clock, Julia's best friend had arrived at Highfield Manor, laden with luggage and gift-wrapped presents. Caroline Drummond had first met Julia at St Mary's School, Wantage, when they'd both been twelve, and they'd stayed close ever since. Both had got engaged in the spring of 1971, when they'd been nineteen, and both had married that same summer. The following year Julia gave birth to Anna, but Caroline suffered a miscarriage, and from that moment on their respective lives veered in different directions, though this did not affect their friendship. In some ways it strengthened it, as Julia offered comfort and support to her less fortunate friend who, after an acrimonious divorce, went on to marry twice more. Each husband proved to be more disastrous than the last, but now, at forty-eight, she was once again single, having made a career for herself as a successful jewellery designer with a shop in Knightsbridge's Beauchamp Place and a clientele who thought nothing of spending thousands of pounds a year on decking themselves out with sparkling personal adornments.

As Caroline unpacked in the wisteria room, so called because Julia had decorated it with wisteria-patterned wallpaper and pale green silk curtains and canopied bed, she realised, almost to her surprise, that she felt no envy for her friend's good fortune. She'd have liked to have had children herself, and, she supposed, a steady relationship, but being single and having a thriving career held huge compensations. It was both exciting and satisfying to paddle your own canoe, as her late father would have described it. It was having no one to think about except herself that was such a relief at this stage in her life. No obligatory dinner to cook every evening; no shirts to iron; no having to watch rugby matches on the TV when she'd been looking forward to a film; no sex when she wasn't in the mood; no boring post-mortems to listen to of what had happened at the office. She could do as she liked and that made her wake up every morning with a glorious sense of freedom. The ability to make the day hers and hers alone.

A gentle tapping on the bedroom door brought Caroline out of her reverie.

'Come in.'

'It's me,' Julia announced, opening the door. 'I've brought you a drink to have while you're getting ready for dinner.' She'd already showered and changed into a long flower-patterned wraparound skirt which she wore with a tight-fitting long-sleeved stretch top. Her dark hair, swept up with combs on each side of her face and tumbling to shoulder length at the back, reminded Caroline of Vivien Leigh in *Gone with the Wind*.

'You're a mind reader. How gorgeous!' she replied, reaching for the fluted glass and taking a sip. 'God, that's good.'

Julia laughed. 'There's nothing like that first glass of champagne in the evening, is there?' She perched herself on the *chaise-longue* at the foot of the bed. 'So how is everything? You're looking marvellous.'

'Look who's talking. You're looking positively radiant.' Caroline glanced out of the window, where there was still coming and going around the marquee, as food and flowers and crockery and cutlery continued to be unloaded. 'It looks as if this is going to be the party of the decade.'

'That's what Douglas hopes,' Julia replied candidly. 'We've got every photographer and diary columnist in London coming down tomorrow night. He's even putting some of them up, as his guests, at the Grosvenor Hotel in Stockbridge, so they won't have to drive back to town afterwards.'

'What are you wearing?'

Julia grinned. 'That's *my* secret! The decorations in the marquee are Douglas's so we're planning to surprise each other.'

'God, what fun!' As she spoke, Caroline unzipped a dark blue canvas travelling bag and lifted out a rich dark green satin evening dress, with gold-beaded shoulder straps. 'I'm wearing this. D'you like it?'

'It's fabulous. Is it Bruce Oldfield?'

'Of course. With his shop opposite mine in Beauchamp Place, it's divinely easy to pop over and try on everything he's got. And I'm going to wear these,' she said, opening two of her trademark dark red jewel boxes. One contained an oriental-style gold necklace set with emeralds and the other matching earrings.

Julia looked at the glittering jewellery. 'My God, Caroline, your designs really are beautiful,' she said with genuine enthusiasm.

'The best bit is they'll go back into stock on Monday,' she laughed.

'And meanwhile you're a walking advertisement for your designs.'

'That's the general idea.'

They both laughed, understanding each other perfectly. Julia rose. 'I must go downstairs again and look after everyone. Come down as soon as you're ready.'

'What are we going to do?' Delia wailed, tears welling in her eyes. 'We haven't even got a mobile phone.'

In the last ten minutes the car park had virtually emptied, except for a solitary group of racegoers who were standing around their cars, finishing off their supply of champagne.

Oonagh felt enraged. This was all Christopher's fault. If he hadn't gone off like that, without a care for what happened to her, she'd have been back in London by now, warm, comfortable and contemplating an enticing menu. Fury propelled her in the direction of the revellers, her high heels causing her to totter on the uneven ground, desperation giving her an adrenalin charge.

'Excuse me!' she called out as she neared them, her voice shrill. At first they didn't realise she was talking to them and so continued jesting and drinking, oblivious of her standing there, a distraught figure with a large silken rose drooping over her pink-tipped nose.

'*Excuse me . . .*'

In sudden silence they turned to look at her but said nothing.

'Have you got a mobile phone in your car, by any chance?'

One of the men looked at her blankly. 'Yes. D'you want to use it?' he asked off-handedly.

'Please. We're stranded . . .'

Oonagh took the phone with hands that were white with cold. 'Thanks.' Feverishly she stabbed Christopher's mobile phone number. With any luck he might not have reached London yet. But when he answered with a gruff 'Hello?' he sounded as if he'd been running.

'Christopher? How dare you go off like that and leave me! Thanks to you I'm now stuck in this fucking car park with no means of getting home. You're to fucking well drive straight back here, *now*, and . . . Christopher? *Christopher?*'

She could hear a woman's voice in the background. A woman's laugh. 'What the fuck's going on?' Oonagh yelled. 'Where the hell are you?'

'I'm . . . I told you I had a business dinner. Why are you stranded? I arranged with Richard . . . Whose phone are you using?'

Oonagh knew him well enough to know he was waffling from guilt, and that without a doubt he was with another woman.

'You *shit-head*!' she hollered to the amazement of the revellers, who had gone very quiet as they stood looking at her, wide-eyed. 'You've done this on purpose. Well, for all I care, you can go fuck yourself!'

She switched off the phone and turned to the group.

'Would you be able to give me a lift to London? I'm desperate.'

'Sorry, but we're already jam packed,' said one of the young men with heartless cheerfulness. 'As it is we'll be sitting on each other's knees . . .'

At that moment Tony Hammond, with Delia trailing behind him walked over to join them. If Oonagh was bristling with fury, Delia was drooping with dejection, her straw hat limp, her shoulders slumped in her thin silk dress.

'I say, old chap,' Tony said, taking the phone from Oonagh, 'I couldn't possibly make a quick call, could I? Damned hire car hasn't turned up and we're stranded.'

The owner of the phone nodded silently.

'Thanks most awfully,' Tony replied, stabbing away at the instrument with his short stubby fingers.

The rain, mere tiny droplets a few minutes before, was now descending with purposeful plops, staining Oonagh's pale green silk suit and spangling the veiling on her hat.

'If we can't get the car to come back for us,' Delia informed her in a loud whisper, while Tony talked to the car hire firm, 'the cleaners who are going around picking up all the rubbish say we can put the picnic stuff in a store room for the night. Then we can walk to the station and get the train.'

Standing in an empty field, in heavy rain, with a biting wind and darkness approaching, Oonagh experienced something approaching despair.

The table for dinner had been re-set for sixteen.

'At least it's easier to take away place settings than to add them,' Julia remarked as Morgan made the adjustments.

'Everyone will have more elbow room too, ma'am,' he

pointed out, changed out of his day clothes into pinstripe trousers and a black coat. He was in his element, feeling like the second-in-command of some great military exercise which he intended to execute with the utmost precision. Meanwhile, in the drawing room, Douglas was handing out drinks as if tomorrow's party had already begun.

'Come along!' he greeted Julia, when she entered the room. 'We've done all we can for today. Everyone's packed it in for the night so let's relax and enjoy ourselves.'

'We shouldn't be too late,' Pat pointed out. She looked tired; accustomed to a quiet life, the comings and goings of the day had proved exciting but stressful.

Julia's mother had no such reservations. Fuelled by champagne on top of a gin and tonic and another couple of tranquillisers, she was ready to dance all night and tomorrow night, too. Past the point of panicking about the lump in her breast, she'd reached the stage when she felt empowered to overcome whatever fate held in store for her. If she was destined to die, she would party her way to her grave and show no regrets. She'd go out in a spectacular blaze of courage and be praised at her funeral for her bravery.

Leonora, overdressed in a silver lamé blouse and black velvet skirt, for what was after all only a family dinner and not a trial run for the following night, looked around the exquisite drawing room with envious eyes, comparing it with their living quarters at the school. She ached to have a room like this, but instead had to make do with the shabby furniture and hideous brown-checked curtains provided by the previous headmaster, and considered adequate by Peter.

'Anyway, we can't afford to waste money on fancy

decorations until Cressida and Sasha are completely off our hands,' he'd pointed out. Leonora looked at her daughters, now sitting in the bay window with Anna, Tim, William and Stephanie, and wondered how long it would be before they got married and became someone else's responsibility. She feared it wouldn't happen in a hurry. Compared to Anna's English rose complexion and fair hair, and Stephanie's figure and sex-appeal, Cressida and Sasha looked dull and plain like their father.

Dragging her eyes away from the enviable elegance of the room, Leonora turned to watch Douglas, the provider of all this magnificence. He was dispensing drinks and bonhomie, his broad shoulders and clever face dominating the scene, his laughter ringing as he went around topping up everyone's glass. How lucky Julia was to have married the successful brother, she reflected, looking down into the popping bubbles of her drink. Not that she herself was in love with Douglas; she wasn't sure she even fancied the idea of going to bed with him; it was something else. He was compelling. Exuded a glamorous aura of power. It would be exciting to be married to someone like him. And it would give her the chance, which she so desperately desired, to shine as a great beauty, a fabulous hostess, and a fascinating figure on the social scene. She considered herself more striking than Julia and certainly more voluptuous. And she felt she had much more personality. There was something altogether wispy about Julia, a tendency to be weak and too sweet for her own good. Maybe that was what Douglas liked? Strong men were often attracted to dependent women.

She looked across at Julia now, sitting on the sofa talking to Roger Sullivan. He was throwing back his head, roaring with laughter at something she'd said, and

Leonora had grudgingly to admit that Julia could not be underestimated. Men did seem to find her attractive, although she, personally, couldn't imagine why.

When Morgan announced dinner, they made their way across the large hall to the dining room, where dozens of creamy candles provided the only lighting and the air was fragrant with the aroma of guinea fowl cooked with dried apricots and garlic. There they regrouped around the laden table, with Douglas and Julia at either end, and there was the hum of contented chatter and soft laughter as everyone took their places.

Stephanie grabbed William's hand under the table and squeezed it tightly. 'This is amazing!' she whispered, looking around. 'Your parents have really gone to town, haven't they?'

William smiled proudly, his head inclined towards hers. 'All that's really amazing is that you're here,' he whispered.

She gazed into his eyes, so like her own in their dazzling blueness. 'Your mother's given me a single room.'

He grinned. 'Don't let that worry you.'

She looked almost anxious. 'But are you sure you know which one I'm in? I don't want you visiting Cressida or Sasha in the middle of the night!'

He doubled up with silent laughter, shoulders shaking.

'God forbid! You're in the one at the end of the corridor on the left, aren't you? The holly room?'

Stephanie nodded. 'You will come, won't you?'

'As soon as the coast's clear. Promise.'

Across the table from them, Anna and Tim were still talking, as they'd done ever since he'd arrived earlier, and she was looking more cheerful. But her eyes held a look that hadn't been there the day before, a knowing expression of sadness and experience. Gone forever was the untroubled, confident gaze of youthful innocence. Tomorrow she would be twenty-one, but in the past few hours she'd already come of age.

Further down the table Pammy, with Douglas on one side and Simon Leonard on the other, regarded the table decorations with a critical eye. She would never, she thought, in a million years, have put cream candles on the table with the fruit-laden gilt épergne; they should have been sapphire blue to match the glasses. And the table napkins should have been gold-coloured, and loosely bound with those pretty blue enamel napkin rings you could get at Tiffany.

Pammy sighed inwardly, while pretending to listen to Julia's step-father drone on about New Labour. She was thinking how she could transform this house into something really stylish if Douglas would only commission her to redecorate it.

Caroline, sitting next to Vivien, was having difficulty carrying on a coherent conversation with her. The older woman seemed so distraught Caroline decided she was either very drunk or having a stroke. Vivien had been like a surrogate mother to her over the years, and she was seriously worried about her now.

'Are you all right, Vivien?' she enquired in a low voice.

For a moment Vivien looked at her with a completely blank expression, as if she had no idea what she was talking about, and then she dropped her gaze and her mouth trembled.

'Oh dear . . . does it show?' she asked.

'Well . . . you're not quite yourself,' Caroline replied tactfully. 'Have you perhaps had . . .?'

Vivien reached out and gripped her wrist under the table. She looked at Caroline again, and there was a look of panic in her eyes. 'I think I've overdone the tranquillisers . . . and maybe I shouldn't have had anything to drink . . . *But no one must know,*' she added in an urgent whisper. 'I don't want anyone, especially Julia, to know anything's wrong. I just feel a bit muddled . . .'

Caroline nodded silently, recognising a plea for help.

'Why don't you drink as much water as you can, and eat something? You've hardly touched your smoked salmon. Here.' She reached for a plate of finely sliced brown bread and butter. 'Have some of this. It'll act as blotting paper.' Smoothly and discreetly, Caroline urged her to eat whilst she talked to her about whatever came into her head, so that no one at the table would guess anything was wrong. But what had caused Vivien, usually so level-headed and in control, to get into this state? Caroline looked over at Simon, talking to Pammy Schemmel, but he gave no indication of having noticed anything amiss.

Dinner did not end until eleven o'clock, because Douglas was thoroughly enjoying himself. This, so far as he was concerned, was a unique weekend, one which would never be repeated in the lifetime of most of those gathered round his table tonight. By the time he and Julia celebrated their Ruby or even their Golden Anniversary, their parents would be dead, and God only knew where Anna, William and Michael would be. Whenever Julia caught his eye, suggesting they bring the evening to an end, he ordered more coffee, more drinks, more chocolates in Victorian silver bon-bon dishes, and kept up a flow of conversation, interspersed with amusing anecdotes, so that the gales of laughter coming from the dining room told the waiting staff who were wanting to clear the table that it was indeed going to be a late night.

No one had the heart to end his evident pleasure. His parents decided they would rise late tomorrow and spend the afternoon resting. Vivien, much recovered after some food and several glasses of water, decided that she would go with the flow and rest when she got back to London on Monday. Leonora could have stayed up all night; this, as far as she was concerned, was Living. Roger, puffing a Monte Cristo and sipping a fine Napoleon brandy, rather wished they were near a casino; he felt like a flutter tonight. Even the young ones showed no eagerness to leave the dining room, so enveloped did they feel in the party spirit generated by Douglas.

And all the while Julia sat at the opposite end of the table, talking animatedly to those nearest her and occasionally looking down the table to exchange smiles with her husband. It had been his entrepreneurial spirit that had created all they had, she reflected. When they'd got married, he'd promised her the earth. Well, he'd certainly kept his word. He *had* given her the earth, and more. But how much of his success did he owe to her? Julia had few illusions. The brilliance had undoubtedly been his, but holding it all together . . . their home . . . the family . . . the restaurant empire . . . Douglas himself, had been her doing, and what it had taken to achieve was something she would never regret.

At last he rose, face wreathed in smiles. Friday was over. Now there was less than twenty-four hours to go before the ball. The countdown had begun. Julia felt a frisson, part nerves, part excitement. After all the months of planning tomorrow was the big day. No turning back now. Three hundred people would be descending on them, all filled with anticipation, knowing that with Douglas in charge their expectations would be fulfilled. There was nothing to worry about, she told herself, because the evening had been organised with precision and short of some national disaster occurring nothing could go wrong. Yet she felt nervous without being sure why.

Only later, when she was on the upstairs landing outside her bedroom, did something happen that she found deeply disquieting. She heard voices in the hall below, and glancing over the banister, saw Pammy talking to Leonora. Pammy was gesticulating and seemed to be praising someone in extravagant terms. 'He's the most fantastic man . . .'

Without being told Julia knew Pammy was referring to Douglas. She'd been enthralled by him throughout the whole dinner and her admiration had been obvious. Julia smiled indulgently, a warm feeling of pride filling her heart.

Then Leonora spoke in a whisper sharp with spitefulness. Julia didn't catch the first words but she heard her say: '. . . of course he has affairs.'

Saturday

22 June 1996

Six

It was five o'clock in the morning. The day of the party was about to dawn, pink and misty and dew-soaked, but so far Julia hadn't slept at all. Beside her Douglas slumbered deeply, his breathing even, his face and hands relaxed in perfect repose. He'd fallen asleep the moment his head had touched the pillow some five hours ago, but Julia, in contrast, felt as if she were becoming more alert by the minute.

Lily. That was what was keeping her awake. Memories of Lily. The girl Douglas had had an affair with all those years ago. It had been a brief affair, Julia was sure of that. A mad fling to reassure himself he was still attractive to women. It had happened just before they'd moved into Highfield Manor, after William had been born and when Anna was three. Julia had read somewhere that at that particular stage in a marriage it was called the 'second baby syndrome' when a husband strayed. Douglas had been so excited at the birth of their first baby; the second time around there was less novelty. Their lives would be predictable now, their responsibilities cast in stone, their future set out in detail. When, one day, looking at William in his cot, Douglas had remarked flatly: 'I suppose that's it?' she knew he was experiencing a sense of anti-climax. There would be no more adventures in their personal lives.

Julia, realising she'd temporarily lost her figure and that all her energies were being directed into looking after William, whom she was breast feeding, was aware of alarm bells ringing in her head. The trouble was, she lacked the energy to do anything about it. If Douglas was bored, in spite of having just opened The Kitchen, and appearing on television in his own cookery programme and being a household name, it was something he'd have to deal with himself. It never struck her, until it was too late, that his way of dealing with it would be to have an affair with a young girl called Lily.

Over the years she had put the whole hideous thing to the back of her mind, blocking it out so that most of the time she was even able to persuade herself it had never happened. Douglas belonged to her. Had always belonged to her, and always would. The affair with Lily was something they never talked about. Best forgotten. Swept under the carpet as if it had never happened. Lots of married men had a fling . . . but that wasn't what had upset her last night, Julia thought. Leonora had said: '. . . of course he has affairs.' So had there been others? Was there, dear God, someone else in his life now?

Julia lay in the darkness, feeling the warmth of his virile body next to hers, and was wracked with misery.

But how did Leonora know? Even about Lily? Had Douglas confided in his brother, and had Peter unwisely told Leonora?

The agony of jealousy that consumed her now, at the thought that there might be other Lilys, was like a knife cutting into her heart. Douglas spent every day in

London, supposedly at one of the restaurants. Perhaps he was really at their flat with a girl? Sometimes he stayed in town overnight . . .

Julia crawled out of bed, unable to stand it any longer. She must do something, go for a walk, a swim, anything to put a buffer between her imagination and her mind, lest she go mad. As she pulled on her jeans and a sweater, she could hear the sounds of a waking house. She wasn't the only one up and about. The day of the party had begun.

William felt Stephanie snuggle against him, her hand, even in sleep, reaching for him. He'd slipped into her room shortly after everyone else had gone to bed, and as they hadn't been together for nearly a week, their love making had been swift and frantic, reaching a peak too soon, and then, in spite of their efforts, unable to reach it again. Giggling, they had settled down to sleep in each other's arms, his legs wrapped around hers, her breath soft and sweet against his cheek.

Now, as they wakened, she moved closer and he stroked her breasts, so young and taut, feeling the stiffening of her nipples beneath his fingers. Immediately she started to caress him, gently, tantalisingly, exciting him with her touch. Within moments a quick build up of heat had fused their bodies into one as he slid inside her and heard her gasp with pleasure.

'I love you . . .' he said, through laboured breathing.

'Oh . . . take me, Will . . . now, Oh, God, now!' She writhed beneath him, coming again and again as he plunged relentlessly, reaching, straining, deeper and deeper, until the world seemed to explode dizzily around him, and he lay in her softness, spent and exhausted.

As he came out of Stephanie's room half an hour later, he bumped into Roger Sullivan in the corridor. He was wearing a tracksuit and seemed in a hurry. The two men smiled at each other sheepishly.

'On your way back to your own room?' Roger enquired in a confidential man-to-man manner.

William nodded. 'You too?'

'God, no.' Roger dropped his voice to a whisper. 'Your mother gave Pammy and me a double room. I'm running away to get a bit of peace!'

Anna, who had slept fitfully, with disturbing dreams of being in a decaying old house where everything she touched crumbled to dust, knew that today was going to be an enormous test of her inner strength. For the sake of her parents, William, her grandparents, and everyone else who had contributed to this celebration, she was going to have to appear cheerful, grateful and in good spirits. She'd been brought up to think of others before herself, to be self-disciplined and to get on with it, without complaint. Today she was really going to have to put that teaching into practice, and as she got out of bed to have a shower, she felt thankful for that training. It told her what to do with herself; without it she knew she'd be crying and raging all day, a misery to herself and everyone else. As she washed her hair and stood rinsing it under the hot shower, she resolved to enjoy herself tonight, if it killed her.

Tim, as if he sensed Anna might need him, was already downstairs, having breakfast and reading the *Daily Mail*. The table had been laid for a dozen people but so far he was the only house guest who had appeared.

'Hi ya!' he greeted her as she breezed into the dining

room a few minutes later, pink and glowing, with her hair still wet. 'Happy Birthday!'

'Hi ya, Tim. Thanks.' It was obvious she was pleased to see him. 'Sleep well?'

'Brilliantly, thanks. I think I overdid the red wine last night. I'd say I passed out more than slept,' he joked.

Anna went over to the sideboard and helped herself to a grapefruit, already prepared in a glass bowl, before coming to sit down beside him.

'What time are your parents turning up?'

He shrugged. 'Haven't the faintest. What are your plans for the day?'

'I haven't the faintest, either. Daddy's got everything so highly organised, I don't know what there *is* to do. At the moment there are more hired staff around than there are guests.' She glanced out of the window. Already there were people working outside. 'Thank God it's going to be a fine day. Daddy has planned a barbecue lunch by the pool for us all.'

'Good idea. It'll save on the washing up and we can all help ourselves.'

At that moment Cressida and Sasha came into the dining room, washed-out-looking without make-up and wearing baggy, ill-fitting tracksuits. No sooner had they helped themselves to cereal and coffee and seated themselves opposite Anna and Tim, than they began questioning her about Petroc.

'So, what's keeping him away?' Cressida asked nosily.

'He's decided he doesn't want to come,' Anna replied as if it were a stupid question.

'On your twenty-first birthday?' Sasha exclaimed incredulously. 'You must have quarrelled.'

'I did tell him what I thought of him,' Anna said

carefully, since that much at least was true.

Cressida looked across the table, her eyes small and mean, reminding Anna of Leonora's. 'Mummy says he's dumped you,' she said maliciously. Anna flushed.

Tim leaned towards Cressida, his expression angry. 'No one has dumped anyone. Anna and Petroc have decided to cool it for a while, and I think we should all mind our own business and let them get on with it. Don't you?' he added aggressively.

The sisters had the grace to look embarrassed.

'We're only concerned for her . . .' Sasha said lamely.

'Like hell,' Tim muttered under his breath.

'Well, I'm not concerned,' Anna said brightly. 'It's my birthday. We're giving the party to end all parties tonight, and I for one fully intend to enjoy myself.'

'That's my darling girl,' boomed a voice in the doorway, and there stood Douglas, beaming at her, his arms held wide.

'Hello, Daddy.' She jumped to her feet, and he hugged her as if he could never bear to let her go.

'Happy, happy, happy birthday, sweetheart.'

'Thank you, Daddy.'

'You'll get your present from Mummy and me tonight. By the way,' he continued, releasing her, 'where *is* Mummy? I can't find her anywhere.'

Anna shook her head. 'I've no idea.'

'Oh, well . . .' He sighed regretfully. 'I'll grab a cup of coffee then I must go and see how they're getting on in the marquee.' He glanced at the others. 'Everyone else all right? Most of the others seem to be having breakfast in bed.'

'Not me, old chap,' Roger announced, bounding into the room, red-faced and sweating. 'I've been for a run and now I'm starving.'

'Is Pammy with you?' Douglas asked.

Roger's eyebrows shot up and he looked at his best friend as if he were a half-wit. 'Is she hell! Pammy never gets out of bed until she hears the ice clinking in the first dry martini of the day.'

'You haven't seen Julia, have you?'

'Don't tell me she's walked out on you on your anniversary?' Roger joked.

Douglas reeled, slapping his forehead in pretend dismay. 'God forbid!'

Douglas found his wife in the summer house. Michael was sitting on her knee and she had her arms around him.

'Hello, you two,' he said in surprise. 'Why are you hiding in here? Everyone's having breakfast, and I've been looking for you.'

'I found Michael wandering around the place on his own, so we thought we'd come in here for a little chat,' Julia explained, smiling up at Douglas. Her dark eyes were calm and nothing in her manner betrayed the inner turmoil she'd suffered all night.

He dropped to his haunches and stroked Michael's head. 'What's up, old boy?' he asked gently.

His son turned away from him, face buried in Julia's sweater, refusing to answer.

'He's feeling a bit miserable,' she explained, 'because he thinks everyone has something to celebrate today except him. I've told him it's only Anna whose birthday is today, and that actually William's birthday is in two weeks' time and our anniversary not until next Tuesday, but he still feels a bit left out, so I was explaining to him that this is a party for us all – a family event.'

'Of course it is,' Douglas agreed swiftly. 'Come here, Michael.' He lifted the boy from his mother's arms, and held him close. 'Can I tell you something?' he asked softly.

The little boy nodded in silent acquiescence.

'When you were born,' Douglas continued, 'at a time when Mummy and I feared we'd never have any more children, we were so thrilled we didn't know what to do with ourselves. To this day, we rejoice that you came to us, to make our family complete. This party is to celebrate your being born, just as much as Anna and William.'

Michael looked into his father's face. 'But does everybody know that?' he asked in a small choked voice.

'Of course they do! And they'll know it even more by the end of the evening when I propose your health, along with Anna and William's.'

'Are you going to make a speech, Daddy?'

Douglas grinned roguishly. 'A short one.'

'Is Mummy going to make a speech?'

'She can if she wants to.'

Looking up at them, Julia's eyes filled with tears. Douglas was such a marvellous father. In a few moments he'd transformed Michael from a sad little boy into one who was rosy-cheeked and giggling, hanging round his neck, restored to happiness and reassured he was loved.

'There's something else, too,' Douglas was telling him. 'Although your birthday is still three months away, there'll be a present for you tonight, when the others get theirs.'

'Cool!' He wriggled out of his father's arms. 'Can I go and have breakfast now?'

They watched him scamper off, yelling to the dogs to

148

go with him. Then Douglas dropped on to the wooden bench beside Julia. 'I was looking everywhere for you, darling.'

'Were you?' He met her gaze as if he had nothing in the world to hide. 'I just went for an early-morning walk,' she said lightly. 'The house is so full of people I had to get away for a few minutes.'

'Is anything wrong?' He looked concerned.

'What could be wrong?' she replied gaily. 'It's going to be a glorious day. We can all have a swim before lunch.'

He grabbed her hand as she rose to go. 'Kiss me good morning before you rush off.'

As she bent to kiss him, he took her face in both hands and held it, while kissing her long and hard on the mouth.

'Don't go far away again. I need you,' he whispered.

'Do you?' Julia tried to keep the wistfulness out of her voice. God damn Leonora and her vicious gossiping! She'd probably only said it to annoy Pammy Schemmel. Julia determined to put the whole episode out of her mind. What mattered was that Douglas was here, now, for her and the children, and whatever it took, she'd make sure it always stayed that way.

Pat and Reggie stayed in their room until eleven o'clock, as did Vivien and Simon. Leonora, determined not to miss a moment's fun, joined the younger ones for breakfast, and wondered why Julia seemed to be ignoring her. Well, who cares? she thought, helping herself to a home-grown peach to have with her coffee. She was looking forward to the arrival of Oonagh and Christopher. Oonagh was smart and amusing, and Leonora enjoyed hearing about the latest restaurants and plays, and what was happening in what she regarded as the sophisticated metropolis. Maybe Oonagh would invite her up to London for a few days? A light lunch at Daphne's? A saunter around Emporio Armani? Drop into Voyage, to see what was new? Bump into Joan Collins shopping in Harvey Nichols? It was all that she'd ever wanted and Leonora sighed with longing.

'Hello,' Caroline said, strolling into the dining room at that moment. 'Are we the only oldies to be down for breakfast?'

Leonora flinched visibly at this description. 'It's too nice a day to stay in bed,' she replied defensively. 'I thought I'd top up my tan by the pool after breakfast.'

'Terribly ageing,' Caroline remarked warningly. 'Where's Julia?'

'God knows. She's running around like a blue-arsed fly. I'm letting her get on with it.'

Caroline had never liked Julia's sister-in-law, and now she realised why. She was a spiteful, jealous woman who would have given anything to have been in Julia's place. And she'd brought up her daughters to be just as objectionable.

'Julia is such a brilliant organiser she doesn't need our help,' Caroline replied sweetly.

'You mean Douglas is. He's arranged this whole weekend, every detail of it. Julia hasn't done a thing.' Leonora's mouth was set in stubborn lines.

'And how would you know? Have you been a fly on the wall for the past three months?' Caroline's smile was as charming as ever.

'I *am* married to Douglas's brother. I do know what's going on.'

'Oh, really?'

'Of course.'

The two women looked at each other across the breakfast table with undisguised hostility.

'I know exactly what Douglas is like,' Leonora said, in a superior tone. 'He's the brains behind . . . all this.' She spread her hands, with their almost black nail varnish, in an expressive gesture. 'Julia would be lost without him.'

'Well then,' said Caroline, rising unhurriedly to her feet, 'isn't it fortunate that she'll never have to be?' Then she turned and left the dining room, a tall and languid figure in her white trousers and top, pointedly taking her coffee into the garden with her.

Later, as she sat by the pool, she saw Vivien coming out of the house through the french windows. As soon as she saw Caroline she came over and sat down beside her.

'How are you, Vivien? You look much better.'

'My dear, I must apologise for last night.' She was wearing a smart navy blue linen dress, and her face was carefully made-up. 'I was out of my skull! I really thought I was going to pass out. Do you think anyone noticed?'

'At the most they thought you were a bit merry, perhaps,' Caroline assured her. 'What happened, exactly? Why were you taking tranquillisers?'

Vivien's eyes were pained. 'I don't want anyone to know until after the party, especially not Julia . . .'

Caroline looked at her sharply. 'What's wrong?'

'I've discovered a lump in my breast and I'm absolutely terrified it's cancer,' she replied, voice thick with unshed tears.

'Oh, Vivien! But it may not be. It's probably a cyst. When did you discover it?'

'A few days ago. Oh, Caroline, you don't know what a

relief it is to tell someone. I've been going crazy with worry . . .'

'What? You haven't even told Simon?' she asked, appalled.

Vivien shook her head. 'I'm determined not to spoil Julia or Simon's weekend. That's why I've been taking tranquillisers – to help get me through the next few days.'

'But it's dangerous to mix them with alcohol. That's why you felt so dreadful last night.'

'I know. It was stupid of me. I've decided to stop taking them, actually, because I do want some champagne tonight.' She sounded wistful and the look in her eyes broke Caroline's heart.

'But you will go to the doctor as soon as you get home?' she urged gently, taking Vivien's hand which was still smooth for a woman of her age, without blemishes or raised veins.

'Yes, I will. I must know one way or another, for my own peace of mind. But promise me you won't tell a soul, darling?'

'I promise,' Caroline said, knowing Vivien was right. Julia would be distraught if she knew, and Simon would be desolate. The whole family, in fact, adored Vivien for her sweetness, her kindness and her beauty. Even now, her white hair tinted a soft ash gold, with her clear skin and slim figure she was exquisite; a blonde edition of Julia and not much older-looking. If anything were to happen to her, they'd all be deeply upset.

'I'm sure it will be OK,' Caroline added comfortingly. 'And remember, whatever it is, you've caught it early.'

Douglas was thoroughly enjoying himself. The decorating team had arrived at seven o'clock that morning with three vans loaded with more blooms in boxes and buckets; there were also branches of trees, ferns, yards of freshly cut ivy, pineapples sprayed gold, and garlands of greenery threaded with ribbons and strands of fresh redcurrants.

'How's it going?' he kept asking eagerly, as he watched them working with swift expertise, using large blocks of oasis and wire to get the desired effect.

'Fine. It's all going very well.'

'Good, good. I'll send out more coffee for you all in a minute.'

Then he charged off to see the head chef, who was hard at work supervising a dozen sous-chefs in the tented kitchen. Tonight's dinner was underway, and Douglas wanted to make sure there were no hitches. Gripping his clip board, he cornered Laurent, who was supervising the preparation of one hundred and fifty lobsters.

'Can I run through the menu for tonight with you?' It was a command, not a question, and Laurent, head chef at Butterfly, knew better than to say he was too busy.

'Of course, Monsieur.' He wiped his hands on a cloth and led the way to a table set up in a corner with phones, a fax, and a heap of delivery notes.

This was what Douglas liked best; his *raison d'être*, in fact. The business of food and how it should be prepared; the devising of a menu and the selection of wines to go with it. He grabbed a folding chair, sat himself opposite Laurent, and got to work.

'Right. We're starting with warm scallop, leek and oyster terrine,' he said, reading his notes.

'Yes,' Laurent agreed. '*Terrine tiède de coquilles Saint-Jacques au poireau et aux huîtres*.'

'And with that we're drinking the Riesling Geisberg

Grand Cru 1994. Then we're going on to the *Schnieders-paetle* noodles with pan fried frogs' legs scented with chervil,' Douglas continued, 'and the Riesling Grand Cru Brand 1988.'

'Oui, Monsieur. The frogs' legs, they arrive this morning. They will be exquisite with the *cerfeuil*.'

'Good!' Douglas beamed. This was heaven. A menu to die for, in fact. People would be talking about it for years to come . . . and no doubt booking tables at Butterfly so they could enjoy the experience again. 'After that comes the roasted lobster with chestnuts and fennel in a spicy *jus*. Correct?'

'*Oui*, the lobster, served with Pinot Noir-Herrenweg 1994. A very fine wine. They will go beautifully together.'

'Now what comes next?' Douglas consulted his notes. 'Ah, yes. The Alsace pigeon with *foie gras* and green cabbage. Are you rolling the pigeon and *foie gras* in a cabbage leaf?'

'Oui, Monsieur. The pigeon will be pre-cooked, boned, and stuffed with the *foie gras*, and then wrapped in the cabbage and cooked for just a few more minutes so the leaves will stay green. And with it there will be tiny steamed carrots and celery.'

'That's excellent. Make sure the pigeon *jus* is strong and meaty. Now, with that we're drinking Château Lapelletrie, Grand Cru St Emilion 1993. And we're ending dinner with the warm candied apple with a pistachio cream and vanilla ice cream.' Suddenly he frowned doubtfully.

'*Oui*, Monsieur?' Laurent looked at him warily.

'Humph!' Douglas slumped as if in pain. 'I'm not sure . . .'

Laurent looked alarmed. 'Everything is prepared, Monsieur.'

154

'I know.' Douglas screwed up his face and Laurent could see his boss was wrestling with a desperate dilemma.

'Strawberries are so clichéed in June . . . so are raspberries,' he lamented. 'I wanted to give them something different . . . original . . . but now I'm not so sure.'

'It is too late to change anything now,' said Laurent in a panic. 'The apple, it look very pretty. The flesh is red from being poached in wine . . . the pistachio cream is most unusual . . .'

'But apples are so *ordinary*!' Douglas suddenly bellowed. 'How could we have thought we could do anything original with apples?' He glanced at his wrist watch and grabbed one of the phones. 'You're too busy to do anything else, and there aren't enough facilities . . . Hello? Get me Marco. Quickly,' he barked into the phone.

'Marco? At Smart's?' Laurent gasped, prepared to be offended.

'This is my fault, not yours,' Douglas assured him, patting him on the shoulder.

'You ask Marco . . . to come here?'

Douglas could tell there'd be blood on the walls if he wasn't careful. The two chefs were deadly rivals, to the extent that Douglas had given orders that neither must ever be told what the weekly takings were in each other's restaurants.

'Marco, is that you? Listen, I've decided to offer my guests a choice of pudding tonight. Yes – tonight. Can you prepare and arrange to send down three hundred miniature summer puddings? With gallons of double cream . . . no, forget the cream. Just the summer puddings, with red currants, raspberries, strawberries . . . and loganberries and blackberries if you can get . . . yes, I know it's June, but you can work miracles, Marco. I know you can, and I'm depending on you. What? You've got several dozen in the freezer? Well, there you are! Make a few more, but we do need three hundred down here by eight-thirty, at the latest. OK? Is everything going all right? How many covers have booked for lunch . . .'

Laurent sat in dejected silence, like a great artist spurned. When Douglas came off the phone the chef looked at him with sad eyes.

'The printed menu, Monsieur . . . it say only the apple pudding but now you want to give them summer pudding. From the freezer.'

'We're giving them both, Laurent. Don't worry. You've done a magnificent job, and tonight, when I make my speech, I want you to come into the marquee so I can thank you publicly in front of all the guests. I'm sure a lot of them will want to see who has provided such a magnificent dinner.'

It took the chef a few minutes to recover from his hurt pride but as Douglas showered him with praise and gratitude, he slowly relented.

'We'll have an apéritif before the evening starts, right, Laurent?' his boss coaxed.

'*Oui*, Monsieur,' he replied, smiling broadly once again.

'Chefs!' Douglas groaned to Julia, when he bumped into her in the garden a few minutes later. 'Bloody primadonnas, the lot of them.' He told her what had happened.

She gazed back at him, stunned. 'How could you do that, Douglas? No wonder Laurent is upset.'

He shrugged. 'It's not causing him any extra work and he'll still be getting the praise tonight. I don't know what all the fuss is about.' He flashed her his most beaming smile, reserved for when he knew he was in the wrong but didn't want to admit it. 'Can't stop. The table napkins that were supposed to be sent down have gone missing and I've got to locate them.' And with that he charged off in the direction of one of the caterers' delivery vans.

'You'll be exhausted before the party even starts,' she shouted after him. He waved jauntily in reply and disappeared inside a van. At that moment a car came slowly, almost reluctantly, up the drive. Julia recognised it at once.

'Chris! Hello, how lovely you're here in good time,' she called out, hurrying forward as it drew to a halt by the main entrance. Christopher climbed out first. He looked tired and grim, but his face broke into a crooked smile as Julia threw her arms around him and hugged him. 'How are you?'

'Great,' he replied briefly, obviously not meaning it. Oonagh was stepping out of the car too, elegant in cream trousers and jacket with a long purple scarf. Her face had the set look of carved ice, her hair the black gloss of caviar.

'Hello, Julia.'

'Oonagh, my dear.' Julia kissed her on both cheeks.

They'd never been close, never shared a moment of intimacy. Christopher was all they had in common apart from Tim, of whom Julia was genuinely fond. But they managed to sustain a cordial relationship and few would have guessed at the abyss that lay between them. Today, however, their froideur was as nothing compared to the open hostility between husband and wife who had obviously had a flaming row.

'Come and see Mummy and Simon,' Julia suggested. 'They've been longing for you to arrive. They're by the pool, with Tim and all the young ones.' As she spoke, she led them along the terrace and down the stone steps.

'So, how's it all going, Sis?' Christopher asked, falling easily into step beside her. He looked across the lawn. 'Are you sure that tent's big enough?' he teased.

'It is enormous, isn't it?' She smiled up at him, so happy to have him here. Then she turned to Oonagh who was trailing behind, looking sulky. 'With so many people coming, not to mention Douglas's decorations, we're going to need every inch of space.'

Oonagh raised her eyes and looked at her as if she'd said something mad. She *always* does that, Julia reflected, remembering that whenever she made a jokey remark or light-hearted observation, Oonagh stared at her as if she were talking gibberish.

'What has Douglas dreamed up for tonight? A theme of some sort?' Christopher asked, ignoring his wife.

'It's a surprise and we're not allowed to go into the marquee until the last minute,' Julia replied. This time she didn't even include Oonagh in the conversation.

Anna, William and Michael were in the pool with Tim, Cressida and Sasha, playing water polo. There were shrieks of laughter and much splashing as the two sides slugged it out, watched by Simon Leonard, who had joined Vivien and Caroline, and Pat, Reggie, Leonora and Roger. There was no sign, Julia registered with mild surprise, of Pammy.

After Christopher had greeted his parents and Tim, the flutter of greetings and kisses spread to include everyone else. Oonagh followed suit politely, but she was too groomed, too smart, too icy for the warm-hearted grand-parents and friends. Even Leonora seemed reassuringly cosy by comparison.

Morgan brought out coffee, jugs of orange juice and cans of Coca-Cola and the young ones clambered out of the pool and came, dripping and laughing, to sit around and drink and chat. It was a gloriously hot, sunny day. A good omen for tonight, Julia thought, glad to see Anna bearing up with remarkable stoicism.

'Peter will be here soon, won't he? And then the family will be complete,' Pat remarked.

Leonora looked at her fake Gucci wrist watch. 'He should be here in a couple of hours.'

Pat stretched her toes in their white sandals, and leaned back in her sun lounger, smiling contentedly. 'It's nice here, isn't it?'

'Very nice,' Leonora agreed, her voice sharp with envy. 'I'd love a place like this.'

A few yards away, Christopher and Tim sat talking as they sipped coffee.

'Is everything all right with you, Dad?' Tim asked, in a reversal of the usual roles between father and son.

Christopher looked up, surprised. 'Yeah. Great. How about you? Are you liking Edinburgh?'

Tim nodded. 'It's fine. I've made a lot of new friends. I think I'll be spending most of August in Italy, actually. I meant to tell you and Mum – I've been invited to stay in a villa and it sounds cool.'

The bird has flown, thought Christopher with a pang. It seemed only a short time ago that Tim was a toddler, dependent on them for everything. Eventually, when he got up to go off and change out of his swimming trunks, Christopher tried to catch his sister's eye.

'I must talk to you,' he said in a low voice when she looked over at him. Giving an almost imperceptible nod, she rose to her feet, murmuring something about getting on with things indoors. Her brother had confided in her since he'd been a small boy, and she could sense he was troubled about something.

Christopher flashed her a grateful look. She'll tell me what to do, how to cope with the mess I'm in, he thought, as he followed her slowly so as not to arouse his wife's suspicions.

'Is there anything I can do to help?' Pammy asked, waylaying Douglas as he came rushing out of the marquee, a mobile phone in one hand and a sheaf of papers in the other. He stopped in his tracks and looked at her blankly.

'*Help* me?' he echoed, as if she'd suggested something extraordinary.

Pammy was not fazed. 'Decor *is* my business, you know. If you need any advice . . .'

'My dear, you're most kind, but John and his team have got everything under control. Now, if you'll excuse me, I have to make a call to . . .'

She laid a restraining hand on his arm. 'Let's talk tomorrow, Douglas, when the party's over. I have a proposition to put to you. *House Perfect* magazine, in the States, are doing a feature on me and my work, and they want to show me to be an international interior designer. I've already done up a flat in Paris, and a *palazzo* just outside Rome – my dear, I put in *acres* of pink marble – but what I need now is a British country house. What do you say? I could do over all your ground-floor rooms, and as you're Roger's best friend I'd give you a discount, of course. It would be good publicity for you and all your restaurants, too, wouldn't it?' Her narrow face and dark eyes reminded him of an over-eager marmoset.

Douglas beamed his most benign smile. 'What a girl you are, my dear Pammy! Listen, it's a lovely idea and it's so sweet of you to suggest it, but Julia only had the main rooms redecorated a year or so ago, and there's no way we can afford to have anything done again for absolutely ages. But thank you for thinking of us. I do appreciate it. Now I really must dash. I've got to make an urgent phone call . . .'

With a wave of the papers and the broadest of grins, he jogged off in the direction of the house. Pammy stared after him, half in irritation at being fobbed off and half in admiration at what she could only see as his sheer chutzpah.

'I don't know what the hell to do,' Christopher confessed, having told Julia all about Barbara. 'I'm crazy about her, can't think of anything else. She's so different from Oonagh. So amazingly warm and responsive, and she really loves me.'

'And now Oonagh knows about her?' Julia replied, pale with shock.

He nodded. 'She phoned me from Ascot and heard Barbara say something and then laugh. Neither of us had any idea it was Oonagh. If only I'd remembered to switch off my mobile . . . But anyway, I never imagined Oonagh would call me. For one thing, she didn't have a phone with her.'

'But she was stuck in a car park, in the middle of Ascot, and not surprisingly quite desperate by that time,' Julia observed. 'That was awful of you, Chris, to leave her there like that. I can't believe you'd do such a thing. Frankly, I don't blame her for being furious. And then to find you'd rushed off to be with another woman . . .!'

'All right. All right. You don't have to rub it in, but I had fixed a lift for her. Of course I didn't just abandon her there. Richard promised me he'd give her a lift home, and they were going to take her out to dinner, too,' he replied indignantly. He was rattled that, for once, Julia wasn't being sympathetic and siding with him.

'So she finally got to London . . .?' his sister prompted. 'And where were you by then? Still with your girlfriend?'

He looked at her with hurt eyes. 'I was waiting at home for Oonagh. The hired car had to drive down to Ascot again and pick them up, and she didn't get home until nearly eleven o'clock. Then all hell broke loose.'

'I can imagine!'

'She called me all sorts of names, and said she wanted a divorce and was entitled to everything. She said she'd ruin me in every way she could. At least,' he added as if he were doing Julia a favour, 'I persuaded her to hang on until after this weekend, and not let Tim know anything was wrong, but what am I supposed to do on Monday when we get back to London? I badly want to spend the rest of my life with Barbara but I can't afford to get divorced.'

Julia rose from her seat. She was shaking all over, her face white and eyes glittering darkly. 'I'm not going to pretend I'm fond of Oonagh because I'm not, but she's your wife; you chose to marry her, and if there's one thing I cannot abide, it's a cheating husband! I'm really sickened that you should behave like this, Chris. And disappointed, too.' Tears gathered in her eyes.

'Hang on a minute,' he said angrily. 'Why this sudden high and mighty attitude? You know I've been unhappy for ages. I'd have left her long ago, but what with Tim, and knowing how much a divorce would cost me, I've stuck it out. But I'm forty-two, Julia. I'm still young enough to start again, have more children even. And I'm in love with Barbara.'

'That still leaves Oonagh,' she said, more quietly.

'What's that to you?'

Julia looked into his face and saw man in all his sex-driven selfishness embodied in her brother's features. 'Because someone gets hurt in this situation. Whether it's the man or the woman, someone always gets hurt.'

'Just because you're celebrating twenty-five years of marriage this weekend,' he said harshly, 'doesn't mean you have to be holier than thou!'

She turned away, deeply upset by what he was doing. Did marriage vows count for nothing these days? She wondered. 'What about Tim?' she said aloud.

'He's nineteen and I expect most of his friends have parents who are divorced.'

'So that makes it all right, does it?'

'Julia . . .' Christopher sighed. 'I came to you for advice, not a lecture.'

'Well, I wish you hadn't. I'm not the right person to talk to about infidelity. It's something I really can't stand.'

He frowned, perplexed. It was unlike her to be so self-righteous and he wondered what lay behind it. They glared at one another for a long moment then Julia turned and hurried out of the room without a backward glance.

Once alone in her bedroom, she seated herself at her dressing-table, and automatically, because her thoughts were miles away, started brushing her hair. Last night's words, spoken by Leonora, came back to her: '. . . of course he has affairs.' They made her feel physically sick, ill with a terrible sense of insecurity, of being abandoned, of fear. Somewhere, deep inside her, a little girl was screaming, 'You can't leave me, I need you', but it was all mixed up with the memory of her mother, mad with grief when she heard Guido had been killed. Vivien's broken-hearted sobs had been so terrible, so uncontrollably wild, that they'd imprinted themselves on Julia's mind, etching themselves so deeply into her psyche that she felt as if the tragedy was hers and hers alone, and that her father had died on purpose in order to deprive her of his love. She'd been advanced for a child of four, but not old enough to understand everything, and although Vivien had been quickly sedated, while Julia had been whisked away by her nanny, she'd nevertheless been left with that terrible echo of her mother's suffering in her own heart. Now, in adulthood, death and infidelity were forever linked in her mind, for they were both a kind of death.

How could Chris be having an affair? she thought, knowing she was being unreasonable but unable to help it. And what a terrible way for Oonagh to find out. That was the sort of agony she would not wish even upon those she hated.

Applying more lipstick and a quick spray of Eternity, Julia made a supreme effort to pull herself together. Now was not the time to examine the darkest reaches of her mind. She had guests to look after, and already she could smell the delicious aroma of steak and sausages being cooked on the charcoal brazier by the pool. It was time for lunch.

Nancy Graham returned to Cherry Tree Cottage at twelve-thirty, dropped off by Mr Miller in his taxi. She, too, could smell lunch being cooked on the Rutherfords' barbecue, and her nose twitched like a terrier scenting something interesting.

Nancy glanced out of her drawing-room window, from where she could see the top of the marquee. The activity and noise from next door had been building over the past days, and tonight would reach its crescendo. Nancy smiled to herself, her eyes glittering with malice. Tonight, when she brought that dreadful family down, was going to be deliciously satisfying. And there was the added piquancy of knowing that their humiliation would be witnessed by the press, whom she gathered from village gossip were rumoured to be coming in droves. For the first time in years, Nancy Graham laughed aloud. Serve the Rutherfords right, for the three years of stress they'd caused her! She'd confirmed the arrangements this morning, on the way into Stockbridge, and Mr Miller had been given his instructions. Now there were only a few more hours to go before, as she called it, the Big Bang.

Pat waylaid Anna as she came running downstairs from her bedroom, changed into a pale blue linen shift for lunch.

'Darling, these are for you,' she said, handing her a flat dark blue velvet jewel case. 'They're from Grandpa and me, and I thought I'd give them to you before tonight.' She didn't add that emotion would have overwhelmed her if she'd presented her gift in front of all the others.

'Grandma!' Anna flushed with delight. 'I keep forgetting it's my birthday.' She opened the case carefully, realising by the soft density of the velvet that it was probably Victorian. They didn't make silk velvet like that nowadays. Her guess was correct. On a bed of fragile white satin lay a row of pearls with a solitaire diamond clasp.

'Grandma!' She stared unbelievingly at the necklace, realising how much it must have cost, and knowing how very little money her grandparents had to live on. 'Oh, Grandma, they're beautiful.' She flung her arms around Pat's bony frame and hugged her tightly. 'Thank you. Thank you so much.' Her eyes were starry as she looked into her grandmother's face. 'I'm going to wear them tonight.'

'You don't have to, Anna. I shan't be offended if they don't go with your dress.'

'But of course I'm going to wear them. I've never had real pearls. Oh Grandma, they're lovely. I shall wear them all the time. Where's Grandpa? I want to thank him, too.'

Pat smiled tenderly at her favourite grandchild. Anna's young face was filled with earnest pleasure, and her smile was genuine for the first time since she'd heard that Petroc wasn't coming.

'He's in the study, having what he calls a snifter with your father, before lunch.'

'I'll put them on first.' Anna hurried to the mirror that hung at the far end of the hall, and gently lifted the pearls from their case. A moment later she turned to face Pat again. 'Look! Aren't they perfect?' They lay in a glistening row round the base of her neck, softly iridescent against her tanned skin.

'Are they really all right, darling?'

Anna kissed the wrinkled cheek again. 'They're the nicest present I've ever had. Let's go find Grandpa and the others. I can't wait to show everybody,' she said eagerly.

★ ★ ★

Oonagh slowly walked the length of the camomile path in solitary martyrdom, wanting to be alone with her thoughts. She could hear Julia calling to everyone to come and have lunch but she'd lost her appetite. Her life was in ruins, and the strain of having to pretend everything was all right, in front of Chris's family, was killing her. Why had she come? In the hope that his affair would blow over and then no one need ever know what had happened? To see Tim? She thought about this for a moment, then acknowledged that she and her only child had never been close. Not even when he'd been small. His birth and babyhood, which had unfurled into boyhood and adolescence, had somehow passed her by, leaving her untouched. It was almost as if she'd never really had a child . . . except in some distant dream that allowed her to refer to him socially, and with a touch of pride when faced by women with problem children. Tim had never been a problem, never caused them any worry or anxiety. He'd been a clean and quiet child, he'd excelled at school, and now he was doing well at university. Perhaps, she reflected with a slight sense of shock, it was because he was so nice that he bored her to death?

'Hello there! Oonagh?'

A man's cheerful voice, coming up behind her, caused her to stop and turn. It was Roger Sullivan, sun-toasted and shiny-faced, in white cotton trousers and an open-necked blue shirt.

'Lunch is ready,' he announced. 'Are you coming?'

She hesitated, realising it would look odd if she didn't. 'In a minute. I was just looking around the garden,' she replied, glancing at the borders of lavender that edged the path. 'It's very pretty.'

Roger nodded vigorously. 'Douglas keeps it ship-shape, all right.' He looked at the flowers as if seeing them for the first time. 'Glad the weather's fine for tonight.'

'Yes.' She stood, hand on hip, looking at the lavender, a smart angular-looking woman with short neatly coiffeured black hair and scarlet lips. She reminded Roger of one of those magazine drawings of a fashion model, dashed off in bold strokes by a flamboyant artist. That was until her shoulders started to heave and he realised she was crying.

'Oonagh? Are you all right?'

She swung away from him, almost losing her balance in her high-heeled sandals, one hand covering her eyes.

He stepped closer and dared to put his arm around her shoulders. Normally he wouldn't have dreamed of being so familiar but she was obviously distressed.

'Have you had a fight with Christopher?'

'Worse . . . he's having an affair!' she sobbed, tears splashing on to her immaculate white dress.

Roger had to admit to himself he wasn't in the least surprised. Oonagh looked as if she could be an iceberg in bed, so frigid that to make love to her would be like plunging into the Arctic sea. If Christopher were having a bit on the side, he could hardly be blamed. He was unlikely, though, to want a divorce. That could well be an expensive luxury.

'I'm sure it's only a passing phase. He'd never leave you,' Roger assured her, making it sound as if Christopher loved her too much. 'An awful lot of husbands kick over the traces, you know.'

'But not Chris,' she replied.

'Then he's probably going through a midlife crisis. What I suggest you do is woo him back. Try some of the old seduction tactics. It always works. Men love a bit of flattery.'

'As someone who's been married twice and had count-less girlfriends, I'm not sure you're in any position to give advice,' Oonagh retorted, as she wiped her cheeks and tried to appear calmer. 'Chris has humiliated me in front of our friends, and I don't intend to forgive him. I only came here because I didn't want to let Julia down, but as soon as we get back to London I'm going to file for divorce.'

Roger looked taken aback. 'Isn't that a bit rash? Don't you think you should give him another chance?'

The pale chiselled face that turned to look at him was unforgiving. 'Certainly not. No one makes a fool of me and gets away with it.'

'But, Oonagh . . .' Roger tried to keep up with her as she strode back to where Christopher and the others were grouped around the barbecue. 'Don't do anything hasty. Think about Tim. He'll be devastated if you and his father split up.'

'Then Chris should have thought of that before he went after his floozie.'

'Has he admitted he's having an affair?' Roger asked, appalled. To him the Eleventh Commandment was 'Thou Shalt Not Get Caught', and if you are, 'Don't Admit Anything'.

'He didn't have to.' The words were tossed over her shoulder. They joined the others and, in silence, Roger got her a glass of Pimm's. Oonagh seemed completely in control of herself again, so much so that he noticed her engaged in conversation, in a perfectly normal voice, with Vivien a few minutes later. Had those been crocodile tears he'd seen her shed, or had wounded pride bitten deep?

'Where have you been, honey?' Pammy rasped in his ear as she came up behind him. She was chewing a drumstick and her lipstick was running into the fine lines around her mouth. 'What were you talking to Oonagh about? You were gone ages.'

'Nothing much,' he replied off-handedly. 'I'm going to get something to eat.' He moved towards the hot, smoking rack of juicy steaks that rested above the glowing charcoal, and speared himself some meat.

'You do that, honey!' Pammy's voice was almost a growl. 'You've gotta keep up your strength for tonight.'

Sitting side by side on the terrace steps, with plates on their laps, William and Stephanie found themselves on their own for the first time since they'd got out of bed that morning. They kept their voices low because their discussion centred around whether or not they would live together when William returned from his world travels.

'But we're going to different universities,' Stephanie pointed out. 'I'll be at Newcastle and you'll be at Edinburgh. I thought you were going to share a flat with Tim?'

'I'm talking about the holidays,' William explained. 'Why don't we get a studio flat in London? Then we can be together for four months of the year anyway.'

Stephanie's eyes sparkled. 'We'd both have to get jobs to pay for a flat, but that would be OK, wouldn't it?'

William looked less sure. 'Dad would up the readies for a place for us to live.'

'You can't let him do that,' she said decisively, her blonde ponytail wagging as she shook her head. 'We'll both be nineteen by the time you get back. Time we stood on our own feet.'

'But we'll still have to study in the holidays.'

'So? We'll get part-time jobs. Maybe we could wait tables at one of your father's restaurants? Or wash up? I wouldn't mind.'

William looked faintly appalled. 'I don't think Dad would like that.'

'Then we'll work in someone else's restaurant. Come on, William. Brace up! Don't tell me I've got involved with a spoiled little rich boy?'

'Of course not,' he retorted. 'Nevertheless . . .'

'Oh, God, Will darling, you do need to go backpacking around the world to toughen you up, don't you?'

He flushed deeply and got to his feet. 'I don't want to jeopardise my education while I scrabble around for cash,' he said with all the dignity he could muster.

Stephanie jumped to her feet, too. 'You prissy little brat!' she yelled, not caring who heard. 'Don't think you're getting back into my bed until you *grow up!*'

Peter Rutherford arrived at three o'clock, full of apologies for being late.

'I thought I'd never get away! Some parents insisted on seeing me about their son's progress, and then the traffic from Salisbury was dreadful,' he explained.

Peter, at fifty, had not worn as well as Douglas. Although two years younger, he looked much older. They were also different in other ways. Peter's sedentary life caused him to stoop, giving him a constantly burdened look, while Douglas bounded around, light-footed in spite of his bulk. Their voices differed, too; both were commanding in tone, but Peter's was measured and pedantic, while his brother's was rich and ebullient. It was as if Douglas was a growing tree, flourishing, with shiny leaves, and Peter a withered branch, reduced to brittle dryness by some long-forgotten lightning strike. There was no doubt about it: Douglas had charisma and Peter definitely didn't. And no one was more aware of this than Leonora. Today, however, she greeted her husband with a smug attitude, as if to say: He may not amount to much but at least he's mine.

She'd noticed the rift between Oonagh and Christopher, and guessed at its cause. Peter might not be the sort of man she liked being married to, but he was better than no one, and at least he hadn't dumped her. Smart enough to realise she'd be worse off without him, she greeted his arrival with gushing enthusiasm.

'Hello, dear,' he said, with a faint look of surprise. 'Did you and the girls get here all right yesterday?'

She decided to ignore the banal stupidity of the question. 'Yes. We've been having a lovely time. It's a pity you couldn't get here sooner.'

At that moment Douglas came up and pumped Peter's hand in his ferociously firm grip, slapping him warmly on the back and booming that it was jolly good to see him.

'The parents are dying to see you too, Peter. Come along. Have you had lunch? Can I get you something? A drink?'

Julia watched the brothers stride off together, shoulder to shoulder, and then she caught Leonora's eye. Her sister-in-law was smiling.

'They like being together, don't they?' she observed.

Julia nodded. 'I'm so glad Peter's arrived. Pat and Reggie have been waiting for this moment ever since they arrived.'

'They're not the only ones,' said Leonora, to her own surprise.

172

By five o'clock the day had become balmy and the house
guests had left the poolside to go indoors and have cups
of tea, talk, watch television, take baths, and, for the
older ones, have a rest in their rooms. Even the activity on
the lawn had ceased; the frantic preparations had been
completed. The marquee was like a great ship at anchor,
her large crew settling down to work through the night.

Bryn Williams, Toast Master at all the best functions,
was 'walking the course' with Douglas, being shown the
layout of the house and garden, and given instructions
about announcing each guest whom Douglas, Julia,
Anna and William would receive in their drawing room.

'After we've received them they're to go out through
the french windows for the champagne reception in the
garden,' Douglas continued. 'You know the form better
than anyone, Bryn. That's why you're here tonight. To
keep us all on time and the whole night running to
schedule.'

Bryn, tall and imposing with white hair, smiled confi-
dently. 'Well, it's very straightforward. Reception at eight
o'clock . . . and thank goodness it's going to be a fine
night! Dinner to be announced at nine, with Grace being
said as soon as everyone is seated. Then the Loyal Toast
at approximately eleven o'clock, followed by your speech.
Will there be any others?'

'Yes. After I've said a few words, my brother Peter is
going to speak and propose a toast. Then it's on with the
dancing.' Douglas rubbed his hands together, feeling
them begin to tremble with a mixture of excitement and
nerves. He felt like a theatrical producer tonight. The
scenery was ready. The lights would soon go on. The
band would strike up and then the grand production,
with its cast of hundreds, would start. Cecil B. De Mille,

eat your heart out, he thought with satisfaction.

'Which band have you got?' Bryn was asking, breaking into his thoughts.

'The Dark Blues, of course. Wouldn't have any other.'

'Yes, they're the best.'

'Now, I want you to keep everyone out of the marquee until dinner is announced. The decorations are a surprise.'

Bryn nodded, knowing Douglas's strong sense of drama.

'The rest of the family are to be allowed in at seven-thirty, for a preview and a drink before we go back to the house to await the guests,' he continued. 'Now, what else? You'll have dinner when we've started ours, of course. So will The Dark Blues and the electricians who are looking after the lighting. I've got six people to help park the cars . . . there are a dozen portaloos over there.' He pointed to the far end of the lawn. He was on overdrive, the adrenalin pounding so that he felt as if he were flying. Tonight was going to be the best night of his life. A reward for all the years of striving ambition and grinding work.

At that moment John Plested appeared, looking exhausted.

'We've finished,' he croaked, after he'd greeted Bryn whom he knew well from the party circuit.

'My dear fellow, I can't tell you how grateful I am! You've done a magnificent job,' Douglas enthused. 'Listen, I've got drinks for you all in the house. Come along. Where are the others?'

'They're packing stuff into the van.'

'Give them a call then. I'll get those bottles opened.'

As if he were thrilled to have something else to do,

Douglas hurried towards the house. Crossing the lawn, he met The Dark Blues' road manager with his two assistants. They'd just arrived and were about to see where they'd be playing before unloading their van and assembling their amplification equipment.

'Go ahead into the marquee,' Douglas said, after he'd greeted them. 'I've had a huge platform built for you. Room to spread yourself. Great lighting effects, too. Just wait until you see it all!'

His enthusiasm was infectious. With a cheery word here and an appreciative pat on the shoulder there, he was reviving those who were tired and inspiring others who were about to start their long night's work. Within minutes he'd found Julia and got Morgan to open a few bottles of champagne and bring in platters of smoked salmon on brown bread and butter. Then he rounded up what family he could find, eventually getting William, Anna, Christopher, Peter, Leonora and Julia. Stephanie was still refusing to talk to William after their lunchtime quarrel, and had decided to go for a walk with Cressida and Sasha.

'Ah, there you are!' Douglas exclaimed, busy handing out brimming glasses when John and the others appeared. 'Come along, all of you, have a drink. Isn't this splendid? A party before the party!'

They collapsed gratefully around the room into various sofas and chairs while Douglas stood in the middle, entreating them to eat the hurriedly made canapés and have some more to drink.

'Thank you all so much,' he said. 'I really am grateful. Everyone is going to remember for years to come what you've created tonight. Here's to you all!'

John and his team just felt thankful it was all done, and

on time. It had been a hell of a job, and Douglas was a very exacting person to work for, but one thing was certain: the guests were going to gasp when they entered the marquee in three hours' time.

Seven

Anna walked slowly up the stairs to get ready. The house
was quiet at the moment, the florists departed, the band
busy getting set up in the marquee, the caterers and
waiters assembling in the mobile kitchens, and the house
guests in their rooms, preparing themselves for the
evening ahead. She fingered the string of pearls around
her neck, and wished she felt in a party mood. Instead, a
weary torpor had come over her, and instead of looking
forward to this night of nights, she felt herself faintly
dreading it. Why had Petroc chosen this moment to
dump her? Somehow she'd managed to get through the
day, largely because dear, kind Tim had never left her
side, never let her sink into depression. But now, for the
first time since she'd got up this morning, she was alone,
and the enormity of what Petroc had done almost took
her breath away. He'd been cruel and selfish. In his shoes
she'd never have behaved like this, never have deliberately
hurt anyone on the eve of a celebration.

Tears stung her eyes as she reached the landing. Stop
it, she told herself fiercely. Stop it at once. But the pain
didn't go away, and although she suppressed her feelings,
she still felt cold and sick inside.

Even the prospect of putting on her new evening dress

didn't cheer her up. It was in Petroc's favourite shade of blue. He'd said it brought out the colour of her eyes. With it she was going to wear her new pearl necklace, the diamond and pearl earrings her parents had given her a few minutes ago, and the pearl bracelet from Vivien and Simon – all perfect to wear tonight but not enough to lift the dark cloud that hung over her.

At that moment, Stephanie, with Cressida and Sasha, came running up the stairs behind her, glowing healthily from their walk.

'Hi, there!' Stephanie greeted her. 'Where's William?'

'He was with Dad in the drawing room a few minutes ago. Are you talking to each other again?'

She shrugged. 'Only if he's matured since lunchtime,' she retorted with a wicked grin.

'What's that you're wearing?' Cressida asked, pointing to the pearl bracelet on Anna's wrist.

'It's my birthday present from Granny and Simon,' Anna replied, stroking the lustrous beads.

Her cousin looked glum. 'Lucky you.'

'*And* you've got new earrings,' Sasha exclaimed, accusingly.

Anna nodded, embarrassed. 'They're from Mum and Dad.'

'You're going to look terrific tonight,' Stephanie said warmly, giving the others a scathing, God-you're-pathetic look.

'I'm not going to look anything unless I get a move on,' Anna replied, hurrying off to her room.

'Anna! Anna!'

She turned to see Michael tearing along the corridor towards her. He was red in the face as he shoved a badly wrapped parcel into her hands.

'This is for you.' He was breathless.

'For me?' She hadn't really expected a present from her little brother. 'What is it?'

'You've got to open it and see!'

From out of the folds of Christmas wrapping paper, because that was all he'd been able to find, emerged a ceramic horse's head, which Anna could see had been moulded by loving little hands. Painted brown and glazed, it had livid red nostrils and a rather wild expression.

'Oh, Mikey, it's lovely,' she exclaimed. 'I'll treasure it forever.'

'I made it,' he said importantly, 'and I fired it in the kiln at school. It's signed, too.'

She turned it over, seeing M.R. '96 scratched deeply into the clay. She hugged him impulsively.

'I think this is the nicest present I've ever had,' she said, deeply touched. 'Thank you very much.'

Looking suitably gratified he charged off, shouting over his shoulder, 'Mum says I've got to have a bath but I don't see why. I had a swim earlier.'

Anna looked at her watch. It was half-past six. One hour to go before it all began.

Through a gap in the trees Nancy Graham realised the Rutherfords' garden was deserted for the moment. She supposed everyone was indoors, getting ready for the night's revelry. The little gilt clock on her mantelpiece said it was a quarter to seven. Stepping down from the footstool which she now kept permanently in front of her bedroom window, she decided it was time to start her own preparations. Her black lace dress was pressed and hanging outside her wardrobe. Her black suede court shoes with diamanté buckles had been taken out of their box. On her dressing-table she'd already placed her pearl choker and earrings. But before she had a bath and got changed, there were two phone calls she had to make. Just to make sure there had been no change of plan.

Stephanie, wearing a bath sheet like a sarong and another towel wrapped like a turban to dry her hair, tapped on William's door. He opened it immediately and looked at her warily, undecided whether or not to forgive her for her earlier outburst.

'How are you doing?' she asked conversationally, strolling past him into the room. Then she saw the half-empty glass of champagne on his chest of drawers. 'Been drinking already?'

He looked sulky. 'Dad gave the florists a drink so we all had one, too.'

'Nice of you to invite me.' She dropped on to his bed, bouncing up and down provocatively.

'You were out walking.'

'So, can I finish yours?'

He avoided looking at her. 'If you want.'

'Pass it to me then, Will. Please.'

Reluctantly, he handed her the glass. As she took it from him with one hand, she grabbed him with the other and pulled him down on to the bed beside her. Then, in a flash, she loosened her towel and splashed the champagne over her bare breasts.

'Now you can lick it all off,' she commanded, throwing her arms around his neck. There was a moment's silence in the room. Then Cressida, passing along the corridor on her way to the bathroom, heard Stephanie's voice, gasping between giggles, 'Oh, Will! It tickles . . . I love it! More . . . lick me more!'

Back in her own room, she turned to her sister in disgust. 'What a tart that Stephanie is! I don't know what William sees in her.'

By seven o'clock Julia was ready. Douglas, coming out of the bathroom, pink and hot from his shower, with a towel slung round his hips and his hair standing on end, stopped in his tracks, staring at her.

'My God, Julia!'

'Do you like it?'

'*Like* it?' He took a deep breath. 'I've never seen you look so . . . so fabulous.'

She was like a shimmering nymph, frosted and fragile in a backless, long-sleeved dress of silver tissue, delicately embroidered with strands of silvery glass beads which hung down like icicles. With her dark hair swept up on either side of her face, she reminded him of a fairy figure in a Paton painting.

'I thought I should look silvery,' she said, smiling at him.

Douglas's eyes were tender as he moved towards her. Then he put his hands to either side of her slim waist and looked lovingly into her face.

'My darling girl, I'm so proud of you. Thank you for all the happiness you've given me.'

With a small convulsive sob, she put her arms around his neck and pressed herself close against him.

'I love you so much, Douglas.'

'And I you, sweetheart.'

'Nothing will ever come between us, will it?' she said impulsively. 'Promise me?'

'What could ever come between us?' he asked softly. 'The next big party we give will be to celebrate our Ruby Anniversary, and you shall wear red. And then there'll be our Golden celebration, and I shall buy you a gown of cloth-of-gold and golden stars for your hair.' He might have been reassuring a child that, even in real life, everyone always lives happily ever after.

She withdrew gently from his arms, Leonora's words forgotten again. 'Hadn't you better get dressed? It's nearly ten-past seven.'

'My God, you're right. You and I are going over to the marquee in a few minutes.' He grabbed his compact mobile phone from the bedside table. 'Hello? Douglas here. We're coming over in five minutes. Is everything ready? Good. Thanks.'

'Who were you talking to?' asked Julia, mystified.

'The electricians. They're here for the night, to make sure nothing goes wrong.' As he spoke, he started getting dressed. It never took him long, and once in his dinner jacket, hair brushed and cologne dabbed on his cheeks, he grabbed Julia's hand and led her hurriedly out of their room. 'Come on! Be prepared to be surprised. I've been waiting for this moment for bloody months!' he exclaimed, ebullient once more.

In the other bedrooms of Highfield Manor, the rest of the family were still getting ready. Pat, in her dark blue silk dress and crystal bead necklace, and Reggie, spruced up in a dinner jacket that he hadn't worn for several years but which mercifully still fitted him, were sipping glasses of milk with which to line their stomachs in readiness for the intake of champagne.

In the next-door room, Vivien was putting the finishing

182

touches to her make-up. It was still possible to see what a beauty she must have been when she'd been young. The fine bone structure was still there, and her figure was only slightly more blurred at the edges than it had been in her heyday. Tonight she wore an exquisite black gown, a Dior original she'd had for years, and round her neck clasped a wide pearl choker. Once or twice her hand stole secretly to her breast. Perhaps the lump had gone . . . but it was still there. Always there. She glanced over at Simon, lounging on the *chaise-longue*, waiting for her. How was he going to manage on his own?

Along the corridor Peter and Leonora got dressed in silence, but it was a companionable silence. She was pleased with her brightly coloured spangled dress and glad she'd chosen it. And she hoped lots of nice young men would ask Sasha and Cressida to dance tonight. Nevertheless, she couldn't help feeling mollified by the fact that if her girls didn't have a special young man in tow, neither did Anna.

'Are you nearly ready?' she asked Peter eagerly. They hardly ever went to parties and she didn't want to miss a moment of this one.

He looked up from tying the laces of his old-fashioned patent leather evening shoes. 'What's the rush? I'm not ready. You go ahead if you're so keen.'

In the room opposite, the silence was heavy with hostility as Oonagh slipped into her dramatic white crêpe ball gown, which had a huge black velvet bow on the left shoulder. She hoped she resembled Audrey Hepburn tonight; certainly her colouring and flat-chested slimness, and the sheer flamboyance of the dress, was a reminder of *My Fair Lady*, but thanks to Chris her dark eyes looked flat and dull, the lids puffy, and for once she lacked the confident glow that usually made people turn to look at her. She shot him a look of pure hatred as he fussed with his cuff links, trying to assume a casual air.

'I want to leave tomorrow morning,' she said suddenly.

He dropped his arms to his sides and stood gazing at her with a pleading expression. 'For Julia and Douglas's sake, darling, if not for ours, why don't we bury the hatchet for the weekend? It's going to be a fabulous party. Tim and my mother and Simon are here, and we don't want them upset, do we? Can't we just forget our problems for a while?'

'But you won't be forgetting *her* all weekend, will you?' Oonagh's jaw was white and sharp as she turned on him. 'How do you think that makes me feel? Here I am, trying to look good . . .'

'You do look good, you look marvellous. Really. I mean it.'

'But you still want to leave me . . . for some little tart!'

'Did I say I wanted to leave you?' he challenged.

Oonagh looked confused for a moment, wrong-footed by a man she knew was cleverer than her. 'It's . . . it's obvious . . .' she stammered.

'It's not obvious to me,' he replied firmly, turning and walking into their adjoining bathroom. He had to be careful what he said. Julia's reaction to his news had shaken him badly. Later, he'd had a private chat with Roger, as they walked through the woods after the barbecue lunch.

'Oonagh will crucify you!' his friend had said succinctly. 'She'll go for everything you've got, Chris. How long have you been married? Twenty-one years? Yeah. Take the word of a man who's been there twice! You'll get fucking creamed.'

But could he give up Barbara? God, what a nightmare the whole thing was. He stood in the bathroom and looked at his reflection in the mirror, and decided he needed a drink. A strong one. It was nearly half-past seven. They were due in the marquee in a few minutes, but there was time for a quick brandy in the study. He swung back into the bedroom, where Oonagh was applying a final spray of Poison.

'We'd better get going or we'll wreck Douglas's carefully laid plans and he'll never forgive us,' said Christopher, grabbing his dinner jacket and keeping his voice light. 'Come along, darling.'

She followed in silence, smoothing her long white gloves, giving her hair a final pat, refusing to look at him.

God knows what the future holds, he thought, trying to blot Barbara from his mind as he followed Oonagh down the stairs to the hall below. But how can I ever be truly happy again without her? She's filled my life with joy in the past few months and given me back my youth. The thought of saying goodbye to her made him feel physically sick.

'Where are you going *now*?' Oonagh's nagging tones grated on his ears as they always had done.

'I thought we could nip into the study for a quick snifter before the evening really gets under way.'

She sighed theatrically. 'I don't want anything. There's going to be enough drink around once the party starts.'

'Will it distress you if I do?' he asked sarcastically.

Oonagh shrugged and followed him into the study, where Roger and Pammy had already sneaked in for a fortifying nip.

The two men laughed when they saw each other, and Pammy grinned conspiratorially.

'I like a little lift before a party,' she confessed, raising her glass of vodka and tonic.

'You like something else, too,' murmured Roger, raising his eyes to heaven behind her back. 'We'd better be quick, though, or Douglas will be furious.'

Fifteen minutes before, Douglas had taken Julia by the hand and led her slowly into the marquee. He'd given orders no one else was to be around.

'This night is dedicated to you, my darling,' he whispered, as he drew her forward, 'as a thank you for the twenty-five years you have dedicated yourself to me.'

'Oh, Douglas . . .' She felt deeply moved, looking back on the years through the glow of her present happiness. Now it seemed as if the path she'd trodden had been smooth, though it hadn't always seemed so at the time; that nothing had been too much trouble nor the work too hard, although memory reminded her that there had been moments when she'd been so exhausted and harassed she'd felt like dropping. Now it seemed that the years had flown by on silken wings, and no sacrifice had been too great; in fact, she felt at this moment as if she hadn't really made any sacrifices at all. No matter what, it had all been worth it. Every second of it. Douglas was still here by her side and that was all that mattered, or had ever mattered.

When the tears were brushed from her eyes, she was able to see clearly again, and then she looked around, gasping aloud from sheer surprise and delight. It was as if she were in Venice, where they'd spent their honeymoon.

The marquee had been transformed into the interior of a *palazzo*, with statues and fine tapestries and antique

186

mirrors hung on the scarlet silk walls. And there were flowers everywhere: garlanded on the back of every dining chair, entwined in the great chandeliers that hung on red silk ropes from a darkened ceiling, so that the air was heavy with the scent of roses, lilies, stock and paeonies. The thirty round tables, set with gold-rimmed glasses and plates, were also decorated with a profusion of flowers mixed with fruit, and in the centre of each a pyramid of cream wax candles rose from a wrapping of dark magnolia leaves.

'I don't believe it!' Julia kept saying. Wherever she looked she was astounded by the beauty of the setting, by the subtle effects of spotlights trained on statues, and the hundreds of candles that flickered in gold wall sconces.

'Do you like it?' he asked, never taking his eyes off her face.

'*Like* it? It's magnificent, Douglas. I never imagined it would be like this.' Nor had she. Never in her wildest dreams had she expected this illusion of Venice, in all its ancient grandeur, to be recreated on their back lawn. She held his hand, eyes wide as they walked around slowly, looking at everything.

'I wish we had longer,' she said. 'I'll never take it all in, and once everyone arrives it won't be the same.'

'Come and look at the tables,' Douglas urged, his voice filled with pride. Tonight was going to cost a fortune, but he didn't care. It would show Julia, their families and all their friends how well he had done. He led her to one of the tables.

'Oh . . . masks!' she exclaimed.

'Yes, and very carefully distributed to each place setting to suit the wearer. See? The ladies' masks have pale delicate features and are trimmed with flowers and ribbons, while the men's are more dramatic. Some are painted gold or silver.'

'It's a total fantasy,' she said, gazing around. 'I feel as if I'm in a dream . . . Oh, I can't wait for the children to see it all.'

'But first . . .' Douglas led her to the table where she'd be sitting and pointed to an exquisite mask, edged with diamanté and with white egret feathers sprouting from either side to frame her face. 'This one is for you.'

Laughing, Julia picked it up and held it to her face flirtatiously. 'How do I look?'

'Wonderful, of course. But look what's under it.'

She turned back to the table and saw a little velvet box. She'd already given Douglas his present, four silver candlesticks especially designed for the occasion by Theo Fennell; this must be his gift to her. She opened the box and there was a solitaire diamond ring set in platinum. She gazed at it, speechless.

'OK?' he asked gently, his smile quizzical.

'If I say anything, I'll start crying again!' she whispered, slipping it on to her finger.

Purposely he kept his voice matter-of-fact. 'Well, we've come a long way since we opened Lots, haven't we? Here, have a glass of champagne and you can thank me properly tomorrow. It's time to get this show on the road . . . as they say.'

The next twenty minutes seemed to pass in a flash as everyone came over from the house for their preview of the decorations, and there were shrieks and exclamations from the young ones as they rushed around, discovering new delights.

'It's cool. Really, *really* cool,' William kept saying, while Pammy kept repeating in her American drawl: 'It's awesome. *Awesome!*' Michael, tearing about dodging behind statues and then reappearing again, could only gasp: 'Wow, Dad! Wow!' Only Anna was quiet, drinking in the atmosphere and wishing Petroc was here. It all seemed so hollow without him, she thought. Was everything going to be wasted on her because he was not here to share it with her? Drinking deeply of her glass of champagne, she decided to get slightly drunk. It was the only way, she thought, to blunt the edges of her pain.

'In five minutes we must go back to the house,' Douglas announced loudly. 'The photographers have arrived and Morgan is giving them drinks in the hall, but the guests will be here in a few minutes. The rest of you can spread out on the lawn, but Julia and I, with Anna and William, must get to our posts to receive the guests.'

'Yes, sir!' William stood to attention, grinning, and gave his father a mock salute.

'All right, all right,' Douglas said good-naturedly. 'I know I sound like a Sergeant Major, but we have to welcome everyone. Ah, here comes Bryn Williams. It's all right, Bryn, we're on our way.'

Looking imposing in his scarlet Toast Master's tail coat, Bryn would now make sure the evening ran to plan, that everyone was seated at the right time, that the toasts were proposed and the speeches announced, and that there were no hitches; and if there were, that nobody should know about them.

'Now I can really relax and enjoy myself,' Julia told him. 'I'm leaving it to you to keep us all in order.'

From the rich decadent setting of an opulent *palazzo* in Venice, it was a cultural shock to walk out into an English country garden on a balmy summer's evening. The guests were arriving, their cars forming neat rows in the adjoining field. Douglas went first to the hall where he welcomed the photographers, amongst them Richard Young, Alan Davidson, Dominic O'Neill, Alec Galbraith and Dafydd Jones, who were in demand every night of the week to cover the best parties. They'd already been given a typed list of the three hundred guests, with a potted biography of the more interesting ones, and there was a press table set aside for them in the marquee, with a waiter specially assigned to see they had everything they wanted. Douglas had left nothing to chance. Tonight's party would be featured in all the newspaper gossip columns and the glossy magazines and he was going to make damn' sure he was portrayed in flattering terms.

There was a ripple of excitement and anticipation in the atmosphere. Bryn stationed himself in the drawing-room doorway, ready to announce the guests. Waiters stood holding trays laden with glasses of champagne. Anna, smoothing the skirt of her ball dress as she stood in the receiving line with her parents and William, was unaware of a figure standing in the french windows, watching her. Then she heard her mother speak.

'Petroc! How lovely to see you.'

Anna spun round and the most extraordinary and thrilling frisson shot through her. Petroc, smart in his dinner jacket, was looking at her sheepishly, a nervous smile on his face.

'May I come in?' he asked diffidently.

'Of course.' Again it was Julia who spoke, going over to kiss him on both cheeks and lead him into the room, while Anna stood dumbstruck.

'Welcome, old chap,' Douglas said, pumping his hand. 'Glad you could make it. Have a drink. You'll find everyone on the lawn.' It was as if nothing had happened and they'd been expecting him all along.

Then he turned and came to Anna, looking down into her face. 'I'm so, so sorry. Can you forgive me?'

'I don't know,' she said stupidly, angry that he'd put her through three days of hell, yet filled with joy that he was here now.

'Please, Anna. I don't know what happened. I sort of . . . couldn't cope . . . it was like a breakdown. Suddenly everything got on top of me and seemed so complicated. Life was just one hurdle after another. I couldn't handle anything: my job, my finances, the future. It was all too much. But I'm all right now.'

'I'm not sure I am,' she retorted, shaking her head.

'. . . Mr and Mrs Henry Banks.' Bryn Williams's voice was strong and resonant. 'Lord and Lady Mavers . . . Mr George Cooper and Miss Lucy Bagshot . . . Mr Peter Townend . . .'

The party had begun.

Petroc slipped away into the garden, muttering that he'd catch up with her later. His expression was anxious and his eyes filled with regret, but Anna suddenly looked radiant. Never before had she felt such a sense of power. For the first time in their relationship, she was the one in control; it would be up to her now whether they parted or not. It was a heady thought.

'Mr and Mrs Charles Wentworth . . . Mr and Mrs Duncan Crow . . . Miss Joan Collins . . . Lord Etchington . . . Sir John and Lady Wright . . . Mr John Rendall . . .'

The pace was hotting up. Bryn was announcing people as fast as he could while on the table behind the hosts, a stack of extravagantly wrapped presents was growing. William, on Anna's right, much cheered by Stephanie's visit to his bedroom, was making sotto voce remarks as people appeared, and reducing his sister to uncontrollable giggles.

'Here comes The Ferry,' he muttered as a much married, titled lady hove into sight with her new husband.

'Lord and Lady Archcombe,' Bryn announced.

'Why?' Anna whispered back.

'Because she moves from peer to peer,' he quipped.

Through the french windows from the garden came the animated hum of voices and laughter and the clink of glasses, while in the drawing room they continued to welcome a steady stream of guests. The Prime Minister and his wife and several members of the Cabinet arrived together, then came the American Ambassador and his wife, followed by the French and Italian Ambassadors, and several members of the Greek Royal Family.

'Lord and Lady Tredwell . . . Prince Georgio Lichtenstein . . . Mr Rodney Lonsdale . . . the Duke and Duchess of Portanova . . .'

Bryn Williams was still going strong. 'We've got one hundred and eighty-two guests so far,' he informed Douglas, during a short lull between arrivals.

Michael, looking unrecognisably clean and polished in dark trousers, a white shirt and a blazer, bobbed up between them.

'How do you know?' he asked Bryn. 'Did you count them two by two as they walked in? Like in the Ark?'

Bryn smiled, and showed him the small numbering instrument in the palm of his hand. 'This was originally called a hand tally,' he explained. 'It was used on ships in the old days when passengers went ashore. As they came down the gang plank, a sailor would count how many there were, and when they came back on board they would be counted again.'

'So no one would get left behind when the ship sailed?' Michael asked, intrigued.

'Exactly.' Bryn turned to Douglas. 'If your guests continue to arrive at this rate, they should all be here by nine o'clock. Would you like me to announce dinner at nine-fifteen?'

Douglas nodded and turned to greet the chairman of the Royal Opera House. 'I'm so glad you could come.'

The steady stream continued, and soon the lawn was packed. Douglas signalled to Bryn that the moment to announce dinner had arrived.

'It's going to take twenty minutes to get everyone seated, as it is,' he commented, leading the way to the marquee.

The magnificence of the Venetian theme astonished the guests, and loud exclamations of delight drowned out the melodious strains of a mandolin. The rococo decor of the *palazzo* was reminiscent of a Tiepolo painting, rich with silk damask and gilding. In a corner designed to resemble a courtyard, a fountain splashed softly into a dark pool, and beyond the balustraded balcony, a back-drop of the Grand Canal and the Rialto bridge glittered under a star-lit sky. Dry ice drifted across the floor, uncoiling mysteriously as if rising from the *Canale della Giudecca*, revealing a golden gondola, filled with crimson velvet cushions.

'I've never seen anything so fantastic . . .'

'Jesus, what did this lot cost?'

'I don't believe it, it's like an opera set.'

'Trust Douglas! It's a bit over the top, don't you think?'

'Over the top? It's outrageously vulgar!'

'But divine.'

'Oh, yes, my dear, quite divine.'

'What a public relations exercise! With the Prime Minister here, what's the betting Douglas gets a K after this?'

'Well . . . an OBE perhaps, for his services to catering.'

'Good luck to him, I say.'

'He's certainly worked hard in his effort to arrive.'

'He's the master of grand gesture, isn't he?'

Bitching and praising in equal measure, the chattering voices rose to a crescendo as the guests took their places, twisting their heads this way and that to see if any of their social rivals had been placed at a better table than them – 'better' in this case referring to tables occupied by high-ranking and more celebrated guests.

Julia, shimmering in her silver dress, darted here and there, making sure people had found where they were supposed to be, ensuring they had everything they wanted, praising the women for looking wonderful and flattering the men by telling them how well they looked. A trail of compliments followed in her wake as she moved from table to table.

'She looks amazing!'

'Have you ever seen such a fabulous dress?'

'A born hostess, of course. What on earth would Douglas do without her?'

At last everyone was seated, the first course served, the first glass of wine poured, the volume of voices more muted, the real enjoyment of the evening settling on everyone like a warm cloak of happiness. This night would be remembered as the most lavish and outstanding party of 1996, if not the decade.

On his way to his own table, Douglas stopped to have a word with, to him, the most important guests of all: the social editors of *Tatler*, *Harpers & Queen*, *Vogue*, *Hello!*

and *OK!* magazines, and the gossip columnists from the *Daily Mail*, *Daily Express*, *Daily Telegraph*, *Evening Standard* and the *Globe*. Knowing they wouldn't want to be lumped together, he'd placed them strategically at eleven different tables, with a variety of prominent guests, so each could get 'exclusive' stories. The photographers' job was different; they all had a friendly working relationship with each other and liked to relax together when not actually taking pictures.

'Did you get my list of acceptances?' Douglas asked each journalist. That morning he'd faxed them the final list of guests who were attending, knowing it would make their job much easier.

There were nods and smiles all round and, satisfied, he made his way to the table he was hosting.

The night to remember had begun.

Eight

Bryn Williams, always alert and never far from the host, noted Douglas's subtle signal and moved smoothly to his side.

'I think we'll have the speeches in five minutes, Bryn.'

'Very well.' There was a fractional pause. 'But shall we wait until the coffee has actually been served, Mr Rutherford? You don't want to be drowned out by the rattle of three hundred cups and saucers being put on the tables.'

Douglas nodded, grinning. 'Good thinking, Bryn.'

He placed the microphone on a stand in front of Douglas. 'Is your wife going to be standing beside you when you speak?' he asked in a low voice.

Douglas looked nonplussed. 'Oh! I hadn't thought . . . you see, we're hosting different tables. What do you think?'

'I imagine you're thanking everyone for coming tonight to share this celebration with you?'

'Yes. Absolutely.'

'Then I think it would be appropriate if you and Mrs Rutherford stood together, just for the speeches,' Bryn suggested.

'You're right.'

A few minutes later, as everyone relaxed with coffee,

petits-fours and cigars, Bryn tapped sharply with a spoon on a side table, bringing the room to silence. Then he announced in a strong authoritative voice: 'Your Excellencies, Prime Minister, Your Highnesses, My Lords, Ladies and Gentlemen, pray silence for your host, Mr Douglas Rutherford.'

A spontaneous burst of applause greeted Douglas as he got to his feet, with Julia standing beside him. A bank of photographers crouched low among the tables, cameras poised. There was an expectant hush.

'My dear friends . . .' he began. 'I think it was Zsa Zsa Gabor who said: "A man in love is incomplete until he has married. Then he's finished . . ." ' He paused until the laughter died, and then, taking Julia's hand, kissed it and continued.

'But that's when my life really began. Twenty-five years ago this month . . . and no one can ever say Julia married me for my money, because I came to her with an overdraft of six hundred pounds and an old wreck of a Ford Escort. We got married, for better or for worse, and I truly thought for poorer and poorer. I think Julia thought the same because she insisted on keeping on her secretarial job until, in a career move, she went on to washing dishes in our first restaurant, Lots, where we offered lots of food, lots of drink . . .' Douglas paused and looked around. 'Nothing's really changed, has it?' he asked deadpan. The guests roared their approval, and as he continued to captivate them, Julia was laughing by his side, especially when he quoted the late Lord Mancroft: 'Happy is the man with a wife to tell him what to do and a secretary to do it.'

When it came to talking about Anna, William and Michael, he ceased to banter wittily but spoke of them with genuine pride, smiling at them as they hosted their tables, noting Anna's eyes overbright with emotion, William's ears pink with embarrassment, and Michael suitably gratified at being mentioned when he'd felt left out of the celebrations earlier.

'I would like to propose a toast to our children,' he continued, 'for the joy they have brought to our lives and the love they have shown us.' His voice caught and Julia squeezed his hand.

'The toast is Anna, William and Michael,' Bryn Williams announced.

'Anna . . . William . . . Michael . . .' everyone chorused, raising their glasses, and William blushed deeper than ever.

Then everyone settled down to hear the end of Douglas's speech and the marquee fell silent again.

'I would also like to propose a toast of thanks to Laurent, my chief chef at . . .' he began, when the distinct *chink-chink* of a spoon tapping on a glass made him pause and look around, frowning with slight irritation. Bryn Williams, always sharply alert and ready to deal with any untoward disruption which sometimes occurred from a guest who had had too much to drink, stepped forward and indicated the entrance to the marquee.

'Over there, Mr Rutherford,' he told Douglas. 'The lady in the black lace dress.'

Douglas looked, and gave a sharp intake of breath when he saw who it was. Nancy Graham was looking back at him with a triumphant expression, chin raised arrogantly. Her voice rang out loud and clear in the sudden silence.

'It was most touching to hear you speak of your children so fondly,' she said, 'and I'm sure all your friends were very happy to drink a toast to them.' She paused and Douglas, face rigid with fury, glared at her in a long moment that held the room spellbound.

'But . . .' she continued '. . . don't you think it would be nice to express your feelings towards your *other* daughter, and suggest that your friends drink to her as well? It was her sixteenth birthday a few months ago, but of course there was no grand celebration for her. So shall we welcome her tonight instead?'

Nancy Graham turned, and a figure stepped forward from the shadows.

Julia, standing by Douglas's side, felt dizzy, her heart pounding so fearfully that, thinking she was going to faint, she clutched hold of his arm.

'What's up, Mum?' William asked, bounding up to them. Everyone was turning in their seats, craning their necks, some at the back of the marquee even standing to look at a waif-like girl with skin as pale as candle-wax and long blonde hair which straggled around her shoulders. So thin she looked anorexic, with high jutting cheek-bones and a pointed chin, she was dressed in a frilled and flounced white ball gown which looked as if it had been designed for some theatrical production. Grey eyes, wide and startled-looking, gazed in terror at the hundreds of faces staring at her.

'Lily!' Julia croaked. 'Oh . . . my . . . God . . . Lily!'

The guests closest to the top table swivelled their heads to look at Julia and wondered why her face was so white and pinched-looking. Douglas, his expression aghast, as if he'd seen a ghost, was supporting his wife as she swayed, close to collapse.

The photographers were closing in too, forming a ring around them and the girl, intent on capturing every second of this drama on film.

Nancy Graham spoke again, louder this time, striving to be heard above the growing murmur of voices which filled the marquee.

'Not Lily,' she said in a clear voice, 'but Rose. Her daughter. Douglas's daughter.'

'*Lily*!' Julia insisted wildly, as if her mind had broken loose and become unhinged. 'How could I forget Lily?'

Rose stood looking at them all like a terrified animal. A frenzy of flash bulbs engulfed her and half-blinded those around her, seeming to brand her image on the very air.

Flash . . . flash . . . flash . . . And Rose stood there, twisting her bony hands, not knowing what to do. Then she wailed: 'I didn't never want to come, but her over there, she made me. Gave me the money to hire this dress, she did.' Her voice was uneducated. She looked close to tears. 'I told her, like, that I wouldn't fit in.'

'What do you say to that, Mr Rutherford?' Nancy demanded. 'You paid this child's grandmother to bring her up and look after her, but you've never accepted her as your own flesh and blood, have you?'

Douglas looked at her silently, a man bereft of words, deep in shock. It was Julia who seemed to rally, drawing herself up and raising her head defiantly.

'This is a pack of lies. Lily never had a child. What are you trying to do – get money out of us, is that it?'

Silence fell again. The onlookers seemed to hold their breath.

'Lily was me mum,' Rose said plaintively.

Julia frowned, perplexed. 'But she was only a young girl herself when she came to work here . . .'

'Twenty-three, actually,' Nancy Graham butted in

loudly. 'Rose was six months old at the time.'

'But . . .?' Julia turned to Douglas, eyes stricken. The query hung in the air between them like poison that would only be released when the truth was revealed. Their whole future seemed to rest upon what he said now. Anna, William and little Michael, not comprehending everything but understanding enough to sense that something terrible was happening in their family, stood helplessly by, like passengers on the deck of a stricken ship. And beyond them, Douglas's parents, Julia's too, the rest of the family and all their friends, and last of all the press, getting a scoop on the famous millionaire restaurateur Douglas Rutherford, Perfect Family Man, Mr Cleaner-Than-Clean, waiting for him to explain himself.

The photographers pressed forward. To hell with an anniversary party! Here was a news story breaking before their hungry lenses. Who *was* this young girl, so pale and bony and pathetic-looking in her pantomime dress? Was she really the secret daughter of Douglas Rutherford?

Bryn Williams turned swiftly to Douglas. 'Shall I tell everyone to take their partners for the first dance?' he whispered. 'Nigel Tulley and the band are all ready.'

Douglas looked dazed. Then he nodded dumbly and went forward as if to pacify Rose. But before Bryn could make the announcement, a shrill, piercing voice sent a chill through the assembled company.

'Get away from me!' Rose screamed. 'You murderer! If it wasn't for you, my mum would still be alive.'

Then, with a frightened howl, she turned and fled, running away across the floodlit lawns, the skirts of her ridiculous gown trailing behind her. A moment later she'd vanished into the woods beyond.

Douglas quickly regained his composure.

'Get the security men to remove Mrs Graham from these premises immediately,' he barked at Bryn Williams, 'and tell her I'm suing her for wrongful entry, trespass, defamation of character, slander . . .' His expression was grim, mouth tight with fury.

'Dad, what the hell's going on?' William asked in agitation. 'Who was that girl?'

His father raised his hand in a calming gesture. 'It's all right, I'll explain everything. I'm going to hold a press conference in the drawing room, and will issue a statement on behalf of your mother and me.'

'I'm coming, too,' William declared, 'and so's Stephanie.'

'And so am I,' Anna affirmed, clinging to Petroc's arm as if there'd never been any trouble between them. Julia stood, gazing ahead, immobilised and dumb with shock.

'I'll tell the press what you're going to do and get them into the house,' said Bryn Williams. The Dark Blues had started playing a jolly bopping number, and the younger guests were already making their way on to the dance floor. The party was in full swing now, like a runaway big dipper, and Douglas realised that whatever their private suffering they were going to have to go through with it.

The nightmare of tonight was not yet over.

In the hurried scramble of the press to get over to the house and into good positions to hear what Douglas Rutherford had to say, only one held back. Harry Clegg, diary editor of the *Globe*'s gossip column, hauled his photographer away from the surging pack and almost dragged him across the lawn, towards the drive.

'Where are we going?' Jim Polack asked, jogging to

keep up, cameras dangling from their straps around his neck.

'We're going to get an exclusive from the fount of all knowledge,' Harry shot back. Then Jim realised they were following the dumpy lace-clad figure of Nancy Graham, who was being frog-marched down the drive by two security men. 'We'll find out what Douglas Rutherford said afterwards. No doubt it will be a load of fucking crap!' Harry said cheerfully.

A minute later they saw Nancy enter the gate of Cherry Tree Cottage.

Harry pulled Jim into the shadows of a ten-foot-high rhododendron. 'Don't let the security chaps see you,' he whispered.

Under the stars in a dark blue sky, and to the distant strains of 'Yellow River', Harry and Jim waited until the security men had walked back up the drive and disappeared inside the house.

'OK, let's go.' Harry led the way. When they arrived at the brightly painted front door of the cottage, he rang the bell.

Almost immediately they heard a familiar voice, coming from inside. 'Yes? Who is it?'

'Harry Clegg, diary editor of the *Globe*, Mrs Graham. And my photographer, Jim Polack. We're very interested in what you had to say just now, and we'd like to talk to you about it.'

The door opened with such speed they both recoiled, startled.

'Good evening,' Harry said, showing his press card.

'Do come in,' Nancy gushed, and led the way into her overfurnished drawing room. 'Can I offer you a drink?'

'No, thanks, I'm driving.'

'I'm fine, thanks,' Jim mumbled.

Nancy arranged herself on a chair and looked at them brightly. 'What can I tell you? You must have been in the marquee just now. What I had to say made quite an impact, didn't it?'

'You obviously know a lot about this,' Harry said smarmily. 'Could you tell us some more?' He took his notebook out of his pocket. 'First, and most importantly, can you give me your full name . . .?'

The silken thread of entrapment had been spun, and Nancy Graham was only too willing to deliver herself into captivity.

'Douglas, I can't. Don't make me . . .' Julia didn't need to ask him if it was true Lily had had his baby. She'd seen the guilt in his eyes as soon as Rose had appeared.

He drew her into the study, and put his arms around her to pull her close.

'Sweetheart, it's you I love . . . always have done. Lily was never a threat to our marriage, you must believe that. The baby was an accident, and I promise you I haven't seen her since she was born. Until tonight. We've got to handle this disaster with dignity and I need you by my side, darling. Please,' he begged, looking into her eyes, willing her to be strong. 'Please, darling. I know it's a lot to ask, but please do it . . . for me.'

'Oh, God.' She rested her forehead against his shoulder. 'I feel sick . . .'

'I know, my love. I know. I'll get you a brandy.'

'I don't want anything.' Julia stepped back, looking up at him. There was pain and hurt in her dark eyes and her lips trembled. 'If we're going to do this, then for God's sake let's get it over with,' she said brokenly.

Douglas's face puckered with anguish. 'Christ, I'm so sorry, Julia. I'd have given my soul for this not to have happened.' He took her hand and led her gently back into the hall where Anna and William, with Petroc and Stephanie, were hovering, white-faced, wondering what was happening. From the drawing room came the excited murmur of voices. Like hounds closing in for the kill, Julia thought with revulsion.

'Let's go,' said Douglas, squaring his shoulders and raising his chin as he led his family in. His grip on Julia's hand was like a vice, but his voice was steady and his eyes unwavering as he braved the very people he'd been so anxious to invite to his party tonight.

They stood waiting in a semi-circle, journalists and photographers alike. 'Could you tell us . . .?' one of them began, but Douglas silenced him and the others with a sweeping look as he stood with Julia close to his side and the rest of the family grouped around him.

'I know it's too much to ask that you should forget what has just happened or destroy the pictures you have taken,' he began. 'But I hope you will not lose sight of the fact that tonight was supposed to be . . . *is* in fact . . . a celebration of twenty-five years of happy marriage, and the birthdays of our daughter Anna and son William.

'Lily was a servant we had, many years ago, who suffered a terrible accident. Tragically, she was alone in this house when she was stung by a bee. It was known by her family that she was allergic to bee stings, and she was supposed at all times to carry a syringe of adrenalin with her. Alas, on this particular day, she must have forgotten, because she died from anaphylactic shock before help could be got to her.

'It was a terrible tragedy for her and her family, and of

206

course we offered them financial help as they struggled to bring up her baby daughter. That is all I have to say. I deeply regret the evening has got off to this very bad start, thanks to the vengeful actions of my neighbour, Mrs Nancy Graham, who obviously coerced that poor young lady into gate-crashing this party tonight. But I sincerely hope this incident will not ruin the enjoyment of my guests, and in particular my family, who mean a great deal to me. Thank you for your time. Now I hope we may all get on with the evening.'

Douglas turned to leave, and William realised with surprise that his father had cleverly evaded any mention of Lily's having been his lover or of their having had a child.

At that moment a chorus of voices seemed to ring in their ears.

'But was that girl your daughter?'

'Can you tell us if . . .'

'Was Lily your mistress?'

'What was the verdict at the inquest?'

'What was Lily's full name?'

'Is this the first time you've seen your daughter?'

'I'm not answering any questions,' Douglas boomed, and Julia broke away from his grasp and ran from the room, her head bowed.

'I've made a statement and you must be content with that. This is not a big story or a family scandal. It is about a poor, unfortunate young woman who died in a tragic accident, many years ago. Now I'd be grateful if you'd leave me and my family alone. And if you can't, then I'd like you to go, please.'

In the drawing room of Cherry Tree Cottage, Nancy Graham was in full spate.

'I have long had my suspicions about Douglas Rutherford,' she said vehemently. 'He is a bombastic, arrogant man . . .'

'I know,' Harry Clegg agreed, trying to sound sympathetic. 'But how did you find out he had a daughter? And what makes you think he killed her mother?'

Nancy Graham looked surprised that he should even be questioning what she'd said. 'Everyone in the village knows he's a most disreputable person,' she said dismissively. 'Mr Harris, who owns the village store, used to employ Lily, and she lived in a room above the shop at that time. Douglas Rutherford was carrying on with her from the moment he bought Highfield Manor, before he and his family moved in. He kept the builders working for months, so he could keep seeing her,' she added. 'Then Lily got pregnant and he dumped her. Typical of that sort of man, of course.'

'But what about him murdering her?' Harry insisted, glancing at his watch. Time was running out if he was going to make the first edition.

'After she'd had the baby and they'd all moved in to Highfield Manor she went to work for them as a cleaner, and Douglas Rutherford locked her in the larder when she was stung by a bee and left her there to die. She was allergic, you see.' Nancy made it sound as if it was fearfully common to be allergic to a bee sting.

Harry frowned, perplexed. 'What happened then? Was he accused of her murder? Did it go to trial?'

Nancy shrugged. 'I don't know. I wasn't living here at the time. All I know is, he's capable of anything. A really nasty man. He paid the witnesses off to buy their silence, I shouldn't wonder.'

208

The party was continuing relentlessly, with the guests determined to do justice to their host's hospitality. The Prime Minister and several Ambassadors had slipped away, blaming 'an early start in the morning' for their departure, but the majority had no intention of leaving the best party of the year. The champagne was still flowing. The Dark Blues' music was terrific, and the setting kept producing further delightful discoveries. In quiet corners, and among the older guests, there was whispered speculation and gossip about what had happened earlier, but Anna and William's friends, a new and more caring generation than their parents, hugged them in sympathy, sharing their shock at the unexpected appearance of a hitherto unknown half-sister.

It was the grandparents who were the most shaken, retiring to the deserted summer house beyond the pool in order not to be overheard.

'I can hardly believe this has happened,' Vivien said wretchedly. 'It couldn't have been some dreadful practical joke, could it?'

Simon slipped his arm through hers. 'That was no practical joke, darling. You only had to look at Julia's face to know she was devastated.'

Pat and Reggie looked at him almost angrily.

'But it's a pack of lies!' Pat retorted. 'Douglas never had an affair, and he certainly didn't have a love child. It's a monstrous suggestion!'

Reggie nodded, his expression doleful. 'It's that wicked woman next door. She's trumped up this whole thing to spoil the evening . . .'

'Yes, she has,' Pat affirmed. 'Didn't that girl, whoever she was, say she'd been made to come?'

'And that woman gave her the money to get a dress.

She said that too, didn't she?' Reggie cut in.

Simon looked at Douglas's parents and knew that, come hell or high water, they were never going to believe their beloved son had done anything wrong. He remained silent, not convinced.

'But Julia would have told me if . . .' Vivien began, then stopped, knowing she wouldn't. Julia had always been a very private person, never talking about her feelings. Even as a child, she'd kept things to herself. Like me, Vivien reflected, realising that she, too, was keeping a secret this weekend. If Douglas had been an unfaithful husband, Julia would never have wanted anyone to know.

At that moment he appeared, striding along the side of the pool with an expression of fierce determination on his face.

'Come along,' he said briskly. 'We've got to put a good face on things. It'll look terrible if we all go into hiding.'

'Where's Julia?' Vivien asked.

'She'll be along in a minute,' he replied brusquely.

'Is she all right? Shall I go to her?'

'She's fine. Just angry with the old bitch next door.'

'But who *was* that young girl?' Vivien persisted.

Simon gripped her arm more tightly. 'Leave it, darling,' he said under his breath.

'Did you know your father had once had a mistress?' Petroc asked sympathetically as he and Anna sat on a wrought-iron bench, in the mock Venetian courtyard, where the fountain splashed gently and the air was heavy with the scent of jasmine. The disaster of this evening had brought them close together again, and having forgiven him, Anna was grateful for his presence.

'I'm not sure that he did,' she replied loyally. 'You don't

know Nancy Graham. She'd stop at nothing to cause trouble. She promised to wreck the party tonight, and she did. I never thought she'd go this far, though,' she added angrily. 'I could kill the old cow! It's absolutely ghastly for Daddy.'

'Not much fun for your mother, either,' Petroc said drily.

'I know. But Mummy wasn't accused of having an affair, giving birth to an illegitimate baby, and then committing murder, was she?' she retorted. 'That's libellous, you know.'

'Slanderous,' he corrected her.

'Whatever,' Anna said dismissively. 'Poor Daddy. He's worked so hard to make tonight a success and he wanted everything to be perfect.' Her eyes, so like her father's, glittered with unshed tears.

Petroc took her hand. 'I know how you feel, Anna, but there's no point in denying this. The facts are . . .'

'We don't *know* what the facts are! Daddy never said, when he talked to the press, that he'd had a girlfriend or a baby.'

'I know he didn't actually *say* . . .'

'Well, there you are then. I think we should wait until the party's over before we jump to conclusions.'

Petroc looked at her closely. He liked this new, spirited, assertive Anna so much more than the old, passive one. He'd been really shocked when she'd rung him back and told him what she thought of him but it had made him see her through new eyes. In the old days she'd never have done that. She'd have slunk away into a corner, to nurse her hurt and sulk.

'Daddy's strong,' she continued, giving him a quick smile.

Petroc leaned sideways and kissed her lightly on the corner of the mouth. 'And so are you. And exciting, too,' he whispered. 'Am I invited to stay for the rest of the weekend?'

'I'll think about it,' she teased, a sudden wicked gleam coming into her eyes.

On the far side of the marquee, in a grotto hung with vines, from where they could watch the dancing, William sat with Stephanie.

'I hope Mum's all right,' he said worriedly.

'Would you like me to go and find her? See if she's OK?'

'Thanks, but I'll go myself in a minute, if she doesn't appear.' He looked around the crowded marquee. 'I suppose she will come back?' He was trying to be mature about the whole thing; married couples often strayed, it was a well-known fact. But not your parents. Not your own dad, betraying your mother like that, and having a baby too. And what would happen now? Would they separate? Get a divorce? He felt cold and sick and lonely, unable to come to terms with such a thing happening in his own family.

'Your mother obviously knew all about it,' Stephanie said, breaking into his thoughts.

William looked at her sharply, frowning. 'What makes you think that?'

'As soon as she spotted that girl, Rose or whatever her name was, your mother recognised her. Or *thought* she did. She called her Lily.'

William didn't like that at all. He dabbed his mouth nervously with his handkerchief and gulped his wine, almost emptying the glass. 'Why do you say that? Did she ever talk to you about it?' he asked harshly.

'No, of course not.' Stephanie watched as William struggled with his emotions, his cheeks flushed and his fists clenched. She knew he'd always been especially close to his mother, and this was obviously a very painful time for him.

'Then what makes you think . . .' His voice was thick with unshed tears.

'A woman's intuition. It never fails,' Stephanie replied, reaching for his hand. 'She's stronger than you think, Will darling. And she has you.'

He shot her a grateful look. 'And I have you.'

Tim, still at the table he was hosting, looked around at the other guests, none of whom he knew. They had no idea he was Douglas's nephew either, and so there was much open speculation about what had happened. For a while he listened, thinking that they sounded no different from a bunch of gossiping twelve-year-old school boys, but gradually he became angry. The guests struck him as being a smug bunch of socialites, whose only interest in life was indulging in salacious gossip. So far as they were concerned, Douglas was now the centre of a delicious scandal which would be in all the tabloids the next day and give the chattering classes a juicy topic of discussion for weeks to come. It was obvious they had no compunction about eating his food and drinking his wine as they speculated on the dramatic appearance of a 'daughter' no one seemed to know about, but the worst thing of all was that Douglas's downfall seemed to have made them feel so much better about themselves.

Suddenly he could stand it no longer.

'I'd advise you all to be careful what you say,' he

shouted above the noise of the band. 'My uncle will be seeking legal advice on the accusations made tonight, and will have no compunction about suing people who have been heard to make slanderous remarks or spread wild rumours.'

There was a stunned silence, then gasps of embarrassment and red faces all round. Then they all began talking at once, about something else, to hide their confusion.

Julia found Michael huddled at the top of the stairs, sobbing quietly.

'My darling boy,' she said softly, gathering him into her arms as she sat down beside him. 'There's nothing to cry about. Mummy and Daddy still love each other and always will, and we love you and Anna and William, too. Don't pay any attention to what that nasty Mrs Graham says. She just wanted to upset us all tonight.'

'But who w-was that girl in the funny dress?' His face was tear-stained and his mouth drooped at the corners.

'She's got nothing to do with us,' Julia said firmly. 'Daddy has sorted everything out, so there's nothing for you to worry about.'

He sniffed. 'I don't want her to be my sister.'

'You'll never see her again so I'd forget about her, if I were you,' she assured him, knowing she must protect him from becoming involved in this family crisis.

'Have you got a hanky?' he asked in a small voice.

'Let's get a tissue from my bathroom, sweetheart,' said Julia. 'I have to powder my nose, anyway.'

'Are you going back down? I don't think it's much fun anymore.'

Julia evaded the question. 'Shall we watch the fireworks from my bedroom window?' she asked instead.

'Will you stay with me, Mummy?'

'Of course, darling,' she replied as she took his hand. I'll always be here for my children, she thought. Whatever happens now.

Pammy Schemmel eyed Roger scathingly. 'Why is everyone so surprised?'

'Because Douglas and Julia have always been such a devoted couple,' he replied. 'I'm in shock, I can tell you.'

'Not all *that* devoted, it seems,' she retorted. 'But you can see it a mile off.'

'See what a mile off?' Roger was getting fed up with Pammy. She'd done nothing but criticise since they'd arrived at Highfield Manor, and if she wasn't finding fault with everything and everyone, she was demanding sex.

'See that Douglas is horny, of course,' she said impatiently. Her dark brown Fortuny-styled evening dress, with its tiny pleats, made her look more like a marmoset than ever. She turned her round, dark eyes on him. 'He's been making a play for me all day,' she retorted, biting into a grape from the arrangement of fruit on the table.

Roger gulped, choking on his champagne. For once he couldn't think of anything to say.

Christopher, watching the dancing with mild interest while he enjoyed a glass of Napoleon brandy and a cigar, suddenly felt that everything about tonight captured the very essence of decadence. Was it the Gothic effect of the hundreds of glimmering candles rising out of their dark wrappings that created this atmosphere of carnality and self-indulgence? Or the extraordinary fancy masks that transformed the guests into macabre creatures, eerily sinister and watchful, eyes glittering through the narrow slits? As he watched them dance, they seemed to loom out of the darkness, emerging from the decaying ruins of an ancient city in a demonic parade which was reflected, over and over, in the mirrors that hung from the blood red walls. He heard laughter, loud and shrill, and caught snatches of conversation, like autumn leaves spun past on a gust of wind.

Christopher was neither religious nor fanciful but a line from the *Book of Common Prayer* came back to him, dredged up from a distant memory of Bible studies at school: 'All the deceits of the world, the flesh, and the devil'.

Something evil had been unleashed into the atmosphere tonight with the appearance of that strange girl called Rose, and Christopher found himself shuddering as an icy frisson of foreboding surged through his body. Suddenly he knew what he must do if he were not to be forever seduced by 'the flesh and the devil'. Tonight was not only a tragedy for Julia; it was also an omen for him and its prophetic significance was not lost.

At that moment Julia floated past, wearing the magnificent feather-trimmed mask Douglas has chosen for her, and it did not strike him as at all inappropriate that stuck to one of the painted cheeks was a single crystal tear.

He rose and followed her, catching her hand and finding it clenched into a tight fist.

'What's happening? Where are you going?' he asked, as they left the marquee with its pounding music and stepped out into the cool sweet night.

'I was looking for Anna and William. I wanted to see if they were all right.' Only her eyes were visible through the mask, and even then she turned her face away from the spotlights that cast their silvery beams across the lawn, so that Christopher could not see the pain she was suffering. Not that he needed to. Very gently he prised open her hand and saw the angry red marks where her nails had dug deeply into her palm.

'God, Julia, I'm sorry,' he said, distressed. 'I'd no idea . . .'

She stood quite still, gazing up at the house. 'I managed to cope somehow when I discovered Douglas was having an affair with Lily, but I don't think I can bear the idea of her having had his baby.'

'I know. And now I understand your anger this afternoon. You were right, Julia. I mustn't leave Oonagh. But if only . . .' His voice drifted away and he was silent.

'There's no such thing as a perfect life. It's all about compromises, Chris, and deciding what's the most important thing to you. I love Douglas and always have. Seventy-five per cent of a cake is better than no cake at all. It's up to me to come to terms with what's happened, if I want to stay with him.'

'And will you be able to?'

'I need time. I'll have more to lose if I leave him now than if I stay. I've always realised that.'

'But isn't this one crisis too many? Can you forgive this? A baby? Maybe . . . murder?'

Julia's hand reached swiftly up to his mouth, covering it with her fingertips. 'I must go and find Anna and William. I promised Michael I'd only be a couple of minutes.'

He let her go then glanced at his wrist watch. It was eleven-thirty. Too late to ring Barbara? She'd still be awake, probably in bed watching a video. A healthy intake of champagne had made him reckless and given him the Dutch courage he needed to end their affair, but could he actually do it? Walking slowly towards the house, he tried to suppress the memory of pale young breasts and soft hidden places that had given him such pleasure. Could he? Could he phone her and end it all?

Nine

Strolling back into the house to get away from the noise and heat of the marquee, Simon bumped into Douglas coming out of the study, which was out of bounds to the guests.

'Like a brandy?' his host asked, shortly.

'Yes, why not?'

Douglas re-entered the room and strode over to the drinks tray where he half-filled a brandy balloon from a decanter.

'Are you having one?' Simon asked.

'Am I having another one?' Douglas corrected him, tersely. 'Yes. Might as well. Got to get through the night somehow.' He looked bloated and heavy, face red, eyes fathoms deep in distress.

'How serious is it?' Simon asked.

Douglas sighed gustily. Then he shrugged. 'It depends. Julia's the one I'm worried about.'

'That girl really is your daughter, then?'

'Yes. She's been brought up by her grandmother. I've been sending them money every month, but I've not seen Rose since she was born.' He downed his brandy then reached for the decanter to refill his glass.

Simon sat down suddenly, as if his legs had given way. 'I'd no idea. And, you mean, Julia never knew of her

219

existence?' he asked, appalled.

Douglas rubbed his forehead distractedly. 'Rose was born before Lily came to work here.'

Simon looked horrified. 'Douglas, I don't believe I'm hearing this. You get a girl pregnant, she has your baby, and then you have her working here as a servant? What the hell did you think you were doing?'

'It wasn't as simple as that,' Douglas retorted angrily.

'It rarely is,' his step-father-in-law said cynically. 'But moving your mistress into your house as a maid really stinks, Douglas.'

'It wasn't me who took her on . . .'

'Then who the hell else decided to employ her?'

'Julia,' he replied quietly.

'*Julia*?' Simon's jaw dropped. 'Didn't she know?'

'Of course she didn't.'

Simon assumed a sarcastic expression. 'Oh, bad luck! But having her on the premises all the time would have been much more convenient for you, wouldn't it?'

Douglas glared at him. 'The whole thing was a ghastly mess, but it happened a long time ago. It's history.'

'How did your neighbour find out, then? And why did she spring this on you? It was an act of pure vindictiveness. What have you done to upset her?'

'What have I done to upset *her*?' Douglas demanded, enraged. 'You mean, what has *she* done to upset *me*? We've had nothing but trouble from her since she moved in three years ago. The woman's off her head. She's evil. I intend to sue her, but right now I have to think about protecting Julia and the children . . .'

'Isn't it rather late for that?'

'Will you get off my case?' Douglas bellowed. 'You're not even Julia's real father! What gives you the right to lecture me?' he added, slamming out of the study and walking straight into Vivien, who was looking for her husband.

'Excuse me,' he said, pushing roughly past.

'Come and sit down, darling,' Simon said when she entered the study. She was pale and looked around nervously, as if searching for the reason for Douglas's angry exit from the room.

'Can I get you a drink?' he asked.

'I'd just like a glass of mineral water, dearest.' She lowered herself on to one of the leather sofas by the fireplace, suddenly feeling like an old woman, deeply tired and with aching joints. 'This whole thing has become something of a nightmare, hasn't it? Have you seen Julia? I can't find her anywhere.'

'She's up in her room with Michael. She said they were going to watch the fireworks from there.'

'Did she tell you that? Where did you see her?'

'I bumped into her in the marquee a little while ago. She was looking for Anna and William.'

Vivien looked wistful. 'Julia never tells me anything. Why is she so secretive, Simon? Why doesn't she confide in me, like other daughters?'

He regarded her with thoughtful tenderness. 'Perhaps she feels the need to create her own identity, darling. Cut the umbilical cord, and all that.'

'But if I ask her anything, she makes me feel I'm intruding.'

'And how much, my darling, have you ever let her into your life?'

'But that was different! When Guido was killed I wanted to protect her. She was only four. I couldn't let her see my devastation.'

'But she's not four any longer, Vivien. She's a woman of forty-four, married and with three children. Believe me, she's strong, too. She'd have to be to survive twenty-five years of being married to Douglas.'

Vivien looked down at her hands, twisting the rings on her long fingers. 'Then why does she make me feel shut out, Simon?'

He crossed to where she was sitting, and bent to kiss her. 'How do you know you don't make her feel shut out?' he asked gently.

Before she could stop herself, Vivien's hand flew to her breast. Flushing, she pretended to be fiddling with her long ropes of pearls.

'Perhaps you're right. Maybe I should go to her now. How much truth was there in what that strange girl said, do you think?'

Simon raised enquiring eyebrows. 'Meaning . . .?'

Vivien spoke nervously, her voice lowered. 'Well, she couldn't really have meant Douglas actually *killed* her mother. I mean, she was referring to . . . to something like a broken heart, wasn't she?'

'I've no idea, darling. I didn't even know until tonight that he had ever had a mistress, far less a child, and I can't say I remember hearing of anyone dying in this house.'

There was silence in the room as each of them tentatively explored their own thoughts, scared at what they might come up with, fearful of vocalising their darkest fears.

Eventually Vivien spoke. 'What's going to happen now? It's bound to be in all the newspapers tomorrow, but nobody is going to take the accusation of murder seriously, are they?'

Simon sighed deeply. 'God knows. That girl is either a bit of a loony or Douglas is in deep trouble.' He rose, catching her hand to pull her gently to her feet. 'I think we should get back to the party, don't you? We should put on a show of family unity.'

'You go back. I think I'll slip upstairs to see Julia. Ask if there is anything I can do.'

There was no response at first when Vivien knocked on Julia's bedroom door, and then just as she was going to slip away, privately thankful she would not have to face an emotional confrontation, the door opened and her daughter stood there, looking at her in surprise.

'Hello, Ma,' she said, voice kept deliberately light.

Vivien gazed at her with something approaching awe as she saw the pain on Julia's face, combined with the dignity with which she was holding herself together. 'Come in. Michael and I have been watching the party from the window . . .' Her voice drifted away and she turned back into the bedroom and led the way over to the window. It was a light airy room, decorated in ivory, with a four-poster bed swagged with voluminous folds of natural-coloured slubbed cotton, which also hung in rich folds at the window. Bowls of white flowers, soft lighting and an abundance of creamy linen cushions on the *chaise-longue* added to the atmosphere of simple luxury.

'I wanted to make sure you were all right, darling. Is there anything I can do?' Vivien asked, keeping her voice light, too, realising this was not the time for an intimate *tête-a-tête*, with Michael kneeling on the window seat, listening to every word.

'I don't think so, thank you, Ma. Everyone seems to be enjoying themselves.' Julia had resumed her position beside her son with her arms around him and her back to the room as they gazed down at the lawn. Then, as if she realised that might sound unfriendly, she turned to look at Vivien over her shoulder.

'We'll talk tomorrow, Ma. I'm so glad you're here for the whole weekend.'

'So am I, sweetheart,' Vivien responded warmly. There wasn't anything else to say at that moment, but at least she felt more reassured that Julia might open up when they were alone the next day. She hoped so, for she needed to be needed, and wanted to be a real mother to her daughter, instead of a glamorous figure in the background. But then, with a stab of dread, she realised it must work both ways. If she expected Julia to confide in her, then she in turn must confide in Julia, and for reasons unfathomable even to herself she knew that wouldn't be easy.

'Did you know anything about Douglas having another child?' Leonora asked Peter as they sat in the marquee, he drinking heavily by now, while she watched the dancers with envious eyes, wishing someone would whisk her on to the floor and hold her close while The Dark Blues played 'Lady in Red'. 'You haven't said a word about it all evening,' she added accusingly.

'I was stuck with some of Douglas's business friends,' he replied. 'To them, mistresses and random illegitimate children seem to go with the territory of being rich and successful. I didn't feel inclined to discuss my brother's sexual activities with them.'

Leonora looked sharply at him, seeing as she always did a pale, prissy edition of Douglas.

'But aren't you surprised?' she persisted, opening her evening bag and taking out a packet of cigarettes. She knew he hated her smoking but tonight she didn't care. The fact that Douglas had had an affair had surprised her, although to annoy Pammy she'd said that he had had lots of lovers; this was to suggest she might even have had one with him herself, which gave her an edge over Pammy.

Peter shrugged. 'Not really. He's always lived in the fast lane.'

'It's very hard on your mother and father, though. They're too old to have a shock like this.' Leonora inhaled deeply, feeling the effects of the nicotine tingle deliciously down to her toes.

Peter's voice was dry. 'They'll be fine. Douglas could never do any wrong in their eyes.'

'She wasn't as pretty as Cressida and Sasha.'

'Who wasn't?'

'Oh, for goodness' sake, Peter! That girl. Rose. She wasn't as pretty as our daughters.'

'I can't see what that has to do with anything,' he replied coldly, refilling his glass from the bottle the waiter had left on the table.

Harry Clegg and Jim Polack had left Cherry Tree Cottage and were racing along the M3 in the direction of London, in a determined effort to catch the deadline for the Sunday morning edition. It was a clear fine night and Harry put his foot flat down. The Saab roared through the darkness at such speed the cat's-eyes down the centre of the motorway seemed to slip past in one continuous stream of light.

They were some way behind all the other journalists but they'd got something their rivals hadn't: an exclusive. A story that made sense of the whole extraordinary drama, although there were elements that didn't quite hang together and needed researching.

Grabbing his car mobile, Harry punched the repeat button for the *Globe*'s news desk number.

'Diary, please,' he said succinctly when he got through. A minute later he was talking to one of his colleagues. Unfortunately it was George Moore, a green hack fresh from a provincial newspaper whose idea of a scoop was covering a village fête.

'George? Harry Clegg here. Listen, can you find out the coroner's verdict at the inquest of a woman called Lily Watson, in the village of Stickley, near Stockbridge in Hampshire, who died in August, 1980? What? I know it's the fucking middle of the night. Listen, she died in a house called Highfield Manor, belonging to the famous restaurateur, Douglas Rutherford.'

There was a pause as he listened, gripping the steering wheel with one hand, eyes eagle sharp on the road. Then he made an explosive noise in his throat. 'I *know* the fucking coroner's office will be shut at this time of night . . . so look in the cutting-room files, for fuck's sake! Look under Rutherford. Or Lily Watson. Have you got that? I need to know whether we're dealing with murder or accidental death.'

It was nearly midnight. Unable to sleep, Nancy Graham slipped on her overcoat and went out into her garden. Over the top of the wall she could watch the proceedings, unobserved, so long as no one came too close. She knew there was to be a firework display at midnight, and had decided to watch it. After all, why not? The Rutherfords had excluded her from everything else in the past three years, but they couldn't prevent her watching this: a display of fire and explosives that aptly symbolised the turbulent emotions within that terrible family at this very moment. Huddled under the branches of a hawthorn, she waited, listening to the distant throb of the music, and the soft murmur of voices as people strolled in the garden. This, she thought with satisfaction, is undoubtedly Douglas Rutherford's swan song. And she felt a surge of pleasure to be in at the kill.

The thunderous explosions sent a deep shudder through the earth and split the black sky into a million fragments of tiny glittering fire, as bursts of gold and silver, overlaid with blue and red and green, spun through the air – whirling, floating, dropping gracefully into oblivion – to be instantly replaced by fresh shooting stars to join the non-stop galaxy. The sky was incandescent, lighting the upturned faces of the guests as they stood on lawn and terrace, watching a pyrotechnic display that was costing Douglas thirty thousand pounds. They counted aloud as each rocket produced several starbursts, like giant shimmering chrysanthemums raining down from heaven: 'One . . . two . . . three . . . four . . .' And finally a thrilled: '*five!*'

Amid the laughter and revelry on the terrace, no one realised that Julia stood above them in her bedroom window, a silvery ghost-like figure, illuminated by each shower of sparks. Michael knelt in front of her, leaning out, his expression transfixed.

'Look, Mum!' he kept exclaiming. 'Wow! I've never seen anything like this before.'

Suddenly, she felt a presence behind her and, turning, saw it was Douglas. He was looking at her anxiously, his eyes tender.

'Everyone is missing you, darling,' he said, putting his arm around her. 'Won't you come down to the garden with me?'

She stiffened at his touch.

'I don't think so.' Her averted profile was outlined as a myriad silver streamers cascaded over the garden.

'Please, sweetheart. Just for a few minutes. For the children's sake. Anna's been asking where you are and so has William.'

Ignoring him, Julia spoke to Michael. 'Do you want to go down to the garden?'

He spun round, and was halfway across the bedroom before he spoke. 'Yeah! Let's go! We'll see even better.'

And so it was, a few moments later, that Julia and Douglas stepped on to the terrace through the drawing-room windows. To those who saw them it seemed the earlier débâcle had not affected them too much. Douglas was holding Julia's hand in his firm grip and she appeared pale but composed. Michael held her other hand, and Anna and William came and stood beside them. There was a flash and a photographer caught the moment on film. When the photograph was later reproduced in *Hello!* magazine, readers could be forgiven for thinking it had been taken at the beginning of the party, rather than the end.

It was close to dawn and the garden was deserted but music still throbbed from the exotic depths of the marquee, vying oddly with the dawn chorus. Only Anna and William's friends stayed on, not wanting the revelries to end as they danced frenetically amid the dying glory of the Venetian *palazzo*, while the remaining waiters stood around, wan and wilting and wondering what time the first train left Stockbridge for London.

Six hundred and fifty-two bottles of Moët & Chandon, two hundred and twenty bottles of Chablis and two hundred and eighteen bottles of burgundy had been drunk, while six hundred and fifty scallops, fifteen hundred frogs' legs, one hundred and fifty lobsters, three hundred and thirty pigeons and two hundred pounds of strawberries and raspberries had been eaten. Together with the decorations, including flowers, the band, the fireworks, the elegantly printed invitations, not to mention the chefs, barmen, waiters and the marquee itself, the whole evening had cost Douglas well over three hundred and fifty thousand pounds.

As he stood in the study window, gazing out at the tawdry remains of the night by dawn's cold light, the marquee looked to him more like a drooping grey elephant, flapping sad ears in the breeze, than a tight white circus top, resounding to the laughter of the clowns. The only clown tonight had been him, and tears of rage and regret gathered in his glowering eyes as he stood alone, a final drink in his hand. Then he turned sharply away and put down his glass before trailing forlornly upstairs to bed.

At last the long night came to an end, finally fizzling out as parties do, with drunkenness, disillusion and disappointment meted out in equal measure to those with the stamina to stay to the end, which for some was often bitter. The music had stopped, the field of cars was empty, the exhausted chefs and waiters had vanished. A few personal articles lay abandoned; a chiffon scarf, an evening purse, a waistcoat, and, inexplicably, one gold high-heeled sandal.

Alone at last, Julia walked around the garden, thanking God it was all over. Not for the first time in her life she'd been forced to draw on her own inner strength, but never before had the cause of her anguish been so terrible, or her misery so absolute. Assured that her mother and Simon and Douglas's parents had gone to bed, she slipped away, using the back stairs in case she met any of the others in the houseparty, and hurried up to their dressing room. Douglas was asleep in their four-poster bed, but tonight she knew she could not bear to share it with him. Longing to lie alone in the comfort of smooth linen sheets and soft pillows, she undressed quickly and got into the single Empire bed that was hardly ever used.

At last the stillness of being alone in an empty room. At last the final shedding of the self-control that had kept her going through the night. But there was no peace; while her body rested, her mind continued to rage, and the reality of what had happened sixteen years ago still had to be faced.

Sunday

23 June 1996

Ten

It was half-past seven in the morning when Anna was
startled to hear mournful warbling coming from the
kitchen. She paused in the hall for a moment to listen.

. . . After the ball is over, after the break of morn,
After the dancers' leaving, after the stars are gone,
Many a heart is aching if you could read them all,
Many the hopes that have vanished, after the ball . . .

It was Mrs Morgan, who, when she was on her own, was
inclined to sing sentimental old ballads learned from her
mother, a former music hall singer. This morning, however, the aptness of the words brought tears to Anna's
eyes. Apart from the disastrous scene last night which
had cast a blight over everything, she felt tired, hung over,
and dangerously vulnerable. The slightest thing was going
to make her weepy and she was dreading the coming day,
with a house full of people to be polite to, and Petroc
arguing with everything she said. Well, maybe not everything . . . but she felt very aggrieved that he was not being
more sympathetic towards her father.

Barging into the kitchen, she endeavoured to sound
brisk.

'Good morning, Mrs Morgan. You're up bright and early.'

Caught in mid-warble, the cook's face flushed guiltily, as she wiped the top of the Aga with exaggerated vigour.

'Good morning, Anna. I'm surprised to see you up so early.' She sounded almost accusing.

'I haven't been to bed yet. I thought I'd make some coffee,' Anna replied lightly, taking the percolator off the shelf by the stove, and filling the container with the fragrant grounds of Blue Mountain.

'Enjoy yourself last night, did you?'

'It was wonderful,' Anna replied non-committally.

'Everything all right then?'

'Yes.'

'Have you seen your ma and pa this morning? Are they down yet?'

'I don't know,' she replied, curt for once. If Mrs Morgan was bursting with curiosity and wanted to gossip, Anna had never felt less inclined to talk. Reaching for a mug from the dresser shelf, and then going to the fridge to get out the milk, she remained stonily silent.

'It must have given you all a shock . . . that girl turning up like that?' Mrs Morgan persisted.

Anna shrugged. From the tented extension of the kitchen she could hear the extra staff preparing breakfast for the house guests. The tantalising aroma of grilled bacon drifted on the morning air.

'Do you want something to eat?' Mrs Morgan asked, as Anna sniffed appreciatively.

'No, thanks.'

'Got to keep your strength up, you know.'

'I'm fine.'

But she wasn't fine. She was dying quietly inside, like a

four-year-old child who wanted to run, sobbing, to Mummy and be assured that everything was all right. Last night, swept along by all her friends and a steady intake of champagne, plus the excitement of the whole evening, she'd been able to keep going because a part of her had refused to take in the reality of the situation. Looking back now, there had been a surreal, almost bizarre atmosphere overshadowing the party, from the moment that girl . . . her half-sister? . . . had appeared in her Cinderella costume. The theatrical setting of a *faux-palazzo* had contrived to add to the strangeness, too, but at the time none of it had seemed to matter. She'd floated through the whole night in a daze, remembering now only quick flashbacks, like watching snatches of a film's trailer; Petroc's surprise arrival, Daddy's speech, the tinkling sound of a spoon tapping a glass before Nancy Graham spoke, and then the appearance of a white-faced girl . . . and after that pain and confusion, blurred by glass after glass of champagne.

Now, in the unrelenting sunshine of the next morning, everything was hideously clear. Her father had had an affair some years ago and Anna had a half-sister called Rose.

The police arrived at Highfield Manor at nine-thirty, parking their car in the drive and ringing the front door bell in a civilised fashion. Morgan, without showing a flicker of emotion on his impassive face, showed them into the study from where he'd earlier eradicated all traces of the party, and said he'd tell Mr Rutherford they wanted to see him.

Douglas had got up early, looking incredibly robust and bright-eyed in spite of only having had two hours' sleep, and was enjoying a hearty breakfast in the dining room with several of his house guests when Morgan delivered the message in a low monotone.

'Will you all excuse me? No peace for the wicked,' he observed, smiling blandly around the breakfast table before rising and sauntering off to the study as if he had all the time in the world. He'd already confiscated the Sunday newspapers, having scanned the lurid headlines first with a cold, sinking feeling.

Julia had not appeared for breakfast, and neither had any of the grandparents, but the others watched him go with curious eyes.

'May I be excused?' Michael asked William, in a perilously high-pitched voice. His face was white.

'Have you had any breakfast?' his brother asked.

'I'm not hungry,' Michael replied, sliding off his seat and pushing away his untouched cereal.

'OK.' William smiled at him understandingly. 'Why don't you go and feed your rabbit? I expect he'd like breakfast.'

'I don't think he's hungry either,' Michael retorted, dashing from the room. They could hear his footsteps as he ran up the stairs and back to his own room. Then his door slammed.

'So what happens now?' Pammy Schemmel breathed, agog, her eyes like cold bright marbles. 'Will he be arrested on a charge of homicide?'

Roger turned on her. 'Oh, for Christ's sake, Pammy! Stop talking such crap! Douglas hasn't done anything . . . and as his oldest friend I should know. But the police have to follow up even the wildest accusations as a matter of routine. They'll want to know what the hell that old bitch next door was talking about.' He glared at her with bloodshot eyes. He not only had a splitting headache after last night, he'd also come to the conclusion he no longer even liked Pammy and was wondering how he could get her out of his life without too much of a scene.

'Well, that's not my fault,' she retorted, offended.

Oonagh eyed Pammy with fastidious distaste. Although she herself hadn't gone to bed until five o'clock, she looked groomed to perfection, her make-up immaculate, her cream trousers and silk shirt without a crease. And two Veganine and a glass of Alka-Selzter before she'd gone to sleep had ensured she awoke without a hangover. 'You should be careful what you say,' she remarked warningly. 'Christopher and I were talking last night, and we decided we should all make a pact. None of us should discuss what's happened with anyone . . .'

'. . . and none of us should talk to the press, or be inveigled into giving even an informal interview,' Christopher cut in.

'I don't intend to talk to anyone about it,' Pammy snapped huffily. 'I'd merely like to know what's going on, or is that a crime, too?'

'Oh, shut up,' said Roger furiously. 'Your mouth is as big as the Internet! Tell you anything and it's like putting an ad on satellite television.'

Pammy jumped to her feet, her narrow face puckered with rage. '*Fuck you*!' she hollered, upsetting her cup of coffee. 'I'm not going to stay here and be insulted . . .'

'Good!' Roger yelled back, moustache bristling.

Peter rose, every inch the headmaster disciplining his unruly pupils. 'Now let's not get overexcited,' he said calmly. 'We're all tired after last night, but getting het up isn't going to help anyone. Let's wait quietly until Douglas tells us what's happening, and meanwhile I suggest we stop speculating until we know the facts. This is probably just a storm in a teacup whipped up by a vengeful old woman.'

William looked at his uncle in disbelief. 'We're not a bunch of third-form kids, you know,' he reminded him. 'I agree we should keep our mouths shut in public, but we can't shut our eyes and ears. You only had to look at Dad's face last night to see he's as guilty as hell.'

'I think he's definitely guilty of having an affair, and I'm sure that was his daughter,' Leonora agreed, 'but I don't for one moment believe he murdered her mother.'

Peter glanced warningly at her, as if he thought she had already said too much.

'It's bad enough he had an affair,' William persisted, 'But to have a child as well! Has anyone seen Mum this morning?'

Caroline, always the observer, silent and watchful, said, 'No. She was still up when I went to bed, and that must have been at half-past five. I expect she'll sleep late this morning.'

'She must be exhausted,' Stephanie remarked sadly. She was sitting beside William, and from time to time stroked his thigh under the dining-room table. 'Last night must have been terrible for her.'

'But worse for Douglas,' Roger retorted tartly. It seemed that ranks were already being drawn up, and sides taken.

At that moment Tim, followed by Cressida and Sasha, came into the dining room. He instantly sensed the tension in the atmosphere.

'What's up?' he asked his father.

Christopher glanced at him. 'Nothing's up, old chap,' he said carefully. Then he looked at the two girls. 'Why don't you all come and have some breakfast? I was wondering if you'd like a foursome at tennis afterwards? Cressida? Sasha? What do you say?'

They stared at him, sulky and sour-faced. Bitterly disappointed that last night had not produced a single man who'd shown interest in either of them, they were not in the mood to humour him.

'I'd rather lie by the pool,' Sasha commented ungraciously. Cressida didn't say anything at all.

'Well . . . have some breakfast anyway,' Christopher remarked easily, waving his arm in the direction of the sideboard on which stood an array of dishes. 'I can recommend the bacon and the sausages. They're delicious.'

'Ugh!' Sasha groaned, with a grimace. 'I can't think of anything worse. I'll have a glass of orange juice.'

'Where is everyone?' Tim enquired, looking at the empty places.

'Around,' said Christopher, still trying to sound conversational. 'I don't suppose we'll see any of the grandparents until lunchtime.'

This was greeted with silence. Knives scraping butter on to toast and cups chinking against saucers were the loudest noises in the stifling atmosphere. Cressida sighed as if from acute boredom. The air jangled with dissent, and Christopher realised it was going to be a dislocated sort of day, where everyone felt displaced and in limbo, not belonging here and yet tied by bonds of allegiance. It would be hurtful to abandon Julia and Douglas by returning to London this morning when they'd made arrangements to have everyone stay for the whole weekend, yet it was going to be hell to stay. Then he thought of Barbara, alone in her flat, and knew he must phone her as soon as Oonagh went out into the garden.

★ ★ ★

'We're sorry to disturb you so early, Mr Rutherford,' Detective Inspector Lester Swann said when Douglas swept into the study, head held high, manner brisk, like a man about to chair a board meeting.

'It's no problem,' he replied, indicating where they might sit. 'Would you like some coffee? Tea?' It was obvious to DI Swann and his sidekick, Detective Sergeant Harry Newton, that Douglas intended to try and take charge of the interview.

'No, thanks,' they murmured in unison.

'It's no trouble,' he assured them affably. 'Right now there are about three staff to every house guest, so why don't you make the most of it?'

Once again they refused, more firmly this time.

'Right.' Douglas seated himself behind his vast desk and looked at them expectantly. 'You've obviously come about my vengeful neighbour, last night's gate-crasher, and the wild accusations made about me in the tabloids this morning. So . . . how can I help you?'

'We're looking into the possibility of reopening the case on Miss Lily Watson who died in this house sixteen years ago . . .' DI Swann began.

'On what grounds?' Douglas asked swiftly. 'The autopsy revealed she died of anaphylactic shock as the result of being stung by a bee to which she was allergic. At the inquest the verdict was accidental death.' He shrugged. 'End of story. A very tragic affair, but there's nothing else I can tell you.'

'New evidence has been brought to our notice which suggests her death may not have been accidental,' DI Swann pointed out.

'New evidence?' Douglas laughed. 'What's that barmy

old woman next door been telling you? That someone purposely got hold of a bee, and told it to sting Lily Watson? My dear fellow, that's a bit far-fetched, isn't it?' He paused and looked serious. 'Look, she was alone in the house when she picked up a jar of jam or marmalade or something, and by accident was stung. The local GP told us that if someone is allergic to bees, they can die very quickly after a sting. Fifteen minutes, maybe twenty . . .'

'We know all that,' Swann interrupted, 'but the point is we now have reason to believe she was not alone in the house.'

Douglas looked at him blankly. 'That's impossible. My wife and I were out, our children were too, with their nanny, and the gardener never arrived until lunchtime. In those days we didn't have living-in staff. We had various dailies and Lily was one of them. There was no one in the house. Don't you think if there had been, they'd have rung for an ambulance? Called for help?'

'So you're saying the house was empty, apart from Lily Watson. For how long?' Newton caught Swann's eye. Mrs Graham had told them something quite different.

Douglas's blue eyes were round and candid. 'God, it was so long ago . . . I don't think I can remember all the details. I know I went out immediately after breakfast, to cut the brambles on the far side of our wood, and that I came back to the house around noon. That's when I found Lily.'

'Where exactly did you find her?' Swann asked.

'In the larder. On the floor. I remember several wasps were flying around, after the spilt marmalade. I was told she'd been dead an hour and a half when I found her.' He spoke in a clipped, matter-of-fact tone, his voice devoid of emotion.

Detective Sergeant Newton was making rapid notes. Detective Inspector Swann spoke again. 'What was your relationship with Lily Watson?'

Douglas swallowed. 'We were . . . had been . . . lovers.'

'Were or had been?'

'Had been.'

'And is it true she had a child? Your child?'

'Yes.'

'The young girl, called Rose Watson, who was brought to your party last night by your neighbour, Mrs Nancy Graham?'

'I'd call it "gate-crashed" rather than "brought".'

There was a pause. Douglas and Swann locked eyes, sizing each other up, while Newton scratched away with his pencil.

Then Swann spoke again. 'Did you ever deny this girl was your baby? Or did you take Lily Watson's word for it?'

'She was my baby, all right. There was no one else in Lily's life.'

'Are you sure about that?'

'Absolutely certain.' He thought about Lily, all those years ago, clinging to him, begging him to run away with her and the baby, refusing to believe that he had decided to stay with Julia. She'd looked at him with those blue, rather staring eyes of hers, her face white and pinched, and the tears had slid down her cheeks and dropped off her jawline on to her cheap cotton blouse.

'You can't leave me now,' she'd wept, 'not me and little Rosie. We belong . . .'

But he'd pushed her gently away, saddened that his own desire for her had passed as completely as if it had never been; disillusioned with himself for what he had done and what he was doing.

When she'd turned up for work at Highfield Manor a few weeks later, he'd been appalled. At least she'd left Rose in the care of her mother, but suppose Julia, who had so trustingly and unsuspectingly employed her, found out what had been going on between himself and Lily? He remembered now how angry he'd been with Lily, accusing her of taking the job in order to stir up trouble.

Swann broke into his thoughts. 'And you're also positive there was no one else in the house on the morning when Lily died?'

'I know there was no one else in the house,' he retorted angrily. 'My wife was in the village, shopping . . .'

'What? All morning?'

'Yes. Look, we've been through all this. Why don't you go through the statements we made at the time? Nothing's changed so why go over the whole thing again? It's difficult enough to remember what happened this time last week, far less sixteen years ago, for God's sake!' He'd risen from his swivel chair behind the desk and was walking towards the study door, as if to bring the interview to an end.

'You say nothing's changed, Mr Rutherford. I have to tell you that things have changed, sufficiently for us to consider reopening the case.'

Douglas looked at Swann defiantly. 'What possible new evidence can you have?' he asked challengingly. 'It was a tragic accident. It could have happened to any of us if we were allergic to bees.'

'We have several people we wish to talk to; I believe one of them will be able to tell us exactly what happened.'

★ ★ ★

'Let's sit on the terrace, it's such a fabulous day,' Caroline suggested as breakfast came to an end.

'What a good idea,' Oonagh agreed, rising from the table. 'Do you suppose there are some Sunday news-papers around anywhere? There's nothing I like more than reading the papers on a Sunday morning.'

'Bound to be. I'll ask Morgan.'

Christopher, Tim and the girl cousins also rose, not to play tennis as Christopher had suggested but to lounge around the pool. Pammy had marched off to her room to pack, demanding that Roger drive her back to London immediately.

At that moment Morgan appeared, to ask if anyone would like some fresh coffee.

'No, thank you,' Caroline replied, 'but we did wonder if there were any Sunday newspapers?'

He looked shifty and busied himself clearing the dishes off the sideboard. 'I haven't seen any this morning, madam,' he replied vaguely.

They caught each other's eye, knowing what that meant.

'Perhaps one of us could drive into the village and buy some more?' Oonagh whispered, as she and Caroline strolled on to the terrace where Morgan had already arranged the pastel-coloured cushions on the cane chairs and put up the cream linen umbrellas.

'It's obvious Julia and Douglas don't want us all to see them.'

'Where *is* Julia?'

'I don't know. I hope she's all right.'

'Should we try and find her?' There was something faintly gloating in Oonagh's tone.

'She'd hate that,' Caroline retorted. 'She'll appear when she's good and ready. She's probably awfully tired, in any case.'

Leonora, coming through the drawing-room windows, walked across the flagstones to join them. She was wearing scarlet trousers and lipstick to match and her bra showed through her thin shirt.

'Where is everyone?' she asked in a bored voice. 'The party's really over, isn't it? Peter's gone upstairs to lie down because he's got a headache. Is Douglas still talking to the police?'

Oonagh shrugged. 'Everyone seems to be at sixes and sevens this morning. Not surprising, I suppose.'

'It's going to be a long day.' Leonora sounded depressed. 'And it's going to get worse when my in-laws appear, and Julia's parents. Pat seemed to spend most of last night in tears because her beloved Douglas was in trouble, and I thought Reggie was going to have a heart attack at one point.'

'It's hardly surprising,' Caroline pointed out. 'Vivien and Simon are terribly upset by what's happened, too.'

Leonora moved restlessly. 'I wish there was something we could do. I loathe just sitting around waiting for something to happen.' She got to her feet, using her long red nails like combs to push her hair away from her face. 'I'm going to find Douglas. See what's going on.' Her high-heeled sandals clicked on the York stone of the terrace as she walked away.

Oonagh smiled maliciously. 'She's just dying to comfort him, isn't she?'

Making sure that Oonagh was settled on the terrace, talking to Caroline, Christopher slipped out of the house and got into his car where he dialled Barbara's number on his mobile.

She answered immediately, her voice soft and whispery. He steeled himself. 'It's me, Barbara. How are you?'

'Oh, Chris! How lovely to hear your voice. I've been thinking of you all weekend, and missing you dreadfully. Was the ball fun?'

'It was hellish, actually . . .'

'Oh, darling! Why? Have you been having a dreadful time with Oonagh?' she whispered sympathetically.

He visualised her lying on her enormous bed, sweet as a little kitten, her blonde hair tousled, her arms outstretched in welcome. He knew she was waiting for his return, and for a moment closed his eyes, overwhelmed by longing. Oh, God, he could die inside her, he groaned inwardly. The power her body exerted over him was intense even as he talked to her on the phone, and he knew that if he wasn't careful it could cause him to lose his firm resolve.

'Barbara . . .' he stammered, sweating.

'Darling? What's the matter? Aren't you well?'

'Yes . . . No. I mean . . .' He thought of his sister, shattered to find Douglas had had a mistress; he thought of Tim, who looked up to him and to whom he should be an example of honesty and decency. He remembered the hurt in Oonagh's eyes when she found out he was having an affair. But most of all, and to his own shame, he remembered Roger's words yesterday: 'Oonagh will crucify you . . .'

He loved his beautiful flat, and the antiques and paintings with which he'd filled it. He loved his Rolls-Royce, holidays around the world, his shooting weekends, going to the best restaurants, wearing bespoke suits and handmade shoes from Lobb's. In fact, he loved his whole damn' life style, which he'd worked like a dog to attain, and he had no intention of parting with any of it now.

There was something else too. Sitting in the marquee last night, he'd had a frightening presentiment; a glimpse of hell and what he imagined it must be like. That feeling of decadence and evil had stayed with him and made him oddly unsettled. The memory of Douglas's public shame had seared his conscience, a reminder that it could happen to him.

'Chris? Are you there?' Barbara's gentle voice broke into his thoughts.

He took a deep breath, eyes still closed. 'I'm ringing to say . . . I wanted to tell you . . . we've got to end it, Barbara. We've got to stop seeing each other.'

There was a long silence, and then he heard her crying softly.

'I'm sorry, darling,' he said wretchedly. 'It's the last thing I want to do.'

'You can't afford to leave her, can you?' she wept.

Christopher was startled, caught on the hop by her shrewdness. 'It's not that, sweetheart . . .'

'Oh, it is. It is! It cost my father a fortune when he left my mother. Somehow I never thought that you . . .' She broke off, unable to continue.

'I'd do anything not to have to hurt you.' Empty words and he knew it.

'Will I ever see you again?' she asked at last.

'Better not, darling. Clean cut and all that.' He heard his own voice and wondered, with dismay, how he could sound so callous.

She hung up then. There was a little click and it was all over. Slowly, Christopher switched off his mobile, feeling immensely tired and empty of all feeling. It was as if someone close to him had died and he couldn't take it in. He kept thinking he'd see Barbara again tomorrow. That nothing had really changed. He'd turn up at her apartment as usual and make love to her and she'd lie in his arms and . . . Oh, God! It was going to be so difficult.

Walking slowly back into the house, his hands in his pockets, he wondered when he'd tell Oonagh. Maybe straight away while he was still numb with shock? Yes, that would be best. And then with any luck life would soon get back to normal. Whatever normal was.

Several hours earlier, before Douglas or anyone else was awake, Julia had slid out of the bed in her dressing room and, pulling on jeans and a dark blue polo-neck sweater, had hurried downstairs and out of the house. Although her body was heavy with tiredness, her mind was maddeningly alert. She hadn't been able to sleep and now she couldn't rest. Like poison darts flying through the air, burning questions kept stabbing at her as she took the path that led to the woods.

Where had Douglas been when the baby had been born? she wondered, as if it was important after all these years. Had he managed to be present at the birth, while he'd spun some lie about working in the restaurant? Had he loved that tiny scrap of humanity he'd fathered as much as he'd loved Anna and William and Michael when they'd been born? But most of all, why . . . why . . . why had he let it happen?

Tears held back from last night poured from her eyes, falling in a continuous stream down her cheeks as if a tap had been turned on in her head and she'd forgotten how to turn it off. This was happening to someone else, not her, she thought. Or else she was being taken over by an external force that was operating her by remote control, obliterating her will to resist.

Frightened by the force of these uncontrollable emotions, she continued to stride on in the cool green shade of lime and ash and oak, while beneath her feet the ground was soft and damp, deadening her footfalls. There was no one about at this hour so she had no need to pretend to be in command of her feelings, and the relief that brought was immense. Sometimes sobbing loudly, sometimes stumbling because her eyes were so blurred with tears she couldn't see, she finally subsided on to the same fallen tree trunk that Anna had sat on with Tim a few days before, worn out with exhaustion and grief.

Julia sat there for a long time, gazing into space, her mind free from frantic activity at last, and gradually a soothing sense of calm stole over her. Taking a deep breath, she knew the worst of her emotional crisis had passed. She felt strangely peaceful now, washed and cleansed of the terrible sorrow that had nearly swept her away.

Lily was dead and a threat no more. If she had been able to survive that trauma, and all it had involved, Julia could survive this. Walking slowly now, she made her way back to the Manor. When she saw Oonagh and Caroline sitting on the terrace, she realised she must have been in the woods for several hours. And yet she was not ready to face them all yet. Not even her old friend Caroline. Taking a long route round behind the shrubbery that edged the outskirts of the garden, she made her way towards the marquee. It would be deserted today. Douglas had said the clearing up would not begin until Monday.

Pulling back a canvas flap, she slipped into the kitchen extension and was not surprised to find it neat and tidy, plates washed and stacked, glasses stored in boxes, cutlery piled in racks. The kitchen staff of any of Douglas's restaurants would not be allowed to leave things any other way.

Julia crossed to the other side, entering the main part of the marquee and standing, dismayed, at the sight that met her eyes. Her first thought was: How different it all looks from last night.

There were no spotlights now, cleverly placed to enhance the view of the Grand Canal, the golden gondola or the courtyard and its fountain; there was no flicker of hundreds of candles reflected in the mottled mirrors. Instead, lit only by the daylight coming through the black fabric ceiling which last night had blazed with a million tiny 'stars', the setting looked cheap and vulgar and false. Stained table cloths and dying flowers brought about the final disillusion that seemed to her at this moment to reflect life itself. Nothing is what it seems, she thought, seeing the Venetian *'palazzo'* for what it really was: a symbol of so much else. The gloss put on a marriage to make it appear better than it is. The veneer to cover the cracks in a relationship. Everything is deception and illusion and what is real doesn't bear close scrutiny. We are all conjurors, in our own way, making everything appear better than it is.

A sound behind her made her turn sharply. She saw Douglas standing a few feet away, a lonely-looking figure amid the ruins of last night's spectacle.

The ace illusionist, Julia thought, gazing back at him. The man who gives the appearance of creating miracles.

He spoke, grey eyes never leaving her face.

'I've been looking for you.'

'I went for a walk.'

'Are you all right?'

She shrugged but did not reply.

He came and sat down beside her, leaning his elbow on the table which was now strewn with debris. Someone had abandoned their mask, and it lay splattered with candlewax among the dead flowers.

'The police have been,' he said heavily.

Her head shot up. 'What did they want?'

'What they wanted last time. When Lily died.'

'But why? Why should they be asking questions again?' She sounded nervous.

'They're planning to reopen the case. They want fresh statements.'

Julia gasped. 'But her death was an accident! What more can we tell them?'

Douglas shook his head. 'According to them they've got fresh evidence. There's apparently someone who witnessed what happened.'

'I don't believe a word of it! Nancy Graham got that girl to make her accusation last night just to stir up trouble. Surely the police don't believe her?'

'Wait until you see the newspapers this morning! Especially the *Globe*. They obviously interviewed Nancy and she's gone into overdrive to make trouble for me.'

'But the police aren't accusing you, are they?' she asked, appalled.

Douglas grimaced then shrugged. 'As I'd been having an affair with Lily, I'm obviously number one suspect. Anyway, I've told them all I know, and suggested they go through their old files to look up our statements at the time. As I said to them, nothing's changed.'

There was a painful silence then Julia spoke. 'But something *has* changed.'

His eyes were like hot coals. 'What?'

'None of us, except for you and Lily of course, knew there was a . . . a baby,' she added with difficulty.

Douglas averted his face, intent on trying to scrape some wax off the discarded mask with his thumb nail. 'By the time Lily came to work here, she was living in Longford with her mother, who was looking after Rose as her own.'

How easily he says her name, Rose, Julia thought.

'So no one in Stickley knew Lily had had a baby?'

'That's right.'

'And was that for her sake or mine?' Julia asked with sudden sarcasm.

'It was a mistake,' he said wretchedly. 'You must believe me, darling. It wasn't meant to happen but Lily couldn't bear the idea of having an abortion, so when her mother agreed to look after the baby . . . well, it seemed like the only solution.' He looked at her then, piercing her with the agony in his eyes. 'I wanted to protect you, Julia. I never wanted you to know anything about it. And then you went and employed her as a cleaner!' He sank his head into his hands. 'I simply couldn't believe it.'

She looked defiant. 'You can't blame me for that. When I asked Mr Harris in the village if he knew of anyone who'd like a job, he said yes. Lily Watson, who used to work in his shop, was looking for work. How was I to know what had happened between you? I didn't realise you'd been having an affair with her until just before she died!' Julia added vehemently, and then burst into tears again, just when she'd thought she had no more to shed.

He placed his hand over hers, leaning forward so their heads almost touched. 'I'm so sorry . . . it was madness on my part. I never loved her, you know. Not like I love you. You're my life, Julia. You're everything I ever wanted. You must believe me, darling.'

'That didn't stop you from having an affair with her, did it?' she replied dully. 'You betrayed me, Douglas.'

'But never for a moment was she a threat to you as my wife, the mother of my children,' he added brokenly.

'Except that you had another child! How do you think I felt when I found out about her last night?'

'That's why I never wanted you to,' he bellowed, suddenly angry. 'I could kill that old bitch next door for bringing that girl here . . .'

'Your daughter,' she corrected him.

'Yes, well, she doesn't feel like a daughter and she never did. The point is the police, not to mention the press, are going to dredge up the whole business now.'

'I suppose we were lucky, when Lily died, that the newspapers didn't make a big splash out of it then.'

'Because there was no story! A servant died from a bee sting in a country house. The coroner's verdict was accidental death. There was a one-inch piece in the *Evening Standard*, that was all.'

'Because your PR kept your name out of it,' Julia reminded him. 'You'd just started your cookery series on television, and the BBC didn't think it would look good.'

Douglas grunted disconsolately. 'Christ, what a mess.'

'So what happens now?'

'The police said they were going to continue with their enquiries and that I'd be hearing from them again.'

Julia looked strained. 'I mean . . . what's going to happen about us?'

'Us?' His eyes blazed at her defiantly. 'What do you mean . . . us? We're all right, aren't we, darling? We still love each other. More than ever, in fact. This isn't going to make a difference, is it? For God's sake, Julia, don't look at me like that!'

She was staring at him as if he were a stranger. 'You'll never know how much you've hurt me, Douglas.'

'Oh, my darling . . .' He slid off the chair and fell to his knees at her feet, this powerful burly man, brought down in a rush of remorse and regret. 'My Julia, my Julia,' he wept, burying his face in her lap. 'I'm so sorry. The last thing in the world I want is for you to be unhappy. Can you forgive me? I know I can never forgive myself for what happened, but please say you'll forgive me?'

She didn't answer, but sat staring with unfocused eyes at the backdrop of the Grand Canal, remembering the first time she'd been to Venice as a naïve young woman, wildly in love, determined to keep this ebullient, charismatic man she'd just married by her side as long as they both lived. They would never, she'd sworn to herself, separate or divorce. Whatever effort it took on her part, she would stay with him, become the other half of his soul, the flame that lit his spirit with joy. Together they would face the future, and stay faithful to each other for eternity. Two beings carved from the same stone. Two bodies designed for each other and no one else.

Douglas had lifted his head and was watching her anxiously, waiting for her to speak. But she couldn't. He'd smashed her dreams and betrayed her love when he'd had an affair with Lily seventeen years ago. When she'd found out, there were moments when she thought she'd have a nervous breakdown, and in the secret chambers of her heart she couldn't prevent a feeling of relief when Lily had died. But this was different. There'd been a baby. The fruits of Douglas's loins had impregnated another woman, underscoring the deep intimacy of that relationship.

'I don't know. I need time,' she said, rising and leaving the marquee.

Christopher joined Oonagh and Caroline on the terrace, wondering how he could get his wife on her own for a few minutes. He needed to speak to her quickly, before he lost his nerve, but she seemed settled in for a chat and he knew she'd never agree to his suggestion that they go for a walk. Oonagh never walked anywhere, nor did she play tennis which exhausted her, nor swim because it ruined her hair.

'Anyone like some coffee?' he asked instead.

'I'd love some,' Caroline said immediately. 'All that champagne last night had really dehydrated me.' She jumped to her feet. 'What about you, Oonagh?'

She shook her sleek dark head. 'No, thanks.' She glanced at Christopher. 'He'll get it for you.'

'No, I'll get it,' Caroline said swiftly. 'Can I get you some too, Chris?'

'No, thanks, I'm fine.'

'OK.'

As she walked away, Oonagh said: 'Why were you offering coffee if you didn't want any and weren't prepared to get it for us either?'

He sat down in the cane chair opposite her. 'Because I want to talk to you, alone.'

'I can't imagine why,' she said sullenly.

Her tone irritated him. Here he was, trying to offer the olive branch, but it was obvious she was going to be bitchy. But what was new? He forced his features into friendly lines and spoke.

'I wanted you to know that it's all over between Barbara and me. I'm really sorry I caused you so much distress, but it will never happen again, I promise. I wondered if you'd like us to take a trip . . .'

'You can forget it, Chris,' she snapped. 'I've had it with you. You've humiliated me.''

'How have I humiliated you? No one knows except you and me. Unless of course you've been telling everyone I've been having an affair . . .'

She smoothed the knee of her cream linen trousers and flicked off an invisible speck. 'Everyone can see there's a rift between us. Roger was saying . . .'

'Roger? What the hell has he got to do with it?'

A pale flush rose to her cheeks. 'He was very sympathetic yesterday when he saw I was upset. I'd made up my mind that I'd like to make a go of our marriage, especially after that fearful scene with Douglas and his bastard child, but then . . . well, Roger asked me to dance. He's a very kind man. It made me realise that I don't have to put up with a husband who cheats on me.'

Christopher looked at her in astonishment, realising she meant what she said. 'He made a pass at you, didn't he?'

Oonagh's flush deepened. 'I wouldn't exactly say that.'

'Well, I would. The fucking little creep! I thought he was supposed to be with that bloody American.' Christopher felt incensed.

'Pammy's packing. She's going back to London before lunch.'

'With Roger?'

'I don't . . . I don't know.'

'You bloody well do,' he said accusingly. 'I can see it in your face. So what happened while I was doing my duty dances with Julia's friends? Did you sneak off for a quickie in the summer house with Roger? Or go behind the shrubbery?'

'Keep your voice down,' Oonagh hissed, looking up at the open bedroom windows above them. 'We don't want the entire household to know our business. And anyway,' she continued, black eyes flashing, 'who are you to talk? How long have you been sleeping with *your* bit of fluff? And how many others have there been that I don't know about?'

Christopher gritted his teeth and tried to control the extraordinary rage he felt at the thought of Oonagh being unfaithful to him.

'There have been no others,' he retorted.

'Well, I want a divorce.'

'Don't be silly, Oonagh. Of course you don't. We'll fly to the Caribbean or wherever you want and have a lovely . . .'

'Don't patronise me,' she said icily. 'My mind is made up. We're not suited anyway. You're always working, and I like to socialise.'

As he sat on the terrace, stunned and in shock, all he could think of was that it had been Roger who'd advised him against playing around because otherwise he risked a very expensive divorce.

'Have you seen Julia?' Vivien asked Caroline as they bumped into each other in the hall.

'No. I don't think she's down yet. How are you this morning, Vivien?'

The older woman looked her age today, with puffy

pouches under her eyes. 'I feel terrible,' she admitted. 'I haven't slept a wink. I'm so worried about her.'

Caroline looked at her in concern. 'You should try and rest. You must look after yourself.'

Vivien's smile was wry. 'It's probably too late to worry about my health. I wonder where she can be? I went to their bedroom but she's not there. Oh, I do hope she's all right.'

Caroline linked her arm through Vivien's. 'She's probably in the garden. Have you had any breakfast?'

'Yes, Morgan brought us a beautiful tray . . . far more than I could eat.'

'I'm going to get myself some coffee. Why don't you have some, too?' She leaned closer to whisper in Vivien's ear. 'Christopher and Oonagh are on the terrace. Talking. That's why I've come indoors.'

'I know their marriage is in trouble, although Chris hasn't talked to me about it. I hope he can sort it out. Oh, dear, is there ever a time when one stops worrying about one's children?' she sighed.

'Why don't you sit in the drawing room, and I'll get the coffee?'

Vivien squeezed Caroline's hand gratefully. 'Thank you, my dear. That's sweet of you.'

The drawing room was empty, a breeze blowing in through the open windows, the air fragrant from the vases of flowers Morgan had arranged for last night. Gift-wrapped presents addressed to Julia, Douglas, Anna and William were still stacked on a table, unopened. Vivien sat in a corner of the room, hoping to be undisturbed. She didn't think she could face Roger or Pammy, or that vulgar Leonora with her sour-faced daughters. Her breast seemed to be aching, and she put her hand over it fretfully, wondering whether she would have to have it removed and if she would need chemotherapy which would make her lose all her hair?

'Here we are!' The cheerful voice of Caroline alerted her to put on a smiling face again. She was carrying a small tray with two large cups of steaming coffee and a little plate of biscuits.

'How lovely, my dear,' Vivien exclaimed, making a space on the table in front of her.

'I'm sorry I've been so long, but I've been making a phone call,' Caroline explained.

'Oh, yes?' Vivien looked politely enquiring.

'Would you mind coming for a little drive with me, when we've had our coffee? There's something I have to do. It won't take long, so we'll be back in good time for lunch.'

'Yes, of course. It will be a relief to get out of the house for a little while, actually. The atmosphere's tense, isn't it . . . or is that my imagination?'

Caroline smiled. 'I don't think it's your imagination, Vivien. Apart from last night's débâcle, and something brewing between Chris and Oonagh though I'm not sure what, Pammy Schemmel is packing right now, and Roger is taking her to the station.'

Vivien's eyes widened in astonishment. 'Have they had a fight?'

'By the look of it, they've broken up.' Caroline didn't add that Oonagh might have something to do with it. She'd seen her dancing with Roger in a very cosy fashion last night, and then they'd vanished into the garden, hand in hand, and hadn't reappeared for ages.

'Simon wondered where we're going?' Vivien asked, as

she climbed into Caroline's car.

'Stockbridge,' she replied vaguely.

'What? An antique shop or something? I do love poking around and seeing what I can find.'

'One can pick up some very interesting pieces. I've found several antique boxes, beautifully inlaid with mother-of-pearl, which look fabulous in the shop, especially if I fill them with ropes of pearls.'

Vivien remained silent. Her thoughts were elsewhere. There'd still been no sign of Julia, or Douglas either, by the time they'd left Highfield Manor and she wondered what on earth was happening. She couldn't even find a Sunday newspaper to see if they'd reported the incident.

Caroline drove through the charming little town of Stockbridge and then, on the far side, turned up a lane, overhung with leafy branches and high hedgerows.

'Where are we going?' Vivien asked.

At that moment Caroline turned in through a white gate and drove up a short drive to a newly built redbrick house. 'This is where we're going,' she said gently, bringing the car to a standstill opposite the white front door.

Vivien frowned. 'Darling, I don't want to go visiting people. I don't feel well enough. I'd never have come if I'd known we were . . .'

Caroline laid a hand on her arm. 'Don't be angry with me, but I've made an appointment for you to see the local doctor. You can't go on like this, worrying and wondering whether your lump is malignant or not.'

Vivien started to protest, but Caroline silenced her by tightening her grip. 'No one knows we've come here. Absolutely no one, I promise you. I remember Julia mentioning Dr Hickey ages ago, and how wonderful he is, so I looked up his number in the phone book and he agreed to see you right away.'

'Oh my God!' Vivien started to tremble. 'Oh, Caroline, I'm scared. What if . . .?'

Caroline put one arm round her shoulders and gave her a comforting hug. 'I'll come in with you. And isn't it better to know, one way or the other? Nowadays cancer doesn't mean the end, you know. As you've only just discovered the lump, your chances of a complete cure are good. That is, if it's cancer in the first place. It may not be, but you'll never know unless you find out.'

Vivien gave a shuddering intake of breath. 'If it is . . .?' She paused, struggling for composure. 'Will you help me keep it a secret until this weekend is over? I don't want Julia upset.'

'Don't you think she might be more upset at being shut out? She's a grown woman and she's strong, Vivien. If you were my mother, I'd want to know what was happening.'

'You're probably right, dear.' Vivien got out of the car slowly, her face drained of colour, hands visibly shaking. Caroline took her arm and they walked to the front door.

'We'll do this together,' Caroline promised, as she rang the brass front door bell.

Detective Inspector Swann and Detective Sergeant Newton arrived at the cottage Nancy Graham had had such a problem finding, but had finally discovered, with the help of Mr Miller, the taxi driver, to be Wishford Cottage, Cranberry Lane, Longford. An elderly, rather stout woman came to the door. She had a rosy weather-beaten face and a mass of fluffy grey curls.

'Mrs Watson?' DI Swann asked.

'That's me.' She looked unsurprised to see them.

Swann held out his identification which had an unrecognisable picture of himself stuck to it. 'Detective Inspector Swann and Detective Sergeant Newton,' he added.

'You don't look like policemen, but I suppose you'd best come in. I'm cooking the dinner but I expect it's Rose you want to see, after last night,' she said, standing to one side so they could enter.

Swann gave her his most charming smile. 'It's you we've really come to see.' His nostrils twitched as the glorious aroma of roasting beef assailed them. 'What a wonderful smell! I can tell you're a great cook.'

Mrs Watson beamed with gratification, and led the way into a small living room. They followed her, bending in order not to hit their heads on the low lintel.

'We won't keep you long, but there are one or two things we want to clear up, concerning your daughter's death in 1980.'

'Sit down and I'll get Rose.'

'We don't need to talk to her at this juncture . . .'

But Mrs Watson was paying no attention. '*Rose*!' she yelled up the narrow stairs. 'Get down here. The police have come to ask some questions.'

'I don't think she can help us,' Newton pointed out, 'because she'd only have been a baby at the time.'

'But it was Rose who let that busybody, Mrs Graham, rake the whole thing up again. I didn't want it brought up. Let my Lily rest in peace, I say. But, oh, no! Mrs Graham waltzes in here, with offers of money, wanting to take Rose to a grand ball . . . even give her the money to hire a dress, she did . . . and I says, for what? The past is past. Mr Rutherford's been good to us. Sent us money every month without fail, and a bit extra at Rose's birthday and Christmas. Let sleeping dogs lie, I says.'

Rose appeared at that moment, pale and frightened-looking in a skimpy cotton frock, her legs bare, white sandals on her feet.

'Whatcha want?' she asked grumpily.

'Sit down, Rose. The gentlemen want to ask us some questions about your mum.'

'I don't know nothing,' she quavered.

Swann smiled reassuringly at her. 'We don't need to ask you anything, Rose.' He turned to Mrs Watson. 'All we want to know is what happened on that last day your daughter went to work at Highfield Manor? How did she get there, by the way? It's a good four miles away.'

'She cycled every morning. Left here at about a quarter to seven, rain or shine. Never missed a day, she didn't. Then she cycled back again, in the late afternoon. I looked after Rose, took her under my wing, I did, from the moment she was born.'

Mrs Watson, they realised, once started, couldn't stop talking. They only hoped that amid the voluble flow they'd find a tiny nugget that might help their enquiries.

'Why was your daughter living in Stickley before Rose was born?' DS Newton asked.

'Worked in the village store, she did. Started when she was seventeen, and lodged with Mr Harris in a room over the shop. A lot of her friends went to work in Stickley, which made her want to go. Tracey worked in the bakery then, and Deirdre got a job in the Swag and Tails. And then there was Mabel . . . she worked in the little café on the . . .'

'Yes, I see,' DI Swann said, loudly enough to bring her dissertation to a halt. 'What I need to know is, was there anything different about that particular morning? Was Lily late in getting off? Did she feel quite well? Did she mention Mr Rutherford at all?'

Mrs Watson now went into overdrive. 'She never *stopped* talking about Mr Rutherford! Morning, noon and night she went on about him. Terribly cut up she was when he said he couldn't see her anymore. I told her from the start: "Lily," I said, "he's just using you." Like all these rich men – and him with a wife and two children, too! Of course he was using her. But she was that in love with him, there was no telling her. When she came over to see me on a Sunday, she was full of all the things he'd said. He used to take her all over that big house he'd bought. Show her how the builders were getting on. Ask her what colours she liked. He was still living with his wife in London then, and coming down several times a week to see the progress of Highfield Manor. I tells her, again and again, that as soon as his family moved in he'd chuck her. But would she listen? And then Lily falls pregnant.' Mrs Watson paused only long enough to sigh. 'She had this fancy idea that he was going to marry her and set her up in that big house, her and the baby! Huh!'

At this point Rose, who'd been sitting quietly in the corner, said shrilly: 'He's a sodding bastard! Who wants him?'

DI Swann and DS Newton were stunned by this outburst, but Mrs Watson didn't seem to notice.

'Like I said, he dropped Lily even before Rose was born. His wife and their children were about to move into the house, of course. The youngest was only a baby at the time. William, I think he was called. Anyway, here we are, Lily, Rose and me, all getting along nicely, when along comes a big posh car, and out steps Mrs Rutherford. You could have knocked me down with a feather, and Lily got in a panic, thinking she'd found out about her and Mr Rutherford. But not a bit of it!' Mrs Watson spread her plump hands expansively. ' "Lily," she said, all refined like, "I need help in the house, and Mr Harris tells me you might be looking for work. Would you be able to come and work for me on a daily basis?" '

'What do they need to know all this for, Gran?' Rose intervened.

'I'm just filling the gentlemen in,' she replied, before continuing. 'That's when Lily and I realised Mrs Rutherford didn't know anything about her husband and his carrying on. Rose was asleep upstairs so she didn't even know Lily had a baby. Well! You can imagine how I felt. I didn't want Lily to take the job, but she insisted. Said she might even win him back. Fat chance! That sort of man never marries his bit on the side and I told her so, but would she listen?'

'Right, Mrs Watson. Now can you tell us about the actual morning in question?' DS Newton asked, getting desperate. Time was getting on, and the fragrance of the roasting beef was starting to make his stomach rumble.

For a moment she looked blankly at him, and then she turned to DI Swann.

'I was just telling you. Lily left just before seven. I can still remember, she was wearing a pretty blue skirt and a white blouse I'd bought her. Nearly forgot her handbag, she did! "Lily," I said, "you'll forget your head one day." "No, I won't, Mum," she said, and then she checked she had everything she needed, including her syringe of adrenalin.'

DS Newton felt icy prickles swarm up the back of his

neck. He was a keen fisherman, and had the same sensation now as he felt at that first tug on the line.

'Lily had the syringe and the adrenalin with her that morning?' he verified in a quiet voice.

'Yes. She always had to have it with her,' Mrs Watson confirmed cheerfully.

'Then can you tell me why, Mrs Watson, when she was stung, she did not use it? She did not even seem to have it with her. The report I have seen says it was not found in her handbag. In fact it could not be found in the house at all, although a thorough search was carried out.'

Mrs Watson nodded. 'I remember. This was brought up at the inquest. It's something I never understood either. She definitely had it with her, I remember quite clearly.'

'What sort of handbag did she have?'

She rose to her feet. 'I kept all her things, you know. They gave them back to me, afterwards like, and I kept them. I'll show you.' She bustled out of the room and they heard her go slowly up the creaking narrow stairs. There was an awkward silence in which Rose sat staring at them.

'Last night must have been very distressing for you,' DI Swann remarked kindly.

'It was bleeding awful,' she replied, 'seeing them so rich and la-di-da. I wish he wasn't me dad. He's a great fat toad!'

A minute later Mrs Watson returned, carrying a worn and flattened navy blue plastic handbag with a tarnished gilt clasp. DI Swann examined it then opened it to look inside. He winced at the pathetic possessions of a girl long dead: a broken comb, a lipstick, a clean tissue, a purse containing a few coins, and a cheap powder compact. There was no sign of the little beauty bag he'd heard about that had contained the syringe and adrenalin that Lily took with her everywhere.

With a snap of the gilt clasp he closed the bag again and handed it back to Mrs Watson. He'd found out what he wanted to know.

Eleven

No matter what, Reggie hated staying in bed in the morning. At nine o'clock he got up, being careful not to disturb Pat, and sitting in an armchair in the window, read until Morgan came in with their breakfast trays at ten o'clock. Not that he'd been able to concentrate on what he was reading. Last night's scene had been a terrible shock for both of them, and Pat had sobbed when she'd got into bed.

'How could anyone say such dreadful things about Douglas?'

Now, as she propped herself up against a mound of snowy pillows, and put on her pink crocheted bedjacket, she was ready to take on the world. If anyone said a word against Douglas today, she'd give them a piece of her mind. She felt like telling that next-door neighbour what she thought of her, too.

Having something positive to do, like defending her son, had energised Pat who felt ten years younger.

'I hope Douglas sues that woman,' she said suddenly as she balanced her prettily laid tray on her knees.

Reggie, who preferred to sit up at a table when eating, and had in any case chosen grapefruit, eggs and bacon, toast and coffee, while Pat had only ask for tea and a

269

croissant, mumbled something about expecting it was all under control.

'How could she have brought that girl to the party?' Pat continued, cheeks pink with indignation.

'At least she didn't stay,' Reggie said calmly.

'I should hope not! Who does she think she is, anyway? It was the most disgraceful thing I've ever seen.'

She continued to rail against the gate-crashers for some time until, exhausted, she asked Reggie to move her tray.

'Pop it on the table, will you, pet? Douglas said we needn't get up early. In fact, he said he'd see us at lunchtime, so I think I'm going to stay in bed this morning. It's not often we're in such luxury, is it?'

'You're right. Douglas has done marvellously. We couldn't be more comfortable in Buckingham Palace, could we? I think I'll go downstairs and read the Sunday papers. Might sit on the terrace. Looks warm enough.'

After he'd bathed and shaved and put on his cream cotton trousers, a white shirt and his navy blue blazer, Reggie went downstairs, leaving Pat to snooze. The house was quiet, which surprised him. Where was everyone? He went straight to the study, expecting to find Douglas, but the room was empty. He glanced around, looking for the newspapers which were usually arranged on a round table in the window by Morgan. There was no sign of them. Then he went to the drawing room but that was empty too. Through the french windows, though, he saw Tim, with Cressida and Sasha, lying by the pool, and in the distance what looked like Simon and Peter, strolling along at a leisurely pace.

Hearing the chink of silver and glass, he wandered next into the dining room, and found Morgan and two of the waiters from London laying the long table for lunch.

'Just the person I wanted,' Reggie exclaimed. 'Have you by any chance seen the Sunday newspapers? I can't find them in the study.'

Morgan busied himself with a place setting and did not look up. 'I can't say I have, sir.'

'Didn't they come today?' There was disappointment in Reggie's voice. Of all the newspapers in the week, the ones that came out on Sunday were his favourite.

'I believe they did, sir,' the butler replied evasively.

'Could my son have them? Do you know where he is?'

Again the butler's manner was elusive. 'I haven't seen Mr Rutherford for some time, sir, but I know he's around somewhere.'

Reggie went back to the study, feeling rather lost. No one about to talk to, and he couldn't find the papers either. He glanced at his watch. It was a quarter to twelve. Too early for a snifter? He considered this for a moment, concluding that this was a special weekend, and he didn't have to go anywhere this afternoon, and anyway a weak whisky and soda would be good for him.

There was plenty of whisky in the cut-glass decanter which had a silver label hung round its neck from a fine chain, but there was no soda water. Not to worry, Reggie said to himself, knowing where Douglas kept the mixers. He went to the cupboard which formed the lower half of the bookcase and reached for a bottle, but instead encountered a stack of paper. Bending down, he realised with surprise it was the Sunday papers, all scrunched together as if they'd been hurriedly hidden.

'How odd,' he muttered aloud, but then he drew them out, unfolded them, and his heart contracted with a painful lurch when he saw the first headlines.

271

Christopher, coming into the study a few minutes later, found Reggie standing stock still, reading a copy of the *Globe*. Christopher gave it a cursory glance, then picked up another newspaper which Reggie had dropped on to a chair.

'Bad show, isn't it, old chap?' Christopher said sympathetically as he skimmed what had been written. 'If only the press hadn't been here last night, no one need have known what happened. They do sensationalise everything so. Mind you, I suppose it was bound to come out sooner or later.'

Reggie's face was red, almost swollen, with rage. 'What was supposed to come out? All these lies?'

Christopher was taken aback. Surely Douglas's father didn't think it was a made-up story?

'Can I pour you a drink?' he said instead. 'I'm going to have one even though it is a bit early. It's not every day one's wife asks for a divorce.'

Reggie didn't appear to have heard him. He was still reading the *Globe* as if he couldn't believe his eyes and his hands were shaking.

'This is the most disgraceful thing I've ever seen,' he thundered, collapsing on to one of the leather sofas.

'Are you all right, Reggie?' Christopher asked, alarmed.

'Yes.' But he looked agitated. 'Where's Douglas?'

'I haven't seen him since the police came to . . .' Christopher broke off, realising he'd said too much.

'The police?'

'Well, you know what it's like.' Christopher did his best to sound casual. 'If someone makes a wild accusation, like that girl did last night, the police have to check it out. It doesn't mean anything, though.'

'But they were the words of an angry child!' Reggie

protested, throwing the newspaper on the floor. 'A girl who had been put up to it in the first place.'

'Quite,' Christopher agreed, nodding. 'I'm sure Douglas will sort it out.'

'Pat mustn't know about this. I suppose that's why Douglas hid the newspapers. It'll upset her very much if she finds out people are saying all these dreadful things about him.'

'Quite,' said Christopher again. 'Ah!' He turned as the study door opened and Douglas walked into the room.

'Where have you been?' Reggie demanded.

He looked from Christopher to his father and then to the crumpled copy of the *Globe* on the floor.

'I see you've found them,' he remarked, impassively.

'Your mother mustn't see them.'

'I'm not wild about anyone seeing them,' Douglas said dryly, 'especially Michael.' He bent to pick them up, gathering them clumsily and stuffing them back into the cupboard.

'On the other hand,' he continued, shutting the cupboard door with a bang, 'everything's going to come out now, so there's not much point in pretending it isn't happening. How are your drinks? Want a top up?'

'What do you mean? Everything's going to come out?' Reggie demanded. 'There's nothing to come out. This is all a pack of lies.'

Douglas went to the drinks tray, poured himself some whisky, added a dash of Malvern water, and then turned to face his father.

'It's not all lies, Dad,' he said quietly.

Christopher, watching, noticed how Reggie's florid colour faded and his skin suddenly looked as if someone had rubbed chalk into it.

'What do you mean, Douglas?' he asked hollowly.

'I'm afraid it's true that I had an affair with a woman called Lily. It happened a long time ago and was the greatest mistake of my life. Something I will regret forever.' He paused painfully, trying to gauge how much his father could take. Reggie was looking at him like a child who hopes he is not going to be disappointed but somehow knows he is.

But it had to be done. Said and got out of the way.

'Unfortunately she got pregnant,' Douglas continued. 'That girl who turned up last night *was* my daughter, Rose. She's sixteen, and it's true that I've been sending money every month to her grandmother since she was born.'

Reggie continued to sit and stare at his son in stunned silence. Christopher went forward and took the empty tumbler from his liver-spotted hand.

'Let me give you the other half,' he suggested gently.

Reggie relinquished the glass as if he hadn't heard.

Douglas continued. 'It's also true that Lily died in this house, but I certainly wasn't responsible for her death and neither was anyone else. It was a tragic accident, but of course, thanks to Nancy Graham next door, the police came to question me this morning. The coroner's verdict at the time was accidental death, so I don't suppose we'll hear any more about it,' he added reassuringly.

For the first time Reggie spoke. 'Oh, dear God! What is your mother going to say? This will kill her, Douglas.'

Christopher handed him back his refilled tumbler. 'Pat's very strong, though, Reggie. And very supportive. It'll put her in a fighting mood but she won't let it get her down.'

Reggie shook his head gloomily. 'I'm not so sure.' He

suddenly looked shrunken and old, sitting huddled on the sofa, his wrists and ankles bone thin. Douglas went over and sat down beside him.

'I'm sorry, Dad. I really am.'

'What does Julia say?'

Douglas paused before answering. 'She needs time. Time to get used to the idea of Rose. She already knew about Lily, but not about Rose.'

'Where is she?' Christopher asked. He could tell by Douglas's manner that things weren't right between them, and then he remembered his sister's reaction on Friday night when he'd told her about Barbara. No wonder she disapproved so strongly of infidelity! She'd been hurt, all those years ago, and that hurt still lingered.

'I don't know where she is,' Douglas replied dispiritedly.

'I think I'll go and look for her,' Christopher said, glad of an excuse to get away.

'I saw Oonagh just now,' Douglas called after him. 'She was in the garden. Is everything all right?'

'Far from it,' he replied laconically as he walked out of the room.

'I'll be back soon,' Roger whispered to Oonagh, who was standing in the drive, looking down at the swimming pool which was on the lower level of the garden. She could see Tim splashing around with Petroc, Cressida, Sasha and Stephanie, but there was no sign of either Anna or William. She smiled as soon as she heard Roger's voice.

'Hello. How are you this morning?'

'I'm taking Pammy to the station. She's going back to London . . . thank God!' he muttered, hurrying over to his car as he saw her emerging from the front door, her face a mask of injured pride behind huge dark glasses, her narrow shoulders swathed in a Pashmina shawl although it was a hot day.

Oonagh watched him march over to his car, remembering the feel of his arms holding her close last night, and the thrilling way he'd kissed her. It was the first time in twenty years that she'd allowed herself to flirt so outrageously. It was also the first time she'd wanted to take the flirting a stage further.

Anna watched her father prowl around the house like a restless beast in a zoo, not knowing what to do with himself. Needlessly, he checked that the dining-room table was laid for enough people, and that the drawing room had a tray of drinks set up in readiness for pre-lunch apéritifs. Then he went to the kitchen, fussing that the huge side of beef wasn't being overcooked.

'It must be crusty on the outside, and really pink in the middle,' he told Mrs Morgan, who'd been cooking their traditional roast beef Sunday lunch for the past seven years without once getting it wrong.

'It'll be all right as long as no one's late for lunch, Mr Rutherford,' she replied with dignity.

'And the vegetables *al dente*,' he added.

'Yes, Mr Rutherford.' Her sharp-featured face looked particularly spiky and her eyes darted coldly in his direction. 'The Yorkshire pudding will be done to a turn, too.'

Douglas retreated, recognising the sarcasm in her voice.

'Daddy, do come out into the garden and relax for a bit,' Anna suggested.

Douglas slung his arm around her shoulders and hugged her as they went outside. The sun was so hot now, blindingly high in a gin-clear sky, that it was like stepping under a giant spotlight.

'How's my girl?' he asked tenderly, as he steered her towards a bench which stood under a large chestnut tree.

Anna averted her face so that he would not see the pain in her eyes. 'I don't know, Daddy. It's all such a shock. I can't bear to think of you loving anyone besides Mummy.'

He turned to her, his face grave and anxious. 'I've never stopped loving Mummy. Never for one moment,' he told her. 'This was just . . . I don't know . . . madness. Something that happened, and God knows why. God knows why,' he repeated.

'But she had a baby. It must have been more than a fling if she had a baby.'

Douglas shook his head slowly. 'No, it was no more than a reckless fling. The baby was never meant to happen.'

'But it *did* happen,' she pointed out. 'Did you . . . did she think of having it aborted?'

'I did,' he replied honestly. 'I certainly did.'

'But she wouldn't agree?'

'No, she desperately wanted to keep it.'

'What's going to happen now?'

'I think the whole thing will gradually blow over, with any luck.'

'But nothing will ever be the same again, will it? From now on there will always be this other girl, your child, in the background. A constant reminder of what happened.' She paused and then said wistfully, 'And we used to be such a happy family.'

Then she started sobbing, little throbbing sobs that tugged at her chest. 'I'm not sure I can bear it. I don't think

Mikey will be able to, either. He's been in his room all morning. He won't speak to anyone. Not even William.'

'Oh, Anna . . .' He pulled her close, lips pressed to the crown of her head. 'This won't change anything, I promise you. It happened so long ago, it's got nothing to do with our lives now. Michael wasn't even born at the time. William was only a baby. Remember the last sixteen years and how happy they've been. We must all try to recapture that feeling.'

She drew away from him. 'But it changes everything. We're no longer the family we were. Last night I was so sure Mrs Graham had made up the whole thing, just to ruin our party, I nearly had a fight with Petroc about it. I was refusing to believe it was true.'

'And then you found your father had feet of clay. He was a sinner, an adulterer, the father of an illegitimate child.' Douglas's voice was harsh.

Anna winced at his words, unable to look at him. 'How's Mummy this morning?'

'How would you expect her to be?' he asked bitterly. 'She terribly upset. And shocked. And, like you, disillusioned. I think that's the hardest thing I have to bear, the knowledge that I've let you all down.'

'You and Mummy are going to be all right, though, aren't you?' she asked in sudden panic.

'Of course we are, darling,' he replied smoothly, although privately, at this moment, he wasn't entirely sure. He'd never seen Julia as devastated as she'd been this morning and he couldn't blame her. To them this was a new blow, something that had zoomed out of nowhere and knocked them for six. But he'd had sixteen years to get used to the idea of having another child, and so for him last night's shock was lessened.

Anna turned and flung her arms round her father's neck, taking him by surprise. 'I'll always love you . . . I just wish this hadn't happened, Daddy.'

'So do I, my love,' he replied, greatly touched. 'Dear God, so do I.'

After Anna had left him, to go in search of Petroc, Douglas remained seated in the shade, deep in thought. For the first time guilt overtook him, seeping like a slow haemorrhage from his heart, leaving him feeling drained. And the object of that guilt was Rose. Poor bloody child, he thought in sudden anguish. She didn't ask to be born. How could she have felt last night, faced with the lavish opulence of Highfield Manor, knowing that only a whim of fate had prevented her from sharing all the advantages Anna, William and Michael enjoyed? *How must she have felt?*

No wonder, he reflected, that she had turned on him like a wild cat. Not only had he denied her all that he had so readily given his three other children, but she must believe he had also been instrumental in depriving her of her own mother.

Sitting alone by the pool, a damp towel draped around his shoulders to protect him from the sun, Petroc watched Anna walking slowly towards him. He could see she'd been crying and wondered what he could say to comfort her. This new Anna, who had suddenly emerged from the acquiescent girl he'd always known, was exciting but required him to act differently. She couldn't be patronised anymore, or talked down to. Neither was she prepared to do as she was told.

'Hi!' he called out, keeping his tone light. 'Come and

get a bit of sun. This is better than the Caribbean. The climate in England really is changing, isn't it?'

Anna spread a towel on the flagstones, and lowered herself beside him. 'What's the time?'

Petroc glanced at his complicated-looking wrist watch. 'Nearly noon.'

'Oh, good. We've got an hour until lunch.' She lay back, hands under her head, eyes closed.

'Where have you been? I've missed you.'

'Messing around. Talking to Daddy. I suppose there's no sign of Mummy?'

'No, I haven't seen her. William had a swim a little while ago but he's gone back into the house with Tim.'

'What about the dreaded cousins? Where are they?'

Petroc laughed at the derision in her voice. 'Gone to wash their hair before lunch. They'd be all right, you know, if their mother would just stop trying to turn them into something they're not.'

'That's what's so sad!' Anna exclaimed woefully. 'I try to be nice to them, but they're so sulky.'

'They'd like to be like you, and have everything you've got, and I suppose you can't blame them. It's jealousy that makes them the way they are.'

'Yes,' she replied thoughtfully. Then her brow puckered. 'If *they're* jealous . . . what must Rose have felt last night?'

'The whole situation is very tough for everyone concerned,' he said carefully. 'It's going to take time before the dust settles on this one.'

'What a hideous weekend this had turned out to be.' Her voice was laden with regret. 'And Daddy had planned every moment of it with such care. I'm dreading lunch with all of us trapped around the table, without any means of escape unless we make a scene. What are we all going to talk about?' She cast him a despairing look. 'We'll all be thinking about one thing only, and it's the one thing no one will want to mention.'

'At least we're spared the resident nightmare.'

'Who's that?'

'Need you ask? Pammy Schemmel, of course.'

'Then let us be thankful for small mercies!' she retorted mockingly.

Vivien and Caroline arrived back at Highfield Manor shortly after twelve o'clock. Vivien went straight upstairs to her bedroom, while Caroline was waylaid by Oonagh who seemed to be hovering as if waiting for someone.

'Where have you *been*?' she asked.

'I just went for a drive,' Caroline replied vaguely. 'What's happened? You look like the cat that's found the cream.' It was true. Oonagh's normally opaque paleness was tinged with a hint of pink and her dark eyes were glowing.

She slid her arm through Caroline's. 'I must talk to someone. Let's go into the drawing room and I'll tell you everything. My dear, my life is about to change completely! You see, I found out Chris was having an affair . . .'

The drawing-room door closed behind them just as Leonora, coming in from a walk, entered the hall. But not before she'd heard the last few words. Walking on tip-toe right up to the door, she leaned closer, hoping to hear more. Christopher having an affair? How riveting! But why had Oonagh sounded excited about it?

Leonora felt a physical pang of frustration and bitterness. Why did everyone else seem to have affairs, but never her? God knows, she longed to have a passionate man in her bed. How long had it been since Peter had last made love to her? Life was passing her by, and all her seductive powers were going to waste. If she didn't get a move on, she'd be hit by the menopause and then it would be too late.

'Hello, there,' a voice called out just behind her.

Leonora spun round, starting guiltily and flushing crimson. Roger was standing, hands on hips, watching her attempts at eavesdropping and laughing at her.

'I'm . . . I'm looking for Cressida,' she stammered. 'I thought I heard her in the drawing room.'

'Can't help you there, I'm afraid,' he said breezily. 'I've just come back from the station. Any sign of Oonagh?'

'Oonagh?'

'Yes.' His expression was bold and he was looking very pleased with himself.

'No.' Leonora widened her eyes in an attempt to appear truthful. 'I've no idea where she is. I've been out walking, and now I'm on my way upstairs to get ready for lunch.' Then she turned and hurried across the hall and up the stairs, feeling quite put out. It was obvious, by the eager way Roger had spoken, that now that Pammy was out of the way, he was after Oonagh. If he was looking for someone to screw – and let's face it, she reflected, that's all he wants – why had he picked Oonagh? Why hadn't he picked *her*? Why didn't men fall at *her* feet? Her anger at that moment was like heartburn; hot, painful and unrelenting. She was stuck with a dreary, dried-up old stick, who didn't know the meaning of having fun, and who was as ineffectual in bed as a few drops from a tepid shower in a heatwave.

Leonora didn't find Peter still nursing his headache in

their bedroom, as she'd expected, because while she'd been out he'd come downstairs again and settled himself for a quiet hour or so before lunch in the study. To his relief he'd found it empty. He scanned the shelves that filled the walls from floor to ceiling, and wondered if Douglas had read any of the books, so neatly displayed. At last he took down a copy of Emile Zola's *J'accuse* and, taking it over to the window, settled himself in an armchair. A gentle breeze came wafting in from the garden, and apart from distant voices from the tennis court and pool, it was marvellously peaceful there.

Peter began to feel less ruffled. He was used to noise; who wouldn't be with four hundred little boys constantly exercising their larynxes at full volume, but last night's racket had jarred him. The pounding music and babble of voices, combined with alcohol, heat, and the shuddering vibrations underfoot as couples stamped and gyrated on the dance floor, had made him long for some cool glade, green and lush, where the loudest noise was the whisper of the wind, stirring the leaves. And then, of course, the shock thrust upon them all by Douglas's next-door neighbour. It was as if a grave had burst open, right there in the middle of the gathering, and the skeletal form of Lily had come surging up out of it, risen from the dead to come back and haunt them. Peter put down his book, finding it difficult to concentrate. He'd always known about Lily because Douglas had confessed to him in an unguarded moment that they were having an affair, but he hadn't known about the baby.

At that moment his brother came loping into the room, reminding him of a tired old lion.

Peter looked up. 'Hello there. How are you doing?'

Douglas went and sat down heavily behind his desk.

283

'What a fucking nightmare this all is,' he replied tersely.
'Of all the weekends for this to happen!'

'It's because it's a special weekend that it *has* happened,' Peter told him. 'You don't expect your neighbour from hell to spring something like this on you when no one's around, do you? That woman was out for blood.'

'And she certainly got it. Christ, I feel like killing the old bitch!' He slumped on his desk, the first time Peter had ever seen him so inert. 'This is an unholy mess.'

'Are you carrying on with the farce of a formal lunch?'

'What else can we do? Serve roast beef and Yorkshire pudding by the pool? Get everyone to leave? For God's sake, this is the family.'

'Caroline Drummond isn't family, nor is Anna's boyfriend, or William's girlfriend, or Roger what's-his-name?' Peter pointed out.

'Oh, stop being so pernickety,' Douglas roared, with a sudden return of his usual vigour. 'We can't very well ask them to leave, can we? Most of them are going home this evening anyway.'

Peter rose, and with careful precision returned his book to the shelf. 'So what are you going to do about this business?'

Douglas shrugged. 'There's nothing much I can do. I'll send Rose's grandmother some extra money, but otherwise I've got to wait and see if the police are going to reopen the case.'

'Do you think they will?'

'They say they may have fresh evidence. According to them there is someone who claims to have witnessed what happened, but I don't think they've talked to them yet.' He sighed wearily. 'It all happened so long ago.'

Peter frowned. 'Who could have seen what happened?

She was alone in the house, wasn't she?'

Douglas spread his large capable hands in a gesture of helplessness. 'Yes, I'm sure she was.'

'Who else could have been here?'

'God knows. If someone did see what happened, they kept it bloody quiet at the inquest.'

'What does Julia say?'

Douglas didn't reply, but rising from the desk went and stood in the french windows, gazing into the garden with unseeing eyes, hands deep in his trouser pockets. After a few moments he spoke.

'I don't know,' he said simply. 'I don't know what Julia thinks about Lily's death.'

Julia, having asked Morgan to bring a pot of coffee up to her bedroom, had a very deep hot bath laced with her favourite gardenia-scented oil, and then set about getting dressed with as much care as if she were going somewhere special. Lunch would be announced in forty-five minutes and she was determined to be composed, if only for the sake of Anna, William and Michael. She'd spent some time with Michael in his room, after her talk with Douglas, and had managed to reassure him that he had nothing to worry about, and that both his mummy and daddy loved him and each other, but she still had to appear cheerful and supportive of Douglas, no matter how she privately felt.

She was putting the finishing touches to her make-up when she heard a gentle tapping on her bedroom door.

'Mikey, is that you? Come on in, darling,' she called out.

The door opened slowly and Vivien appeared.

'It's not Michael, it's me. Do you mind if I come in for a moment?'

'Hello, Ma! Come in. How are you this morning?' Julia sprang to her feet in greeting, kissing her mother on the cheek.

Vivien didn't answer immediately but, after returning Julia's kiss, came into the room and then sat down on the *chaise-longue* at the foot of the bed.

'More importantly, how are you, my darling?'

Julia resumed her seat at her dressing-table and applied her lipstick. 'OK, I suppose,' she replied flatly.

'It will take time, sweetheart.'

'I know.'

'The shock as much as anything is a killer. When your father died, the shock of it all seemed even worse than what had happened.'

'I know what you mean. I feel . . . sort of stunned.'

'That's hardly surprising,' Vivien sympathised. She paused, watching Julia fix her gold stud earrings, then she spoke again. 'I've been out . . . with Caroline, this morning,' she began hesitantly. 'I went to see your Dr Hickey.'

Julia turned sharply, a gleam of alarm in her eyes. 'Why? What's wrong?'

Vivien took a deep breath, nervously stroking the skirt of her linen dress. 'I was worried about something. Caroline persuaded me to . . . well, take the bull by the horns and go and see a doctor. So I did. I found a lump in my breast at the beginning of the week . . .'

'Why didn't you tell me?' Julia demanded, appalled. 'For God's sake, Mummy, why didn't you tell me?' Unconsciously she'd slipped into her childhood mode of addressing Vivien.

'I didn't tell anyone. Even Simon doesn't know. The last thing I wanted to do was cast a blight over this weekend.' She paused to smile wryly. 'But in the end I'd have been upstaged anyway, wouldn't I?'

'But what did Dr Hickey say?' Julia burst out, her voice choked.

'He's ninety-nine per cent certain it's only a subcutaneous benign cyst. Quite harmless. He suggested I have a mammograph when I get back to London, just to be on the safe side, but he's certain it's nothing to worry about.' Vivien was smiling now. 'Isn't it wonderful news? It seems I jumped to conclusions and got in a panic over nothing.'

'And you didn't tell me? You went through all that worry and fear without saying a word to me? Why, Ma? *Why*? I'm your daughter. I should be the person closest to you . . . apart from Chris. I suppose you haven't told him either?'

Vivien shook her head.

'And you haven't told Simon, and yet . . .' Julia's rush of anger escalated '. . . *you told Caroline*?'

Vivien looked embarrassed. 'I didn't tell her. Well, not exactly. She sort of found out. I was drinking too much on Friday night, and I'd taken some pills, and then I felt a bit woozy. She guessed something was wrong.'

'When was this?' Julia asked, puzzled.

'During dinner. She made me drink lots of water and eat some bread. I was soon all right again,' Vivien added.

'What sort of pills, Ma?'

'The ones the doctor gave me when Bouncer died.'

'Tranquillisers and drink? Oh, God, Ma! And you never told me.'

'We're not in the habit of telling each other our secrets, are we?' Vivien pointed out, carefully.

'You shut me out when I was small,' Julia shot back, relief that the doctor had said her mother was all right causing her to react angrily now. 'When Daddy died, you wouldn't come near me for weeks! I can remember being stuck with my nanny, and every time I asked for you, she told me you were sleeping. I needed you then, and you never came near me.'

Vivien sat looking at her daughter, and some of her joy at discovering her lump was benign seeped away.

'I suppose I have to accept what you say,' she said sadly. 'Every child sends its mother on a guilt trip, sooner or later.'

'Oh, Ma, I don't mean to, but you must see how it seemed to me when I was a child?' Julia said, blowing her nose and reapplying a little face powder.

'I do see,' Vivien agreed, 'but at the time I was trying to protect you from pain. And that's why I didn't tell you I had a lump – to spare you the worry.'

Julia got up and went over to where her mother sat. She put her hands on Vivien's shoulders and looked down into the beautiful familiar face which had been a part of her life ever since she could remember.

'Ma, I do understand. Really, I do, and thank God Dr Hickey said you're all right. That's what matters most of all. But in the future, *please* tell me if anything's wrong. I mean it. I'm a grown woman now, not a little girl who needs protecting. I want to know what's happening in your life.'

Vivien smiled up at her, reminded of Guido on seeing those dark eyes and creamy-olive skin.

'I promise, my darling,' she agreed. 'And is it going to work both ways?' she added wistfully.

Julia sank on to the *chaise-longue* beside her, looking thoughtful. 'I think I always have, apart from things happening in my marriage.'

'Like Douglas having an affair, when William was a baby?'

'Exactly. That wasn't just about me, which is why I didn't tell you or anyone. It was about Douglas and what he was doing in his private life. I felt it would be disloyal to him to tell a living soul what he was up to. Of course, I didn't know he and Lily had had a baby until last night. Now the secrets of our marriage have been all dragged out into the open, haven't they?'

'I'm afraid so, sweetheart.'

Mother and daughter looked at each other with a new and deeper understanding, as if the air between them had been cleared. Julia leaned forward suddenly and kissed Vivien.

'I didn't mean to make you feel guilty, Ma.'

Vivien smiled then, a real smile, radiant and joyful. 'I'm sure you didn't, my darling. And remember that when *your* children start saying their failings are your fault.'

For the first time, Julia gave a little laugh. 'I will. Oh, I will! Now, let's go downstairs. It's almost time for lunch.'

Vivien got to her feet lightly and with a spring in her step. 'I'll be right with you, but I must go and tidy myself first. It's such a lovely day, and I feel so well now, I might even put on my new white trouser suit. What do you think?'

Julia grinned. 'I think it's a smashing idea. You're still a model at heart, aren't you? Go for it, Ma! You'll look great.'

DI Swann and DS Newton emerged from Neville Barton's bleak-looking semi-detached villa on the outskirts of Stockbridge at twelve-thirty. They'd spent the past hour with the retired gardener, in his small front parlour, rank with the smell of pipe tobacco and an ancient dog of uncertain lineage who slept at his feet. Dressed in a pair of worn corduroy trousers, a grubby shirt out of which his scraggy neck emerged like a tortoise from its shell, and carpet slippers, Neville was more than prepared to talk.

At first his memory of what had happened at Highfield Manor on the day Lily had died was as crystal clear as if he'd witnessed the incident the previous week.

'I gets there early that day,' he said, puffing away at his malodorous pipe. 'I remembers it well. The Rutherfords weren't expecting me until the early afternoon, but it was a fine day so I thought I'd get on with mowing the lawn. Damn' big lawn they've got up at the Manor, you know.' He nodded chattily, his wrinkled face wizened as a nut.

'How early did you arrive?' DI Swann wanted to know. 'Can you remember what time it was?'

'About ten-thirty,' Neville shot back, voice suddenly loud in the low-ceilinged room.

'As early as that?' DS Newton queried.

Neville waggled his head like a nodding dog in a car window. 'Yes. Ten-thirty. Definitely.'

'Was there anyone about? Who did you see?'

'I never went into the house that morning, because I wanted to get on. I just went to the garage to get out the lawn mower.'

'So you didn't see anyone?' Newton asked, watching Neville closely. His powers of recall seemed amazing in such an elderly man.

'Not 'til I passes the kitchen window.'

'And what time was that?'

'Eleven o'clock.'

'You've very sure of that, Mr Barton? Did you have a wrist watch on you?'

'I've never had a wrist watch in my life!' he barked triumphantly, as a cloud of acrid blue smoke rose around his head. He started fishing in his trouser pocket. 'I've got me old dad's army watch, haven't I? Here it is! Still working as good as ever.' He withdrew a round flat watch, made of dull metal, with a screw winder on the top. 'Never misses a minute, this doesn't.'

'And what exactly happened at eleven o'clock?' Newton asked, secretly impatient. This old fart with his stinking pipe was getting on his nerves and he wanted to get away from this depressing little house. 'What did you *see*?'

'I happened to be passing the kitchen window, on my way to the garage, and I see Mr Rutherford in the kitchen.'

Swann and Newton tensed. They glanced at each other. Swann was the first to speak. 'What was he doing? Was he alone?'

'Yes. He was on his own. I saw him go and open the larder door. It looked like he unlocked it first.'

'Are you sure it was the larder door he opened?'

Neville looked offended. 'I always had a cup of tea in the kitchen, around teatime, so of course I know it was the larder door.'

'What happened then? Did Mr Rutherford go into the larder?'

Neville waggled his head from side to side this time, and with a matchbox tamped down the tobacco in his pipe. 'He never did nothing,' he replied bluntly. 'I thinks he *looks* in the larder, but then he turns and walks out of the kitchen, and that was that. I never thought no more about it. Until afterwards,' he added slyly.

DI Swann glanced through the papers on his lap, read something with care and then looked up at Neville again.

'How come you didn't mention any of this in your statement, taken down at the time?'

Neville shuffled his feet, accidentally kicking his dog. Several minutes were taken up in bending down to reassure Rover that he hadn't meant to hurt him. Then he straightened up and looked blandly at Swann again.

'What was that?' he asked.

Swann repeated the question.

'Oh, I was took ill,' Neville replied. 'Terrible ill I was, with pleurisy. I was in bed for three weeks. Didn't remember much about it. Must have slipped my memory, I suppose.'

'Slipped your memory?' Newton, less sympathetic, looked incredulous. 'You witness what could be the missing link in this case . . . and you suppose it slipped your memory?'

Neville started to whine. 'I was a sick man. I was in me bed. I tells you, I forgot! I didn't want to get the sack, neither. Mr Rutherford's a hard man, he is. And I had four children to support then.'

'So you forgot to mention this vital piece of information?'

'I suppose I did,' Neville admitted sulkily. 'I was ill.'

There was silence in the horrid little room, broken only by DS Newton scribbling away on his notepad.

'We'll want to talk to you again,' Swann told Neville, as they rose to leave. The old gardener made no reply but continued to puff on his pipe.

Outside, sitting in their car, Swann and Newton gave each other knowing looks.

'It's Douglas Rutherford we're after, isn't it? He had the motive and the means,' Swann remarked. 'He obviously wasn't expecting Neville to turn up until the afternoon on that day, so I reckon with Mrs Rutherford shopping in the village, and the nanny out with the children in Stockbridge, Rutherford nipped back to the house, from where he'd been cutting brambles in the wood, and Neville saw him unlocking the larder door after Lily Watson was dead. Eleven o'clock, Neville said. Yet Douglas Rutherford officially "discovered" her body at twelve-forty-five.'

Newton frowned. 'Unless he made a mistake about the time? On the other hand, Rutherford's original statement said he found the larder door open, and Lily lying just inside.'

'One thing's certain, this wasn't a planned murder. I think Rutherford came back to the house, knowing she'd be alone and wanting to talk to her; get her to leave her job in case his wife found out about them . . .'

'Don't you think Mrs Rutherford already knew?' Swann asked.

'I'm not sure about that yet. Why employ the girl if she knew Lily was Douglas's mistress? No, I'm convinced Douglas Rutherford wanted Lily out of the way. I expect he planned to pay her off, once and for all, and urge her to leave the village and go back to her mother's, where her baby was living. I suspect he entered the kitchen, some time after ten o'clock, and heard Lily scream from the larder that she'd been stung. Instead of going to help her, I think he slammed the door shut and locked her in. He could then have removed the syringe from her hand-bag . . . after all, everyone seemed to know about Lily's allergy so he'd know she carried the antidote everywhere with her. Then he would have destroyed the syringe, which is why it was never found. Finally he went back to unlock the larder door half an hour later, *and that was when Neville saw him.*' Newton drew a deep breath of satisfaction at his theory.

DI Swann remained silent, deep in thought, privately annoyed and even jealous that these days Newton, his assistant, seemed more on the ball then he was.

'You could be right,' he said with reluctance. 'Douglas Rutherford did have the means and the motive . . . and a lot of luck, too, if he happened upon Lily just as she'd been stung. But then, he has a reputation for being an opportunist, doesn't he? That's how he built his restaurant empire. I've heard he always bought into property in a buyer's market, and latched on to every new fad in the restaurant world, then sold his first company when the market was booming. And now he's doing a copy-cat of the Conran restaurants, and is making a fortune at it, too.'

He grunted, switched on the ignition, and put the car into gear. 'Maybe the bugger's luck is running out, though. I think we should check up on a few things, then ask Douglas Rutherford some more questions.'

'God Almighty, this is a right carry on,' Mrs Morgan whispered to her husband as she hid the Sunday newspapers in the cupboard under the sink, in case any of the family came into the kitchen. Morgan had slipped into Stickley to buy them, having only had time to glance at the ones delivered earlier. As soon as lunch was over, they planned to retreat to their own quarters, to have a good read.

'Mr Rutherford with a love child!' Mrs Morgan continued, her thin frame quivering with a mixture of nerves and excitement.

'There's more to it than that,' he muttered darkly. 'They

think he may have done the mother in. That's why the police were here this morning. He's under suspicion, he is.'

'He's never!' Mrs Morgan's eyes looked as if they might jump out of her head.

Morgan looked around to make sure no one could overhear.

'She died right there, in the larder,' he told her, pointing through the open door at one end of the kitchen which led to a cold oblong room, thick-walled and marble-shelved, with one tiny window covered with mesh high up on the wall, and a stone floor on which were stacked sacks of potatoes and onions.

'Who did?' Mrs Morgan gasped.

'Lily, his mistress. The one that had the baby. Questioning Mr Rutherford, the police were, while everyone was having breakfast.' He put his mouth to her ear. 'I was listening, outside the study door.'

She looked shocked. 'You never! Supposing you'd been caught?'

'There's nothing wrong with my hearing. I'd have heard someone coming,' he replied loftily. 'Old Mrs Graham seems to know a lot about it. I wonder how she found out?'

'And I thought they had the perfect marriage?' Mrs Morgan lamented. 'And the party being for their Silver Anniversary, too. Oh, dear, oh, dear. I hope things aren't going to change. We don't want to have to leave here, do we? This is the best place we've ever had.'

Morgan shrugged. 'Who knows? If he has to go to prison, they might have to sell up. Well, you never can tell, can you?' he added, seeing his wife's expression of horror.

'I dare say they'd give us good references, but it wouldn't be the same, would it? I'd miss it here, with all the entertaining they do and everything. Livens things up, it does.'

'We're lucky about one thing, though,' he reminded her.

'What's that?'

'We've only been here for seven years, right?'

'So?' She looked puzzled.

'All this happened sixteen years ago. The police won't be questioning us, because it was before our time. Right?'

'Right,' she echoed, looking relieved. 'And if they ask us anything, we can say Mr Rutherford's a very nice, devoted family man and we've never heard no scandal about him.'

'Exactly.' Morgan glanced at the big electric clock on the wall above the Aga. 'Glory be, I'd better get a move on. They'll be going into the drawing room for drinks in a minute. I'd better get the champagne out of the 'fridge and take it in there.'

Tim, white-faced, looked at his father in shock.

'*Divorce*?' he croaked.

Christopher put his arm around his son's shoulders as they strolled across the lawn, back towards the house. 'It looks like it, I'm afraid, old chap,' he said sympathetically. 'I wanted you to be aware of what was going on, before you heard it from anyone else.'

Tim stared down at the grass, his head hanging dejectedly. 'But it's so sudden. Are you sure? Maybe Mum's in a bad mood or has PMT. That can affect women, you know,' he added, as if it was something his father might not have heard of.

Christopher's grip tightened. 'It is sort of sudden, but

when you think about it, we haven't really been getting along for years.'

'But lots of couples don't necessarily hit it off and still manage to stay married. Lots of my friends have parents who lead different lives and sleep in different rooms, but they don't get divorced,' Tim argued. 'It seems so drastic.'

'I know.' Christopher nodded understandingly, feeling sorry for Tim but also slightly relieved that he could well be a free man within a few months. The only thing that was bugging him was the financial aspect. Oonagh wouldn't settle for a farthing less than she thought was due to her. And then there was Barbara. Was she the right woman for him if he did get divorced?

As if by telepathy, Tim asked; 'Is there someone else, Dad?'

Christopher hesitated for a moment, but decided he might as well be truthful. If he didn't mention Barbara, Oonagh most certainly would. In fact, she might well cite Barbara as co-respondent.

'There has been, Tim,' he replied carefully. 'I'm not sure if the relationship is going anywhere. Only time will tell.'

'And Mum?' Tim's voice was hoarse with pain. 'Has she got someone?'

At that moment, the study french windows opened on the terrace and a couple almost tumbled out, they were laughing so much. Clutching glasses of champagne, they seemed to cling to each other, heads thrown back in mirth. And then suddenly they stood quite still, and the man leaned forward and kissed the woman lightly on the mouth. It was Roger and Oonagh.

Lunch was a subdued affair, and the tension was almost unbearable. Pat came downstairs with Reggie to join everyone for champagne in the drawing room beforehand, but her poor little face was blotchy from crying and although she made an effort to be brave, it was obvious she was heart-broken at her son's fall from grace. Reggie stayed beside her all the time, as if to protect her from further pain, and they both seemed to have aged ten years since the previous day. Vivien and Simon stayed close, too. She'd told him about her lump, and together they'd thanked God and embraced each other with fervent relief that it had been a false alarm.

William and Stephanie held hands as he pointedly ignored Douglas and hovered around Julia as if she'd been ill and might have a relapse at any moment. Anna, turning her back on Petroc, laughed too loudly at her father's attempts at being amusing, and did her best to make the occasion jolly.

'We must play tennis after lunch,' she insisted. 'Why don't we get up a foursome, with me, Cressida, Sasha and Tim? What do you say, Tim?'

But Tim looked grim and ashen, eyes suddenly set in bruised hollows. 'I think I'll pass on that, Anna. I'm still hung over from last night,' he lied.

While Douglas did his customary and by now jaded performance of *mein host*, Christopher drew Julia into a corner.

'You'll be glad to hear I've finished with Barbara,' he murmured, so the others wouldn't hear.

Her face, in spite of looking tired and drawn, lit up as she smiled at him. 'I'm glad, Chris. Really glad. Did last night make you decide to end it?'

'It isn't all good, Julia.'

'Why? Is Barbara going to make trouble for you with Oonagh?'

'Oonagh wants a divorce . . .' He paused at Julia's sharp intake of breath. 'But it's not entirely to do with me and Barbara,' he continued, and turned to survey the rest of the house party. Leonora and Peter were talking to Oonagh and Roger, but his wife had a look of belonging to Roger by the way she stood close to his side, listening to everything he had to say and laughing when he was being amusing. 'Haven't you noticed what's going on?'

Julia frowned, not knowing what he meant. 'No.' She drew out the word wonderingly. 'But I've not been around this morning, so this is the first time I've seen everyone.'

'Oonagh and Roger,' Christopher mouthed.

'Oonagh and . . .? Oh, don't be so silly, Chris.'

'I'm dead serious. Pammy has gone back to London after a bust-up with Roger, and he and Oonagh have been inseparable ever since . . . well, it really started at the party last night.'

'You can't mean it! How could he do a thing like that? He's supposed to be Douglas's oldest friend. Surely he'd never try to go off with my sister-in-law?'

'It's happening, I promise you. I've already told Tim, and he's taken it very badly.'

'I'm not surprised. Oh, these poor children. What are we doing to them, Chris?' she said in distress. 'Anna, William and Mikey – especially Mikey – are in a real state after last night. And now Tim!' She turned away, eyes brimming. 'I'm not sure we deserve the children we've got. They're so good, and they try so hard to please us and become the sort of people we want them to be, and how do we treat them? As if they don't matter, so long as

299

our own desires are gratified and we get everything we want.'

Christopher watched her as she tried to control her emotions which were already on edge. He regretted ever telling her now about himself and Oonagh, but telling Julia everything had become a habit, started when he was a small child and she had been his big sister. When he'd been six, a twelve-year-old half-sister, already showing beauty and sophistication, had seemed like a grown-up to him.

'It may blow over,' he told her, trying to comfort her. But in his heart of hearts, he didn't believe it.

'Lunch is served,' Morgan told Douglas in his quiet way.

'Good! Good! We're all starving,' Douglas responded robustly. 'Come along, everyone. Grub's up!'

They all trooped into the dining room, talking to each other in low voices, as if they'd spent the morning at a funeral. Morgan had once again gone to a lot of trouble laying the table and in the centre had placed a large bowl of fresh sweet peas, their pastel frilly skirts like a group of ballerinas brightening the formal room. Douglas, taking his place at the head of the table, seated his mother on his right-hand side and Vivien on his left. It was a correct placement from an etiquette point of view, something Douglas was very keen on, but for him a brave one. Pat sat like a subdued dormouse, occasionally dabbing her nose with a tiny handkerchief but not talking. Vivien, on the other hand, was poised, cool, and kept up a constant flow of small talk, white-washing over the uglier moments such as when William made a snide remark to his father about betrayal.

Caroline, everyone's friend, sat quietly observing the

group. What struck her was that while they represented, on the whole, a united family, each of them was pursuing his or her own agenda and there were deep divisions, like ploughed ridges through a previously smooth field. It had not escaped her notice that Oonagh and Roger were exchanging smouldering looks, much to the annoyance of Leonora, or that Anna was ignoring Petroc's desperate attempts to distract her. Below these fissures lay the deeper rift; those who were understanding of Douglas's past infidelity, and those who were appalled that he could have been unfaithful to Julia.

It was going to take a long time for this family to recover from such a blow, Caroline reflected, and it wasn't over yet. She, too, had bought the *Globe*, when they'd stopped on the way home from the doctor to get petrol. She'd put it in the boot of her car so as not to upset Vivien, but once up in her bedroom was appalled by what she'd read. There was no doubt the police were going to be forced to review the case again and she dreaded to think how it would affect Julia, for deep in her heart she had this terrible feeling that Douglas might well be responsible for Lily's death. Not by actually killing her, but maybe by omitting to save her when she was in a life-threatening situation.

William followed Douglas into the study when lunch was over. Closing the door behind him, he turned to face his father with an expression Douglas had never seen on his face before. They watched each other warily as Douglas automatically went and sat behind his desk while William stood with his back to the fireplace.

Douglas was the first to speak. 'What is it, old chap?' he asked genially.

William was shaking with pent-up hostility. 'What do you *think* it is?' His face was scarlet. 'You've wrecked this family. Broken Mum's heart. Devastated your own parents . . . and you ask what's wrong? Dad, don't you realise what you've done? We all looked up to you. I thought you were the greatest father anyone could have. I was *so* proud of you.' His voice broke. His hands were shaking as he plunged them deep into his trouser pockets.

Douglas watched him silently, his face impassive. To his shock he realised that his son had grown into a man in the past twenty-four hours, still green and untested but nevertheless a man.

'How could you betray us like this, Dad?' William continued, gaining control of himself again. 'Did you never, for one moment, stop to think what this might to do to Mum? Think what it is doing to her *now*? It would serve you right if she walked out of this house and never came back.'

'What happens between your mother and me is our concern,' Douglas said, voice dangerously quiet. 'Please do not interfere in matters which do not concern you.'

'Not concern me?' William shouted, his voice ragged with emotion. 'For God's sake, what you did with some wretched servant girl concerns us all! Affects us all – Mum, Anna, Mikey and me. I thought we were supposed to be a family? Well, you've made it clear it's a family in which you have no part. You don't belong to us, not anymore. Go back to your womanising and your bloody restaurants and your whole glamorous life which is just one big publicity stunt from beginning to end. Last night you got more than you bargained for, didn't you? Well, serves you right! But leave us out of it in future, because we don't bloody need you.'

Douglas was enraged. He rose to his feet, a towering man with broad shoulders and eyes which flashed with fury, determined now to penetrate with angry words any chink in William's apparent maturity.

'You were quite happy to enjoy the benefits from my bloody restaurants until last night!' He waved his hand towards the garden beyond the open windows. 'I built all this for my family. You've had everything you could ever want since you were born. *Everything!* And I was about to finance you to go around the world for your gap year, and then give you a car for when you went to university. But now, of course, I can hardly burden you by asking you to accept these spoils, seeing you so despise the means by which I pay for them,' he added sarcastically.

'That suits me fine,' William shouted. 'I don't want another penny of your fucking money! I'll earn my own living. Get a job. And when Stephanie and I get married, you can be sure I won't be following in your footsteps, by betraying her . . .'

The study door opened and they both turned to see Julia standing there. She came into the room like a thunderbolt, slamming the door loudly behind her.

'How dare you talk to your father like that?' she stormed, glaring furiously at William. 'Let me remind you that you owe everything to him and his hard work. Let me also remind you he did it for *us* – you, me, Anna and Mikey . . .'

'Don't give me that, Mum,' William jeered, on a roll now, unable to stem the abuse that had been building up in him since the previous evening. 'Dad's on one big ego trip. Everything is to the greater glory of *him*. Even us. Last night's extravaganza was to show the world what a beautiful wife *he* had, what splendid upright children *he* had, what a marvellous house and . . .'

He reeled as he felt the stinging slap of Julia's hand on his cheek.

'Never forget that he's your father,' she continued. 'And I don't want to hear you talk about him like that again. It's disgusting and I'm ashamed of you.'

Without a word, William brushed roughly past her and marched out of the study, banging the door behind him.

Douglas came over from behind his desk to put his arms around Julia, and she clung to him for a moment, leaning against him.

'I didn't enjoy doing that but William had no right to speak to you in that way.'

'That was very, very sweet of you, my darling,' Douglas murmured, seeing how hurt she was beneath her angry exterior. 'He'll get over it. When the dust settles we'll make friends again.'

'I hope so.' Then she gently extricated herself. 'I've got things to do,' she said, leaving the room hurriedly.

Douglas went back to his desk, seeking the familiar security of his lair. His own hurt was deep and painful. Whatever William might say, he loved his children dearly, and Julia had been right: most of what he'd done had been to give them the best education and a style of living that was denied most people. If that was a sin, and if it was wrong to want the world to see how well he'd done, then he was indeed a vain, self-seeking man but that was something he'd long ago learned to live with.

Lying on her bed, resting, while the rest of the house party spent the afternoon playing tennis, croquet, swimming or relaxing on the terrace, Julia felt like a patchwork quilt, not like a person at all. She seemed to be made up of a dozen different personas. Like separate pieces of fabric, they all varied in colour and texture but were haphazardly stitched together in an effort to make an integral whole.

Her mother still saw her as a little girl who must be protected from harsh reality, while her son saw her as a helpless victim whose battles he must fight because she was not able to defend herself. Anna was more critical, a rival for her father's attention; maybe in her subconscious she even blamed her mother for Douglas's affair and secretly swore she'd never let *her* husband stray when she was married. Pat and Reggie probably felt she'd let Douglas down, too; did a devoted and dutiful wife cause her husband to have an affair? And then there was little Mikey, weeping in his room this morning while trying to be brave. To him she was just Mummy, source of warmth and unconditional love, uncomplicated until this moment by events beyond the nursery and the school room.

And what about Caroline, to whom she'd been a staunch friend and a source of strength during her debilitating divorces? And Leonora, who had always been jealous of her, and Peter, kind and remote in his dry scholarly way yet looking upon her as an ignoramus? And Christopher, her loyal brother, who looked up to her and to whom she was chief confidante and adviser . . .

Julia's mind started to reel, so fragmented did she feel as she thought of all these people, each claiming a part of her, each thinking they were the one who knew her best. And all under her roof at this very moment. How was she supposed to hold herself together? she wondered. The threads were breaking, the fabric fraying, and she was disintegrating, no longer whole.

Monday

24 June 1996

Twelve

If the weather had been glorious over the weekend, it changed with a vengeance on Monday morning. Rain lashed down in torrents, like the strands of a beaded curtain, making the dismantling of the marquee a wet and muddy job.

Julia and Douglas were both up early, having spent a sleepless night on the farthest edges of their vast bed. Their conversation was one-sided with Douglas trying to coax Julia into talking to him, while she stonewalled his advances politely, but coolly. Once dressed, they went downstairs; she to have a word with Mrs Morgan about domestic matters, and Douglas to supervise the packing up and removal of the kitchen equipment back to London. Town and County flowers had also returned to dismantle the decorations, with all their hired scenery and props, and by lunchtime another company would arrive to take down the marquee. Months of preparation and a week of solid hard work was about to be demolished, and within a few hours the glory and the glamour of the night, the whole illusion of Venice, would be gone, as if a beautiful richly hued bubble had burst.

'Good morning, Mrs Morgan,' Julia said, striding into the kitchen. She looked slimmer and even more fragile this morning in black trousers and a black turtleneck sweater. 'What a terrible day.'

Mrs Morgan looked gloomily out of the kitchen window as she put on the kettle. 'The lawn's going to be a mud patch by the end of the afternoon,' she observed.

'At least let's be thankful it was fine for the weekend, otherwise we'd have had everyone indoors the whole time.'

'So how many are there for breakfast?' Mrs Morgan was sole cook now, as all Douglas's chefs had been dispatched back to London the previous evening to resume their normal duties in Smart's, Trendy's, Futures and Butterfly.

Julia perched on a high stool, having poured herself a glass of freshly squeezed orange juice.

'We need trays for my parents and Mr and Mrs Rutherford. And there'll be six of us downstairs. Let's use the breakfast room, it's so much cosier.'

'Very well, ma'am. And will that make ten for lunch?'

'Yes. What can we give them, Mrs Morgan? We want something simple. I think everyone has overdosed on rich food for the past couple of days.'

'What about a nice shepherd's pie? Mr Rutherford always likes my home cooking,' she added, as if all the grand young chefs from London had deprived him of the finer things in life. 'I can make a bread and butter pudding to follow.'

'Perfect,' Julia agreed, getting down off the stool and going into the breakfast room which led off the kitchen. It had originally been a small conservatory, but Douglas had converted it into a warm sunny retreat for informal family meals, with a round table covered with a splashy floral cloth, cane furniture, and an abundance of plants.

Over the weekend, he'd used it for storing extra kitchen equipment, but his junior kitchen staff from Butterfly had already cleared it. Mrs Morgan followed Julia and they surveyed the tidy room.

'I must say,' she admitted grudgingly, 'them people from the London restaurants are quite efficient.'

Julia smiled. 'I don't think they'd last long with my husband if they weren't.'

The rest of the house was tidy too, thanks to Morgan. It was also silent and had an empty atmosphere. Julia frowned, feeling an unaccustomed loneliness in her own home. It was the contrast, she supposed, to the build-up to the party and the presence of so many people. Normally she'd have welcomed this quiet but today she was not sure she liked it.

Last night the mass exodus had begun. Peter and Leonora, with Cressida and Sasha, had departed for St John's Court, ready for Monday morning assembly. Christopher had also left, dragging a very reluctant Oonagh with him. She'd wanted to stay on for another day, presumably to be with Roger, but Chris had insisted they leave.

Anna had also gone back to London, to her job and the flat she shared with her three friends. She'd been very sweet when she'd said goodbye, thanking them for her presents and the party, but there had been sadness in her eyes and she'd hugged her father far more fiercely than she had Julia.

Petroc had gone with her, but still looked anxious, their relationship not yet resolved in a way that satisfied either of them. Everything had changed between them from the moment he'd announced he wasn't coming to the party. His profound sympathy for Julia, which Anna had taken as a criticism of her father, hadn't helped either. She'd clung to him from habit when the trauma was at its height, but as soon as she'd regained her equilibrium, had pushed him away again so that he felt more friend than lover.

Tim, tense and miserable-looking, had also left the previous evening, to catch the last flight back to Edinburgh. He barely kissed Oonagh goodbye, but in a reversal of William's attitude, hugged his father warmly and seemed genuinely sorry to leave him.

Families, Julia reflected, as she sat at the escritoire in her little sitting room, were an extraordinary mixture of love and discord, loyalty and betrayal. Until this weekend, she'd been naive enough to take her family at face value, while deliberately obliterating from her mind Douglas's affair with Lily all those years ago. With the passing of time she'd come to feel inviolable, secure and unafraid; but who had she been fooling? While she'd been bringing up their three children, in the belief that they were special because they were Douglas's babies, another child had been living only four miles away, brought up by her grandmother but financially supported by Douglas.

Shocking to her, too, was the swiftness with which the dynamics between them all had changed since Saturday. But had everything been perfect before the party? She wondered. Or had the cracks always been there, thinly disguised by diplomacy and social convention?

Michael came tearing into the room at that moment on his roller blades, miraculously restored to high spirits after a good night's sleep.

'When's breakfast, Mum?'

'Quite soon. We're having it in the breakfast room,' she

replied, hugging him as she marvelled at his recuperative powers.

'Cool! I'm starving. I didn't have any supper last night.'

'You fell asleep, sweetheart, and I didn't want to disturb you.'

'Can we go into Stockbridge after breakfast? I want to get some elbow pads. Look.' He pulled up the sleeve of his shirt to show her a dark bruise on his funny-bone. 'That's where I fell over on Saturday.'

'All right, Mikey, but on one condition.'

'What's that?'

She looked lovingly into his fresh open face and kissed his smooth cheek, loving the smell of his skin and hair; so familiar, so dear. 'On condition you stop roller blading in the house. You know you're not supposed to.'

'Yeah, OK,' he agreed reluctantly, turning and whizzing off.

'*Now*, Mikey, not tomorrow,' she called after him.

'How are you bearing up?' Roger said later that morning as he joined Douglas in the marquee, stripped down now to bare white canvas as if the delights of Venice had never been. Both men wore raincoats and Roger had put on a tweed trilby to protect his thinning hair from the rain. 'Everything OK?'

Douglas didn't answer immediately. The damp bleakness inside the marquee seemed to match his mood of desolation. He dug his cold hands deeper into his raincoat pockets.

'I'll survive,' he replied succinctly.

'I know you'll survive, but how are things between you and Julia?'

'Not good. We're treading carefully around each other, like walking on broken glass. This thing isn't going to go away either.'

'What do you mean? Lily's death was an accident. No one killed her.'

Douglas looked at his friend, knowing he could trust him but wondering how much he should say.

'It seems the police no longer believe that. They're coming to see me again later today.'

Roger turned to look at him, startled. 'Why?'

Douglas nodded. 'They've reopened the case. They told me they have cause to believe Lily was allowed to die, which certainly constitutes manslaughter if not murder.'

'And they think *you* did it?' Roger asked, appalled.

'If not me, someone else who wanted her out of the way.'

'But who . . .?' The question hung in the air like an evil vapour. The two men looked at each other. Roger spoke again.

'Christ, surely not . . .?' He couldn't say it. Didn't want to consider it. It was out of the question.

'We'd better go back to the house,' Douglas remarked, walking slowly towards the open flap of the marquee, through which the rain, driven by gusts of wind, sent an icy chill into the empty space. Then he turned to take a final look. Forty-eight hours ago the splendour of the setting had thrilled him even more than the opening of a new restaurant. Designed to show his family and the world how successful he was, it had been a glorious manifestation of style, imagination and wealth. And now it had vanished. Together with his happiness and reputation.

★ ★ ★

Pat had hardly slept, so troubled was she by what was happening to her beloved son, and when Morgan brought in their breakfast trays, she realised she wasn't hungry either. In fact she felt vaguely nauseous, but out of politeness let him place the tray on her knees as she sat, propped up in bed.

Reggie, as usual, was having his at a table in the window, and so did not notice that she only sipped a little tea and pretended to nibble some toast.

'We'll be indoors today,' he observed, looking out of the window. The far end of the garden was hazy through the veil of rain.

'It feels much colder.' Her hands were icy.

'It's warm in here.' He didn't feel cold at all. He poured himself a second cup of coffee, hot and strong, just the way he liked it.

'Has Douglas made any plans for today?' he asked his wife.

'Not that I know of. Everyone's gone home, except for us and Julia's parents. And I believe her friend Caroline and Roger. I expect we'll have a quiet day. Just the family.'

'A pity Peter and Leonora had to rush off last night.'

Pat nodded but said nothing. As long as Douglas was around she was content. At the thought of him her lips began to tremble and she felt the tears rising again, like an inexorable tide, surging through her body, trickling behind her throat and spilling slowly out down her cheeks.

'What's going to happen?' she asked hoarsely.

'Now don't upset yourself, dear,' Reggie soothed. 'You know Douglas. He'll be all right. He didn't do anything wrong so he's nothing to fear.'

'He certainly *didn't* do anything wrong, but it's terrible

that this has happened. So unfair!'

'Whoever said life was fair? Now eat up your breakfast, dear, and stop fretting. Everything's going to be all right.'

Pat tried to lift her teacup but her hands were so cold it was difficult.

They stayed in their room until nearly noon. Reggie read his book contentedly, looking up every now and again to watch the rain, while Pat stayed in bed with her eyes closed. She wasn't asleep but hoped that if she kept her eyes shut the feelings of nausea would pass and she'd recover. At last he closed the book with a snap and looked over at her.

'Better get up, love. Lunch will be in an hour, and you know Douglas likes us all to get together for a drink beforehand.'

She opened her eyes. 'You're right.' With a supreme effort she sat up and got slowly out of bed. Her feet were as icy as her hands. 'The weather's changed,' she remarked. 'I think I'll have a hot bath.'

'Good idea. I might have one after you.' He felt good today, the result of hardly drinking at dinner last night. He was looking forward to a glass of wine with lunch, though. Douglas always served beautiful wines, perfectly chosen to go with the food. But then, of course, that was his business.

After a while, he got up and padded on bare feet to the bathroom. If Pat didn't get a move on, they'd be late.

'Pat?' he called, through the open door. There was no answer. Frowning, he pushed the door open and caught his breath. Like someone who had lain down to sleep, his wife lay on the bathmat, still and white, a towel clutched to her chest with both hands.

'Pat!' He crouched down beside her, held her wrist, but did not need anyone to tell him that she had died, slipping away quietly and without fuss because her great and generous heart was no longer able to bear the sorrow and strain of Douglas's downfall.

'Oh, Pat . . .' He stroked her face, gently pushing back the grey hair from her forehead. They'd been married for fifty-four years and during that time had never been apart for more than a few hours. Fifty-four years of companionship, closeness and compatibility. They'd been friends as well as lovers and now it was all over. She was gone from him. How was he going to manage without her? He was missing her already.

Reggie rose slowly and stiffly to his feet, wanting to weep but unable to. Shock, the body's ultimate means of protection from the onslaught of immediate grief had locked him into a trance-like state. Without conscious thought, he tightened the belt of his dressing-gown, and went downstairs to find Douglas.

The rest of Monday passed like a nightmare for the Rutherford family. Dr Hickey hurried round to confirm what they had all presumed: Pat had died from a heart attack, which had struck swiftly and fatally, but as he wasn't her regular practitioner, a second doctor was called in to sign the death certificate.

Douglas, his face as grey as putty, eyes red-rimmed, marched grimly around, trying to get things organised. It was agreed that the funeral should take place at St Olaf's, the little fourteenth-century church in Stickley; Douglas had already been on to the vicar to ask if he could buy adjoining burial plots, so that eventually Reggie could be laid to rest beside his wife.

He himself, still in his dressing-gown and moving as if in a dream, with a glass of whisky permanently in his hand, looked heartbreakingly lost. He hardly spoke. Words of sympathy and condolence went unheard. He shuffled around the house as if he were looking for Pat and was perplexed he couldn't find her. At last Julia, wrenched by pity and sadness, went and put her arms around him. Pressing herself against his burly frame, she looked up into his face.

'Reggie, I want you to know this is your home now. Douglas and I would really love you to live with us. You can't go back to Derby on your own. Stay here and live with us all.'

'That's right, Dad. You must stay with us,' Douglas agreed. 'We'll all look after you.'

Reggie looked from one to the other of them and then took a gulp of his whisky. 'I'd still be near Pat then, wouldn't I? I could visit her grave whenever I wanted to.'

Julia hugged him closer. 'Of course you could,' she assured him warmly. 'And you'd be with Douglas . . .' Her voice broke. Too much was happening. At any moment, according to her husband, the police would arrive to question him further. They'd said they'd want to question her, too. They were extremely sorry to hear about his mother dying but they had to continue with their enquiries which wouldn't take long . . .

William, coming into the room, the row with his father forgotten, had a message for them.

'Anna's coming back. She'll be here later this afternoon.'

'Oh, good,' Julia replied with relief. She had a feeling that so long as they could all stick together, everything would eventually come right. They'd be a family once again, divisions forgotten, betrayals forgiven.

'This has been a doomed weekend,' Caroline whispered to Roger, as they sat on the window seat at the far end of the drawing room, wanting to be helpful and supportive but at the same time feeling they might be intruding in what were strictly family matters.

Roger sighed gustily. 'Poor old Duggie. He's had a double whammy this weekend, hasn't he? I'm surprised he's coping as well as he is. Julia seems to have softened a bit towards him, though, so that's something.'

'She's been to hell and back since Saturday night,' Caroline pointed out, loyally. 'How would you feel if you discovered your wife had secretly had a child? Julia's had the most enormous shock. And the accusation that Douglas may have killed the mother of that girl was the last straw,' she added vehemently.

'Not killed . . . allowed to die,' Roger corrected her. 'But that will soon be sorted out. He isn't guilty. He didn't let Lily die.'

'You seem very sure of that?'

'There's no doubt about it.'

'But according to the *Globe* it wasn't an accident.'

'I never said it was.'

Caroline's brow became furrowed as she looked at Roger, perplexed. 'But who else could have it been?'

He shrugged and remained silent, face averted, watching as William put his arm round Julia's shoulders in a protective way as she stood talking to Douglas and his father.

Then he spoke. 'I must go and make a phone call. I was going back to London this evening, but I think I'll stay another day in case Douglas needs me.'

Caroline nodded absently, not listening, her mind in

turmoil. She should get back to town, too, to attend to her business. It was almost a relief, she thought guiltily, to have a valid reason to leave.

'Roger! Oh, God, how nice to hear from you.' Oonagh had picked up the phone on its second ring as if she'd been waiting for his call. 'How are you?'

'It's all a bit tense down here.'

'What's the latest?'

'Douglas's mother has died.'

'*What?*' She sounded stunned. 'Pat? Pat's died?' she repeated incredulously. 'My God, what happened?'

'She had a heart attack. It was very sudden. Poor old Douglas and Reggie are shattered.'

'I suppose she was upset about Douglas's other child turning up at the party.' Oonagh sounded slightly disparaging.

'Well . . . yes.' Roger felt disconcerted by her cool manner.

'Oh, well . . . when am I going to see you again?' she asked in a seductive voice, as if he'd told her about something no more important than a change in the weather. Taken aback, he paused before answering.

'It depends how long Douglas needs me here,' he said. 'He's pretty cut up, as you can imagine, and on top of everything the police want to ask him some more damn' fool questions.'

'But what about me? I thought we'd arranged that as soon as I was back in London, you'd come back, too, and we'd meet?' Oonagh suddenly sounded cold and nagging, her voice harsh.

Roger underwent the quickest change of heart in a long lifetime of falling in love and allowing his emotions to rule him. He must have been mad. Julia's sister-in-law, and a cold bitch at that! Deciding to put it down to too much champagne at the party, coupled with the sexy music of Nigel Tulley and The Dark Blues, he realised he'd been about to make an even bigger mistake than getting involved with Pammy Schemmel, and *that* took some beating.

'While Douglas needs me I must stay down here,' he said firmly. 'It's going to be a tough week for the whole family. Anyway, I'll see you around sometime . . .' He was cut off in mid-flow by Oonagh's slamming down the phone, and imagined her, sharp white face set, scarlet mouth tight, swearing at him furiously.

Julia had begged her mother and Simon to stay on for a few more days, and they needed no persuasion.

'Of course we will, darling,' Vivien exclaimed, glad that Julia appeared to need her. They'd grown closer since their talk on Sunday morning, as both came to realise that their reason for not communicating was based not on a lack of understanding, but perhaps on understanding each other too well. Even now they were being tenderly careful with each other's feelings, because both realised that if the walls of reserve they'd built around themselves were to break, they could both be swept away in a torrent of emotion that dated back to when Guido had been killed.

'Tell us what we can do,' Simon offered. 'Douglas is under terrible stress at the moment, and I'd like to help.'

'Darling Simon,' she replied. 'Your just being here is a help. You know what Douglas is like. He's a workaholic. I sometimes think he needs to work in order to survive. He'll have to stay down here this week, for his father's sake, but knowing him, he'll be glued to the phone and the fax machine, trying to run all the restaurants at a distance.'

'Perhaps we could help with Michael?' Vivien suggested. 'Maybe take him out for the day?'

'That would be marvellous, Mama. Pat's death has been an awful shock for him, he was really fond of her. You could take him to the cinema in Andover . . . Oh, and there's a bowling alley as well. He'd love that.'

Simon's face lit up.

'Splendid!' he said. 'We'll take him out for the day. What is it these youngsters like to eat? Hamburgers and chips? Hot dogs and Coca-Cola? Right. We'll go to McDonald's for lunch, and that will give you a bit of a break.'

Julia kissed his cheek. 'I'm really grateful, and it will do Mikey the world of good.'

'Is Peter coming back?' Vivien enquired in a low voice. 'Shouldn't he be here?'

'There's a governors' meeting this afternoon and he can't get away, but he's driving over later this evening.'

'He wasn't as close to his mother as Douglas, was he?'

'No, Mama. Douglas was her favourite.' Julia spoke wistfully. 'I've always felt sorry for Peter. He simply couldn't win. Nothing he did ever compared with Douglas's achievements.'

Anna arrived in the late afternoon, tear-stained and exhausted. Roger had gone to meet her at the station, and when she got back to Highfield Manor, she flung herself, sobbing, into Douglas's arms.

'Oh, Daddy! Poor Daddy. I'm so sorry. I can hardly believe Grandma's gone. How's Grandpa? Is he all right?'

Douglas hugged her close. 'He's bearing up although

he's pretty shattered. He's going to stay with us indefinitely, and I think that's cheered him up a bit. To know he won't have to go home alone.'

Anna cried even harder. 'And Grandma gave me those lovely pearls for my birthday . . . Oh, how could this have happened? It's so cruel.'

He patted her back, affected by her grief. 'We were expecting you earlier than this,' he said. 'What happened? Roger said you weren't on the first train he met.'

'I was trying to find something black to wear for the funeral, and I couldn't find anything suitable. I'd never get into any of Mummy's clothes, and there are no shops around here that sell anything decent. In the end I managed to find a black linen suit. I hope that will do.'

'It will do splendidly, sweetheart, and Grandma would have been very touched to know you went to so much trouble. Is Petroc coming back?'

Anna shook her head. 'No.'

'Not even for the funeral?' Douglas sounded hurt.

She blew her nose, tears subsiding. 'He doesn't know about Grandma because I haven't told him,' she said succinctly. 'We had a blazing fight last night when we got back to London and I'm not seeing him again. It's over. I've really had enough of his on-off behaviour. He can't make up his mind whether he wants me or not. Finally he said last night that he couldn't decide whether we should get engaged or not.'

'And what did you say to that?'

Anna gave a watery smile. 'I said to him: "Allow me to make up your mind for you, Petroc. Get out of my flat and don't come back, I never want to see you again." He was a bit surprised, but he left.'

Douglas gave a throaty chuckle. 'Good for you! I like your style. So it's all over, is it?'

'Absolutely,' she replied stoutly. 'I won't be messed around anymore.'

Half an hour later, DI Swann and DS Newton arrived. Morgan showed them into the study and a few minutes later Douglas joined them, making no secret of the fact that he was in a distressed state. Holding a large white handkerchief, he wiped the outer corners of his eyes.

'You must excuse me if I don't seem to be co-operating but I have a lot on my mind. In any case, I don't know what more I can tell you,' he said gruffly.

Swann and Newton were cordially sympathetic, but it was obvious they had no intention of abandoning their line of inquiry and leaving him in peace.

Swann spoke first. 'There are some further questions we have to ask you, sir, about what happened on the day of August the twenty-third, 1980. Neville Barton, the gardener you employed at the time, has made a statement to the effect that he arrived early that day. He says he saw you through the kitchen window. You were unlocking the larder door, and then you opened it. He told us this happened at eleven o'clock. Yet, in your statement, made at the time, you claimed to have returned home from the woods at twelve-forty-five, and that you discovered Lily Watson's body then by finding it lying on the larder floor – *through the open door*. Can you explain that, sir?'

'Easily,' Douglas retorted. 'The man's lying.'

Swann was poker-faced and unamused. 'That's not a very constructive attitude, sir.'

'Well, you tell me what my attitude should be,' Douglas

barked. 'I have an alibi for that whole morning. The farmer who owns the adjoining land was mending the fence between his property and mine. He saw me.'

'Unfortunately, Mr Maxwell, the farmer in question died last year, so we are unable to verify this,' Newton said dryly.

'He'd have said the same thing,' Douglas argued. 'Why don't you read the statement he made at the time, for God's sake?'

There was a long silence. Swann and Newton looked at each other. Knowingly, it seemed to Douglas.

'When, to your knowledge, did Neville Barton arrive for work that day, sir?'

Douglas raised his eyebrows in surprise. Then he frowned, thinking. 'D'you know, I've no idea.' He sounded genuinely puzzled. 'Frankly, I don't remember seeing him at all that day. Mind you, it was all so chaotic, so tragic. Most of it seemed to pass in a blur.'

'Were you still in love with Lily Watson?'

'No, I was not,' Douglas swiftly rejoined. 'But the death of anyone young is a tragedy.'

'It must have made the situation easier between you and your wife, though, when Lily wasn't around anymore.'

'There was never a problem between myself and Julia in the first place.'

Swann leaned forward, eyes watchful. 'But your wife knew you were having an affair?'

'We never talked about it.'

'But did she know?'

'I believe she learned of it through village gossip.'

'But I imagine you went to great lengths to hide this affair from your wife, sir. It must have been a great blow to you when she engaged Lily as a servant. You must have been nervous your wife would find out then?' Swann asked slyly.

Douglas looked stubborn, eyes hard. 'Lily wasn't a kiss-and-tell sort of person. I provided generously for her and the baby. Anyway, she knew our affair was over. There'd have been no point in telling Julia.'

'Except for vengeance.'

'She wasn't like that. Now, is that all?' he asked impatiently. 'I have to get back to my family. There are so many arrangements to be . . .'

DS Newton interrupted him. 'There is also the question of the syringe and antidote which Mrs Watson swears was in Lily's handbag that day. But when her body was discovered the handbag was only a few yards away and the syringe was missing. That syringe and the adrenalin it contained could have saved her life. Can you shed any light, Mr Rutherford, on why it was missing?'

'I'd like to shed some light on why people are now saying something quite different from the statements they made at the time,' Douglas roared, pounding his fist on the desk in front of him. 'This is a farce, and I'd like to bet Nancy Graham has something to do with this ludicrous state of affairs.'

'We make our own enquiries, sir,' DI Swann said icily. 'We don't listen to tittle-tattle.'

'Well, you're making a bloody good job of it now.'

'I must warn you, sir . . .'

Douglas shook his head from side to side. 'All right. All right. You don't have to lecture me.'

Both Swann and Newton rose to their feet and Douglas looked up at them expectantly, thinking they were leaving. His hopes were dashed by their next words.

'Mr Rutherford, I have to inform you that we are

arresting you on a charge of manslaughter in connection with the death of Lily Watson, on August . . .'

'You're *what*?' he bellowed, jumping up from his desk. 'What the hell are you talking about? You can't just overturn a coroner's verdict. There was never any question that anyone had deliberately tried to kill Lily.'

'We are reopening the case in the light of fresh evidence . . .'

'What bloody fresh evidence?' Douglas was scarlet with rage. He stood like a boxer, feet planted wide, fists clenched, glaring at them as if challenging them to lay a finger on him. Then he spun round and grabbed the phone on his desk. 'I'm getting on to my solicitor. We'll soon put a stop to this rubbish . . .'

'Douglas, what's happening?'

The three men spun round and saw Julia standing in the doorway, eyes wide with alarm. 'What's going on?' she demanded, shrilly.

Swann and Newton stood stiffly, aware of their own height and bulk beside this slim, fragile-looking woman. Before they could say anything, Douglas spoke.

'They're arresting me,' he said flatly. 'They seem to think I was responsible for letting Lily die.' His upper lip curled in a sneer. 'They think I hatched some clever plot to entice a bee to sting Lily, and when it had carried out its mission, I locked her in the larder until she was dead. Having, of course, remembered to steal her syringe from her handbag and hide it somewhere afterwards. And then, not content with that, they think I opened the larder door again, so no one would realise she'd been shut in. And then, guess what?' He was incandescent with rage by now, towering over her while she stood quite still, watching him intently. 'Guess what happened next? I discovered her *all over again*, an hour and a half later, having pretended to have just come in from working in the woods. What do you think of that?'

Julia's hand flew up to cover her mouth. She looked terrified.

'But that's how it happened!' she gasped.

Douglas crumpled, wrath deflating as he stared at her. It seemed he couldn't believe his ears.

Newton stepped forward, frowning. 'Are you saying you've always known your husband was responsible?'

Julia collapsed into a chair, both hands covering her face now.

'No. *No!* It wasn't Douglas who let Lily die. It was *me*. You've got the wrong person. You can't arrest Douglas. It was *me*. I wanted her out of the way . . .'

Ashen, Douglas looked at her, as if he were seeing her for the first time. 'Julia . . . what are you saying?' he asked wildly.

She dropped her hands and stared at him unflinchingly. And when she spoke it was as if they were alone in the room.

'You didn't think I knew about you and Lily when she died, did you? But I did. Not when I first employed her, I had no idea at that time, but then the gossip started and I heard you'd been . . . lovers. I couldn't bear it. I'd never have asked her to work here if I'd known but once I knew . . .' There was a long pause.

Swann and Newton continued to stare at her as if they, too, could hardly believe their ears. 'Oh, God. Oh, God,' Douglas kept saying under his breath. Then Julia took a deep breath, as if she'd made up her mind about something.

'I came back from shopping in the village shortly after

ten o'clock,' she continued in a dull voice. 'The house was empty and as I entered the kitchen I heard the crash of something falling and then Lily cried out: "I've been stung!" She was in the larder, and I rushed to see what had happened. She was standing there, just standing, looking at the palm of her hand. A bee was still sticking to it. She seemed mesmerised with shock. I acted on impulse. I just ran out and slammed the larder door behind me, locking it. Who would think it wasn't an accident? Everyone knew she was allergic to bee stings. She'd told everyone that if she didn't have an injection of adrenalin immediately, she'd be dead within twenty to thirty minutes. It was a perfect way to put an end to a situation I could no longer bear,' she added sadly.

'So you took the syringe out of her handbag and destroyed it?' Newton asked gently, almost as if afraid of breaking Julia's flow of memories.

She raised her head, looking at him in confusion. 'No,' she replied uncertainly. 'I just left the kitchen and went upstairs. Lily was . . .' She bowed her head. 'Lily was screaming . . . and choking . . . I couldn't stay and listen . . .'

'Oh, Jesus Christ!' Douglas groaned, as if he too was in physical pain.

'Then what happened?' Swann prompted.

'After half an hour I came down to the kitchen again. I listened at the larder door and there was no sound. So I unlocked it. And opened it.'

'And?'

'I couldn't look. I went straight out again, drove down to the village, went into all the shops to buy something and stopped for coffee at the little café on the corner. Everyone saw me. Dozens of people. I had an alibi and that was what I needed. I didn't return here until nearly one o'clock and by that time Douglas had discovered Lily's body.'

'We need you to come down to the station to make a statement, Mrs Rutherford, where you will be formally charged with the murder of Miss Lily Watson,' DI Swann informed her, stiltedly.

Julia nodded silently. Then she looked over at Douglas, who was sitting at his desk with his head in his hands.

'I'm sorry, darling . . . so sorry,' she told him brokenly. 'But I had to do it. I couldn't risk losing you to her.'

'But it was over between us. I was never going to see her again,' he exclaimed furiously.

'I didn't know that, Douglas. I wasn't sure it was over between you. People in the village were calling her your mistress. How do you think that made me feel?'

'Oh, God, Julia.' His cheeks were wet.

She turned to Swann and Newton and spoke as if what she was going to say next was the reason for everything.

'I love my husband more than life itself, you see. I couldn't let anyone take him away from me.'

Vivien found Michael in his dimly lit bedroom, standing leaning against the wall, crying silently, in an attitude of total despair.

'My darling boy,' she said, putting her arms around him. He didn't resist her but allowed her to guide him over to his bed, where he instantly curled up in a foetal position, with his face buried in his Spiderman pillowcase.

'It's going to be all right, sweetheart,' she told him, amazed at her ability to lie so smoothly.

'I want my mum,' he whimpered. 'How long is she going to be in prison?'

Vivien stroked his dark hair and remembered Julia at this age. Of her three grandchildren, Michael was the most like his mother.

'She's not in prison,' she tried to reassure him. 'She's at the police station, answering lots of questions. Daddy will make sure she doesn't stay there. He's already been talking to his solicitor.'

He rolled on to his back and looked up at her, his dark eyes gazing into hers. 'Did you ever know Lily?'

Vivien was taken aback, unaccustomed to the direct manner and maturity of modern children. Julia, when she'd been nine, had still played with dolls and had had no idea even how babies were born.

'No, I never knew her,' she replied.

'Daddy must have loved her. They had a baby together,' he said. His small face puckered, disturbed by this thought.

'I'm certain he never loved her as much as he loves your mummy.'

'Then why did he do it?' His manner was so direct, so grown-up, so masculine, it brought home to her the great difference between little boys and little girls.

'Grown-up men do all sorts of silly things,' Vivien said lightly. 'Now, would you like some supper? Mrs Morgan has made a lovely pasta, and we could have it in the breakfast room, all cosy. And then a yoghurt or some chocolate ice cream. What do you say? There's Coca-Cola to drink, too.'

He turned his face away, indifferent to temptation. 'I'm not hungry.'

'You will be if you don't have supper.'

He looked at her again. 'Where's William?'

'He's downstairs, talking to Anna.'

'And where's Grandpa?'

'In the study with your daddy, Roger and Simon.'

'Granny?' He gazed through the window. It had stopped raining and the garden was shrouded in the blue cloak of twilight.

'Yes, my darling?'

'Do you suppose Grandma has met up with Buster, in heaven?'

'Buster?' Vivien asked carefully.

'Yes, you know. My hamster. He died last year.'

'Oh, I'm sure they're together! Looking after each other.' She was near to tears but knew she must control them for his sake.

'That's all right then,' Michael commented philosophically.

She stroked his cheek, firm and soft as a ripe peach.

'Soon everything will be all right,' she said comfortingly, praying it might be true.

'I think I'll go and talk to William.' He clambered off his bed, shirt tails hanging out of his cotton shorts touchingly, his hair ruffled. 'He'll know when Mum's coming home.'

'What a good idea,' she told him. When he'd gone, Vivien went back to her own bedroom, feeling exhausted by the nightmare events of the day. Julia's confession had been a terrible shock; she didn't believe it, yet. Couldn't take it in. Her Julia, so gentle and kind, so generous and warm . . . But deliberately to let someone die when they could so easily have been saved? It didn't seem possible. Not Julia. Not her beloved daughter.

Vivien lay down on her bed for a little rest, refusing to believe what had happened.

Christopher, arriving home from the office, heard the phone start to ring just as he entered the flat. Striding across the hall to grab it, thinking it might be Barbara although he'd had no contact with her since they'd spoken on Sunday morning, he was surprised to hear his father's voice.

'Hi, Dad,' he said conversationally.

Simon spoke with difficulty, as if he didn't know how to phrase what he had to say. He decided to break the news of Pat's death first, not to get it out of the way so much as to build up to the news which would really upset his son.

'Pat?' Christopher said, shocked, when he was told. 'Oh dear, poor old Reggie. He's going to be lost without her. And poor Douglas. God, what a terrible weekend it turned out to be, and it all started as such a joyful occasion.'

'I'm afraid there's more, and it's much worse.'

'*What?*' Suddenly he had a premonition Simon was going to say something had happened to Julia. 'What is it?' asked Chris, half afraid to hear the answer.

'Julia has confessed to killing Lily.'

For a moment he almost laughed. It was the most preposterously bad joke he'd ever heard.

'Come on, Dad. That's not funny,' he rejoined sharply.

'It's no joke, Chris. The police came to question Douglas, and were on the point of arresting him when Julia burst into the room and said she was the one who'd locked Lily in the larder.'

'I don't believe it!' Christopher exclaimed loudly. 'It's not possible, Dad.' At that moment Oonagh came into the hall from the drawing room, wondering what was going on.

'What's happened?' she mouthed. Chris gave her a cursory glance, and could see she'd been crying. Her eyes were swollen and her cheeks blotchy instead of their usual perfect shade of ivory.

He put his hand over the mouthpiece of the phone. 'Did you know about this?' he asked coldly.

She blinked, looking blankly back at him. 'What?'

'That Julia's confessed to killing that woman . . . Lily what's-her-name?'

The shock had a curious effect on Oonagh. That someone was in a worse mess than herself, because she now knew Roger would have nothing more to do with her, revived her flagging spirits so much that a malicious gleam immediately lit up her eyes.

'God, no! How awful! Who's that on the phone?'

'My father,' he replied curtly before resuming his conversation with Simon. Oonagh continued to loiter in the hall, looking pensive as she listened.

'I'll drive down right away, if only to give Douglas moral support. I can recommend a friend of mine who's a barrister. Actually, he's a Q.C. and excellent. How's Mum bearing up?' Christopher added.

When he'd hung up, he felt Oonagh's hand on his shoulder. 'I'll get my coat and come with you. I won't be a moment,' she said in a tone which suggested they were off to an interesting social event.

He stood looking down at her. 'No, you won't,' he said, firmly but quietly. 'You wanted a divorce and you're getting one. Why don't you run off to Roger? He'll give you some fun and the sort of life you really want. But count me out from now on.'

Oonagh started, as if she'd been slapped in the face.

'What do you mean? I thought you said . . .' Her

334

expression turned nasty. 'I suppose you've seen that tart again? You can't give her up, is that it? You're going to leave me, after all, for *her*.'

'I have not spoken to Barbara since Sunday,' he replied calmly. Inwardly he was surprised. Only yesterday she and Roger . . . but then he understood the reason for her tear-stained face and guessed what had happened. 'Anyway I must go. I'd better take a few things because I'll probably be staying at Highfield for the time being.'

As he hurried off to their bedroom to pack, Oonagh stormed after him, screaming obscenities and threatening to ruin his career if he left her. Suddenly he'd had enough. He turned on her in fury.

'You were happy enough to throw yourself at Roger all weekend, embarrassing Tim and making a complete fool of yourself. Now, suddenly, you want to stay married to me. What's happened? Has he chucked you? Are you afraid you'll miss out and have no one?'

Her face crumpled and she slumped on to the bed beside his half-packed suitcase. 'Don't leave me, Chris. We can work something out,' she wept. 'I can't be on my own. I hate being on my own.'

He threw his sponge bag into the case and clicked it shut.

'Well, now's the time for you to learn. I've had enough. Over twenty years of nagging, unfeeling sex and a round of boring parties, just so you can have your photograph in the magazines.

'I'm getting out, Oonagh, and I can assure you this has nothing to do with Barbara, whom I shall probably never see again.'

After Julia had made a statement confessing to the

murder of Lily Watson, and had been placed in a holding cell prior to being formally committed in court at the first hearing on Friday, DI Swann turned to his colleague.

'I could have sworn it was him who did it, y'know.'

'Douglas Rutherford, you mean?'

'Yes.' Swann felt dazed. Was he slipping? Getting too old for this job? 'She looks like such a gentle sort of woman. The type that wouldn't hurt a fly.'

'They're usually the worst,' Newton replied dryly. He was hungry for promotion, ready to step into Swann's shoes. 'Douglas Rutherford is such a blusterer, such a swaggering windbag, that although I knew he had a motive, I always felt there was something missing . . . some flaw in the case. I can't say I'm surprised it was the wife.'

Swann shook his head, angry with himself for getting it wrong.

'We've got to prepare for the hearing in four days' time. That doesn't give us long,' he remarked, determined to keep a grip on the case. 'We've got to go through all the statements, and check up on everything. It may mean visiting the witnesses again.'

'What about Nancy Graham? She's moving house tomorrow. Going to live at Egbury.'

Swann considered this for a moment. 'Let's see how we go. She's only an informant really. The witnesses are Lily's mother, Neville Barton, and Mr Harris.'

'OK.' Newton sounded impatient. With a confession in hand, what was the point of doing all this work on the witnesses' statements? He said as much to Swann, who looked horrified.

'Supposing Mrs Rutherford chickens out and says she didn't do it after all? Suppose she says she was framed?

She might even say we framed her, or trapped her into confessing.'

'But we didn't.'

Swann sighed pointedly. 'If it's promotion you're after, that isn't the attitude to take. We must be prepared for every eventuality. For all we know, she may be bitterly regretting having confessed.'

Newton nodded, knowing old Swann was right. He thought of the beauty of Highfield Manor, and the life of luxury the Rutherfords led there, and felt quite sad at the waste. 'She's got a lot to lose.'

'You can say that again.'

It was late evening and Christopher had just arrived. Douglas, distraught and drinking heavily, was in his study, while his father lay sleeping upstairs, worn out by the events of the day. Vivien, together with Mrs Morgan, had moved Reggie into another bedroom, a cheerful bright room overlooking the swimming pool, so that the memories of that morning could be softened, and for this he expressed his gratitude.

'You're very kind, my dear. When I wake up in the morning, I'll try and remember not to reach out for Pat. And as I've never slept in this room before, that might be easier.'

He looked so lost, so utterly ravaged by grief, that Vivien's heart went out to him. Gently, she laid her hand on his arm.

'All Pat's things are just as she left them in the other room, and I'm sure Julia would understand if you wanted them kept that way until you're ready to deal with them,' she said gently.

Reggie nodded mutely, unable to speak. Vivien left the

room quietly then, sensing he would prefer to be alone. On the way back downstairs, she looked in on Michael, and found him fast asleep. So the oldest and the youngest members of the family had retreated to the safety of their beds, to seek the blessed oblivion of sleep which is the greatest healer of all.

But Vivien couldn't contemplate going to bed yet. Her thoughts were with Julia, locked in a cell, and she felt sick with fear at what was going to happen. Stunned, too, by her daughter's confession. How she must have suffered all these years, Vivien reflected, making her way downstairs to the study again. Her heart physically ached for her daughter, as if someone had punched her in the chest. And at this moment, so intense were her feelings of sorrow that she paused at the bottom of the stairs and closed her eyes. Not a churchgoing woman, she nevertheless turned, with a homing instinct, to a deity with whom she had only a vague acquaintance.

Dear God, she prayed, wondering if He would do a trade-in, let me die if you'll only stop Julia from having to go through this torment. She did it because she loves Douglas. She did it because she thought she was protecting her children from a broken home. Please, God. Please. I'm not afraid to die, if you'll only let Julia be set free. She clutched the banister tightly, eyes closed, willing God to listen to her.

'Granny! Are you all right?'

The voice startled her. Anna had come out of the study and was standing looking up, her expression anxious.

Vivien smiled wanly. 'I was praying for a miracle,' she replied, without embarrassment. 'I was trying to do a deal with God, but I have a feeling He's not listening.'

'Oh, Granny, I don't think He works in that way. For a

minute I thought you were ill. I'm going to make some more coffee. I think Daddy needs it. Would you like some?'

'Thank you, sweetheart, that would be lovely. Can I help?'

'No, you go and sit down. Christopher's on the phone trying to get hold of his barrister friend, but he's out at a dinner party.'

A few minutes after Anna had made the coffee and was pouring everyone a cup, Peter arrived, stooping more than ever, eyes bloodshot in his long grey melancholy face, his suit crumpled and shabby, giving him the appearance of an out-of-work grave digger.

Douglas greeted him with a silent but emotional bear hug, to which his brother responded feebly. The others rose to greet him, Simon with a sympathetic pat on the shoulder, Roger with a firm handshake and Christopher with a brief embrace. William shook hands and murmured embarrassed words of condolence, while Vivien and Anna kissed his chilly cheek and invited him to sit down and rest after his long drive.

'You've come alone?' Douglas asked after a moment.

'Yes. Leonora's tied up with visiting parents tomorrow, and of course Cressida and Sasha are back in London, working.'

'What would you like to drink?'

Peter looked at the tray on which earlier in the evening Morgan had arranged bottles of Famous Grouse, brandy, vodka, gin, sherry, Cinzano, and a quantity of mixers.

'I think I'll just have a cup of tea,' he said morosely.

'I'll get it,' offered Anna, glad to be kept busy.

Peter lowered himself into a chair. 'How could Mother

have died? She was so well yesterday. I don't understand it.'

Douglas was pouring himself another drink with his back to the room. It was as if he hadn't heard. Simon spoke instead.

'The doctor said it was her heart. It was very sudden. She probably wouldn't have felt anything.'

'Where's Father?'

'In bed, asleep,' Vivien told him. 'He's being incredibly brave, but of course it's been a terrible shock.'

Douglas had turned round and was watching them, but his unfocused eyes seemed to gaze at an interior landscape which the others could only surmise was bleak.

'I suppose the funeral will be down here?' Peter asked.

The others nodded.

'Probably on Saturday,' Simon vouchsafed, wondering why he'd suddenly become the spokesman.

They were suddenly startled by an eruption, drunken and passionate, from Douglas.

'It's all my fault. All of it,' he burst out, crashing a glass down on his desk. 'I'm to blame for everything! None of this would have happened if I'd never taken up with Lily.' He started sobbing. 'Oh, God, what have I done?'

Peter looked at him, bewildered. 'What are you talking about? That's got nothing to do with Mother's death.'

'It's got everything to do with her death,' his brother lamented remorsefully. 'I've let her and Dad down. The shock of Rose's arrival at the party was bad enough, but being accused in the press of killing Lily! And then the police coming to the house yesterday morning . . .' Wracking sobs prevented him from continuing. He collapsed in the chair behind his desk and buried his head in his arms, muttering, 'Julia . . . Oh, God, Julia.'

'I don't see . . .' began Peter, lugubriously.

Simon interrupted him, managing to speak evenly while he reached for Vivien's hand. 'The police came back earlier today and were on the point of arresting Douglas on a charge of murder when Julia confessed that it was she who locked Lily in the larder.'

Peter looked at him, and then at the others, too stunned to say anything.

'She's being held by the police,' William said, his voice wobbling dangerously.

'In prison?' he whispered hoarsely.

William nodded. 'She's going to be formally committed at the local assizes on Friday when a date will be set for the trial.'

'It should be me,' Douglas moaned wildly. 'It's my fault she was driven to . . .' He started to sob again.

Simon and Roger looked at each other, both realising it was late and that Douglas was very drunk. Nothing was going to be gained by further discussion tonight.

Roger rose and went over to him, patting his shoulder.

'Come along, old chap. Time we all went to bed. You need to be fighting fit for tomorrow.'

'I'm not going to bed. How can I go to bed?' Douglas demanded querulously, wiping his eyes with the back of his hand. 'I shan't sleep. What's the point of going to bed?'

Christopher came into the study at that moment, and took in the scene at a glance.

'I've got hold of Quentin Bartholomew at last,' he informed them. 'He says of course he'll represent Julia. Wants to see you at his chambers in London, Douglas, first thing tomorrow morning.'

Douglas raised his head, his features woebegone, his eyes blurred with tears and alcohol. 'Tomorrow, eh?'

'That's good news,' Roger commented sturdily. 'Come on, Douglas. I'll drive you up to town, first thing. Now let's get to bed before we all collapse.'

Tuesday

25 June 1996

Thirteen

With superhuman stamina, Douglas was the first up the next morning, his head clear after a few hours' fitful dozing, energy restored. He, Roger and Christopher had a quick breakfast at seven o'clock, and left Highfield by seven-thirty in a determined effort to get into London before the rush hour, for their appointment with Quentin Bartholomew.

Peter, on the other hand, seemed to be in a state of depression so profound he was almost catatonic. He sat in the breakfast room, with William, Anna and Michael, hunched over his toast and Marmite as if unaware of their presence.

'Where's everyone else?' Michael asked.

'Grandpa's having breakfast in bed,' William told him. 'And so are Granny and Simon. They'll be down later.'

'What are we doing today? Can I go and see Mummy?'

Anna intervened. 'Granny and Papa are going to take you out for the day. I think they have a treat in store for you.'

'But I want to see Mummy,' whined Michael, getting flustered, eyes brimming.

'You'll see her very soon. Daddy, Roger and Christopher have gone to London today to talk to someone who will help us get her home as quickly as possible,' Anna assured him.

Michael squirmed in his chair as if he itched all over. 'I want to see her now,' he whined.

'Brace up, old lad,' William told him with brotherly authority. 'Mum will be home soon.'

Breakfast over, Anna turned to Peter, who was sitting gazing into space.

'Shall I take you up to see Grandpa? He doesn't know you arrived last night and he'll be so pleased to see you.'

'I rather doubt that,' her uncle remarked, 'but I'll go up anyway.'

'He's in a different room. I'll show you where it is.'

'You needn't. I can find it for myself.' He heaved himself to his feet and left the room without another word.

Anna and William looked at each other with raised eyebrows.

'He's very upset about Grandma, isn't he?' William observed, sotto voce.

Anna nodded, indicating they should not discuss him in front of Michael. Afterwards, when they were on their own, she explained what she thought was the reason for Peter's acute grief.

'He's never really got on with Grandma and Grandpa, you know. Daddy's always been the favourite. It's a shame, really. Parents shouldn't have favourites. I bet he's especially upset because he wasn't here when she died. He never really got to say goodbye. Not properly, I mean. I think he'd have liked some reassurance that she really did care for him.'

'She probably did. Just not as much. He can comfort

himself with the thought that we were all together for her last weekend, though.'

Anna looked at her brother askance. 'Yes, but it wasn't exactly a weekend of happy families! A granddaughter she never knew she had gate-crashed the party and then Daddy's accused of murdering the girl's mother.' She paused to analyse her feelings. 'I'm not sure whether I'm glad she died before she knew Mummy had . . . well, confessed, or not,' she added painfully.

'At least she'd have known Daddy was innocent,' William pointed out.

'Oh, she knew that already,' Anna rejoined swiftly.

DI Swann was meticulous in the way he went through the witnesses' statements. When something wasn't quite right, years of experience sent warning signals to his brain. He began by asking DS Newton to get in touch with the meteorological office to find out exactly what the weather had been like on 23 August 1980.

'Neville Barton kept stressing it was such a fine day that he wanted to get on with mowing the lawn,' Swann said. 'In my opinion he rather overstated it.'

'It probably was fine, though. It was August, after all. Douglas Rutherford was working in the woods all morning, and Julia Rutherford was shopping in Stickley. Wouldn't there have been muddy footmarks in the kitchen if it had been raining?'

'That's not the point,' Swann replied, rattled.

'And there's no mention of wet weather in the old police reports.'

'Yes, all right, Newton.' Swann knew there was something amiss but was unable to put his finger on it. 'I'm going to do some research on Neville Barton. He's lived in the same cottage all his life. There must be plenty of people who can give me a profile on him. What worries me is this. Why is Barton – and Lily's mother for that matter – so keen to put the blame on Douglas Rutherford all of a sudden? Now we know it wasn't him, why did they make these statements? And why now, after sixteen years? If Douglas Rutherford had gone down for this, the money he sends for Rose would obviously have stopped. Why should they want that to happen? And why is Neville Barton swearing he saw Rutherford unlock and then open the larder door, an hour and a half before he supposedly came back to the house, when it's Julia Rutherford he should have seen, at that time?'

Newton's mind raced. Had he missed something after all? 'I'll get on to it right away,' he told Swann.

By lunchtime, Newton had found out several very interesting things. In the past week Lily's mother had taken delivery of a washing machine, a tumble drier, a new television and video recorder, and a compact disc player, while Rose had a wardrobe full of clothes. The new items were squeezed into their cottage and looked incongruous beside her shabby three-piece suite, damp-stained walls and worn carpets. Her explanation, grumpily given in a tone of whose-business-is-it-anyway, was that she'd been saving up and that now Rose was sixteen she'd needed these things and surely no one was going to grudge the poor child a few comforts?

Newton's next call was to Neville Barton. They found him once again in an acrid cloud of pipe smoke, watching the racing from Doncaster on a brand-new sixteen-inch television set, which was also linked to a video recorder. Further 'comforts' extended to a microwave oven, a fridge-freezer, a mobile phone, an electric toaster, kettle, and a fancy new armchair which tipped back, had a rising leg rest and an adjustable head rest and did everything, as DS Newton later remarked to Swann, 'except give you a wank on a Saturday night'.

When questioned, Neville Barton, too, talked about spending his savings on a few little luxuries, which at the age of seventy-six, he thought he deserved. So the two main witnesses on Newton's list had, strangely, decided at the same moment to indulge in a massive shopping spree.

'Let's have a chat with one or two of his neighbours,' Swann suggested when told of these developments. 'I don't for a moment suppose he won the Lottery, but they might have something interesting to tell us. Like if he's had any visitors in the past few weeks, or if anything unusual has happened.'

They struck lucky almost immediately when they called on Mrs Parrish, an eighty-year-old widow who had lived next to Neville for twenty-three years. Glad to have someone to talk to, she invited them into her clean little house which smelled of lavender and furniture polish. Quickly realising that although she walked with the help of a stick, her brain was as sharp as a new pin, Swann decided to try out her memory.

'You'd have been living here when Lily Watson died at Highfield Manor, back in 1980.'

Her small grey eyes, bright and interested, positively sparkled.

''Course I remember,' she said. 'Terrible shame it was. Her so young, too, and with a baby.'

'Have you ever met the owners of Highfield, Mr and Mrs Rutherford?'

She smiled, yellowing skin breaking into hundreds of

tiny lines all over her face, a lot of them laughter lines.

'Not likely! They're rich folk, they are. Ever so rich. Got three kids, I think. Live the life of Riley, they do, in that big house.'

'Heard all about it, have you, from your neighbour, Neville Barton?' Newton threw in casually.

She nodded, and in the sunlight streaming through the window, her scalp, pink and shiny, was visible through her fine white hair.

'He's retired now, of course, but he used to work there every day. Full of it all he was. He'd tell his wife, Alice, all about the house, and how beautiful the rooms were. And Alice, she was a friend of mine, so she'd tell me. Big parties they give. Were you at their ball at the weekend?'

Swann's smile was wintry, while Newton looked wistful.

'We're not exactly guest-list material,' Swann pointed out. 'To get back to Lily Watson's death . . . I suppose Neville Barton was full of it, seeing as he was working there the day it happened?'

Mrs Parrish shook her head. 'No, he wasn't. He missed all the excitement. He was at home in bed all that week with bronchitis. I remember Alice telling me he was proper poorly. Had to get the doctor for him, she did. Makes you think, doesn't it?'

'It makes you think indeed,' Swann remarked ironically as they got back into their car. 'That clinches it so far as I'm concerned. Neither Mrs Watson nor Neville is going to admit it at this stage, but someone anxious to discredit Douglas Rutherford has bribed them into making false statements.'

'Is it worth talking to Mr Harris again?' Newton

suggested. 'He's got it in for the Rutherfords because they bring down all their supplies from their restaurants in London. Apparently the previous owners of the Manor spent hundreds of pounds a week with him. I should think he'd be glad to see the Rutherfords move out.'

'He probably would, and we'll go and see him right away, though my money's not on him. But I bet he's able to confirm who is behind all this.' Swann sounded triumphant, back in control again.

It was nearly lunchtime and it was warm and dry again, the countryside refreshed by yesterday's rain. Anna suggested they have lunch on the terrace. Eating out of doors was so much more informal than staying in their grand dining room, and today the last thing she could face was the thought of them all having to make stilted efforts at polite conversation.

Douglas, Roger and Christopher had returned shortly after twelve o'clock and were holed up in the study once more, with Reggie and Peter. The morning had been spent dealing with the unbelievable situation concerning Julia; the next few hours were to be devoted to arranging Pat's funeral.

Vivien and Simon had gone off with Michael for the day, promising to indulge and distract him.

It was a simple lunch, but Anna had put flowers on the garden table, and a bright linen cloth, with matching china, and she'd asked Morgan to chill her father's favourite white wine. When Douglas saw the effort she'd made, he squeezed her hand in gratitude.

'Thank you, my darling.' He looked tired and stressed, although he tried to hide his worry about Julia.

'Daddy, you must rest this afternoon or you'll collapse.

Mummy's going to need you on Friday when she appears in court.'

'I can't rest, Anna,' he said desperately. 'In twenty-four hours I've lost my mother . . . and my wife.'

'You haven't lost Mummy, Dad. This QC you've been to see won't let her go to gaol. She can plead diminished responsibility or . . . or . . .' Her voice broke, as she suddenly doubted her own words. Did someone automatically get sentenced if they confessed to a crime? She daren't ask her father. He'd seated himself between Reggie and Peter, and they were talking about which hymns to have at the funeral. Reggie looked better today, calmer and more rested, and kept patting Douglas on the arm saying: 'I can't tell you how grateful I am to you for letting me stay on here for a bit, you know, m'boy.'

'Stay for as long as you like, Dad, and I hope that means forever,' Douglas replied with sincerity.

Peter, on the other hand, hardly spoke at all, so steeped in misery did he seem.

Douglas looked at him sympathetically. 'And I hope you'll stay on until after the funeral, Peter. You could do with a break.'

He seemed to come to life, as if awakened from a deep reverie. 'Thanks, but I must get back to school this afternoon. This is a very busy time of year, just before the boys break up for the summer holidays. I'll be driving over for the funeral on Saturday morning and then going home again afterwards.'

'Are you sure? Wouldn't it be better if you stayed with Dad and us for the rest of the week?' Douglas suggested persuasively. Inwardly he was ashamed to admit to himself that he felt quite relieved at the thought of his brother's going home. Peter's grief at their mother's death was actually making him feel worse and he had a niggling feeling their father felt the same.

'No, I must get back,' Peter said firmly.

Suddenly, they heard raised voices, the clanging of heavy doors associated with a lorry and the revving of a heavy engine.

They all stopped talking and eating, and listened intently. The noise seemed to be coming from the other side of the old brick wall that divided their property from the neighbouring one.

A man shouting, 'Back a bit!' came floating towards them on the balmy summer air. 'Back a bit more . . . stop! That's it.'

'What on earth's going on?' Anna asked.

'Yeah!' yelled William, thrusting his fist into the air. For the first time in days he looked happy. 'That bloody woman is moving out at last!' he crowed. 'Good riddance to bad rubbish, I say. Let's hope we never have to set eyes on her again.'

Douglas nodded. 'The damage she's done to this family is incalculable,' he admitted soberly. 'When I was talking to the QC this morning we discussed instituting legal proceedings against her for trespass and slander.'

Anna leaned forward, elbows resting on the table. 'She's been awfully quiet since Saturday night, hasn't she? Suspiciously quiet, I'd say.'

Douglas thumped his fist down on the table. 'She's got what she wanted – ruined the party and my reputation. She did her damnedest to bring us all down, but by God I won't let her succeed. I'll see the old bitch in hell first.'

'That's fighting talk, Douglas,' Christopher commented approvingly as he helped himself to some more wine. 'I've no doubt Julia will get bail tomorrow, which is something.'

The bleakness returned to his brother-in-law's face. 'Yes, but she's confessed! Even Quentin Bartholomew admitted that makes it difficult. Christ, why did she have to do that?' he growled in despair. 'If she'd kept quiet, the whole thing might have blown over. The police could never have proved I was guilty on the evidence of Neville, and there was no one else about.'

They sat on in the silence of profound regret, all wishing in their different ways that they could turn back the clock. Reggie blew his nose, Christopher drained his glass and promptly refilled it. Roger put a comforting arm around Anna's shoulder, remembering her as a small child, so happy and lively, riding her pony. William stared down at his plate, appetite gone, while his father and Peter seemed to have withdrawn into themselves, united in their grief in a way they never had been in normal life.

At two o'clock, while the Rutherfords were still sitting around the lunch table, Swann and Newton left the back room of the village store where they'd been interviewing Mr Harris. Newton's stomach was rumbling and he thought if he didn't have something to eat soon, he'd keel over. The problem with a small village like Stickley was that there was no Pizza Hut, no McDonald's, no fish and chip shop. He looked up longingly as their car approached the local baker; at least there you could get warm jammy doughnuts encrusted with sugar, scones dotted with sultanas, fancy pastries filled with squelching custard.

He pressed his foot down gently on the brake.

'Why are you slowing down?' DI Swann demanded.

'I thought, sir, we could maybe stop for a bun or something? It seems a long time since breakfast.'

'Not yet, Newton. We've got to make one more call. Drive to Cherry Tree Cottage.'

'Why are you so late?' Nancy Graham demanded angrily, when the removal van, with Fast Flit Ltd painted on the side, arrived at noon, instead of the scheduled time of nine-thirty.

'I've been waiting all morning,' she continued ranting. 'There's no excuse for this gross inefficiency. I rang your firm five times and they kept saying you were on your way, so where were you? Having a leisurely breakfast at a service station? Stopping early for lunch? This is terribly inconvenient. I wanted to be settled in my new house by this evening, but it looks as if I may have to go to a hotel for the night at this rate. Well, let me tell you something. If so, your firm will have to pay my hotel bill. I'm not paying it. Your charges are too high as it is . . .'

The foreman stood with his hands on his hips and spoke in an apologetic voice which did not match his aggressive body language.

'I'm sorry, ma'am. There was nothing we could do. The traffic was terrible. As soon as we got out of Southampton we ran into a solid jam. Stretched as far as Winchester, it did. There'd been an accident.'

'You could have taken another route if you'd shown any initiative!' she shouted. 'I'm not used to being treated like this.'

The driver of the van, listening outside the front door with the two other removal men, tossed his head and made a grimace.

'She ought to be by now, the way she's carrying on,' he

quipped. 'Come on, lads. Let's give Fred a hand. If we want to get home tonight, we'd better get a move on.'

Faced by four burly men with muscles like a stevedore's, Nancy Graham backed down, but only in volume.

'Well, get on with it then, and there'll be no tea breaks until everything is in your van,' she said nastily.

Retreating to her bedroom, she stood in the window looking out over the Rutherfords' garden for the last time. By tomorrow she'd have a different view: a patio furnished with vulgar garden furniture, owned by a young couple with a dog. Already she couldn't help having misgivings about them. Dogs barked. And in time they'd probably have a baby who cried . . . and relatives who visited . . . and barbecues on a Sunday . . .

Two hours later the removal men had finished packing up the china, silver, ornaments, cooking utensils and linen, into large wooden tea chests, when Fred, who'd managed a quick swig of tea from his thermos while crouching low in the driving seat, hurried into the house to have a warning word with the others.

'Hey,' he whispered, 'the rozzers have just arrived wanting to see Mrs G. Where is she?'

'Upstairs in the bedroom,' Fred vouchsafed.

DI Swann and DS Newton did not wait to be invited into Cherry Tree Cottage. They marched into the narrow hall, squeezing past the tea chests and rolled up Persian rugs.

'Mrs Graham?' Newton's voice rang loudly through the house. 'Are you there, Mrs Graham?'

A minute later she descended the narrow stairs into the cottage hallway, as if she were coming down a grand staircase in a mansion. 'Who wants to see me?' she asked coldly.

When she saw Swann and Newton she stopped in her tracks, and regarded them with hostility.

'What do you want? Can't you see I'm extremely busy?'

'We'd like to have a few words with you, Mrs Graham,' Swann said with exaggerated politeness.

She frowned, pulling down the jacket of her plum-red suit as if to smooth her image. 'What about? I'm moving house this afternoon. It really is most inconvenient.'

'I can see that,' Newton said evenly, 'but we have to talk to you. Shall we go into the living room?'

'*Drawing* room,' she corrected him. Then she turned to the removal men who were standing with their mouths open. 'Get on with finishing upstairs. You have all my clothes to pack.'

DI Swann didn't beat around the bush. 'We have reason to believe, Mrs Graham, that you have given substantial amounts of money to Mrs Watson and Neville Barton, in order to bribe them to make false statements relating to events that occurred on August the twenty-third 1980. Namely, that you managed to persuade Mrs Watson to say she knew Lily had had the syringe and antidote in her handbag when she left for work that morning . . .'

'But she did!' Nancy Graham exploded furiously. 'That was the truth. She did have her syringe with her that morning. But, at the time, Mrs Watson was frightened that Douglas Rutherford would stop sending money for the baby if it looked as if Lily's death was suspicious. Mr Harris told me that, and Mrs Watson confirmed it. I merely suggested to Mrs Watson that it was time to tell the truth.'

Swann continued as if she had not spoken. 'We also believe that you bribed Neville Barton to say he was working at Highfield Manor on the day in question, and to state that he actually saw Douglas Rutherford unlock and open the larder door, shortly after Lily died, and not an hour and a half later which was when he actually found Lily's body on his return from the woods.'

'But . . .' she began again.

He raised his hand to silence her, face set as if it had been carved in stone.

'It may interest you to know, Mrs Graham,' Swann continued coldly, 'that Neville Barton was at home, ill in bed with bronchitis, *all that week*. He was never even near Highfield Manor that day. Apart from which we now know that if he had been, it would not have been Douglas Rutherford he'd have seen.'

Her face was suffused with a dark red colour, blending with her plum suit, and her eyes were darting around the room, unable to meet Swann's.

'I must ask you to come to the police station where you will be formally charged with trying to pervert the course of justice by bribing witnesses to make false statements . . .'

'I want my solicitor!' she screamed, arms flailing as Swann and Newton moved closer. 'I will not be humiliated like this by a pack of country bobbies . . .'

'What are we supposed to do now?' the removals foreman asked DS Newton, following him out to the police car. 'We're in the middle of moving her out of here.'

'Have you actually loaded anything into your van yet?'

'A few packing cases of china and the like.'

'Right. Unload them and bring them back into the house. Then you might as well go, because there's no way she'll be able to move house today. I'll ask her for her keys so I can lock up.'

The foreman grinned. 'Rather you than me. At least we'll get back to Southampton in time for our tea now.'

William came rushing into the house, breathless. 'Dad!' he yelled. 'Dad? Where are you?'

The study door was flung open and Douglas stood there, an alarmed expression on his tired face. 'What is it?'

'You'll never guess in a million years.' He looked jubilant. 'I've just seen Nancy Graham driven away in a police car. When she saw me, she looked *daggers*! What d'you think has happened?'

Douglas turned and wandered back into his study. 'They probably only want her to make a statement,' he replied wearily.

'She was with the two blokes who came here to talk to you . . . they wouldn't want her down at the station because of what she did, would they? I mean, she's an evil old bag but she hasn't committed a crime . . . or has she?' William wondered aloud.

Swann and Newton weren't the only ones who'd been busy that day. Swann had detailed Constable Noel Barnes to go through all the statements taken after the death of Lily, paying special to attention to witnesses who had seen Julia Rutherford in Stickley that morning. In her 1980 statement Julia had said she'd been in the village between nine-thirty in the morning and twelve-forty-five, yet in her confession, made two days ago, she'd admitted returning to Highfield Manor in the middle of the morning.

Some of those who'd seen her had long since moved away from Stickley, and others had died, but there were still several people who remembered the details of that day with the clarity that all tragedies leave in their wake.

By lunchtime something had emerged that was to put a completely different aspect on the part played by those at the centre of the incident.

'They all said the same thing, sir,' Constable Barnes informed Swann and Newton. 'Mrs Rutherford was seen in the village by a lot of people, doing her shopping . . .'

'In the village store? Did Mr Harris see her?' Swann interrupted.

'Yes, he did, but only passing his window on the way to the coffee shop next door . . .'

'Right. Well, get on with it.'

'She shopped at the little haberdashery shop, and spent some time in Morton's, the antique shop, then she went to the chemist and . . .'

'OK, OK. I get the picture.' Swann was frazzled, tired after a long morning, hungry, and thoroughly pissed off by Nancy Graham's behaviour. 'What's the bottom line, Barnes?'

'Mrs Rutherford has alibis exactly as she said in the original statement made in 1980. She was in the village from approximately nine-forty-five that morning until twelve-thirty. I've traced and spoken to several people who made statements at the time and they're sticking by them. For one thing, her car was on the forecourt of Endfield's Garage between those times, having two new front tyres fitted. Then at twelve-thirty-five she drove back to Highfield Manor.'

Newton, who'd been listening intently, spoke. 'And while she'd been out, Lily had been stung by a bee at approximately ten-thirty, and her body was discovered by Douglas Rutherford at twelve noon. Or so he said.' He paused, mind racing. 'Then why is Mrs Rutherford confessing to a crime she obviously didn't commit?'

Constable Barnes remained silent, but he could feel the frisson of excitement that was sweeping through Newton.

'Is there anything else, sir?' he asked, addressing Swann.

Swann looked up, surprised, as if he'd forgotten Barnes and Newton were there.

'Yes, Barnes. Mrs Rutherford is in the holding cell. Bring her to me. I want to know who she's trying to protect.'

The car slid almost silently through the twilight, took a right turn, drove swiftly through the gates of Highfield Manor and up the long drive where the towering rhododendrons that Julia had always hated cast long shadows over the gravel. Then it drew up to the front door and stopped.

A moment later a slim figure in black trousers and a black sweater scrambled out of the back and hurried up the steps, pushing open the heavy front door.

'Douglas?'

For the second time that day he came bursting out of the study then stopped dead, staring as if he'd seen a ghost.

'*Julia*!' His voice was hoarse, his face ashen.

'Oh, Douglas!' She flung herself at him, sobbing with relief and unable to speak.

They held each other with a frantic urgency, as if they could not believe they were together again. A moment later William and Anna came rushing out of the drawing room, followed by Christopher, Roger, and more slowly Reggie. Everyone was asking questions, trembling and shaking, Anna in tears, and Christopher and William both talking at once.

On a tidal wave of love and relief, with arms and hands holding and patting her, Julia was borne into the study, where Douglas made her lie down on one of the leather sofas.

'I'm all right. I'm not ill,' she kept protesting. Then she looked around. 'Where's Mikey?'

'Your parents have taken him out for the day. They'll be home in about an hour,' Douglas explained.

'Lucky Mikey.'

'So what's happened?' Christopher asked. 'We thought you were appearing in court on Friday morning . . .'

'They've dropped the case,' she replied quietly.

'They've . . .!' Douglas stopped. 'You mean the original verdict of accidental death still stands?'

She nodded, still too emotional to talk, overwhelmed by her welcome home. Douglas took her hand and, leaning over her, gazed with loving concern into her eyes. 'Why don't you go and have a bath, darling? You may not feel tired but you probably are. The great thing is you're home again and I can't tell you how happy that makes me.'

'Me, too,' she replied with feeling. 'Me, too.'

He went upstairs with her, as if he could not bear to be out of sight of her for a moment, and as she undressed then slipped into her blue towelling robe, he spoke, unable to contain his curiosity any longer.

'So what exactly happened, sweetheart? William saw the police taking Nancy Graham off in their car.'

Julia nodded. 'That's why the whole case has fallen apart. She bribed both Rose's grandmother and Neville to make false statements. For a start Neville wasn't even working here that day. I could have told them that, if anyone had asked me.'

'That's right. When the police asked me about Neville, I couldn't remember seeing him that day, but I couldn't be absolutely sure. It was all so chaotic.'

'It certainly was.' She sat down at her dressing-table and started brushing her hair, making long downward sweeps with the brush. 'So . . . without those two main witnesses to say that Lily had her syringe in her handbag, and that Neville had actually seen you unlocking the larder door . . . well, there really wasn't a case. Apparently they checked on my movements and discovered I was in the village all morning and couldn't have come home if I'd wanted to because my car was in the garage. So that blew my confession out of the water. They're very angry with me for wasting police time, but at least they let me go.'

Douglas dropped on to the side of the bed, watching her face in her dressing-table mirror. The room felt very still, as if shut off from the rest of the house. Her eyes caught his in the reflection, held them for a long questioning moment, and then he asked with controlled intensity: 'Why did you do it, Julia? Why did you confess?'

She looked away, laid down her silver-backed brush, remained silent.

'Why, Julia? Did you think I was guilty?' he asked, his voice becoming harsh with pain.

'No, but the police did,' she replied, turning to face him. 'The whole business was disastrous for you, Douglas. Even if you'd been found innocent, it would still have ruined you and all you've worked for. I couldn't let that happen.'

'But you did, in your heart of hearts, believe I'd deliberately let Lily die?'

'Did you think I had?' she countered swiftly.

He hesitated, unable to meet her direct gaze. 'You were terribly convincing,' he said at last. 'But it was so out of character. At the same time I can't come to terms with the thought of you confessing wrongfully. Why, in God's name, did you?' He was angry now; angry with himself for half believing she was guilty, and angry with her for confessing to something she hadn't done. 'It was such a dangerous thing to do, Julia! Doubly so now we know that old bitch next door had set the whole thing up out of revenge. What the hell would have happened if it had gone to a full-blown court hearing with a jury and you'd been found guilty?' He was bellowing now, guilt and relief mingling with a sense of fear at what might have happened. 'Why, Julia? Why did you do it? Isn't it enough that you sought to protect me from public disgrace?'

She looked away again, and her voice was small and weary. 'I confessed because I love you. I couldn't let you suffer because of the death of a girl who was no good for you. I love you more than anyone or anything in the world. Always have and always will. If I had to give my life for you, I would do so, and willingly. I love you so much that maybe I *am* capable of killing someone . . . if I thought they were going to hurt you or take you away from me.' She paused before adding, 'But how Lily came to die that day, I don't know.'

Douglas was staring at her, understanding something he'd never fully appreciated before; the intensity of her obsessive love for him. Such love was a responsibility to be borne with care; not taken advantage of, cherished even. But it was also a burden. At that moment it crossed his mind that, perhaps sub-consciously, he had been aware of it seventeen years ago, and that was what had thrust him into the arms of Lily, for a little light-hearted fun. But then, she had become obsessive, too . . .

'What are you thinking about, Douglas?' Julia was watching him closely.

He took a deep breath and smiled at her. 'The fact that you confessed to killing Lily . . . because you loved me. Even after you'd discovered we'd had a child? That's the most forgiving gesture I've ever heard of.'

'It wasn't a case of forgiveness. I felt so hurt. And humiliated. And so jealous of what you must have had with Lily, even if it was only for a short while.' She paused, voice breaking before she could continue. 'But when the police came, and they were going to arrest you and charge you . . . well, I couldn't let that happen.'

'Oh, God, darling.' He was by her side now, clasping his arms around her, bringing her to her feet, burying his face in her neck. 'Oh, dear God, I don't deserve someone like you.' His tears felt wet against her skin as she held him close.

'Should we do something for Rose?' she whispered tentatively. 'You and I, and Anna and William and Mikey, are so lucky, we have so much, but that poor child . . .'

Douglas drew back, stunned. 'W-what sort of thing?' he stammered.

'Nothing too overwhelming at first. Ask her over, with her grandmother, when we're on our own. Take an interest in her. I don't mean we should swamp her with money and . . . and things, that would be the worst thing to do. But maybe we could gradually draw her into the family. After all,' she added, looking up earnestly into his face, 'none of this is her fault. She shouldn't be allowed to suffer because of what's happened.'

'You are the most amazing woman,' Douglas said slowly.

Clinging to him, as she found his mouth and kissed him hungrily, Julia felt a deeper sense of peace than she had ever experienced before, a sense of rightness and belonging and of finally laying to rest all the doubts and fears that had lingered ever since she'd learned about his affair with Lily, all those years ago. It was like coming home.

Wednesday

26 June 1996

Fourteen

Douglas summoned the local vicar, Reverend James Spencer, to Highfield Manor the next morning, to discuss the service for Pat's funeral on Saturday. When he arrived at nine-thirty, Morgan ushered him into the study where he found Douglas sending faxes off to the managers of his restaurants, with instructions for the rest of the week.

'Good morning,' said Reverend Spencer breezily. He was young, referred to as 'swinging' by the local teenagers for the way he ran the youth club and played cricket for the local team, and was gradually acquiring the trust of the older members of his small congregation.

'Good morning,' Douglas replied, rising from behind his desk. 'Sorry it's a bit chaotic, but this has been a helluva weekend, and now I've just seen the morning tabloids. What a rotten bunch they are, aren't they? We put nice dignified notices about my mother's death in *The Times* and *Telegraph*, and look what this bunch of gutter-snipes write!' He flung down several newspapers on to the desk, with the *Globe* on top.

ACCUSED MAN'S MOTHER DIES AFTER WEEKEND PARTY, screamed the headline.

'It's enough to make you sick, isn't it?' James Spencer agreed. 'The best thing to do is to ignore them. Can you stay down here for a while or do you have to get back to London?'

'I'm trying to run the business from here, at least until next Monday. As you've probably heard, the case they were going to bring against us, and which my wife very nobly confessed to, thinking she was protecting me, has been dropped . . .'

'Yes, I heard about all that, and I'm terribly sorry for what you and your wife must have gone through. Has Mrs Graham left Cherry Tree Cottage?'

'You must forgive me, but I hope that woman rots in hell!' Douglas said explosively.

'I can understand how you feel. I think I'd feel the same if I were in your position. But I've got to try and see past her behaviour, sympathise with a sad, lonely and bored old lady, who deeply resents anyone having any happiness.'

'I wish you luck,' Douglas retorted. 'It's more than I could do. Now, I'll go and get my father. He's got some ideas for my mother's funeral, and I know he'd like us to sing "I Vow To Thee. My Country".'

'That's a beautiful hymn,' James Spencer agreed, taking a small notepad out of his jacket pocket.

Douglas returned a few minutes later with Reggie, who was carrying several sheets of paper.

'Let's have some coffee,' Douglas suggested, knowing this was going to be an ordeal for both his father and him, but hoping he could ease the pain by making it as comfortable and relaxed as possible. *Peter should be here*, he thought, *helping us arrange Mum's funeral*.

They sat on the sofas to either side of the coffee table in front of the fireplace, and then Douglas looked at James expectantly.

'I have to confess I've never arranged a funeral before,' he said with unaccustomed diffidence.

The fresh-faced young vicar smiled. 'People usually start with a hymn, then we have the service, then either a reading or a psalm . . .'

Reggie leaned forward, holding out a sheet of paper.

'My wife always requested that Douglas should read this at her funeral,' he explained, his hands and voice shaky.

'I've never been able to find out who wrote it. I don't think anyone knows, but it was found in an envelope addressed to his parents, from a soldier who was killed on active service in Northern Ireland, to be opened in the event of his death. Pat was very touched by the story.'

James Spencer looked at the typewritten lines briefly. He knew the poem well. 'That's beautiful. Very appropriate,' he remarked, handing the sheet to Douglas.

> Do not stand at my grave and weep,
> I am not there – I do not sleep.
> I am a thousand winds that blow,
> I am the softly falling snow,
> I am the gentle rains that fall,
> I am the fields of ripening grain,
> I am the morning hush,
> I am the graceful rush,
> Of beautiful birds in circling flight,
> I am the starshine of the night
> I am the flowers that bloom
> I am in a quiet room
> I am in the birds that sing,
> I am in each lovely thing.
> Do not stand at my grave and cry–
> I did not die.

The print was blurred as he got to the last line, and he knew that to read this aloud, in front of dozens of people, was going to be the most difficult thing he'd ever had to do. But he would do it. Somehow. Because she'd asked him to, and because he'd never let her down.

'I must leave you to your work,' Reverend Spencer said, rising, when they'd concluded their meeting. 'I can see you've got faxes spewing out like machine-gun fire. Things are obviously hotting up at your restaurants.'

Douglas grinned. 'No peace for the wicked, as they say, so I'm probably going to need you around for a long time!'

When he'd seen the vicar into his battered little Volvo, and Reggie had gone off to find Julia, Douglas went back to the study, grabbed the dozen or so faxes that had come through while they'd been talking and settled himself behind his desk to go through them.

Lazlo, manager of Trendy's, had a problem with one of the chefs who wanted extra time off; Antonia, manager of Butterfly, had discovered the sommelier had been stealing wine; Marco the head chef at Smart's was worried about their meat suppliers; there was also a letter from Peter. Douglas stopped abruptly and looked again. How unlike his brother to send him a fax when he usually phoned. He started reading.

Dear Douglas,

The events of the past few days have been preying on my mind, as they have been on and off for some years now. I was appalled to hear you were being accused of Lily Watson's death, and quite horrified when I heard Julia had confessed to the crime. I always knew about you and Lily, of course, and about her having a baby, having found out (from her, incidentally) when Leonora and I stayed with you and Julia a few weeks before Lily died. Why she confided in me, I do not know. Perhaps she was distressed because you had recently terminated the affair, and she needed someone to talk to.

Now, I think the time is right for the truth to come out, and I feel a great need to unburden myself.

It is common knowledge in our family that you have always been our parents' favourite child. You were the brightest (if not the most academic, a role I modestly claim for myself), and you were always the one most likely to succeed. Your charisma, personality, and ability to communicate with the man in the street have been your great strengths, coupled with courage and a willingness to work hard. Please believe, Douglas, that while I envied you all these gifts, not least your choice of Julia as a wife, I knew, and there is no doubt about this in my mind, that you were the one our parents were most proud of. You were the son they could look up to and tell their friends about. You were the son that brought glamour into their lives, and knew how to give them a really good time. But I digress.

When Lily told me your affair was over, and she seemed very down and vulnerable at that time, I decided to try and steal a little of your dazzling stardust and grab some excitement for myself.

One Saturday morning I drove over from Salisbury, intending to drop in on you both and perhaps find the opportunity of a quick word with Lily. As it turned out, the house was empty except for her. She said you and Julia were out, and that the nanny had taken Anna and William into Stockbridge.

Are you surprised at my total recall after all these years? A good memory is one thing I do have.

Lily was in the kitchen. She made me a cup of coffee and we talked, and I suggested we meet during the afternoon, having discovered she stopped work at two o'clock. This was not as bluntly done as I'm making it sound. I'd spent some time telling her I thought she was very attractive, and I'd like to get to know her better. Obviously, I'm not as good (or maybe as practised?) at this sort of thing as you, because she rejected me. Outright. She simply didn't want to know. She said she'd need a barge pole to touch me. *And she laughed in my face.*

To be rejected by your leavings was the final straw. I was rude to her; told her she was a slut. She flounced off into the larder to get something, and the next moment she yelped because she'd been stung. I knew she was allergic. Do you remember how we all discussed it at lunch one day just after Julia had taken her on as a daily help?

I think you can guess the rest. After I'd locked her in, I removed the syringe from her handbag which was on the kitchen dresser. Then I buried it under a rhododendron bush on the left, as you go down the drive to leave the house. I stayed in the garden for a while. No one saw me. Then I went back into the house, and unlocked and opened the larder door. She was dead, of course. I thought I'd died with her, but one learns to go on. Somehow.

Please try to understand, Douglas, and do not

think too harshly of me. There must be peace for me somewhere. I have yet to find it.

Your devoted brother . . .

Peter had signed it in his familiar neat writing.

Douglas sat, numbed, not knowing who to tell first. The shock was going to be terrible for their father but at least their mother had been spared this fresh pain.

The telephone on his desk rang and impatiently he picked it up.

'Douglas?' At first he could hardly make out what was being said. But then he caught Leonora's words: 'I've just found Peter . . . he's hanged himself.'

'Dear God . . .!' Douglas clutched the phone. 'No! Oh, no!' he groaned, stunned by this fresh blow. 'Leonora, my dear, what's happened?' As if he didn't know. As if the reason didn't lie before him, on a sheet of shiny fax paper. So Peter had been unable to live with what he'd done and, having confessed, could no longer bear to carry on.

'I f-found him,' Leonora explained, her voice choked with tears. 'He was in his study. He'd . . . Oh, God . . . he'd hung himself . . . with his dressing-gown cord . . . from one of the beams.' Her sobbing increased and she was unable to continue.

'Oh, my dear. I'm so sorry . . . so sorry.' He felt immobilised. Even his heart seemed stilled by shock. But his mind was racing, visualising the terrible scene; trying to imagine the desperate feelings of his brother at the moment when he tied the cord around his neck.

'What shall I do, Douglas? I don't know what to do,' she burst out at last. 'I rang for the school doctor . . . he managed to . . . to take him down. He'd only been dead a few minutes. If only I'd found him sooner . . .'

The last thing he must have done was send me the fax, Douglas realised. He had a sudden thought. 'Has he left a note, Leonora? Has he given a reason . . .?'

'Nothing. Absolutely nothing. His desk is clear. I think he'd been tidying up. There were even ashes in the grate as if he'd been burning old papers. What can have happened? I mean, he was upset about Pat dying, but even so . . .'

Peter had shown the way. Had shown how he wanted things to look and in that fearful moment before he died, had trusted Douglas to carry out his unspoken wishes.

'He was distraught by Mother's death,' Douglas cut in swiftly. 'That is why he must have felt he couldn't carry on. It was a tragedy he wasn't actually here when she died, and I could see he'd taken it terribly badly.'

'You think that's why he took his life?' she asked tremulously. 'I was afraid he was depressed because, well, I have been nagging him a bit lately to buy us a flat in town . . .'

'No, my dear. It was Mother's death. Definitely,' he assured her. 'It's been a terrible shock for me, too, and of course for our father. And this is going to be an added blow to Dad.' His mind was racing, but first there was something he had to do. Making sure that Leonora was not alone, and that she was surrounded by supportive people, he promised to ring her back later.

Alone in his study, Douglas read Peter's fax once more before going over to the fireplace and throwing it in to the empty grate. Bending down, he set light to the fax with a match. He'd loved his brother and there was no need for anyone to know what had really happened on that August day sixteen years ago. The case was closed, the final verdict accidental death. Only he knew what had really happened and that was the way it was going to stay. He gazed through his tears into the fireplace at the blackened fragments of Peter's confession. Ashes to ashes. Dust to dust. It was better that way. He loved his brother and his secret would die with him. Who needed to know the sad and sordid secret that Peter had hidden for so long?

Douglas was pouring himself a drink when Julia came into the room. One look at his face told her something was wrong.

'Darling, are you all right? What is it?'

He turned to face her. This would be the last half-truth he would tell her for as long as he lived, but his conscience was clear.

'Terrible news, darling. That was Leonora on the phone. Peter's been so devastated by Mother's death, that he's taken his own life. It seems he simply couldn't bear to carry on.' He reached for her, badly needing her support at this moment and a second later she had her arms around him, holding him close, whispering words of comfort in his ear.

The burden of guilt weighed heavily, but he knew it was not altogether of his own making. The gods had blessed him, had given him gifts and made him his parents' favourite child, and, as a result, Peter had suffered and, in pain, had taken Lily's life. And now his own.

'Where are the children?' he asked suddenly.

Julia looked up lovingly into his face. 'In the garden, I think. Why?'

'Let's go and find them, darling. We must all stick together. Families are so important.'

'Tell me about it, sweetheart,' she replied, smiling up at him.

If you enjoyed this book here is a selection of other bestselling titles from Headline

WOMAN TO WOMAN	Cathy Kelly	£5.99 ☐
UNFINISHED BUSINESS	Val Corbett, Joyce Hopkirk & Eve Pollard	£5.99 ☐
PASSION AND ILLUSION	Barbara Delinsky	£5.99 ☐
HER ONE OBSESSION	Roberta Latow	£5.99 ☐
HOLDING OUT	Anne O Faulk	£5.99 ☐
A WHIFF OF SCANDAL	Carole Matthews	£5.99 ☐
MISBEHAVING	Sarah Harvey	£5.99 ☐
THE DADDY CLOCK	Judy Markey	£5.99 ☐
FINDERS KEEPERS	Fern Michaels	£5.99 ☐
A CROSS OF STARS	Patricia Shaw	£5.99 ☐
MIXED DOUBLES	Jill Mansell	£5.99 ☐
ANGELS OF MERCY	Lyn Andrews	£5.99 ☐

Headline books are available at your local bookshop or newsagent. Alternatively, books can be ordered direct from the publisher. Just tick the titles you want and fill in the form below. Prices and availability subject to change without notice.

Buy four books from the selection above and get free postage and packaging and delivery within 48 hours. Just send a cheque or postal order made payable to Bookpoint Ltd to the value of the total cover price of the four books. Alternatively, if you wish to buy fewer than four books the following postage and packaging applies:

UK and BFPO £4.30 for one book; £6.30 for two books; £8.30 for three books.

Overseas and Eire: £4.80 for one book; £7.10 for 2 or 3 books (surface mail).

Please enclose a cheque or postal order made payable to *Bookpoint Limited*, and send to: Headline Publishing Ltd, 39 Milton Park, Abingdon, OXON OX14 4TD, UK.
Email Address: orders@bookpoint.co.uk

If you would prefer to pay by credit card, our call team would be delighted to take your order by telephone. Our direct line is 01235 400 414 (lines open 9.00 am–6.00 pm Monday to Saturday 24 hour message answering service). Alternatively you can send a fax on 01235 400 454.

Name ....

Address ....

....

....

If you would prefer to pay by credit card, please complete:
Please debit my Visa/Access/Diner's Card/American Express (delete as applicable) card number:

Signature .... Expiry Date ....